THE GUILEFUL ROSE

The Curoria Chronicles

E.A. Almanza

Sarcastic Cat Writing, LLC

To the pigs that gave me an allergic reaction.

Yes, I imagined you everytime a character was killed, tortured, or otherwise harmed.

Author's Content Note

The Guileful Rose is an adult fantasy novel made for those over the age of 18. Content readers may want to consider beforehand is gratuitous violence, torture, imprisonment, a fake pregnancy and miscarriage used for political gain and personal survival, childbirth, backstabbing false friends, death, death of children, graphic consensual sexual content, minor sexual assault (a kiss on the lips), the death of horses and elephants, and harsh language. These characters are morally grey and as such will do and think awful things.

This is not a romance book. It is a grimdark political fantasy that focuses on war, political schemes, and world building. While there is a romance subplot, *it is a subplot.* If you are expecting a romantasy, where the romance is the forefront of the book—go ahead and put this book down.

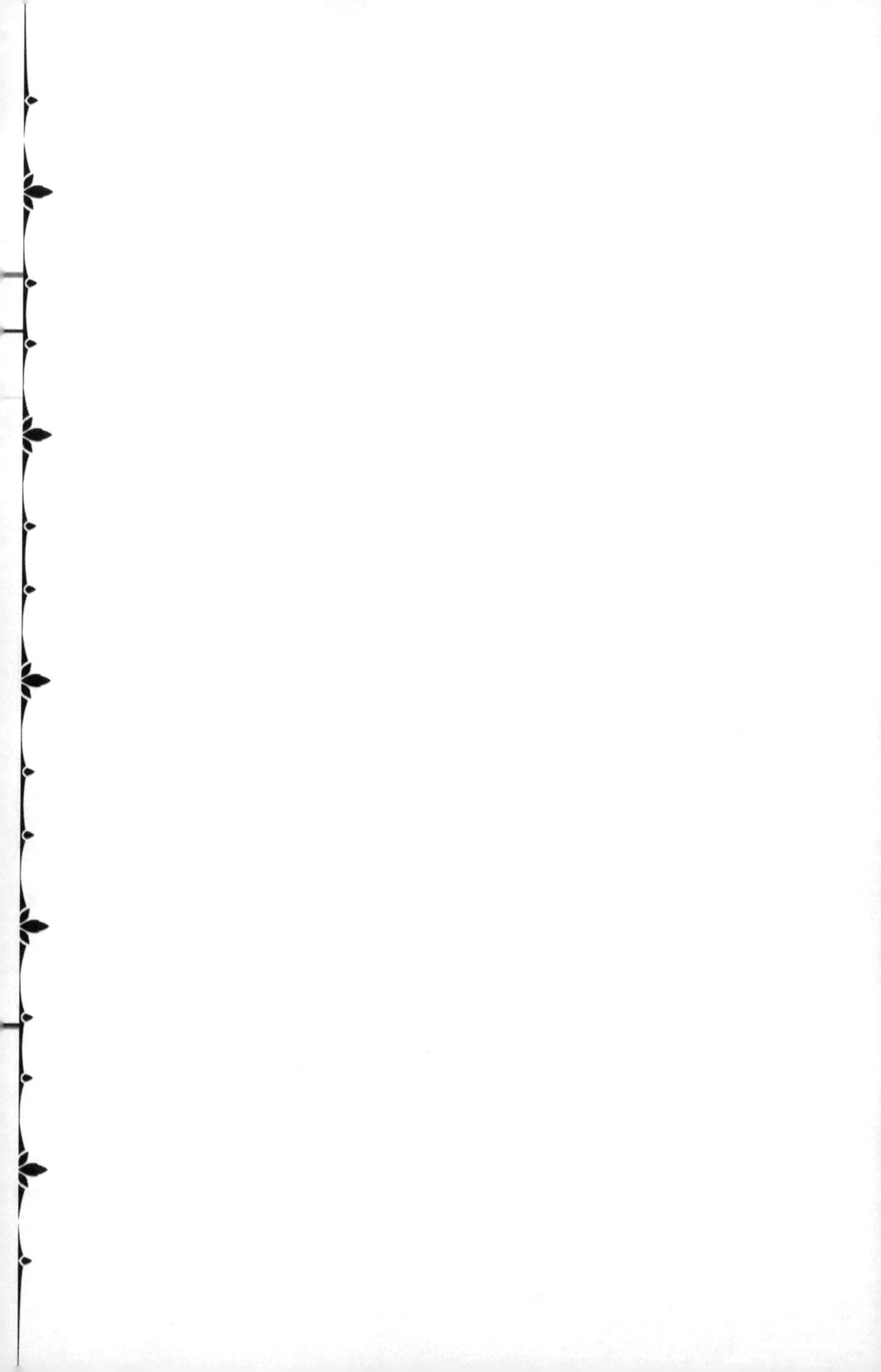

Contents

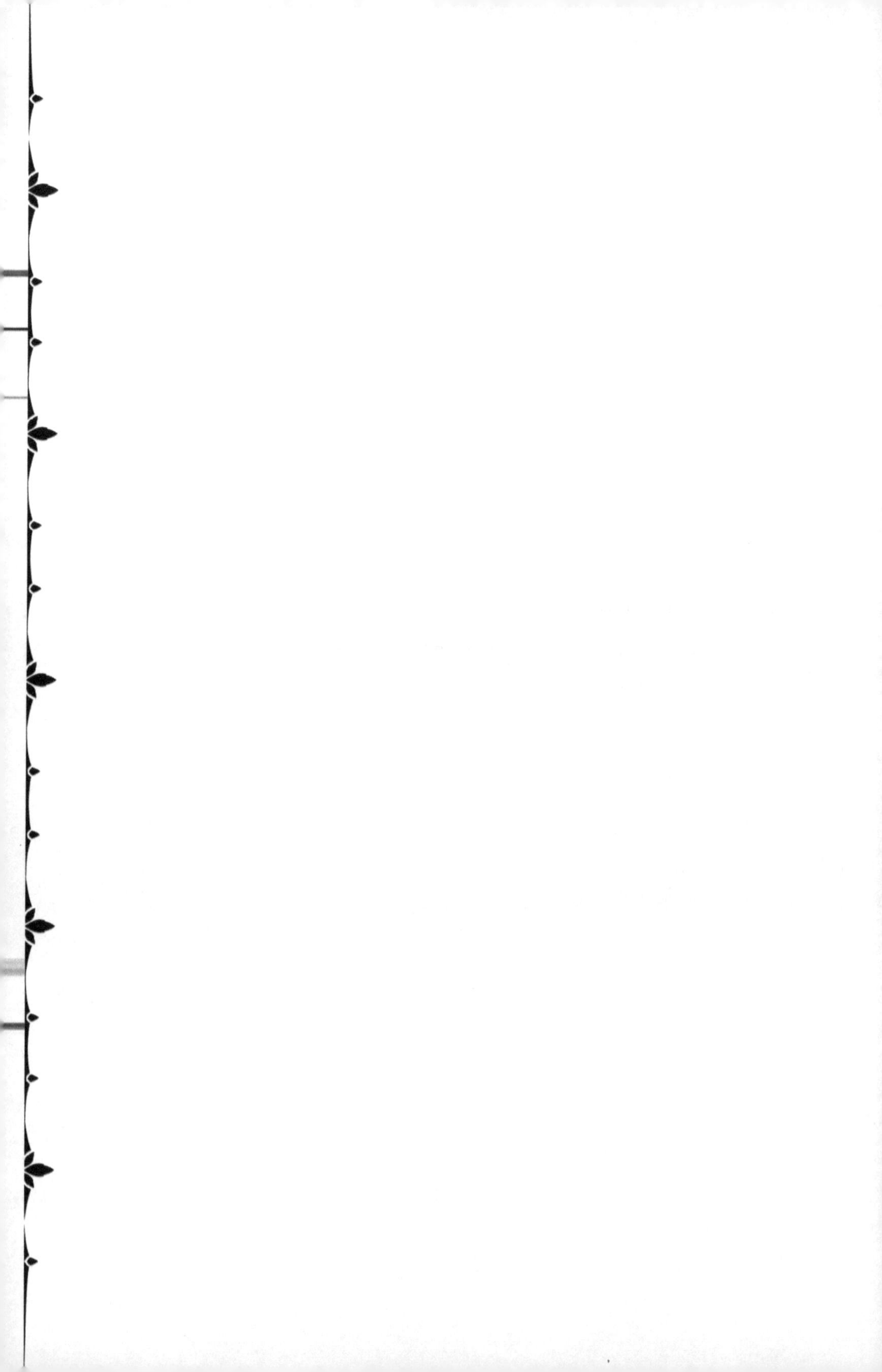

Part One

the beginning

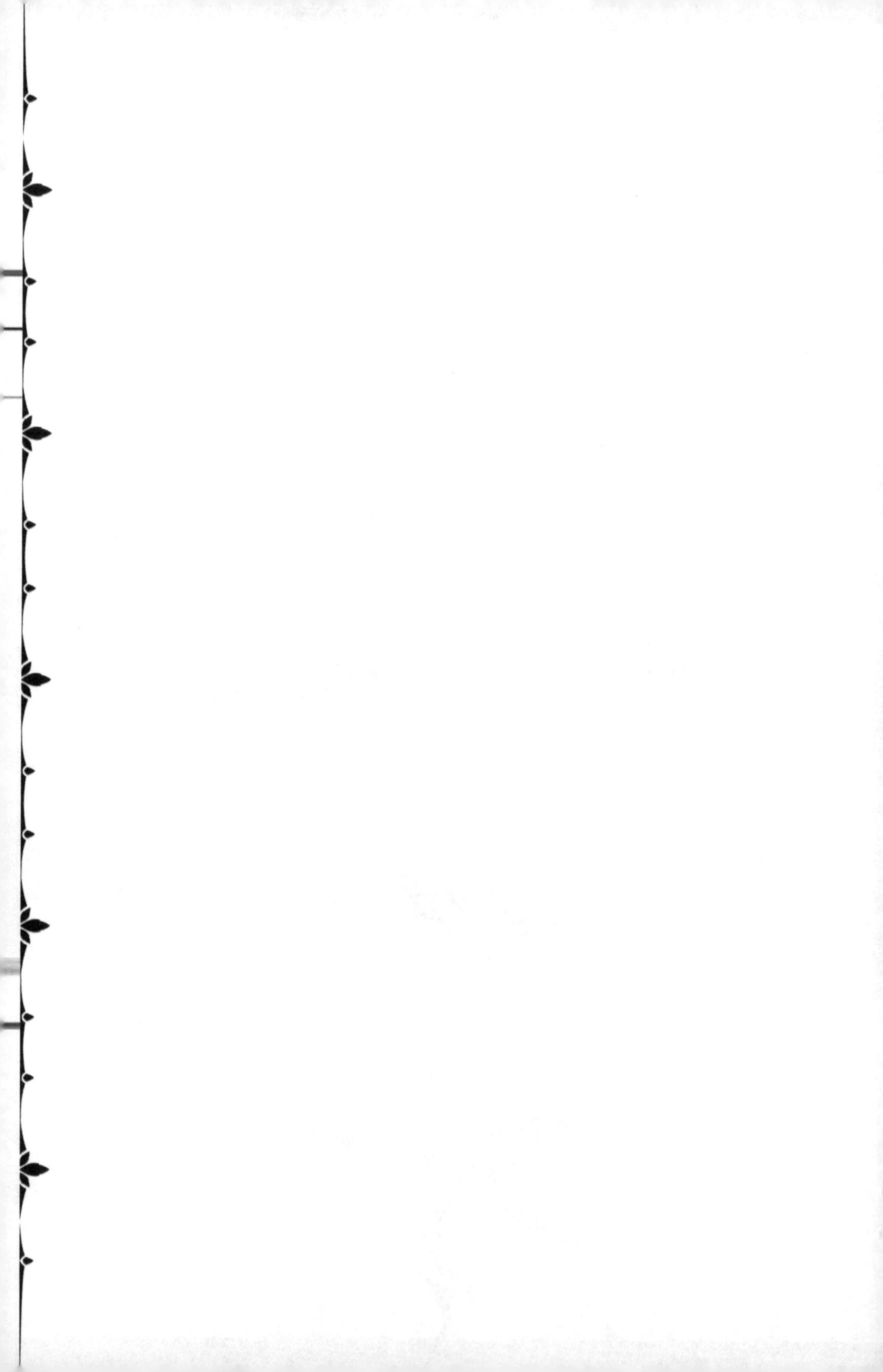

Chapter One

Cool water circled around Amaria as her long, dark hair floated around her, as if she were a siren instead of a human. Perhaps she could be, or at least pretend to be one. She was beautiful, she knew that—everyone knew that. And, even now, she was combining her air and water magic to breathe underwater. It wasn't exactly breathing, but all the same, she could remain at the bottom of the pool for hours.

The day was blistering hot, one where you laid inside to avoid the risk of burning your skin in the sun. The water in this basin inside the palace of Provincia Palencia was the most comfortable place in Raulle right now.

A swish of blonde hair floated past her, the girl waving vigorously. Amaria chuckled, air bubbles blowing out of her nose. Delphina returned the smile, bubbles swirling her face as she broke the surface of the water.

Amaria shook her head, following her to the surface of the water.

"Nice of you to join us." Delphina grinned.

"It's peaceful." Amaria rolled her eyes playfully. "Unlike you."

Delphina threw her wet hair back, the strands sticking to her body. She was covered in red burns—she had stayed outside too long recently. Not for the first time, Amaria was glad that her tanned skin gave her some protection from the Perivinan sun.

"I'm peaceful," Delphina said. "You just don't appreciate it."

Amaria leaned up against the wall of the basin, sitting on the stone stool as she listened to the rest of her ladies-in-waiting chitter. She enjoyed the serenity of the water cradling her. "How long have you been swimming laps? That's not peaceful."

"I find peace in it." Delphina sat next to her, eyeing Amaria with concern. "Is everything alright?"

Amaria closed her eyes, trying to push back the sense that something was wrong. Perhaps it was the scented oils used in the bath? Amaria breathed in, distinguishing the smells of orange and rose.

Everything had roses here. How else would you know that this was Provincia Palencia, the home of the Raulets? Amaria lightly blew air out her nose. Being subtle in matters outside of political threats wasn't one of her family's strong suits.

And she'd have a new family soon. She'd go from being a Raulet to a Chauvignon. Well, *also,* a Chauvignon. She would always be a Raulet, regardless of her legal name. How could she shed that part of herself?

That, and the Raulets were the richest family in the empire. Gods, they were the richest family on the continent. Who'd release a claim to that?

"I'm wondering about my husband," Amaria told Delphina. And she was. Amaria wondered what her new husband's inner faults were. She was aware of the outer faults—he was known as not particularly loquacious, he had blacked out at a battle when he was sixteen killing thousands, and was said to be a cunning deviant, but Amaria did not see those as flaws. However, these outer cracks were known—they existed—but cracks seemed so different when you were on the inside.

"Theodmon Chauvignon seems fine enough," Delphina said. "Better than the last fiancé. Gods, he was a creep."

Lyseno Vypren, Duke of Darcassa, Avondra. He was about thirty years older than Amaria and her skin crawled every time she had the misfortune of seeing him. "I hate that Emperor Aion forced my father to make the match," Amaria said.

Delphina raised an eyebrow. "Your father runs the country—"

"We have to let the emperor think he's doing it," Amaria interrupted, heat rushing to her chest. "My father convinced Aion to let us break off the engagement and I'm marrying Theodmon now."

Delphina's eyebrow didn't drop. "I think you trust your father too much."

"He's my father," Amaria said. "He wouldn't hurt me." She breathed in, letting the scent of orange calm her. "I need this marriage with Theodmon—you know Vypren is telling everyone that he consummated the marriage."

"He's saying he made you bleed on the marriage bed," Delphina said. "There's a difference."

"Yes," Amaria hissed. "And he did, by trying to carve my womb out of me." Her voice shook and she dunked herself under the water to calm down and to hide her tears. She hated him. He had gotten notice somehow that her father was canceling the engagement mere weeks before the wedding. She had arrived early to prepare for the ceremony.

And Lyseno Vypren had drugged her and was about to...pre-consummate...the marriage when her father burst into the room. Vypren hadn't been able to do what he was planning to, but he'd cut Amaria, claiming nobody else could have her if he couldn't.

She had covered his hand in ice and burned it as retribution.

"Look," Amaria said. "We know the blood he's talking about isn't what he claims, but how is the average person supposed to interpret 'bleeding on the marriage bed'?"

"Your family is powerful and rich enough, it doesn't matter that much," Delphina protested. "You could be with several men before marriage and still have a respectable groom because of the size of your dowry alone."

Amaria dunked under the water again. Yes, she had avoided the brunt of Vypren's insults and the fallout of his claims—she was protected enough due to her name. Still, there was only so far her name could shield her. Her father told her this.

"It's better if I marry quickly," Amaria told Delphina when she broke the surface. "My father is trying to protect me. I marry, consummate the marriage, have children, and put this whole situation behind me."

Delphina raised an eyebrow, saying nothing.

Amaria knew she didn't believe her. Delphina distrusted Aaron Raulet. And Aaron was a cunning, conniving snake. But, he was Amaria's father. He valued family, family legacy, or familial protection most of all.

That cunning, conniving snake wouldn't hurt her. She was his daughter.

Delphina nudged Amaria, smiling widely. Amaria could guess Delphina was trying to put this difficult conversation behind them. Amaria appreciated that. She didn't want this to sour her day.

"I bet you a gold dragon that I can beat you to the other end," Delphina said.

She was so competitive. Amaria loved that about her. Amaria was competitive too. Not in the same way Delphina was; Amaria didn't care about sports. But she enjoyed games, especially mind games.

"Do you?" Amaria laughed, not moving from the bench.

Delphina crossed her arms. "I thought you were more competitive than that."

"I'm exhausted," Amaria said. However, she still sat up from the bench. She wanted to beat Delphina. She didn't even need the dragon.

She just liked winning.

"Nicoletta!" Amaria called out to a girl with curly hair. Her skin was a bright pink; she too had never fared well in the tropical sun. Much like Amaria, Nicoletta was also engaged to a Lord in the Westerlands of Thestitiunia. A much more minor one than Amaria's future husband, however. Nicoletta would likely fare much better in the Westanni climate than the Perivinan one. Amaria, however, with her golden skin and natural heat resistance from her fire magic, thrived in the heat of Perivina Fluere. The snowy mountains and forests of the Westerlands, while beautiful, would be a severe adjustment.

"Amaria?" Nicoletta asked as she swam beside her and Delphina.

"Would you time the race between Delphina and I?" Amaria stated.

"Of course, how many lengths?" Nicoletta responded.

"Just down and back," Delphina said, stretching her arms above her head.

Amaria lowered herself in the water, placing her feet on the bench, waiting to push off of it. Others moved out of their way. A perk of being Duke Raulet's daughter. She resisted the urge to roll her eyes.

"On your mark....three...two—"

A clanging sound erupted through the bathing hall. The warning bells were ringing. Amaria stood up abruptly, her eyes widened. "What's happening?"

"I don't know," Delphina mused, pulling herself on the deck. "We should probably dress in case it's serious."

Amaria's mouth went dry. Warning bells could occur for many reasons. Sometimes there was a fire in the city—but that wouldn't cause a warning bell at the palace would it? The palace was stone and isolated from other buildings. Fire may spread quickly in the city, but Provincia Palencia usually remained unaffected.

Perhaps it was a fight. Sometimes those broke out—it likely was two men who had too much to drink so they attacked each other. Even as she thought it, Amaria knew she was being stupid. Warning bells wouldn't be used for a mere fight.

Amaria could not admit the truth. There were dangers inside her home. Something terribly wrong had occurred.

She summoned a warm gust of air, circling herself, Delphina, and Nicoletta with it, drying them as she grabbed a dressing gown. There were no robes here, the servants usually brought them later to protect them from the moisture of the bathhouse. The dressing gown was lightweight, almost sheer. Paired with its cut of no shoulders and almost dropping to a point where you could see the side of her breast, it was revealing. Normally Amaria would never wear this out in public, she would have a robe brought as she went to her rooms.

However, now Amaria did not particularly care how revealing the dressing gown was as long as it covered her long enough to get to safety.

"What do you think's happening?" Nicoletta asked.

Amaria shook her head, summoning fire to her hands as they stepped out of the bathhouse and into the hallway of the first floor of the palace. Amaria didn't know what she was planning. She didn't even know what was occurring.

She flattened herself against the wall as guards ran past.

"What's happening?" Amaria shouted to one.

"Attack!" The guard shouted, barely stopping. Amaria suspected that if somebody else had asked, he would not have bothered. Her position afforded her these small luxuries. "Two guards died near the gemstone hall."

Amaria froze, the shouts and clangs ringing in her ears as the world swirled. She had to get to the hall. She had to know what they took.

She had to know if the Raulet Ruby was safe.

The Raulet Ruby was a bit of an irony, considering that their house colors were blue not red. However, the magical gem had been entrusted to her family's safekeeping for generations, and so the name was donned. She didn't know why it was entrusted to them; perhaps having strong magic and a castle, they were the best people to house the Ruby.

Amaria tried not to investigate the history of the Ruby much. She was never a particularly strong student with her tutors—she didn't see the point of studying things that weren't immediately practical. Needlework, dancing, polite conversation—essential to a woman of her position. Magic, well she had to do that or else her magic would consume her. Politics, economics, torture, and espionage methods—that was where she excelled as a student. Not history.

Besides, the Raulet Ruby was terrifying. Even if Amaria was a student of history, she wouldn't want to research it more. Dark magic swirled around in the Raulet Ruby, and the magic grew, only contained with layers upon layers of magic. Amaria did not know what exactly placed its magic there, only that it scared her.

She wished the Ruby could be destroyed.

It was unfortunate that destroying the Ruby likely would cause a rift in the border between the Badlands and the rest of the continent. Although, rifts were already appearing since the Queen of Avondra had taken over.

Not that many people knew about this. A small convenience of being a good spy master and helping her father with his intelligence network was that she knew a great many things that others didn't.

Most of them were bad.

Maybe that's why she had felt so on edge recently?

Amaria shook her head, determinedly running up the grand staircase. She did not have time to be concerned with her thoughts.

"Stop them!" A guard yelled as two men sprinted down the hall. Amaria turned to see them trying to jump to the railing of the staircase. Breathing heavily, she pulled the moisture from the air, directing a stream of water towards the railing, freezing it.

One of the men tried to grab the railing. His hands slipped from underneath him, and he pitched forward, falling to the ground floor. Amaria heard his neck snap.

The second man turned to face her. "Lady Raulet," he inclined his head almost mockingly as he raised his hands in front of him. He wasn't showing surrender though; Amaria saw him shift his weight. This man was a mage.

"Get back," Amaria muttered to Delphina and Nicoletta. They weren't mages. They did not need to be in what was likely going to be a rather hostile mages' duel. "Find a room, lock it, and stay there."

Amaria did not have the chance to say more as a fireball whizzed past her head. She turned, her eyes glowing silver, glaring at the man as if her hatred alone could kill him a thousand times. His arms were on fire, his eyes a deep red now, and he smirked.

She hated him. She hated that he came into her home to commit a crime. Why else could he be here other than to steal or worse, conduct intelligence activities—it was a stupid way to do it, but Amaria wasn't striking the possibility. She hated him for disrupting her peaceful bath. She hated that he was a fire mage—burning him to death was not a realistic option anymore.

"I want your friends to witness this," the man laughed. He was taunting her. He wanted to anger her. Angering a fire mage was a risky strategy, but if you yourself couldn't be burned, Amaria understood the man's methods. She would have to avoid using fire—that was what he was likely expecting, for Amaria to match his fire magic with her own.

"Just how you witnessed your friend's neck snapping?" Amaria threw a burst of air at him. She intended to extinguish it at the last moment, killing the oxygen needed for his flames. Unfortunately, she was too slow and his flames sprung higher and higher.

"More of an acquaintance," the man threw the fireball towards Delphina and Nicoletta. Amaria dove in front of it, pulling a ball of water around her. Her clothes were burnt, but thankfully, Nicoletta and Delphina were unharmed.

Amaria breathed, taking the water in front of her and flinging icicles from it. The man danced around them, using his fire to melt them as he moved. Amaria gritted her teeth, throwing the entire force of the water at him. She wanted him to drown.

The tidal wave died down. He was on his back. Guards were running, approaching closer. Nicoletta and Delphina, seeing their chance, tried to flee. Amaria approached the man, air circling them. She wished she had a knife. Choking him until a guard with a sword arrived would have to do.

He gasped on the ground. Suddenly, he grabbed her ankle, pulling her down to the ground. "They'd kill me anyways," he stated as he pinned her down.

Amaria couldn't breathe. She felt vomit rise to her throat. Her legs wildly thrashed. The man pulled out a knife.

"Killing a Raulet," he said, smirking. "I'll get an award."

Amaria summoned the air circling her towards her face. She blew outwards in the man's face, forcing him to fly upwards. She quickly rolled out of the way, hitting Delphina's feet. Delphina and Nicoletta could not pass the chaos. Guards were all around.

It was over; he was caught.

The man landed on the ground, his body shaking as he screamed. As he sat up, the guards ran towards him, swords drawn. The man smiled.

Amaria felt her blood freeze—why would he be smiling?

The man threw his knife, the blade whizzing past Amaria's face. She flinched, shutting her eyes as the knife grazed her cheek. Even though Amaria heard the squelch of a sword entering a human body and the man's scream as the air around her settled once the blade passed, she was convinced she would die.

One thud came from the man.

The second one came from behind her.

Amaria's eyes snapped open, as she turned around wildly to see Delphina on the ground, clutching her heart. Next to her, Nicoletta was screaming for a healer.

"Some gems," a guard stated what the man stole, as if that were important. Amaria ran to Delphina's side. She gently moved Delphina's hands from her chest. There was a knife in her heart. He had missed Amaria but struck Delphina.

Screaming, Amaria sank to her knees. Delphina couldn't be dying. They never got to finish that race. Beneath her hands, Delphina shuddered.

"Healer!" Amaria shouted.

Delphina coughed, her eyes fluttering. Amaria was in a pool of blood. It was warm. Delphina was cold. It shouldn't be that way. Amaria felt a burning in her eyes as large, salty tears fell.

"It's alright," Amaria lied. "A healer is coming. They can fix this."

"I'd have won that race," Delphina weakly said, coughing up a stream of blood.

"I know, I know," Amaria hugged her. "You'd have won and been a gold dragon richer. You're an amazing swimmer. How about this? Once you heal from this we will go swim in the sea?"

Delphina closed her eyes.

"No," Amaria said. "Talk to me."

"Mhmm," Delphina muttered.

"She's lost too much blood," Nicoletta whispered.

Amaria's hands tightened over Delphina's. No. Delphina was not going to die. Amaria refused to acknowledge that absurd and stupid possibility, even as no breath came in and out of Delphina's body. She was just holding it, a cruel practical joke.

"She's dead." A guard approached, lowering himself down to lift her wrist.

"No," Amaria said, laying down on Delphina. "She's not."

The guard attempted to lift her from Delphina. "Lady Raulet-"

"No," Amaria screamed. "Leave me alone. Get a healer!"

She closed her eyes. Amaria could not bear to see the pools of blood. If she shut her eyes she could pretend the metallic smell was some form of salt and that they stupidly swam in the shores by the slums for whatever reason.

It was nonsensical but it made more sense than Delphina being dead.

"Amaria." A dark haired and golden skinned man ran to sit next to her. "Are you hurt?"

"Lord Raulet," a guard told her twin brother, "she seems to be in shock. It seems that Lady Delphina Ginsery was-"

"Stop!" Amaria screamed. "Don't say that word, Haerdnor. I'll throw you from the highest tower if you do."

Haerdnor placed his hand on her shoulder. "Amaria, she's gone. A healer isn't what she needs; she needs a priestess or priest of Sadthos-"

Amaria pushed herself off Delphina, swinging her hand towards Haerdnor to get him off of her. She did not need his lies. She did not need the reminder of what she had lost.

"Carry her to her room," Haerdnor directed the guards. "I don't care what she commands you to do. Keep her in her room until my father comes to her."

"You can't order me-"

"I can. And I will," Haerdnor snapped, interrupting her. He extended his hand to Nicoletta as Amaria was pulled off Delphina's body. "Are you alright, my Lady?"

Nicoletta took his hand shakily, silently shaking her head. Haerdnor nodded to the guards, indicating they should take care of Nicoletta as well. Amaria screamed as the guards dragged her through the corridor.

Why was nobody helping Delphina? Why did they dismiss her as dead? A healer approached the guards. Through her shouting and thrashing, Amaria felt a quick breath release in relief. Someone was finally going to help Delphina.

The guard paused and the healer placed his palm on her forehead. He wasn't helping Delphina. Amaria's world spun and turned to a sudden black.

Chapter Two

Amaria heard rustling around her. She was laying on her bed, plush pillows surrounding her head. She breathed a sigh of relief. She had an absurd dream—Delphina would find it interesting when she told her.

And then Amaria smelled the metallic stench of blood.

Her eyes fluttered open. Her previously blush dress was now covered in dried blood. It was burnt as well, a few places charred.

Amaria's heart sank. She didn't have a horrible nightmare that Delphina died. It was real.

Her friend was gone. She wanted to go back to sleep and pretend this never happened. Unfortunately for her, the healer saw her open her eyes and immediately turned to notify the richly dressed man sitting near Amaria's vanity.

"She's awake, Your Grace," the healer said.

"Good," Aaron Raulet, Amaria's father, replied. "You may leave. Check up on the other injured."

Amaria pressed her eyes shut again. Her father in her rooms was only a breeding ground for criticism. And the gods knew he had plenty of mistakes to choose from.

"Amaria, open your eyes," he said. "I know you can hear me."

"I'd rather not," Amaria said, bringing her hands to her temples.

"I understand Delphina's death is upsetting." Aaron stood over her, moving her hands off of her face. "Unfortunately, there are matters of business we must attend to."

"Can't you just let me grieve?" She sat up, looking directly at him. She didn't want to deal with his criticisms and she needed time and space to process what had happened.

Anger bubbled in her throat—with the healer's knocking her out, they were circumventing her healing process. Like that ever turned out well.

"No," Aaron said. "We do not get that luxury. I'll start with the least pressing matter first. Your behavior was unbecoming."

Amaria pressed her lips together. Her friend was just murdered with a knife that was meant for her and he was worried about her etiquette?

"There's also eyewitnesses that said he pinned you under him-"

"Nothing happened." Amaria stood up from the bed. "Don't worry, Father, I won't ruin my chances of marriage."

"It is unfortunate we must conduct a funeral before leaving for Chauvi," her father stated mildly, as if remarking on the weather. "You will conduct yourself appropriately as a bride, I trust?"

"Yes, Father," Amaria said. She forced down the bitterness rising from her chest. "I suppose I must after you called off my other engagement."

"Did you want to marry Lyseno Vypren? I forced Aion to recant his wishes for you to marry him if you don't recall."

"Yes, Father," Amaria repeated. "I'm thankful, truly." She was. Lyseno Vypren was Avonnian. She would be far from home, in a country that wasn't her own. She had been engaged for years to a man who was ancient, all at the commands of the Emperor of Thestitiunia. If one could even call Aion Marion that. Everyone knew Aaron Raulet was the true power behind the throne.

But they all had to flatter the emperor's ego. For propriety's sake.

Lyseno Vypren had claims to the Avonnian throne. Her mission was to marry him and breed while Thestitiunia somehow killed Queen Lynette Edrion of Avondra. Lyseno Vypren would become king and Amaria would rule until her son came of age. Avondra would be a puppet kingdom.

It would've all been perfect except for the fact Amaria hated it.

And she was a powerful mage. That played a part in the revocation of the engagement. The emperor had changed his mind on losing her magic to another country. Amaria scowled at the memory.

After her betrothal to Vypren had been broken, Amaria was almost immediately re-engaged to a Thestitiunian. Her new fiancé was Marquis Theodmon Chauvignon of the Westerlands. Briefly, she had wondered how that had happened, because usually these things took time. But Amaria was a Raulet. She was a good match. Of course, someone would immediately take her.

And it took them time to work out the finer details of the marriage anyways. During the entire engagement, her father and Theodmon had negotiated dowry, additional gifts for the funding of Theodmon's army, who would pay for what at the wedding, and a litany of other finer details.

Amaria had prayed during this that the engagement wouldn't fall through. Despite the title, Theodmon Chauvignon was as equal a rank as her father. There were four dukes, each the king of their own province in Thestitiunia. Because the Chauvignons hosted the faerielands, they fell a few acreages short of the required legal amount for dukehood. All the same, they were de facto dukes.

Theodmon Chauvignon was young, only six years older than her. Nineteen and twenty-five was better than Vypren who was in his fifties. He was said to be attractive as well. Amaria could not complain about a young, attractive husband of equal rank.

She wished her father didn't lord that fact over her head.

"I know how to conduct myself," Amaria said. "I was just…it all happened so fast. I can't believe she's dead; it feels like a bad dream."

Amaria's breath was still tight in her chest from the memory of it. She didn't want to cry or scream in front of her father, so she thought about everything else—the empire, her marriage—anything but the events that had occurred earlier in the day.

"It's worse," Aaron said. "The Raulet Ruby was taken. Those two thieves were a distraction." He looked at her sternly. "Why do you think they engaged you?"

"I presumed they wanted me dead." Amaria's nostrils flared. "Our family has starved and tormented two foreign countries; is it really surprising that some people don't like us?"

"Morroek and Rindria do not deserve sovereignty," Aaron said.

Amaria agreed with that sentiment; both countries should be absorbed into the empire. With their backwards and ill founded views on magic, paired with bordering the Badlands, anytime something with dark magic occurred, other rational countries had to be on the defensive every day Morroek and Rindria were independent. However, she wasn't going to admit this to her father. Not now anyways.

"That may be true, but it still explains why some people may hate us," Amaria said, tears suddenly pouring down her face. Delphina died because she was close to Amaria. Delphina died because Amaria was hated.

"That reminds me, get Theodmon Chauvignon to like you," Aaron told her calmly, as if she wasn't crying in front of him. "To have his army is invaluable. He is the military power behind the empire, and-"

"And you're the economy," Amaria finished, wiping snot from her nose. "Yes, I know. Have tons of children in the marriage, strengthen political connections. Father, I'm not an idiot. I know my job." Her chest was tightening. She couldn't breathe. The speed of her speech was quickening. "Besides, don't you know Marquis Chauvignon better than me? Couldn't I just provide children and you bond. Shared blood-"

"You're clever, despite some of your questionable decisions," Aaron interrupted. "Do you think I want you to be miserable? You and Theodmon Chauvignon may be a good match and not just politically."

Amaria did not know what to think of that confession.

"What about Raulet Ruby?" Amaria dug through her wardrobe. "You said it was taken?"

"Yes," Aaron said dryly. "It seems that someone took it."

"Who?" Amaria asked, her shoulders tightening. "You don't think it was Lynette Edrion, do you?"

Amaria knew it was Lynette Edrion. She did not need that confirmation that the Queen of Avondra had done this–politically, she knew that Lynette Edrion had made an alliance with Rindria and that Rindria was a puppet state of Avondra. Lynette had made Rindria a buffer between her and the Badlands. And the Badlands's magical containment was weakening. With a gem filled with dark magic as old as the continent, it would take someone as powerful, and as mad, as Lynette to shatter the containment spell.

It was a spell placed by a goddess. Ghagyn was the goddess of magic and hope but she also dominated despair and tragedy. The Badlands seemed to exemplify that well.

"Yes. Lynette Edrion likely has them on payroll. Get dressed; the man you fought is in the Drowning Tombs."

Amaria looked at her father in surprise. "What? I thought he died."

"Injured," Aaron corrected. "He'll be dead soon enough. Be ready in an hour. I presume you're capable enough to torture him?"

Amaria's silver eyes hardened, looking as if they were storm clouds and steel. "Yes."

She hadn't enjoyed seeing Delphina suffer, but she had cared about Delphina. She had been training in torture since she was twelve. She should have hated it. Prison was no place for a lady.

Aaron didn't agree. Apparently he had seen that she had the necessary cruelty and precision needed to be an adept torturer. And Aaron Raulet raised his children how Aaron Raulet saw fit. She would be a perfect lady on the surface. Poised. Polite. Wouldn't dare even think about impolite or improper conversation topics.

She would also be skilled at politics and espionage—helping him run his spy network. And prisoners and their information were skills she learned.

Unfortunately for the prisoners, Amaria was more than adept at these skills. She was talented.

And this prisoner had made the mistake of breaking into her home, stealing from her family, and murdering her friend.

Amaria hoped that he was a Thestitiunian citizen. She always enjoyed enacting the punishment for treason.

Chapter Three

Three hours later, Amaria met her father at the entrance of the estate. She had showered, removing the dried blood from her skin, and she had dug out an old black dress and veil reserved for mourning.

"Loose the veil," Aaron said.

"I'm mourning," Amaria protested. "No."

"It'll be ruined at the Drowning Tombs."

Amaria glared at her father wondering how he could be so crass. "Then I'll take it off before we go inside."

The sun danced over Amaria's skin as she and her father stepped beyond the white gates of Provinica Palancia and into the city of Raulle. Delphina would have burned in this heat. Still, Delphina would have still loved an excursion to the city. She had loved Raulle from the portside markets to the mosaics in the street—Delphina loved the hustle and bustle of the city.

Had loved. Past tense. Delphina couldn't love anymore—she was dead.

Amaria shook her head, trying to clear the poisonous cloud taking over her mind. She focused on Raulle, breathing in to take in her surroundings as they walked through the portside markets.

The sailors lowered anchors and tied ropes around posts. Amaria scanned her surroundings. She saw tents and booths—a variety of wares being sold from each location. Shells littered the white sand around the docks, and the water, a clear turquoise near Provincia Palencia, was now a murky blue, the smell of alcohol and dead fish wafting from it. A few scantily dressed women yelled to the sailors, and Amaria felt herself inadvertently turning her head the other way, her lip curling.

Amaria had loved going to Raulle with Delphina. And if she looked only at her surroundings, she could pretend she was walking with Delphina and not her father.

Rapidly blinking back tears, Amaria pushed her way through the crowd of the bustling market, thankful her rich dress and silver eyes made her distinguishable to the Raullian citizenry. They shied away from her, not wanting to push a Raulet daughter over.

Amaria smelled the comforting scent of baking bread wafting over the rafters of the stores and the middle-class residential buildings. She turned her head, seeing wire seats and stone tables in front of a glass-front store, greenery overflowing from its façade.

All seemed well. Amaria could almost forget that life had become a tragedy.

Almost.

A carriage was waiting for them in the middle of the merchant district. Amaria had wanted to walk through the city to clear her mind and distract herself. Her father had humored the idea.

Silently, Aaron and Amaria climbed into the carriage. The task at hand was an ugly one, and neither one of them felt particularly chipper.

The carriage rolled through the streets and after nearly half an hour Amaria noticed a foul smell wafting through the rafters of the carriage. They were nearing the slums, which meant the prison was near as well.

Amaria looked down at her plain blue dress. It was simpler than what she normally wore, but there was no point in ruining a beautiful garment at the Drowning Tombs. The Drowning Tombs was an apt name for the prison, considering most of it was underwater.

The carriage slowed, coming to a stop. The doors were opened and Amaria and Aaron departed from it, walking towards a huge lighthouse, likely ten stories high. It wasn't the only lighthouse in the city. Amaria knew of two more of that size, one near Provincia Palencia and the other near the seaside market. There were smaller lighthouses too, she supposed.

Her dress swept over the sand, causing miniature dust clouds to form near her feet as they approached the lighthouse, the waves lapping against the rocks surrounding it. Amaria clenched her hands together, forcing the lump in her throat down.

She wanted to make this man pay. She was happy to avenge Delphina.

She just hoped that she didn't disappoint her father.

A few guards ran by, casting sharp glances towards the two Raulets but making no effort to approach them as Amaria and Aaron approached a stone bridge with two guards on either side of it.

"I'm seeing the prison," Aaron directed, indicating for Amaria to step onto the stone bridge with him. "Is there a boat ready?"

"Yes, Your Grace," the guard said, his head still bowed.

Aaron nodded curtly, walking briskly across the bridge. Amaria followed. She would make him proud. She was competent. She was good at this. There wasn't much he could criticize with her methods. They were different from his, but they worked.

She walked silently next to her father for a few moments before they departed the bridge, soon approaching the other side of the small island where a dinghy was prepared for them. As they walked, Amaria looked across the narrow channel. Even from where she was standing, she could see a diminutive island, and then a much bigger one, across the way. There was nothing but sand, a few palm trees, and a forest of watch towers on the smaller island.

She remembered the first time she had come to the Drowning Tombs. She had been twelve when her education in torture had begun. Amaria had frozen Haerdnor because he had burnt her embroidery, and her father had decided that perhaps she was already sadistic enough to learn the skill set.

His assessment wasn't incorrect, to be fair. She was shockingly adept at torture.

"What's the plan?" Amaria asked as they climbed into the rowboat. She wanted to know what her father expected from this trip so as to not disappoint him. She wanted to make sure the man who broke into her home and killed her friend over jewels would pay in the most painful way possible.

"His compatriot is a woman. We need to know where she's headed. Who they work for. I figured your style may be more adequate to gaining information," Aaron said.

"Will you be there with me?"

Aaron shook his head. "No, I'll be outside the door."

Amaria sighed. Perhaps this was for the best. She did tire of doing dirty work, but she valued efficiency. If this was what truly needed to be done, she would do it. She surveyed the large gray building looming in front of her. The building was surrounded by a steep wall with as many guard towers as petals on a flower.

It was an ugly flower.

Amaria used magic to manipulate the waters into moving the boat across the sound. Silently, the boat cut through the waves and soon hit the grainy sand of the second island, its texture and coloring unlike the pristine white sand surrounding the rest of the city.

Her hands clenching into knuckles, Amaria felt a chill run down her spine, as her skin was suddenly covered with bumps. Shivering, Amaria wrapped her arms around herself. Her surroundings were darker, and dingier, than they were on the surface, even within the prison. She turned her head to the side to see a murky glass window, algae growing upon it from complete submersion and the likelihood of its never being cleaned.

Not for the first time, she wondered if there were sharks around Raulle, and how the prisoners would feel being face-to-face with one.

Wincing, Amaria forced back a gag. There was a reason the Drowning Tombs was said to be one of the worst prisons on the continent. She could almost feel pity for its inhabitants if they hadn't embezzled, murdered, or committed treason. The Drowning Tombs were filled with criminals who would hurt her if they had the chance. Amaria could not afford to feel pity for them, nor did she want to.

In fact, she didn't want to particularly think about them at all.

"This way, Your Grace and my Lady." The guard's keys jangled as he unlocked another gate with stairs leading further downwards on the other side.

Aaron stepped behind the guard, water lapping around his ankles. Amaria hoped her father didn't slip—he had a bad leg—as she stepped behind him, immediately picking up her skirts above her ankles to avoid the water on the ground.

They continued down further in the half-underwater prison, ignoring the screams and sobs echoing from unseen corridors, the dripping of water on the walls, the stench of seaweed and, perhaps, blood.

"Brief me," Aaron commanded the guard as they walked.

"Prisoner refuses to speak. We've withheld water-"

"Bring me water and wine," Amaria interrupted, "for the prisoner. And a blanket."

The guard turned towards her, his eyebrows arched.

"I think I can get him to talk by initiating kindness," she explained.

Aaron shrugged. "Follow my daughter's lead. She's conducting this interrogation."

"Yes, Your Grace," the guard said as they stepped into the midnight-colored archway.

"Have someone turn the rack on standby," Amaria commanded. "I'll let you know when I need him."

"Yes, my Lady," he said as they stopped in front of a worn wooden door with iron rods over the small opening—Amaria could've slid a thick letter through the gap where the bar covered but not much more.

The door to a cell was unlocked. Amaria clenched her fists, centering herself with the pain of her nails digging into her palms as she stepped into the dingy cell. The overwhelming smell of rotting fish, salt, and urine caused Amaria to gag. She pinched her nose, forcing herself to think of the clear waters near the Provincia Palencia, the crystalline waves lapping against the white sand. If she pretended she was there, she could force herself to wade through this cesspool.

"Hello." Amaria's voice was gentle, emulating a doctor when they were healing a scared patient. She dropped her skirts, letting them drag in the dirty water as she stepped further into the shadows of the cell. "Would you like some light?"

"What do you want?" The man snarled, his eyes haggard. Still, they flashed with hatred as deep as the ocean and as wild as a tsunami. "Is this a depraved trick?"

"I want your name," Amaria sighed.

"I'm not giving you that, *Lady Raulet.*" Contempt radiated in the man's saying of her name. As Amaria stepped closer, she saw he was chained to the wall. Good. He deserved it.

"Why?" Amaria asked. She didn't really care what he had to say about this. "You're already in prison. What more can you lose?"

"Lose?" The man manically laughed, throwing his head back so far it hit the wall. "I'm gaining something."

Amaria's eyes flashed. She wanted to gut this man. She wanted to burn his entrails—as difficult as that may be with him being a fire mage—as she gutted him.

"Gain?" she said lightly, keeping the anger out of her voice. It'd ruin her strategy to show her hatred now.

"When's the last time a fucking Raulet didn't get what they wanted?"

Amaria sighed. She would have to play a naïve fool. However believable that may have been. "I didn't get the perfume I wanted for my birthday this year."

The man rolled his eyes. "What do you want?"

"I want closure." She summoned fire to her palms, illuminating the cell.

The man smirked. "How's your friend?"

Amaria almost threw fire at him. How *dare* he mock her like that? How *dare* he mock Delphina's death in that way?

Her fists clenched as she closed her eyes, forcing herself to do a quick breathing exercise. She had to remain calm. She had to remain in control.

"Better than you," Amaria said. She was proud that her voice remained steady, with no hint of agitation or anger lacing her tone. "I ordered water and wine to be brought to you."

"Why?" The man's eyes narrowed.

"Perhaps this has been a miscommunication." Amaria chuckled pleasantly as fire ran across her palms, illuminating the cell. There was much more water on the floor than she had initially thought. It seemed as if the floor slanted near the door—the further away from the exit, the deeper the water got. "I apologize for these conditions; they're abhorrent."

"I killed your friend," the man said.

"These things happen," Amaria dismissed. She hated herself for the lie. It was exhausting being so manipulative.

"I won't tell you anything," the man spat. "Whatever game you're playing-"

"No game," Amaria said. "Why do people think I am much more nefarious and clever than I truly am?"

Another lie. People tended to underestimate her. That was their first mistake. Haerdnor had once compared her to an oleander flower, beautiful but deadly. Just as the white and magenta flowers looked soothing, Amaria tried to be a docile and calming presence to others before she signed their death warrant.

It made it easier to deny later.

"I apologize for anything my family did to hurt you," Amaria told the prisoner, lowering the inclination of her voice to almost indicate shame.

Amaria hated pretending she didn't like what her family did. She wasn't discomforted by being a Raulet, rather actively participated in bolstering her family's power, no matter how devious or underhanded the reasoning or methods were.

Showing that pride wouldn't work here. Shame, as infuriating as it was, was a better strategy. And she would do it, no matter how much she internally wanted to scream.

The man spat at her, the plopping of the water damning. "Oh, you apologize. Why are you here?"

"As I said, closure," Amaria lied. Perhaps it wasn't a complete lie. She needed closure for Delphina. She doubted she'd ever get it. "My friend died. I need to know why. We can help each other."

The door opened, a guard passing her wine and bread.

"Why should I trust you?"

Amaria shrugged. "You shouldn't." The most effective lies were merged with truth. "I don't mean to harm you, I promise you that. Do you want water or wine?"

Amaria looked at the swirling black water, the smell of sulfur coming from it, and she could swear in the dimming light, she saw debris in the depths. The last place she ever wanted to wade into was that water.

The door opened, a guard holding two jugs.

"Water or wine?" Amaria repeated.

The man looked at her suspiciously. "Wine," he slowly said.

The guard handed Amaria the jug of dark red liquid. Curtly, she nodded, dismissing him. It would be better to conduct this part alone, without the leering presence of someone else around.

"I'll have to feed you," Amaria told him apologetically, as she stepped into the dirty water. She flinched, forcing herself to pretend she was stepping in the near translucent water near the palace.

Forcing back her gags, she approached the man, standing next to him, lifting the goblet to his lips, when she said: "I'm not authorized to unlock your chains...I mean, I'm not even supposed to be here, but this seems like a terrible..."

The man gulped down the wine, Amaria holding it up to his mouth. She flinched whenever slobber hit her hands, but otherwise, she remained chillingly unruffled, seemingly the epitome of charity. She wanted to kill him.

"Why?" Amaria repeated. She knew she needed to get information on his compatriots. She knew that strategically Delphina's death meant nothing. She knew that somewhere out there the Raulet Ruby, and all the dark magic trapped within it, was with somebody it shouldn't be. However, she couldn't find it in her to care that much. And perhaps, this human approach to an interrogation—sharing wounded souls and wine—would work.

"Got paid," the man shrugged. "Had an opportunity to embarrass your family."

"Was your friend who died paid?" Amaria asked.

"I'd assume so," he said. "None of my business really."

Amaria stood silently. She was close; she could feel it. But if she was too heavy-handed, she would lose it all. "We don't have much time," she said, glancing towards the door. "I'm not supposed to be here; my father would likely imprison me if he knew—I'm burying my friend soon. Was it necessary for her to die? Were you aiming for her? Why a knife? Why not fire?"

"I was aiming for you," the man said. "Fire won't hurt you. Steel will."

Amaria breathed. She was close. "Wouldn't killing me hurt your mission?"

"You caught me with the gems anyways."

She wondered if he knew that his compatriot got away. "Fighting with me hurts your mission. You should have ran; you could've gotten away with the gems. Fed your family."

"How do you know I have a family?" he asked.

Amaria didn't know. Not until now. "Most people aren't reckless enough to steal from a Raulet unless they have something more to gain than lose. For most, that's their family. Can I have your name?"

"You won't hurt them?" His voice shot up. Amaria stopped herself from smiling.

"No," she lied, already making a mental note to have the traitor's family arrested and hanged. "But others will. I'm the only one who can protect them from my father and has the inclination too. But I need a reason to do it, to justify my actions." She shrugged. "I have to protect my own skin."

Another truth with the lie.

"Justin," the man said, wetting his lips. "And Giuliana Vero," the man said. "She stole Raulet Ruby. She's a Thestitiunian citizen who lives near the border of Avondra. She was recruited by the Avonnian Queen."

Amaria sucked in her breath. She wasn't surprised Lynette Edrion was behind this. Every dark magic event recently seemed to be tied to her in some way. Or to Rindria. But Rindria was in Lynette Edrion's pocket. It was clear that the country was a buffer, a bridge, between Avondra and the Badlands. Amaria only wondered how the people from Rindria, or Riams as they were called, didn't see that. They had to see that, right?

"And your family?" she asked kindly as a guard stepped in. He handed her a blanket and began to light the torches on the wall.

"I have a wife. She's in Raulle. Haninia Fila."

Amaria beamed. She turned towards the door. "Come in, Father."

The man froze, his eyes widening as Aaron stepped through the door, three guards behind him. One began lighting the torches in the room.

"You're a traitor," Amaria chillingly hissed, throwing the wooden wine goblet to the ground. "And I despise those without loyalty." She turned to the guard, who had finished lighting the torches around the room on the walls, revealing that this cell was not a cell, but a torture chamber. "Rack him."

He had already talked. He didn't need to be racked.

She didn't care. She didn't want information anymore. She wanted his pain. She wanted to hear his bones stretch and break. She wanted to hear his screams.

"Raulet Bitch!" The prisoner screamed as two more guards unchained him and dragged him through the grimy water to the rack table. "May you suffer ten million deaths! May your family die! I'd kill your fr—"

"Hit him," Amaria instructed a guard as they chained him onto the table. The guard did as he was bid, slapping the man across the face.

They had all the information they needed now. This was just for her own validation.

Amaria nodded towards a guard, indicating for him to turn the wheel. The guard complied, a small grunt escaping him as the wheel began to move.

As the rack turned, the man screamed, the sound almost as loud as his cracking bones as his arms were pulled over his head and his legs pulled downwards, the table's rods turning to stretch his joints outwards.

Amaria felt pleasure in the noise. "Hand me a knife, please," she told her father.

Aaron unsheathed the dagger at his side, handing it to her. She placed her hand forcefully on the prisoner's, pinning it down before bringing the blade down on his pointer finger, cutting the tip of the finger off right above the knuckle.

The man screamed, thrashing in pain as red fell into black water.

"Thank you for your cooperation," Amaria smirked as she picked up the finger. "Box," she commanded.

She'd place all his fingers in a box and have them bring the box to the estate as a trophy.

"Where's the gem being taken?" Aaron asked.

"I told your bitch daughter already," the man panted. "We work for Lynette Edrion."

Amaria saw his eyes shift. She saw the spark in them. He thought he was triumphant, even in this cell being racked.

Perhaps they didn't have all the information as she had previously thought. It seemed as if the gem wasn't being brought to Lynette.

And if the gem wasn't going to Avondra, it had to be going to its puppet state, Rindria. Everyone but Rindira itself seemed to understand that it was not truly its own sovereign nation, oh they all pretended but anybody with half a brain cell that wasn't completely delusional knew that Rindria was nothing but an unofficial colony of Avondra. The King of Rindria was fully inept at foreign alliances and he rather allowed his sister, Clarissa Nalaeny, to conduct those for him.

Unfortunately for Rindria, Clarissa Nalaeny was an idiot who believed she was the smartest person in the room. No greater harm had been done by a fool who believed himself to be a genius.

Amaria knew where the gem was. She should feel triumphant. But she couldn't. While Clarissa Nalaeny had no magical power and could not be classified as a true threat, she was unbelievably stupid. Stupidity killed more people than intelligent effectiveness.

She twisted the rack once more, his screams sounding as if it were a sweet symphony. He had killed Delphina.

Amaria swore revenge. She swore she would find the Raulet Ruby. She would hunt down Lynette Edrion and her Riam pawns and tear them limb from limb, forcing them to drink their own blood as they died.

Perhaps she would first tear their skin off to prolong the pain. Each day Delphina could have lived but didn't because of them, Amaria would add a minute of suffering. They deserved more, but she had to be realistic and understand the constraints of time.

She leaned forward, bringing the knife to the man's throat. His blood splattered onto her dress and face. She heard the dripping of his blood and the droplets falling into the water.

"Go bathe and see if the servants finished packing your belongings," Aaron's voice interrupted her thoughts as Amaria leaned her head against the carriage's window.

It seemed that despite Delphina's death, Amaria was still to be shipped off to be a bride as scheduled. "I can't go to the funeral?"

"You have other obligations," Aaron dismissed. "Have you been taking the herbs given to you by the healers?"

"Yes," Amaria said. She had been eating bitter roots to increase her fertility for six months now. Apparently it would be detrimental to her, her husband, and worse to her father if she wasn't immediately swollen with a child after her first time.

She was a Raulet, and Raulet women were docile breeding grounds with outrageously large dowries. At least publicly. Amaria didn't mind that too much—she had accepted the reality, at least. She knew her role and what she had to do. She wasn't an idiot and did not need her father's reminders, which served only to treat her as such.

"When's the funeral?" Amaria asked.

"Tomorrow."

"Traveling can wait," Amaria snapped. "The funeral can be early in the morning and we leave after the body is at sea. I don't need to be there for the feast or whatever else. Let me put her body to rest."

"Amaria-"

"I'll disgrace our family." Amaria coldly looked at her father. "I'll run half-dressed, sobbing to the funeral. I'm going either way; how much decorum I show is entirely in your control."

Amaria and Aaron stared at each other. Amaria's narrowed silver eyes did not break from Aaron's brown. The only noise was the creaking of the carriage's wheels as it rolled through Raulle, the Raulet's ancestral city.

Amaria wished her father wouldn't be so difficult. She wished that he would grow a semblance of healthy human emotion. He was brutally practical, at the expense of any positive emotions or empathy. It was a survival instinct, but still, it was difficult to stomach.

"Fine," Aaron said. "The funeral will be at six in the morning, at sunrise. As soon as the boat is burning and floating to sea, we'll depart."

Amaria slumped in her seat. "Thank you."

She had worried her father would refuse. She wasn't sure she would have actually disgraced her family. She wanted to increase their power. And for her, that meant marriage and children. What alternative did she have? A temple.

While temples would love to have her—she was, after all, a powerful mage—Amaria knew that a temple wasn't a place for her. A temple was a place of peace. Amaria didn't want peace.

She wanted revenge. The man she killed was a puppet. There would always be more puppets.

Unless the master's head was mounted on the city's walls.

Chapter Four

Amaria's mind replayed Delphina's funeral the entire trip up north to Chauvi. She tried to nap. She couldn't think if she was asleep. If she didn't think, she couldn't feel pain. She could pretend she had a horrible dream as they traveled to Chauvi. She was having pre-wedding jitters, and it manifested in a bizarre nightmare.

Amaria didn't believe it. She was too good of a liar to fall for her own delusions. She wished she had more time with Delphina. Delphina should have had more time to live. She was so young. She had so much life left. Delphina should be sitting in the carriage in the seat behind her, or at least in a following carriage like Nicoletta was.

Amaria wondered how Nicoletta was doing. She had seen Delphina die too.

At least the knife wasn't aimed for Nicoletta. The knife was aimed for Amaria. It should have hit Amaria instead of Delphina.

"Should" was a stupid word. The concept of "should" was foolish idealism. Lots of things should or should not happen. Those things did not reflect reality. Life wasn't fair, and Amaria would only hurt herself if she believed in children's fables.

"Are we almost there?" Amaria asked, mostly to distract herself.

"Anxious to meet your husband?" Haerdnor snorted. "How story book of you."

Amaria rolled her eyes. "I'm anxious to be away from you."

A few more days of travel passed. Amaria marveled at the large, looming mountain ranges and the dense forests they passed as she wrapped her cloak tighter around her. The Westerlands had an edge to them, as if the lands were still wild. Everything was neat and orderly in Perivina Fluere, the Westerlands, while it had elements that were also untamed.

And although it was still summer, it was much colder here than it was in Raulle.

The city of Chauvi seemed more separated from the liege lord's castle than Provincia Palencia had been from Raulle. While Provincia Palencia had tall walls to keep out the rest of the city, Forteresse les Blanche was built into the mountain above Chauvi.

Amaria wondered how they would get up to the castle. Could the carriage get them all the way to the top?

Her question was quickly answered when the carriage stopped midway up the mountain. "We'll have to walk," the footman informed them. "It's too steep. Your belongings will go to the off-path, where the pulley system is."

Gingerly, Amaria looked around, seeing green. What had to be thousands of evergreen and pine trees surrounded the mountain and valley below with smoke stacks from Chauvi poofing upward.

Forteresse les Blanche was carved from the mountain. Amaria had worn boots today, knowing this hike was coming. She understood the appeal of having a castle as well fortified as this, but she wasn't thrilled with the effort needed to reach it. Decisively, Amaria determined she probably wouldn't leave the castle much once she arrived. It seemed to be too much of a hassle to go down this mountain path every time.

Amaria's chest already hurt from the hike, her breath wheezing in the colder air. Ahead, she saw guards opening the gates. Bless the gods, Amaria couldn't imagine asking them to open them in between gasps for air. She was more dignified than that.

Smoothing down her dress, she stepped into a white and gray stone courtyard. A few hundred feet away, Amaria spotted a large oak double door, large scratches carved into the face of the wood. She could see the bolts on the door from where she stood, and she guessed it usually was bolted. Forteresse les Blanche was a fortress—it was obvious from the name and the secured position on a mountain.

Amaria imagined that forts were often bolted.

However, this fort was currently open, and a tall, broad shouldered man stood in the middle of the vast doorway. Shyly, Amaria peered at him. He had a shadow of stubble over a defined jawline, and Amaria wondered how much it would tickle when his face brushed against hers in a kiss.

"Welcome," he said, his voice deep, as they approached him. "Duke Raulet, is this my bride?"

"Marquis Chauvignon," Aaron gave a short incline of his head. "This is my daughter, Amaria."

She lowered herself into a curtsy, her veil still over her face—it was bad luck for a groom to see a bride before their vows. She curtsied, raising her eyes slightly to discreetly observe Theodmon Chauvignon. She had seen him at Imperial Events. They had never interacted much but she knew of him. He was handsome, and she could tell he was well-muscled under those clothes. She had seen him spar at court tournaments and such.

She met his hazel eyes. They radiated a fierce, uncompromising intelligence.

Would Theodmon be kind to her? There wasn't much talk of his kindness. There also wasn't much talk of his cruelty. It was as if that topic did not matter in the gossip halls.

It mattered to Amaria.

"It's a pleasure to see you again, my Lord," she said. "I was at the tourney in Aionstown two summers ago. I remember you performed well."

He nodded shortly to her. "I'll have your belongings brought to my chambers. You'll stay in a guest chamber until we are wed. How was your journey?"

"Long, my Lord," Amaria said, ignoring her flaring anxiety. Surely the short nod wasn't intended to be dismissive? Theodmon had people from all over coming to his home—hospitality would be paramount. Amaria hoped he was distracted.

She didn't want to be dismissed for the rest of her life.

"The incline was steep reaching your castle," she said.

"Military advantage." Theodmon's face lit up. Amaria's mouth twitched. He just wasn't good at military strategy, it appeared that he loved it as well. She had always admired passion and conviction. Perhaps she could bond with him, not over military matters per se, but other things. She wanted this marriage to work. She didn't want to be miserable. He was intelligent, she was intelligent. There had to be something they could bond over.

"Invading armies find it incredibly difficult to seize, and it's easier for us to defend," Theodmon continued.

"How do you get supplies into the castle?" Amaria asked. She in part asked to keep him talking to her, perhaps he'd like her if she showed an interest in what he found interesting. She also asked because she was curious.

"A pulley system and earth mages," he said as a slender woman with black hair approached. "I'll explain it in more detail later if you'd like."

Amaria had found military matters boring her entire life. Still, she was honest in answering, "I'd like that very much, my Lord."

Theodmon gave the ghost of a grin. "My Lady, may I introduce you to Lady Juliette Bécharil? She will be one of your ladies-in-waiting as she is married to my bannerman, Lucas Bécharil."

Amaria inclined her head.

"She'll be bringing you to your guest chambers," Theodmon said, stepping away from them. "I'll see you at the wedding, Lady Raulet."

"When's the wedding?" Amaria asked. "I lost track of time in the carriage."

"Two days," Theodmon said. "You should ask Lady Bécharil to answer the rest of your questions. It isn't proper for us to speak further before our wedding—bad luck."

Amaria nodded. She was familiar with the superstition. She wondered how much of it was truly bad luck or a way to mitigate the bride and groom running off because the other was hideous.

Not that Theodmon was bad looking...

He departed without another word. Amaria's face burned. Of course she was fortunate enough to get a handsome, young groom who had no rumors of cruelty.

Of course she would get all of that and for him to be as emotionally hard as a stone wall. Amaria knew she was being greedy, but she had hoped for the chance of happiness. It was unlikely and she would do her duty either way, but to have the chance to have genuine affection for her husband and for her to return the sentiment was all she had ever wanted.

"My Lady," Juliette said beside her, her soft voice disappearing into the night sky. "You must be tired."

"Yes," Amaria sighed. "I'd like a bath."

Perhaps she could drown herself in the bath. She wished she could forget about Delphina.

She paused, turning around to look at the carriages. Nicoletta had followed Amaria to the Westerlands. She would be married in a few months. "I'd like my lady, Nicoletta Fialieno, to join us later."

Juliette smoothed her skirts. "Of course, my Lady."

Amaria watched her as they silently made their way up the steps. Juliette had long black hair, which was tied into intricate braids. She had a kind face, and her eyes meticulously gazed over their surroundings as she and Amaria walked through the castle. It was obvious that they'd both be stuck as acquaintances—Theodmon loved Lucas Bécharil, his childhood friend and bannerman—for Lucas and Theodmon were inseparable. When there was a formal event where one appeared, the other was close by. It didn't take many formal weddings or solstices or whatever fancy party was occurring to know this if one was half-observant.

Amaria didn't want new friends. But she didn't want to be cold with a woman she would be around until one of them died. It was too soon after Delphina. It felt as if a knife was burning and twisting in an open wound.

Still Amaria kindly smiled at Juliette. "I love your hair."

Juliette returned the smile. "Thank you, my Lady."

"You can call me Amaria," she said. "Our husbands are close. I hope we can share that love."

Juliette's shoulders dropped and Amaria heard the exhale that came from her. "I hope so as well. You can call me Juliette."

Amaria laughed, linking her arms in Juliette's. It was entirely too informal, but Amaria knew that if you acted as if you were closer than you truly were to someone, the brain might be tricked into believing it.

Amaria needed a friend. She had Nicoletta, but Nicoletta was scarred by Delphina's death as much as Amaria was. It would be nice to escape into a cloud of mindless pleasantries.

"What's your favorite thing about this court?" Amaria whispered as if sharing a deep secret. "Is it the red griffins everywhere?"

The two passed an enormous statue of a golden griffin as Amaria said this.

Juliette laughed. "Never," she said dryly as her hands rubbed over Amaria's sleeves. "You'll start wearing red soon, I imagine."

Amaria looked down at her dress. The heavy blue fabric draped from her arms, with golden and red roses expertly stitched in. Her necklace hung down over her corset, a thread of gold pulled through a loop in the golden scales. She was perhaps somewhat heavy-handed in showcasing she was a Raulet.

At least she didn't arrive wrapped up in the royal blue banner with the golden money scales balancing the red roses as if they were coins. She had some ability to be subtle.

Amaria didn't think she would ever stop wearing Raulet imagery. However, she did know Juliette was correct. She would soon also wear griffins and red, as it was her husband's imagery and she would have to represent him well.

"I've always enjoyed rubies," Amaria said.

Juliette stopped in front of a door. "These are your temporary chambers. Most of your luggage is being brought to Marquis Chauvignon's chambers, however I'll go get your hair brush, dressing gowns, and other things you'll need before marriage from your belongings," she said. "You're only staying here two nights, so it shouldn't be much."

"Juliette," Amaria called her back, "be honest, what do you think of my husband?"

Juliette smiled softly at her. "The rumors are a mixed bag of falsity and reality. Make your own judgments with caution."

Amaria resisted scowling. What game was this woman playing? It would be best if she explained herself. She wanted to know about her husband from the wife of his best friend. She wanted to know what the rest of her life would be like. It was reasonable to ask, and Juliette was interfering with the information she wanted.

"He's kind," Juliette continued. "He values intelligence and efficiency. But you seem intelligent from what I've heard and witnessed. Be open minded." She smiled genuinely. "Marriage may surprise you."

Chapter Five

"**A**re you ready?" Aaron stood next to his daughter. Amaria stared at the large, white painted double doors in front of her through her sheer veil, the edges tipped with lace.

"No," the truth slipped through Amaria's lips. "I mean, I'll obviously do it with grace, but no, I'm not ready."

Aaron shrugged, holding out his arm. "It could be worse."

Many things could be worse. That didn't make the nasty thing better. There was a quote about her family with similar sentiments: *"I'd trust a starving crocodile before I trust a Raulet with a quill."*

Amaria had once thought that saying was ridiculous. But now she understood it.

Amaria smiled, not voicing any of her thoughts. "Let's just enjoy today. The gods know you paid enough money for it."

"Your dress alone set me back nearly five hundred dragons," Aaron chuckled, glancing over at her. And it was true, Amaria's dress was clearly expensive: with its heavy, draping silk sleeves, a fifteen-foot train, and the bodice of the dress was wrapped in intricate lace, the designs as if it was a rose garden. *Raulet.* A belt of silver rested on her hips, which was connected to another belt of diamonds encased in gold, going up to her lower waist.

Right over the center of the diamonds was a large red ruby, also encased in gold. *Chauvignon.* Connected to the ruby was another jeweled belt, this one encrusted with sapphires. *Raulet.*

Along the rest of the dress, up to the neckline, pearls were sewn into the lace. At the neckline, sapphires and pearls were sewn together, and a heavy silver chain, like a necklace, was also sewn onto the dress. Around that silver chain, there was another necklace, golden and framing several large rubies around her neck. *Chauvignon.*

It was absurdly heavy.

Amaria's earrings were also rubies, matching the necklace in design. At the top of her head was a large diamond tiara, sitting upon her elaborate updo. Even then, several diamonds dangled down from the tiara onto her forehead. Behind her, a veil trailing to the ground fell, and another veil was thrown over the tiara to hide her face.

"Yes, it feels as if it is eighty pounds," she smiled good-naturedly, adjusting the bouquet of red roses in her hands. *Raulet and Chauvignon.* Gods, what if she tripped and embarrassed herself? What if Theodmon wasn't at the altar? What if someone spilled wine on her dress? What if he didn't like her? Her father told her to get him to like her. Would her father scold her?

"Probably is," her father admitted. "But, weddings are a place to forge alliances and, as such, show off power and wealth. It's worth it." As he spoke, the heavy doors creaked open, the sound of music lifting into the air. "That's our cue," Aaron whispered, walking forward with his daughter on his arm. "Smile, it's improper for a bride to look unhappy at her wedding."

"Can a groom?" Amaria joked through her plastered smile, walking slowly down the long aisle, people seated on either side of her. This was generally used as a ballroom, but it had temporarily been adapted into a wedding hall.

"Only if the bride is ugly," Aaron said. "Fortunately, Theodmon cannot look upset."

"Not about my looks," Amaria muttered. "But there's plenty wrong with me."

"Relax." Aaron said as he smiled through clenched teeth. "Do you really think I'd let you go into a bad marriage after Duke Vypren? Aion can rot for what he attempted."

Amaria looked over at her father in surprise. Her father was careful. He wasn't the type to say the emperor could rot with witnesses around—that was nearing treason.

"Be happy," Aaron reminded her as they neared the altar. "The world is watching."

Feeling as if centuries had passed, Amaria and Aaron finally reached the end of the aisle, the song about to reach its final notes. The groom was dressed in a deep red tunic, intricate designs in the fabric, with a dark blue cape and a golden jeweled sash. Marquis Chauvignon nodded politely at Duke Raulet as the older man and his daughter stopped their walking.

Amaria tiptoed upwards, lightly pecking her father on the cheek, before he handed her over to Theodmon. The groom took his bride's hands in his own, leading her up the two steps to where a Priest of Endar and Colene, the god and goddess of marital unions, stood waiting. As they stood above the guests, Theodmon tightly squeezed Amaria's hands, waiting for the final note of the song.

The ceremony went smoothly with the priest giving the traditional speeches and blessings, Amaria and Theodmon responding in kind as they exchanged rings.

Theodmon took Amaria's hand in his, slipping the tear-drop-shaped ruby onto her ring finger. Amaria took Theodmon's hand in hers, placing a simple gold band, a streak of rubies running through it, on his hand.

"Marquis, you may lift the bride's veil, show her off as your wife, and then kiss your new Marchioness for the gods and men to see," the priest directed Theodmon. Theodmon gently smiled at Amaria, his hands reaching for her veil, throwing it over her head, her tiara now plainly visible.

Theodmon put his hand on Amaria's waist, turning her to face the spectators. Amaria felt every eye critiquing her from her dress, to her posture, and her facial features. Whether it was silver eyes, a high and prominent jawline, plump lips, or even her makeup, Amaria was being watched and judged.

"We bless this union," the priest called behind them.

Theodmon silently turned Amaria to face him, leaning down slightly, as Amaria lifted her head up, meeting her new husband's lips.

They pulled away, and briefly smiled at each other. *That wasn't terrible.* Amaria breathed.

"I now pronounce these two lawfully wed!" The priest announced. "Please remain seated as Marquis and Marchioness Chauvignon leave the hall."

"Let's go," Theodmon whispered in her ear, guiding her down the steps. "Our guests will leave to the foyer and dining rooms for hors d'oeuvres as they move banquet tables along the walls for the reception."

"And us?" Amaria asked, smiling as she walked down the aisle.

"We go wave to the commoners of the Westerlands outside," Theodmon was also smiling, though much less exaggeratedly than Amaria was, as he looked around at the guests. "I'm sure they'll want to see their new Lady."

Theodmon quietly led her through the halls, pushing open a door leading to the courtyard. "Forgive the question, my Lord," Amaria ventured, "but your castle is on a mountain, correct?"

"Yes," Theodmon said.

"How will we greet the commoners from the top of a mountain?"

"We won't," Theodmon said, looking over to where a squire was bringing forth a white horse. "We ride down the mountain. At least by the time we return, dinner will be ready."

Amaria nodded silently, looking at the horse apprehensively as Theodmon led the horse down the mountain. She knew that they would swing themselves on the animal's back once they reached a less steep area in the mountain.

Her heart thudded in her chest. "I can't ride," Amaria whispered, cheeks flushing red. "I haven't been on a horse since I was seven."

"I'll help you." Theodmon warmly smiled.

Amaria flashed him a smile. She was tense, her muscles felt as if they were wound on a rack. She wasn't sure how to be informal with him or if she even should be yet. She was weighed down by gems, gold, lace, and silk and her heeled slippers were not made for hiking. She focused on moving her feet down the path and not stumbling down the mountain.

Soon, the mountain leveled out and there was a squire with a stool, ready to help her onto the horse Theodmon was holding by the reins.

"Bring down my boots," Amaria commanded him, already dreading the hike back up to Forteresse les Blanche.

Theodmon chuckled, holding her hand and he guided her towards the horse.

Amaria, not wishing to disobey him, stepped onto the stool, clumsily hopping on the horse. Even as she got on side-saddle, she felt Theodmon stabilizing her so she wouldn't fall off.

"I'm sorry," she said. "I'm ruining everything. I'm not trying to be diff-"

"You're ruining nothing," Theodmon said, his lips brushing over her ears. Clicking his heels, he slowly moved his horse down the mountain path, balancing her in front of him. "Let's pray and greet the citizens."

Chapter Six

Amaria and Theodmon prayed in the temple of Ednar and Colene, the god and goddess of marriage, husbands, wives, and conception, for a fruitful marriage. They had prayed beforehand, but both Amaria and Theodmon agreed that the gods deserved praise.

It was better to tread with caution when dealing with capricious beings.

They waved to the commoners. Amaria was tired of smiling. Her face hurt. Her feet also hurt as they were hiking up the mountain once more. Theodmon was gently guiding the horse the best he could.

"Do you like boar?" Theodmon asked her as they finally walked through the gates.

"What?" Amaria said.

"I hunted a boar for the feast," Theodmon explained. "I hope you like it."

Amaria did like boar. She liked it roasted with herbs. "I'm sure it'll be lovely," she told him sincerely as they stepped into the foyer of the castle. Immediately, the sound of applause exploded in Amaria's ears. She wanted to go to bed; she wanted people to stop staring at her.

A forced smile stayed on her face as she waved slightly to those around her as Theodmon and she walked through the cleared path to the great hall. Some noble social customs truly were a better torture than anything she could have cooked up in a dungeon. Not that she would ever admit that.

Theodmon and Amaria moved towards the center two seats at the head table near the front of the hall. A roaring fire was in the massive stone fireplace behind the table. Amaria beamed. She liked the warmth of fire.

Her smile froze as she remembered the fire mage who attacked her home. She immediately thought of Haerdnor, another fire mage. She thought of her own fire magic. She wouldn't let that man take more from her.

Theodmon pulled out a chair for her. She smiled at him in thanks, sitting down.

"Tell me about yourself," Theodmon directed.

Amaria blinked. She wasn't sure what there was to tell about herself. There was her name, but he already knew that. She had magic, but that was common knowledge. He likely wanted something he didn't know. She didn't remember anything interesting about herself.

"My favorite color is turquoise," she said. She cringed as soon as she said that, wanting to slap herself. Why did she say something so stupid? He likely didn't want to know her favorite color.

"More blue or green?" Theodmon asked.

"What?" Amaria blinked up at him.

"The turquoise you like, is it more blue or green?" Theodmon clarified.

Amaria paused, tilting her head. She brought the memory of the Émeraudes Sea to her mind, visualizing the vibrant coral reefs around Raulle and the water they lived in. "Blue," Amaria said. "Like the sea by Raulle."

Theodmon chuckled. "Mine is orange. Not a bright orange, but more muted. Think of the leaves in fall."

"I bet fall is beautiful here," Amaria complimented.

"I hope you enjoy it," Theodmon told her as the first guest approached their table. "If you want, I'll bring you to festivals."

Amaria would like that, but she didn't get the chance to tell him as a stream of important people came and they were both busy greeting and entertaining them. After a while, Juliette approached with a blond man beside her. Amaria smiled softly at her, genuinely glad to see her again.

"Lucas!" Theodmon stood up, bear clapping the man.

"This is Lord Lucas Bécharil," Theodmon introduced him to her. "Lucas, this is my wife, Marchioness Amaria Chauvignon."

It was odd to hear that name associated with her. She supposed she would get used to it. Amaria didn't hate it, and she may even grow to like it. However, it still felt as if she were wearing a cloak to a masquerade and *Marchioness Amaria Chauvignon* was a costume for Lady Amaria Raulet to don.

"Pleasure, my Lord," Amaria inclined her head towards him. She knew that he was Theodmon's bannerman because she was well-versed in politics to have trite details like who was allied to whom and a shallow appearance of how close those alliances may be. She would see Lucas a lot for the rest of her life. And Juliette as well.

"My Lady," Amaria addressed Juliette. "Would you like to dance later with me?"

Juliette beamed. "I'd love that, thank you, my Lady."

Juliette and Lucas moved out of the way, headed towards a table near the front. Behind them, Aloysius, Theodmon's brother, bowed, pausing to move around the table to sit next to Theodmon.

Amaria was more familiar with Aloysius. He had been close friends with Haerdnor so she had been around him more than she had with Theodmon.

"The formalities are stiff," Aloysius complained.

"We still have to do them," Theodmon chastised, pretending to drink from his goblet to hide his moving lips.

"It's good to see you," Amaria told Aloysius as Celestine and Ophelia Chauvignon—now Ophelia Belegines—approached. Amaria stood up, reaching over the table to hug them. She knew Ophelia better than Celestine as Ophelia was one year her elder and had often been at the Imperial Court the same times she had been. That and they both were to be married to an Avonnian duke. Only Ophelia followed through with that.

"I'll see you on the dance floor," Ophelia laughed, following her husband around the table to sit with the rest of Theodmon's family. Amaria's family would come soon enough and sit on her side.

Celestine followed her sister, smiling warmly at her brother and Amaria. Behind them, Theodmon's mother came to greet them. She warmly hugged her son, yet threw Amaria a hateful glance before moving to her seat.

There was a large gap behind her, as those in line had become distracted in speaking with each other.

"I'd love to go to those festivals with you, my Lord Husband," Amaria whispered to Theodmon, sensing the break in people and knowing it wouldn't last long.

"Theodmon," he corrected. "I don't want us to be overly formal."

Marriages were rarely loving in the nobility, as they were for politics, financial, or military gain with the parties often having little to no choice in the arrangement. Some of them were healthy in that the spouses were friends. A few marriages were fortunate enough to develop love.

Amaria did want to be among the fortunate. She believed that perhaps with Theodmon she could be. She tried to calm her beating heart as she looked into his hazel eyes, the blue flecks within them looking like sparks from a driftwood fire. Was she being stupidly optimistic?

She would only hurt herself if she believed in the chance of loving her husband. And yet, she believed in it, already finding herself liking Theodmon. He was kind. He was handsome. He had a good reputation. He liked the color orange.

"I agree." Amaria placed her hand over his, squeezing it slightly.

"Let's finish greeting the guests." Theodmon said as he leaned into her. "Looks as if the Riam and Morrian delegations are approaching."

Amaria groaned. The thing she hated about weddings was the obligation to invite anybody remotely important, even if they despised them. It would be a social slight of grand proportions to not invite the nobles and royalty of not only their kingdom, but the neighboring ones as well.

And of course nobody had enough discretion to not appear where they weren't wanted. No, if they or their representative didn't appear, then there was now the perception that they were unimportant people.

So they all invited people they despised to their weddings and went to the weddings of others they would rather see dead than have prosperity.

"You've had border disputes for years with both of them, my father and I enacted sanctions on Morroek that have caused famine within their lands, and my brother and father have done similar in Rindria," Amaria said dryly. "This should be a delightful conversation."

"And Clarissa Nalaeny isn't the center of attention," Theodmon chuckled. Amaria laughed with him as the Riam princess approached, her dress a gray so light it was almost white. Amaria thought it was in poor taste, but she didn't mind. She was much more dazzling than Clarissa Nalaeny would ever be.

"Your Majesty," Theodmon greeted the Riam King, Tristan Riarl. "Princess," he greeted Tristan's sister. "Duke Nalaeny," he said to Clarissa's husband.

"Thank you for coming to our wedding," Amaria told them, her smile as wide as a cavern and as fake as the terrible shade of red pigmentation brushed over Clarissa's eyelids.

"Let's talk about the border," Liam Nalaeny started to say.

"This is inappropriate," Theodmon interrupted. "Let me enjoy my wedding, my Lord."

"Cousin," Amaria intervened, knowing that ever since the famines had started in Rindria, the Nalaeny's actively hid their Raulet's roots. She was barely related to Liam, his mother, while Raulet, was a distant cousin. Still, she acknowledged the familial bond to irritate him.

There was no political gain to it. She just liked watching him squirm.

"Marchioness Chauvignon, I'm sorry for your recent loss," Clarissa said, her voice like a snake.

Amaria's hand hovered over her carving knife. It was for the boar but she wanted to plunge it into Clarissa's heart. How dare she come and mock Delphina's death? Amaria knew she had something to do with it. Not directly, but she worked with Lynette Edrion who had hired those damn thieves. Clarissa was implicated by association in Delphina's murder.

She turned to see Liam and Clarissa's children, choosing to not engage with the jab. There were two there. She thought the Nalaeny's had three children—it was unimportant. Rindria was a mosquito-bite of a country. Annoying but not particularly valuable or threatening. "Are these your children?"

The man around Amaria's age stepped forward. "Tesden Nalaeny," he said. "Congratulations on the marriage, Marquis and Marchioness."

"Thank you, my Lord," Amaria said.

"Liara Nalaeny." The girl gave a shaky curtsy. Amaria supposed it was because of her height—she was tall. Or perhaps it was because she was simple; she had a vapid look in her eyes as if she wasn't truly here. "I hope you find happiness."

Yes. Simple. Only an idiot would wish a noble bride and groom happiness in their marriage. A standard *"may the gods bless this union"* or a mere *"congratulations"* would have been sufficient enough.

Theodmon cast Amaria a side glance, so brief she could have imagined it. "I believe I will. Thank you, Lady Nalaeny."

Swiftly, Theodmon greeted King Tristan's wife and son as they approached. The queen appeared emotionally fragile, her hands white knuckled over her son's shoulders. The young prince was pale, shuddering under his cloak even though it was summer. She had heard that he was ill, it seemed the rumors were credible.

The Riam delegation departed and the Raulets came after them, greeting Theodmon and Amaria before Aaron sat next to her. Next to Aaron was Haerdnor, then Catalina, and several cousins she barely knew. Nicoletta also came to greet them and Amaria resented that she had to go eat at the tables below. She wanted Nicoletta here with her. She had preferred Delphina to Nicoletta, yes. But Delphina wasn't here.

Amaria furiously blinked her eyes, forcing back the tears as a redheaded man stepped forward. Bawling at a formal event was wholly undignified.

And Amaria needed her decorum. This redheaded man was Durek Svilas, a Morrian duke, married to the eldest princess of the Morrian king. The king had no sons, and so, Durek was the heir apparent as women could not inherit in Morroek—a backwards and barbaric concept to Amaria. She thanked the gods Thestitiunian woman had property and inheritance rights.

Durek Svilas was one of her least favorite people, and she despised his country even more.

"Pleasure to see you again, Duke Svilas," Amaria said, her voice as sweet as honey.

"I share the same sentiment," Durek said politely. "It's the same delight I have when you visit in Morroek."

Amaria had to admit he was clever. She didn't like to acknowledge it, but she was clever enough to not impute flaws onto her enemies and to see their strengths. "Enjoy the meal," she said politely.

Durek's face momentarily hardened, but he bowed. "Thank you, Marquis and Marchioness Chauvignon."

Behind him, a dark skinned man stepped forward, a hand running through his coiled curls. Theodmon stood up, pulling him into a hug similar to the one he gave Lucas. Amaria knew him well—this was Lord Henri Delaluna. He was another Extractor. He wasn't an elemental mage like Amaria though. Henri could read and alter people's thoughts and memories.

"He despises you," Henri chuckled.

"It doesn't take a mind reader to know that," Theodmon said.

"Congratulations," Henri said, turning towards Amaria. "I'm glad we aren't losing you from our order."

"You know the emperor would never allow that," Amaria said. She did not say the unspoken thoughts. Emperor Aion would never have the foresight to plan for any long term action or care for the consequences. Why would he, when Amaria's father cleaned up all his mistakes for him?

Henri heard her though, raising an eyebrow.

"You know it's true," she thought, staring at him as she felt his magic press against her mind, a swirling sea trapped behind glass. Slowly, Amaria lowered her barriers, letting him enter her mind through a mage link—an invitational ability between trusted mages to communicate with each other privately or over long distances. It was incredibly useful. Unlike the emperor.

"Treasonous thoughts you have there, Amaria." Henri smirked.

"You have the same ones." Amaria resisted rolling her eyes, knowing others were surely watching. It was her wedding, and she was the center of attention.

"You alright?"

"No." Amaria gave him a smile she hoped was reassuring. *"I'll survive though. You should move on. I think I see Lynette Edrion approaching."*

Henri's eyes flashed. *"I'll be nearby."* He bowed once more. "Congratulations to you both."

Theodmon looked at her questioningly.

"I suspect some of our guests killed my friend," Amaria whispered, tears welling in her eyes. It was too soon. She'd ruin her makeup in front of everyone. She blinked furiously, wishing she still had a veil to cover her face and that it would be appropriate to do so now.

"I heard about that," Theodmon said softly, his hand moving to hold hers. "I know it won't bring her back, but I'm sorry for your loss."

Amaria sniffed. "Thank you. Please, not now."

Theodmon nodded, squeezing her hand. "It looks as if we have Avonnian guests approaching. Hopefully there'll be food soon."

Amaria tensed, forcing her muscles around her mouth upwards, directly fighting her involuntary scowl. She hoped she managed to look neutral. She wanted to leap across the table as the queen of Avondra approached, Amaria's former fiancé behind her.

Unfortunately, strangling foreign heads of state in full view of the world tended to lead to *minor* political issues.

"Your Majesty," Theodmon said as Lynette approached. "Duke Vypren." His voice was curt.

Amaria's mouth twitched. She appreciated how brusque he was with Lynette. She knew it was likely not for the same reasons she despised the Avonnian queen, but all the same, she appreciated the shared sentimentality.

"Marquis Chauvignon," Lynette replied, tilting her head slightly. "Marchioness, you look beautiful."

"Thank you," Amaria said. If only Lynette were dead. Bubbling rage surrounded her, she felt her skin getting hot. She needed to calm down for she didn't want to catch on fire. She knew she should continue speaking, say some false nicety, but she could not bring herself to do it to either Lynette or Vypren.

"I see you've healed, my Lady," Vypren said. Amaria felt a flare on her stomach, the white scar suddenly itchy under the layers of fabric. She felt cold as her eyes flashed.

Lynette sharply turned her head towards her countryman, her eyes turning from green to black. A mage's eyes normally changed color when conducting magic. Every mage had their own color, and nobody truly knew where the color came from or how it was determined. There were theories, of course; academics always had theories.

There was one known thing about a mage's color. Only dark mages had black. In a few seconds, Lynette's eyes were green. Amaria wanted to throw her out. How dare she conduct dark magic at her wedding? How dare she appear here at all?

But Amaria couldn't. Lynette was a foreign queen, so there would be complications for throwing her out, to put it mildly.

Theodmon looked over at her, his head tilting slightly towards the two Avonnians. Amaria forced herself to remain still. She was a hurricane. If she moved, she would destroy those around her. She could not speak, or else she'd scream.

Causing an international scene was not the reason she wanted to be the center of attention at her wedding.

Theodmon stood up, holding his hand out to her. "Would you like to dance?"

She took his hand, trying not to squirm under Vypren's beady gaze. "Absolutely."

She breathed in relief as he led her to the floor, the musicians' violins weaving in beautiful notes and harmonies. He took her hand and her waist and they spun around in a waltz.

Chapter Seven

Theodmon led Amaria down the white stone halls. She looked downwards, focusing on the plush red carpet rolling down the corridor. Her neck hurt, the heavy tiara making it cramp. She clasped her hands together, feeling nervous for what was about to happen.

She wished she knew more about this sort of thing. Amaria wished she could have asked her mother. But how could she have asked her when she was only seven? It was stupid to think of the past; Amaria hadn't known about adult things when her mother died, let alone to ask about them. Her mom dying wasn't anyone's fault but the assassins. Still, she wished her mother was alive. She wished she had her mother's advice.

She wondered why her father never remarried. He could have secured an alliance. They were, after all, limited in what alliances they could gain through marriage, what with Haerdnor having proclivities for other men and their hiding the fact for the sake of his reputation. They had solved that by finding a Tressi noblewoman with similar inclinations and engaging them to each other. Haerdnor and his *special friend*, Oliver, seemed thrilled with the engagement.

Additionally, Amaria's sister, Catalina, was joining a temple of healing. The goddess of healing had saved her life as a child—most died when they caught Mal'ora. Catalina didn't. The disease took its toll, coating her face and throat with gold scars, but she had survived. Amaria suspected dark magic was the cause of Catalina's Mal'ora.

Then, the emperor of Thestitiunia had ordered Amaria's marriage to an Avonnian Duke. In Thestitiunia and Avondra, dukes were kings because of the sheer size of the duchies. In Thestitiunia, they were more cohesive. The Dukes worked together for the benefit of the empire. There was a central economy, similar laws, and strong military alliances between the provinces. Avondra had a central monarch, but their laws and economy were disjointed, each duchy acting only for their own interests, rather than for Avondra as a whole.

It wasn't a bad marriage politically per se; she was the equivalent of a princess marrying the equivalent of a king. It was acceptable. But her old fiancé, Duke Lyseno Vypren, was old and cruel. Amaria had dreaded the future. So Aaron had fought it, postponing the marriage age. Now, Amaria was nineteen, nearing twenty, and married. But not to Vypren, thank the gods.

It irked Amaria that the emperor had changed his mind because her magic was too strong, suddenly deciding her magic could not be with another country. She wanted to scream. Amaria had shown magic at three, most mages showed magic at eight. She could control all four elements, while most elemental mages could only control one or two. It didn't take a genius to predict this would be an issue early on.

Her father had tried to protect her. Still, the emperor had insisted.

Mages were semi-common in the empire. Amaria could guess twenty to thirty percent of the population had magic. And magic was common in the other two nations that didn't persecute magic users. However, in places where it was banned, like Morroek and Rindria, magic was rare and when it appeared, it was stamped out.

However, while magic wasn't uncommon in Thestitiunia, powerful magic was rare. There were eight others with Amaria's level.

But her darling cousin did not listen. He was lucky her father was competent and did not want the crown. Aaron Raulet ran the empire. Everyone knew it. And Amaria wondered why he never made it official.

She did not know why she was thinking this. It did not seem like appropriate thoughts to have on her wedding night.

Theodmon looked back at her, and she smiled at her new husband as if nothing was wrong.

"Did you enjoy the wedding?"

"Yes," Amaria said, thankful for the distraction.

"You're a beautiful dancer," Theodmon said.

Amaria smiled at him, too nervous to say anything more as she turned to large double doors, a guard on either side of the doorway. One of the guards nodded at Theodmon, a respectful, "my Lord," coming from him, before he pushed open the door to reveal a spacious room.

A massive fireplace was on the right wall, its embers low. Next to the fireplace there were two oversized red sofas facing each other, only a cherry table separating them. Behind one of the sofas, there was a sizable set of drawers along the wall. Theodmon led Amaria into the room, turning her to face another wall, this one lined with bookcases on either side of another large double door.

"Allow me." Theodmon brushed past Amaria, as she turned to look at the armor near the fireplace, and the barren walls. "You'll embroider a tapestry for the walls?" Theodmon directed as he opened the doors.

"Yes, I'll start on the Union Tapestry as soon as I can," Amaria muttered, knowing the tradition for wives to embroider a design for their marital rooms, symbolic of the union between their ancestral family and their marital family. "I'll need thread and needles though."

Theodmon waved his hand dismissively, pulling her into the bedroom with his other arm. "Welcome to your rooms."

Amaria stood awkwardly in the doorway, her head slowly turning to survey her new bedroom. The room was spacious, even ignoring the separate sitting room that Theodmon's rooms began with. In front of her was a prodigious mahogany bed, nearly twice the width of her bed at home—*ancestral home*. Amaria sighed, forcing herself to remember the distinction now.

The bed was carpeted with rich red and gold draping around it and matching blankets on top. Stepping inside the room, she awkwardly stood in the center, the bed now slightly to her left. Behind her was a large wardrobe, likely big enough for both her and Theodmon's clothes. In front of her was another sofa, the fireplace crackling in front of it. Turning towards her right, she was on an elevated platform, doors to a balcony behind it. On the stone platform there was a suit of armor and a desk strewn with papers and maps. Beside the platform and near the wardrobe was another door.

"That's the washroom," Theodmon said, catching her eye. "We can bathe afterwards, unless you need to use a chamberpot?"

Amaria shook her head slowly, still balancing the heavy diamonds on her head. "I'd still need to be undressed anyways."

"Ah, yes." Theodmon grabbed her hand, leading her towards the side of the bed away from the fireplace. Near the exit to the sitting room, a mahogany desk sat, an ornate mirror on the wall in front of it. "I had a vanity brought here for you."

"Thank you," Amaria pulled out the puffed seat, also in red, sitting down. "There's lots of red here," she said lightly, her hands moving towards her earrings.

"House colors," Theodmon said, removing the jeweled golden sash he was wearing, as well as the deep blue cloak connected to his shoulders. He smoothed down his deep red tunic, looking at the rubies and sapphires encrusted into Amaria's dress as well as her ruby earrings and necklace. "Do you need help?"

"Please," Amaria met Theodmon's eyes in the mirror, her own shining with gratitude. "This tiara is hurting my neck." Theodmon came up behind her, lifting the tiara off of her elaborate updo.

"That's a lot," Theodmon said, looking at the litany of braids, curls, and pins under the tiara. "Do you need a maid to help you?"

"I thought," Amaria wet her lips nervously before lowering her head. "Never mind."

"You thought I wanted to consummate the marriage?" Theodmon finished for her, chucking. "Yes, but I think we would both rather your hair be loose." He moved his hand to the rubies around her neck, unclasping the necklace. "That way we can be alone for the rest of the night."

"I know it's tradition for it to be witnessed," Amaria blurted out. "Forgi–"

"I don't want a bunch of people watching," Theodmon interrupted. "We can hang a sheet from the balcony as proof."

Amaria stared at him incredulously. He wasn't going to have witnesses? It seemed too convenient. She didn't want to be watched—it felt obtrusive.

"Theodmon, what if that's not adequate proof?"

"You're beautiful. The chance to lay with you and the sheets will be enough," Theodmon dismissed. "With the gods' blessing, you'll soon be swollen with a child. Don't worry. I'm not allowing others to watch."

Amaria stared directly at him. "What?"

"I rather not be in a menagerie," he said dryly.

Amaria hugged herself, forcing back the vomit rising up from the depths of her stomach. "I apologize."

"For what?" Theodmon looked at her in surprise.

"I'm not sure," Amaria muttered, kicking her leg up to the opposing thigh, an impressive feat with the sheer weight of her skirts. The dress felt about as heavy as herself, the silk, lace, and gemstones weighing it down. Carefully, she removed her white satin heeled shoe, then moved to the other foot.

She wasn't sure what she should apologize for. She felt as if she were a disappointment all the same. "I want to be a good wife to you."

"I want to be a good husband."

Amaria moved her two sigil rings, one with the symbol of an Extractor and one with her house crest and the initials A.R. carved into sapphire stone, off her right hand. Her hand lingered on her left ring finger, watching the candlelight catch in the large tear dropped shaped ruby, small diamonds twinkling around it. Her wedding ring.

"You are," Amaria responded. "This is beautiful, thank you."

"I'll get a maid to help," Theodmon turned on his heel, quickly leaving the room, the doors thudding behind him.

Amaria sighed, reaching down to pick up her shoes before standing up. Walking over towards the wardrobe, Amaria gingerly opened the doors. Inside she saw some boots, two pairs of her heels, Theodmon's tunics hanging up, and a few of her underdresses and overdresses. She placed her heels down next to her other shoes, closing the door. Her shoulders slumping slightly, she opened a drawer underneath the swinging doors of the wardrobe, seeing Theodmon's pants. She moved down to the next drawer, it was filled with some of her jewelry. The last drawer, at the very bottom, held her bloomers, corsets, and stockings. There was a division in the drawer about halfway down, each side holding either Amaria's or Theodmon's undergarments.

Amaria wandered over to the vanity, sitting as if she were a statute as she waited for the maid to arrive. She didn't know how to breathe; air was racketing in her chest. What if Theodmon didn't like her? What if he was cruel and was exceptional at hiding it? She clenched her fists, using the pain of her fingernails digging into her palm to center her until Theodmon and the maid returned.

"Undo her hair," Theodmon directed, the door thudding behind him.

Amaria sat in silence, letting the maid unpin and unbraid her hair, placing the jeweled pins and veil on the vanity. She stared at her reflection, hating how red her face looked. Perhaps the blush was overdone.

Her eyes darted towards the back of her husband's head, looking at him through the mirror. He appeared to be kind—when he wasn't slamming a door at least. And he was young and attractive. Her father thought this would be a good marriage, and not just politically. It couldn't be that bad, could it?

"Lady Chauvignon," the maid's voice interrupted Amaria's thoughts. "Would you like me to brush out your hair?" Amaria, feeling how stiff her hair felt, nodded sharply. For a few minutes, the maid pulled the brush through her hair, slowly softening and detangling the dark brown locks.

"That's enough," Theodmon directed the maid behind her. "Leave."

As the maid scurried off, Amaria stood up, turning to face Theodmon. Silently, she questioned him. What was he doing? What was occurring? Could he sense her confusion?

"Turn around. You can't get out of this on your own," he said.

Amaria complied, feeling Theodmon's hands run over the buttons and laces on the back of her dress undoing them. As the dress became loose, she felt a cool chill on her back. "Step out," Theodmon directed her. Amaria nodded silently, showing her compliance, as she slowly moved her arms out of the sleeves, stepping out of the heavy wedding dress.

"Thank you," Amaria muttered, feeling the underdress loosen on her. She slipped out of it, and behind her, she heard rustling and footsteps as Theodmon threw her dress on the couch. Silently, she untied the strings around her waist, letting the layered petticoat fall to the ground before bending down to untie the strings holding up her garter and stockings. Wordlessly, she let them fall to her feet before she sat down to remove them. Theodmon was also removing his outer clothing.

Breathing deeply, Amaria stood up again, her hands moving behind her, feeling for the strings to her corset. She found them and quickly untied the strings behind her, pulling them out to loosen the garment before popping open the metal boning at her front. As the corset fell to the ground, Amaria stood in front of her husband, completely naked.

Theodmon held out his hand. "We have to consummate the marriage tonight, but you control the speed."

Amaria did not dare believe this kindness as she stared at him with widened eyes.

"Vypren is notoriously violent and possessive. You have stitches on your stomach from where he stabbed you, and I can guess that he attempted certain things to avoid the engagement."

Amaria blinked, trying not to cry at his unexpected kindness, as her hands hovered over her puckering scar. "Be gentle." She moved to hold his hand.

He nodded, gently leading her to the bed. He lifted up the covers, and Amaria saw the sheets were a stark white. Of course, the blood had to be visible. There were methods to ensure blood certainly appeared—one was marrying when a bride's menstrual cycle was ending. Another was to have a small ring with goat's blood hidden in the gem, just enough for when the gem twisted, blood droplets would appear.

Amaria had hidden that in a small ruby on her Extractor's sigil. Her muscles tensing, Amaria looked down at her hand, realizing she had taken that ring off. And she couldn't get it now; that would be suspicious. Oh gods, what if she didn't bleed?

"Will it hurt?" Amaria asked, feeling heat rise up her neck.

"It shouldn't," Theodmon smiled sympathetically. "Let me know if you're in pain so we can adjust. I've zero desire to hurt you."

"He didn't penetrate me," Amaria blurted out. "He tried, but I'm a virgin!"

"I know," Theodmon said kindly. He gently kissed the top of her hair. "I'll be gentle. Do you want to close your eyes or would it help you to look at me?"

Amaria's eyes drifted over to Theodmon's. She saw his muscular body, his dark hair and hazel eyes, angular cheekbones, and a light well-trimmed scuffle along his jawline. He was young and handsome, and his eyes had genuine concern—she did not know her ex-fiance well, but he had never looked at her as anything but a possession.

"I'll look at you," Amaria decided.

She pressed her back against the bed, trying to relax with each breath. Somehow, she felt as if her muscles were more tense, a betrayal from her body. Amaria licked her lips, trying to bring moisture to them as a lump appeared in her throat.

Theodmon's palm brushed against her cheek. His hand was overpowering, nearly encompassing her whole head. "It's alright," he said.

Amaria closed her eyes momentarily, before opening them again. Theodmon kissed her gently, she couldn't help but notice his lips needed balm as their chappiness felt scratchy against her own.

He sat on top of her, still kissing her. She closed her eyes, it felt awkward to have them open. All of her felt awkward—what exactly was she supposed to do?

"Spread your legs," Theodmon said. Gently, he placed his hands on her inner thighs, pushing them away from each other. Amaria's legs were in a widened V. "It helps to bend your knees."

Amaria's face flushed, but she bent her knees, her hips widening with the movement.

She felt something hard enter her. She tensed up, barely breathing. Still, her lower areas tingled and she wanted more, despite her fear of what was occurring. Amaria didn't like uncertainty.

"You're doing well," Theodmon whispered into her ear, thrusting his phallus into her. Amaria winced at the feeling but did not otherwise move as she continued to watch him as he towered over her. "Open your legs wider. It'll make this easier on you."

Amaria extended her hips, opening her eyes to look at Theodmon for approval. He reached down and kissed her on the mouth, tongue pressing against hers, laying his body on top of hers, violently ramming his penis into her.

It hurt. Must it hurt?

"It's so you bleed," Theodmon told her apologetically, as if he could read her thoughts. She knew he couldn't. "Slightly barbaric, but I don't want shallow-minded questioning."

However it didn't fully hurt now. She felt herself get wet, her body losing under his touch. "Kiss me," she closed her eyes.

"Amaria," Theodmon blinked slowly at her as he rhythmically moved inside of her body.

"Please." Her hands moved up his back, pulling him towards her.

Theodmon sighed and he connected his lips towards hers. Amaria kissed Theodmon back, meeting his tongue with hers. She relaxed slightly, and she felt Theodmon forcing himself harder within her, and she found that it felt good as a soft moan escaped her.

"You're allowed to enjoy sex with your husband." Theodmon said.

Her back arched, Amaria gave a small grunt. Suddenly, Theodmon stopped and Amaria felt a liquid-like substance run inside her.

Theodmon rhythmically pounded against her. She felt something wet explode inside of her, and Theodmon pulled out, his penis still jutting out.

Theodmon pulled himself off her, extending a hand to help her sit up. "It'll get easier. And we will eventually enjoy it, having many children from it." He looked at her unblinkingly. "Welcome home, Marchioness Chauvignon."

She heard the laughter laced through his tone. Amaria wrapped her arms around herself, shaking.

"Will it always hurt?" She looked at his face, trying to ignore how oddly shaped the male body was with an erection.

"No," Theodmon said. "It'll get easier. If it hurts, let me know; I don't want to cause you pain." He held out his hand to her. She took it and he pulled her up to a sitting position. "Do you want to bathe?"

She nodded. She took in his facial features from the sharp jawline, to the small brown curl over his forehead. She stood up, him still holding her hand.

"I'll tell the maids to hang the sheet outside our balcony and to give us fresh sheets. I'll join you soon." Theodmon stated as Amaria wandered over towards the stained-glass doors, a picture of sirens, dragons, hydras, and griffins. Amaria stared blankly at the pictures, as if she were a stranger in her own body.

She had just had sex. It was relatively painless—she hadn't been beaten, choked, or screamed at. Theodmon had been gentle, and it had started to feel good near the end. She wasn't crying, wishing it would all end on her wedding night. And she wasn't dreading the rest of her life.

Amaria hadn't expected this—for years her fate was to be the wife of another. Vypren would have had witnesses. He would have not gently caressed her face, giving soft kisses before thrusting himself inside of her.

She looked over at Theodmon, who closed the door from where he had screamed orders into the hall through the crack in the door. She noticed he had several scars across his chest—how did those happen? Some looked deep.

Amaria averted her eyes as Theodmon opened the chest at the foot of the bed, pulling out a bedroom robe. It was rude to stare. She didn't need to know about his injuries now.

"Go ahead," Theodmon urged Amaria, "I'm just confirming maids are coming."

Amaria nodded, stepping inside the bathing room.

Looking upwards, she saw intricate carvings in the white stone, a scene of a battle, maybe one with Vathar; Amaria was not sure. Lowering her gaze downwards, Amaria walked to the basin, dipping her toe in. It was cold. She pulled her foot out quickly. She supposed it was hard to perfectly time a bath during a wedding.

Amaria tried to push her annoyance aside, not wanting to sour this day. She lowered herself to the ground, her hands outstretched over the water, slowly weaving her magic through the particles, raising the water's temperature.

"I could have called for someone," Theodmon laughed as he opened the door.

"This was more efficient," Amaria said simply, dipping her toe in to test the water. "Apologies-"

"No, don't apologize." Theodmon chuckled, throwing his robe on the counter. "I like efficiency as well."

Amaria turned around, smiling at him, finally feeling as if she could relax. "It's ready," she told Theodmon, turning to step into the basin through the stone steps. "I bet you can't catch me!"

Delphina. The memory of their races hit Amaria as if it were a meteor. She couldn't think of this. Not now. Hurriedly, she broke into a stroke, aiming to reach the other side before Theodmon.

Theodmon laughed and jumped into the basin, forgoing the stairs, before swimming after Amaria, quickly catching her with a few powerful strokes. Standing up, he grabbed her by the waist and twirled her around in the water. "I got you."

Amaria sniffed, unsuccessfully trying to hide behind a laugh. "What are you going to do now that you captured me?"

"Ask you why you're crying."

"Nothing," Amaria shook her head. "It's nothing." She didn't want to sour this moment. They had been getting along, having fun together—almost. She wasn't going to ruin it by bringing up her dead friend.

"It's something," Theodmon said. "Tell me."

"It'll ruin the mood," Amaria protested.

Theodmon's hands tightened around her thighs from where he was still cradling her in the water. "Maybe. But crying doesn't help either."

Amaria sat silently, watching the ends of her hair trail around to where she could see them floating in her peripheral vision.

Theodmon said nothing. Amaria sighed. It would be nice to tell him, she supposed. Someone who understood war and death but wasn't as traumatized as her by this particular incident.

"My friend, Delphina Ginsery, died. The knife was meant for me. Before the attack, we were going to race," Amaria hiccuped, tears falling freely down her face. "It just...I don't know why I'm this way. I'm ruini—"

"You ruin nothing," Theodmon said, gently letting her float in the water, releasing his cradle. "It was recent, and she was your friend. I'm sorry for your loss."

He stepped away, swimming towards the side, where three bars were laid on the ground, something Amaria missed before. "I'll get the sponges and the shampoo bars."

"What shampoos do they have?" Amaria asked, gently floating in the water, blinking away the tears as quickly as she could.

Theodmon smelled the three bars left out for them. "I believe they're lemon, jasmine, and hydrangea. Which do you want—not lemon, that's mine."

"Hydrangea, thank you." She wasn't going to focus on Delphina any more today. She had a kind husband. She was going to enjoy this first night with him and not ruin any chance she had of a good life with him.

She wouldn't let ghosts destroy her future.

Theodmon wadded back to Amaria, two sponges and shampoo bars in hand. Amaria took the sponge and the yellowish shampoo bar from Theodmon's hands, dunking them in the water. "Allow me?" Amaria asked.

Theodmon chuckled and lowered himself into the water, his shoulders peaking out.

Amaria rubbed the bar in Theodmon's hair, massaging his scalp with her hands, bubbles forming up. "Close your eyes please. Soap will get in them."

"Of course," Theodmon contentedly closed his eyes. "This feels good."

"We can do this more often if you would like," Amaria offered. "It's not like this isn't our bath house."

"Would you like that?" Theodmon asked.

"Whatever pleases you." Amaria responded dutifully, almost automatically.

"I asked you what *you* personally would like," Theodmon said. "I appreciate the dutifulness and obedience, but answer the question."

"Yes," Amaria rubbed his shoulders. "I'd like more of this. I enjoy being with you." Immediately Amaria's face turned red at the confession.

"Was that so hard to admit?" Theodmon teased before dipping himself under the water, rinsing his hair off. "Now," he said after he emerged from out under the water, "let me clean your hair. No protests. It'll let me feel my bride more."

Amaria handed him the pinkish bar and lowered herself in the water, dark hair floating in a pool around her. Theodmon approached behind her, gathering the dark tendrils in his hands.

"Why hydrangea?" Theodmon asked.

"These flowers are only native to Perivina Fluere and the islands where the hydras live," Amaria sighed as Theodmon massaged the shampoo into her hair. "It's comforting. Smells like home, uh, my ancestral home, I guess, and I have good memories of it. I used to pick hydrangeas for my parents with Haerdnor and Catalina. Mother would have them placed in vases around the estate before she died. She was so proud of them. I grew a hydrangea as my first sign of having earthen magic."

"I'll see if I can import them," Theodmon offered, letting the ends of Amaria's hair fall back in the water. "I'm not sure how they'd fare in the climate though."

The water cradled Amaria. She felt peaceful. She had expected something worse than this. She wasn't sure what exactly, but she would have never fathomed floating peacefully in a pool on her wedding night.

When engaged to her last fiancé, she tried not to think of the future.

Theodmon picked up the sponges, which were floating in the water, and handed one to Amaria. "Come on."

"Mhhmm," Amaria sighed. "Can I stay here longer?" She lifted her legs up to float, placing the sponge on her chest. "It's peaceful."

"Your wedding night is not nearly as horrific as you imagined?" Theodmon laughed.

"I mean, the bare minimum was to be better than Duke Vypren of Darcassa, so it didn't take much," Amaria dryly said.

"Oh," Theodmon clutched his heart jokingly, as if he were touched. "Such loving words from my wife. I can feel the affection radiating from you."

"Can you not?" Amaria retorted, still smiling. "I thought we established that we share a fondness for each other's company."

Theodmon held up his hands, jokingly conceding. "And I see I lost a battle of the wits."

"I'm sure it has been your first defeat in any battle," Amaria laughed, staring up at the ceiling. "But, if you want to understand losing battles, Haerdnor can advise you on how it goes."

"Your brother?" Theodmon snorted in disbelief. "He became a captain at seventeen, and will likely be an admiral by the time he is twenty-three if the rumors are correct. You don't get that with lo-"

"Oh, I meant to me," Amaria said, feeling more and more comfortable. Theodmon was surprisingly easy to talk to. "Really, how many magical training battles do you think he's won?"

Theodmon chuckled lightly before suddenly grabbing Amaria and dunking her underwater. Amaria raised herself to the surface, wiping her eyes. "What was that for?"

"You just lost a battle to me," Theodmon bowed mockingly, however, not unkindly.

Chuckling, Amaria walked towards the edge of the pool. She was titled. And in Thestitiunia, not a foreign nation. Her husband was kind. She had escaped her engagement to the Duke of Darcassa. She would get to keep her citizenship with this marriage.

The realization hit her hard; she had been so prepared to have to forfeit her citizenship upon marriage as citizen status came from the father or, if a woman married, her husband. It was that way in all of the nations. She took a deep breath. "I know tomorrow we have to show the sheet from the balcony and further sacrifice to the gods, but is there anything else tonight?"

She picked up a towel, drying herself off, using her wind magic to speed up the process with her hair, Theodmon closely following her.

"No," he said. "Only us talking to get to know each other better. "

Amaria smiled at him. "I'd enjoy that." She looked at his muscled chest and took in his appearance. She enjoyed the shape of his eyes—they were almond-shaped almost, framed by long eyelashes. And he had sparks of blue, as if lightning, in his otherwise bright hazel eyes.

Theodmon noticed her surveying him, chuckling.

Amaria lowered her eyes, feeling her face turning red.

Theodmon lifted her face with his hands. "I'd appreciate it if you quickly dried my hair, dear. I think it's amazing you can use your magic in that way."

"Uh, yes," Amaria agreed, her towel dropping to the ground, as she was now completely dry. "Are you ready?"

Theodmon outreached his arms, closing his eyes, laughing. Amaria, suppressing a small chuckle, summoned a warm breeze to run through his hair, watching the wavy locks fall as they dried. "All done," she said softly, moving to open the glass doors.

"No," Theodmon commanded. "Let me." He pushed past her hand to open the doors. "May I carry you?"

Amaria nodded and Theodmon easily lifted her in his arms.

"Can we have candles lit during the night?" Amaria asked, her face burning. "I'm...I'm scared of the dark."

She hated admitting that weakness. But she had always slept with a fireplace or candles lit, and she felt that without a flicker of light she was suffocating.

Theodmon nodded. "Of course." He carried her to the bed, already outfitted with new sheets, these a light gray. On top of the bed was a red nightgown, embroidered with a small griffin on the edges of the sleeves. "The maids laid out your nightgown."

"You...you had a gown made for me?"

"I hope you like it."

"I love it. Thank you. I was so worried you'd despise me, and that you were desperately in debt and that was the only reason you accepted me-"

"I wanted a wife, I wanted to not owe your father money, and I wanted money for my army," Theodmon interrupted. "I wouldn't despise the woman I chose and who gave me all three of my goals."

He set her gently on the bed. "Dress. Then let's talk—I want to get to know you."

Amaria blinked at him. She wanted to get to know him too. Politically, it would be wise if they trusted each other. He was a talented military tactician, she was good with intelligence—it would be beneficial for both their families if they worked well together.

But there was more than politics at play. Amaria wanted to be happy.

Part Two

the extraction

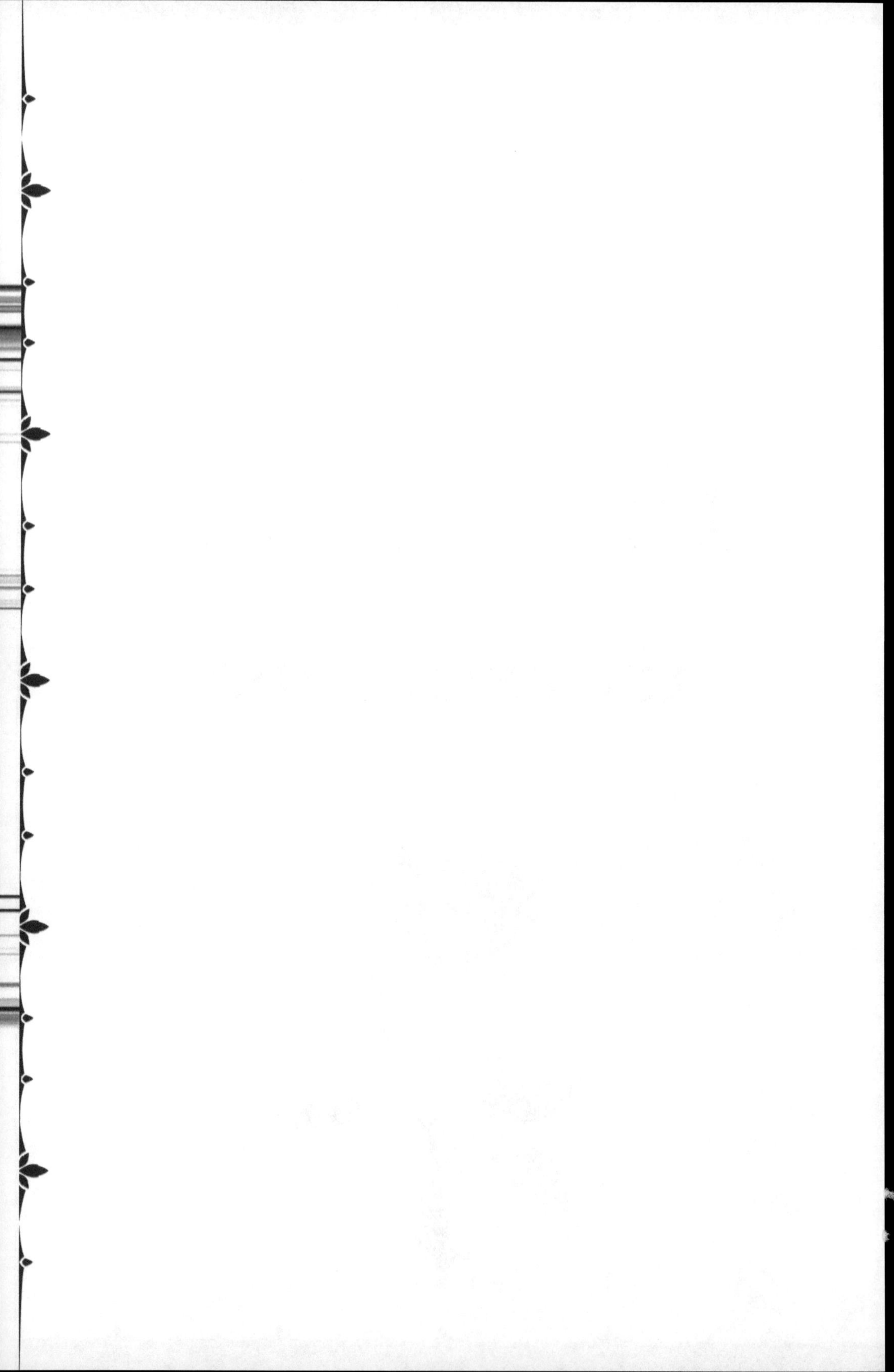

Chapter Eight

A little over a year after her wedding, Amaria woke up in the dead of night, her back arched in pain and covered in a pool of water.

"What?" Theodmon jolted upwards as she screamed, rubbing the sleep out of his eyes.

"Baby," she gasped, seeing black dots across her vision. "It's time." Her groin felt as if it were on fire as she bit her lip.

That was a mistake. Her teeth cut right through her lip. The pain of that was still less than what was occurring elsewhere in her body.

"I'll get the healers and someone to summon your ladies," Theodmon was already walking towards the doors. "Do you need me here with you?"

It was entirely improper for a man to be in the birthing room, unless he was a doctor. "Please," Amaria grunted out, her knuckles white as she tried to get off the bed. She did not want to remain laying in that wet spot.

Theodmon's eyes softened as he looked at her, his hand pushing open the door. He barked out orders to the guards on duty.

Amaria doubled over on herself, a howl escaping her as she felt as if her body were being torn in two and her intestines twisted. Trembling, she wondered if the entire process would be this way or if it would get easier as the baby made its way out. A sharp, hot pain exploded up her back. Was this what it would be like to touch fire without her fire immunity? Screaming, her knees shook, and she was on the ground, tears falling from her eyes.

Theodmon was beside her, rubbing her shoulders. "Hey," he said soothingly. "It's okay. You're doing good."

Was she? She felt as if her body was failing her. She was made for breeding—or so she was told. It should be easier. Why couldn't she stand? She had been trained in torture methods, and not just in being the torturer. Amaria wasn't unused to pain. This should be easier.

She screamed as another contraction came, clutching Theodmon's hand. Her throat felt tight as if she had swallowed sand. Her mouth was dry. Something bubbled in her stomach.

She leaned over and puked. Next to her, Theodmon wrinkled his nose, but he continued rubbing her back.

"Are you staying the entire time?" Amaria asked, wiping the acidic remains from her mouth.

"I can," Theodmon said. "Do you want me to?"

Yes. They had grown close in these past fifteen months. Amaria liked being with him. They had taken four months to travel for their wedding tour. By then winter was approaching, and they were secluded in Forteresse les Blanche until the snow melted. They had become pregnant relatively quickly.

Theodmon was away at the Rindria border during spring and summer. The Riams, those fuckers, decided that attacking their borders was a wise decision. It was amazing how an entire nation was deficient in common sense. Every time they attacked the Westerlands, they lost land. And in retaliation, they were starved via false scarcity. Thestitiunia had money. Bushels of grain were never truly worth twenty gold dragons. But Avonnian and Tressi merchants would sell to the highest bidder. Thestitiunian merchants would be forbidden from selling to Rindria. Rindria had grain, but not enough to feed its population for adequate amounts of time. Its closest ally was mainly a frozen tundra and focused on feeding its own people.

And so, Rindria starved.

Everyone else was happy. Foreign merchants made more money. Her father counted the loss of grain as a credit against the emperor; it was on his orders that money was lost, and nobles were entitled to just compensation for lost property. The credit gained interest, and they'd recuperate the losses, in time. Thestitiunian farmers' grain was given priority in the domestic supply, and bread and alcohol became cheaper in the empire. There were increased holidays to celebrate, with free beer, mead, and bread given en masse.

Everyone was happy but the Riams. Amaria didn't care about them. Let them starve. Let them die. Let the whole country crumble. Their sovereignty hurt everyone else in Cesmassia, including themselves.

Amaria gave off a guttural scream, interrupting her thoughts, her lower areas feeling as if they were lit on fire as a tight wave of cramps went across her abdomen. She clutched her stomach as she leaned over, almost blacking out from the pain wrenching across her back.

"Don't leave me," she clutched Theodmon's hands, her vision breaking into a million pieces, as if it were a kaleidoscope. He had just returned from the border a month ago. Amaria was amazed the Riams had fought for seven months with diminishing food. She hated them for it.

"I won't," he promised, kissing the top of her head quickly.

The doors burst open, an army of healers, midwives, and maids coming through. Juliette and Nicoletta were there, bleary eyed.

Amaria wanted to hug them. Her stomach was on fire. Her asshole was being pulled. She felt as if a million knives cut her. She was crying.

"Breath," Fylla, the midwife, commanded, kneeling next to Amaria. A resident healing mage of the castle, Katerina Montersatt, set out her supplies on a table.

"I'm going to unlace the back of your nightgown," Fylla told Amaria. "It'll make things easier. Put your hands on the edge of the bed and when you feel a contraction, start breathing. Once you are unlaced, I'll check to see how dilated you are."

Amaria nodded, gasping as another wave of pain hit her. She felt the cool October air hit her back, chilling her otherwise sweaty body.

"Marquis, you may leave," Katerina said.

"I'm staying," Theodmon dismissed the healer's words without taking his eyes from Amaria's face.

Katerina, thankfully, did not protest. Amaria gritted her teeth as the contraction subsided.

"Lay down, my Lady," Fylla told her. "I need to see how dilated you are."

Amaria complied, screaming as the pain seemed to be worse as she lay on her back. Fylla's hands made her way up the nightgown, and Amaria tensed slightly. She focused on Theodmon, studying his frown lines. She was uncomfortable with anybody being near that region except for her husband and was trying to pretend it was him there.

"Six inches, you're in active labor." Fylla looked over towards Katerina, who had laid out a variety of herbs on the table, her hands and eyes glowing a mint color.

"Would've never guessed," Amaria sarcastically said before screaming once more, curling into a ball.

"Drink." Katerina pushed a wooden bowl filled with a sticky, brown liquid into Amaria's hands. "It'll help with the pain."

Amaria took a sip, immediately gagging at the tar-like texture. She pinched her nose, threw back her head, and forced herself to drain the bowl before she stood up once more, placing her hands on the bed. Another contraction came.

The medicine did not help with the pain and Amaria wondered if she would die tonight.

She felt someone rub her shoulders, and she turned to see Theodmon.

"You've got this," he told her before Fylla brushed him aside. If Amaria wasn't screaming, she could have laughed. This was a woman's space, and liege lord or not, Theodmon was intruding—Fylla would not engage in niceties.

Amaria was glad Theodmon stayed.

She desperately wanted her mother. Another scream as sharp pains erupted across Amaria's back and crotch, and she felt her muscles suddenly give in on themselves. Her legs shook but she gripped the bed tighter. Katerina knelt under her, letting Amaria remain in whatever position was most comfortable for her labors.

"Push," Nicoletta encouraged.

Amaria bit her lip, tears falling from her eyes, but braced herself, forcing her muscles to release, as if she were pushing something from her. She barely registered large hands closing around her white knuckles, the strong fingers interweaving between her clenched nails. "Squeeze my hand. You can get through this," Theodmon reaffirmed.

His calloused hands brushed over her soft ones. She felt present, centered. Only for a moment and the contraction came once more.

"You're doing well," Katerina said from in between Amaria's legs, her hands coated in blood. "I can see the head."

"Pain medication!" Amaria gasped, seeing black across her vision.

"You've had dangerous amounts already," Katerina told her somberly. "If your child is crowning, you are almost done. Push."

Gritting her teeth, Amaria complied, holding Theodmon's hand tightly.

"One more push!" Fylla said.

"I have the baby's head secured; you can do it," Katerina confirmed.

Taking a deep breath, Amaria closed her eyes and pushed, screaming as Katerina pulled her child out. Exhausted, Amaria collapsed to her knees, Theodmon catching and holding her shoulders just in time.

Katerina passed the wailing child to the midwife as she clipped the umbilical cord separating them.

"Let me hold-"

"Soon," Katerina interrupted. "Fylla is cleaning the blood from him, and I need to get the placenta out from you. Lie back."

"Him?" Amaria looked up at Katerina hopefully as Katerina pressed down on her stomach, a disgusting liquid coming out from Amaria as if she were a pastry filled with berries. "I have a son?"

"Yes," Katerina confirmed.

"Let's get you cleaned up," Juliette said, her hands gently securing themselves on Amaria's back, helping her stand upright. "There is a small tub in the bathroom ready; I can heat the water for you. Once you have washed the blood, sweat, and vomit from yourself, we will get you in bed and you can be with your son as long as you like."

Amaria looked over at her son, being wiped down by Katerina. She wanted to hold him. To hug him.

"Marquis?" Katerina said. "Would you like to hold your son as your wife cleans up?"

"My son," Theodmon said, his chest swelling. He reached out for the small screaming bundle as Katerina gave instructions on how to hold the baby.

"What will we name him?" Theodmon asked. "I can join you in the bathroom with him, if you want."

"What do you think?" Amaria said as she took small cautious steps with Juliette's guidance. Her entire body was sore as if she had tumbled down the mountain.

She turned, glancing over at the small bundle in the gold and cream blanket she had sewn. His face was red, and he was screaming, the trauma of birth still poignant. His tiny fist moved out of the folds, a high pitched wail reverberating through the room.

He was a warrior. "What about Lysander?"

Lysander was a Chauvignon name. She knew Theodmon would like the name. Sure enough, Theodmon nodded. "Lysander," he confirmed.

Amaria cleaned the blood and sweat off of her, changing her nightgown. She soon was in the plush bed, Theodmon handing their son to her.

"Ssshhh," she reached to pick up Lysander. "It's alright, I'm here."

She cradled him, holding him to her chest as she bounced him. She beamed at Theodmon. "He's beautiful."

Theodmon merely smiled back, kissing her on top of her head. Her body relaxed underneath his touch. She had done what was seemingly impossible: she loved her husband. Amaria couldn't remember when she fell in love. Initially they were stiff, awkward even, as they got to know each other. But soon, that initial hesitation melted away, leaving behind tenderness and genuine connection.

She breathed heavily, closing her eyes. She smelt the top of Lysander's head. The scent of the newborn was calming, almost intoxicating. She looked upwards, meeting Theodmon's eyes, the hazel melting as he pushed back a lock of her hair. She noticed his eyes harden, and he seemed deep in thought.

"I'll send for breakfast," Theodmon stood up stretching, pointedly looking at the child in her arms who was blinking lazily up at his mother. "You recently gave birth, you should relax. Give him to the wet nurse."

Amaria sighed, handing Lysander over to the woman who just approached. She wondered what it would be like to breastfeed him herself.

Too many rules had already been broken today. Noblewoman didn't breastfeed.

Noblewomen also tended not to be talented spymasters. Amaria pushed back her scowl. She had a pile of intelligence reports ever growing on her desk. So did Theodmon. There was something being planned by their enemies to hurt them.

Amaria looked over at Lysander, who was latched onto the nursemaid. She promised herself that she would burn down the world before anyone could hurt him.

Like a battering ram against a china cabinet, the same nagging thought she had had every day for fifteen months exploded in her mind. She wasn't safe as long as the Raulet Ruby was missing.

And if she wasn't safe, Lysander wasn't safe. Amaria's smile melted away as her happiness turned to ash. The Ruby had to be found.

She liked the world she lived in unburnt.

Chapter Nine

I nk blots dripped from Amaria's quill onto her parchment as she stifled a yawn. It was only nine in the morning and she had already been working for three hours.

She moved the parchment to the side, deciding to rewrite it later, before lifting a sealed letter, pressed with a golden rose, from the top of the pile.

Amaria broke the seal with a chuckle. Roses perhaps seemed too on the nose for intelligence. Possibly it's why her codename worked. Nobody would ever suspect that a Raulet used one of the items on their House Sigil. Everyone expected them to be more cunning than that.

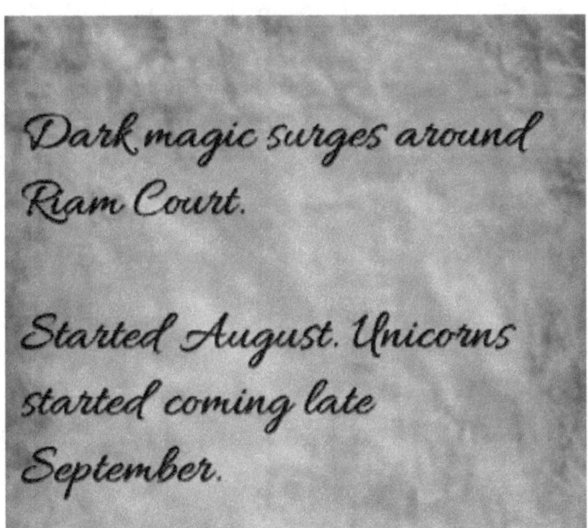

Amaria rubbed her temples, groaning. Rindria was a buffer—no, a bridge—for Lynette in Avondra and the Badlands. But Lynette wasn't dumb. And giving an ancient, powerful gem filled with dark magic to Clarissa Nalaney couldn't be called anything but stupid.

Why did she have the Raulet Ruby? How dare those two banshees come into her home, steal her property, and kill her friend. How dare they still have the gem.

Amaria needed to get it back.

"Morning love." Theodmon strolled into the offices. His shirt was unknitted, the tops of his muscles showing. Sweat glistened off his face and chest, and Amaria knew that he had been training with his sword on the grounds.

"Morning." Amaria grabbed his arm as he passed, pulling him towards her. She tilted her head upwards, her lips connecting with his as her eyes closed.

"You're coming to breakfast?" Theodmon asked as they broke apart.

Amaria shook her head. "No, I mean yes…Theo, I need your help." She thrust the note at him. "Clarissa Nalaeny has the gem."

Theodmon had a litany of intelligence networks and they had been combined with her own networks. If she hadn't heard from her own informants about the information she needed, it was possible Theodmon's networks had the missing piece.

"We'll retrieve it." Theodmon slipped his hand into hers, pulling her to her feet. Amaria protested, but she laughed as he spun her around, guiding her to the couch. Only he could be so playful when talking about this sort of thing.

"Do you have any ideas?" Amaria asked as they sat together on the couch.

"Maybe," Theodmon said slowly, staring at the flames in the fireplace. "Lynette and Clarissa work together. She's only working with Rindria to get access to the Badlands. Tressidil isn't stupid enough to mess with the Badlands. Morroek hates female monarchs too much to work with her…"

Theodmon's eyes lit up as Amaria smiled. Durek Svilas of Morroek was scheduled to come to Forteresse les Blanche within the coming month to discuss trade with Amaria as her father's agent. Svilas was married to the King of Morroek's eldest daughter and, as the king had no sons, was the presumptive heir to the throne. They could use Morroek's hatred of female monarchs to their advantage.

Perhaps, if they were lucky, Morroek, Rindria, and Avondra would destroy each other. It would make it easier for Thestitiunia to conquer them later.

"We pit them against each other without them ever knowing." Theodmon said, his eyes bright.

"I don't think they're that dumb," Amaria said.

Theodmon rushed over to the desk, finding three quills before running back to Amaria. "This is Avondra," he held up a black quill. "This is Rindria," a peacock feather quill. "And this is Morroek," a white quill. He pulled his dagger from his belt. "And this is us."

He placed the black quill and the peacock quill together on the coffee table. "They have an alliance." He set the white quill close to the peacock one. "Morroek is sympathetic to Rindria, as they have similar cultures, fears, and socio-political issues." He placed the dagger down, the blade cutting off the white feather from the other two.

"We can curb those sympathies," Amaria agreed. "If we can get Morroek to ally with us, we can focus on destabilizing Rindria and getting rid of Lynette."

"We'll also run a second scheme," Theodmon spun the dagger so its tip pointed towards the black feather. "The Morrian alliance will be secret. However, we also make a public alliance with Avondra. And when we're attacked by Rindria, Lynette will have to choose: support her public ally or ruin her secret alliance."

"She'd either earn the scorn of the international community or lose her easy access to the Badlands," Amaria breathed, pulling him towards her. The empire had enough resources to conquer if needed, but it was better to allocate fewer resources when possible.

Disgraced rulers didn't garner as many allies as well-loved ones. Disgruntled populations didn't fight as hard for hated leaders. And Thestitiunia, by playing a game of politics and scheming, would gain more resources with less Thestitiunian blood and suffering.

"It's a temporary roadblock," Theodmon admitted, his hazel eyes sparkling.

"It gives us time," Amaria said. It was better than what anybody else was doing. Her mouth curled sourly. Why were they doing more for the country than the emperor? Amaria picked at her nail beds. "How will you get Rindria to attack us? They're aggressive, but they won't attack when it's convenient to us."

"I'm going to frame us for the assassinations of key members of the royal family," Theodmon said. "We'd never leave griffins behind, nor a note signed by my name."

"But it'll be there," Amaria held his hands, a smile breaking across her face. It was brilliant. It was so simple. She moved over towards her desk, picking up another sealed letter. Perhaps there would be more info to further base their plans around. The seal broke and the letter unscrolled.

Amaria's eyes scanned over the sprawling, hastily written words.

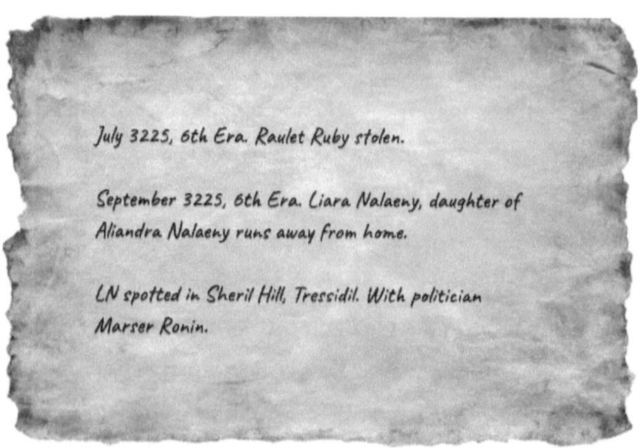

Her hands shook as she dropped the parchment, it floating down to the ground. It wasn't a coincidence that Liara Nalaeny, the daughter of the woman who now had the Raulet Ruby, ran away shortly after Amaria's home was attacked—almost a month after Amaria's wedding. Liara Nalaeny must have fled as soon as she returned home.

Liara knew something. Amaria was going to get that information.

"We have a third plan," Amaria said. "We get Liara Nalaeny and use her to get the Raulet Ruby back."

"What?" Theodmon walked over, taking the parchment from her hand. His jaw hardened as he read. "How hard will it be to convince the emperor not to punish us?"

"The emperor on the throne or the real emperor?" Amaria pointedly looked at Theodmon. Emperor Aion Marion had a big bark, but he was lazy, incompetent, and left ruling Thestitiunia to Aaron in the background. Aion had a son, but somehow the son cared even less for the responsibilities of his position than his father.

Amaria ground her teeth. The empire was centuries old, surviving throughout wars, famines, and plagues. She'd be damned if the current emperor and his heir squandered it all. "My father will support us. That's enough to stop Aion if he is that angry."

One day this system would implode. Amaria knew that. She pushed the thoughts of unwanted potential civil unrest from her mind, that would be an issue for another time. Instead, she focused rather on the wanted destruction they were about to inflict on three other nations.

It was for the good of Thestitiunia. It was for the good of all on the continent.

She pulled out a quill, writing two of her own letters.

"What are you doing?" Theodmon asked.

Amaria was silent, slowly drawing letters across the page. For a few moments the only sound was the crackling of the logs in the stone fireplace and the scratching of her quill. She stepped back, surveying her handiwork.

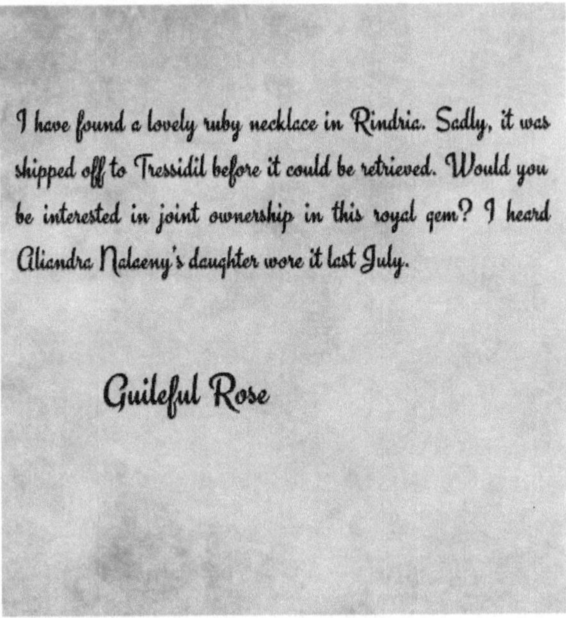

"You're signing this one with me," Amaria told him. "We're going to convince Aion to ward this runaway and immediately marry her off."

Theodmon looked at her, his eyebrows raised. "To whom?"

"You know," Amaria said.

"Aloysius," Theodmon groaned his younger brother's name. "He'll take this well."

"He's twenty-one," Amaria rolled her eyes. "He'll get over it. He'd have to marry soon either way."

"And this helps us get the Ruby back?"

Amaria smirked. "Of course. You should visit your new in-laws with a gift. It is only proper." She twirled a lock of hair around her finger. "And when Rindria falls, if Liara Nalaeny was somehow the only remaining heir...."

Theodmon kissed her, his hands wrapped around either side of her head. Amaria had given them an excuse to go to the Riam court without suspicion. She had given the Chauvignons specifically a way to claim Rindria for the empire and to limit Aion's claim to it.

"You're brilliant, Ammy," he told her as they broke away.

"Let's go to breakfast," she entwined her hand in Theodmon's, smiling up at him as if nothing was wrong.

It wasn't a lie. The world could crumble around her but it would be alright as long as they faced it together.

He broke away. "I have to go to the faerie lands soon. If we're planning more travels...I'm the liaison," Theodmon said.

Amaria nodded, feeling as if she had been punched in the stomach. Marquis Chauvignon had been the liaison between Thestitiunia and the faeries—perhaps even between all humans and the faeries—for centuries. It was why the Chauvignons had stepped down from being emperor. It is why the entrance to the faerie lands, which allegedly transcended space and time, were in the Westerlands.

Amaria knew it was an important duty. Theodmon didn't have to explain the necessity of it to her. Still, she didn't want him gone from her so soon after birth. She didn't want him gone for such a long work trip only to come back and have to travel more.

She understood it and hated it. Fuck duty. If only they could all be as carefree as Emperor Aion. And if only Cedric, his heir, was competent. Sometimes Amaria could swear he was simple. Or perhaps lazy and entitled. He seemed intelligent enough when convincing women to lift their skirts for him.

"When?" Amaria asked.

He kissed her warmly. "Soon. It's not imminent, but soon enough. The relationship is important."

Amaria sighed. Yes, she supposed it was.

Duty was the death of them all. But somebody had to be responsible.

Chapter Ten

"Duke Svilas," Amaria greeted the Morrian duke and presumptive heir to the Morrian throne as he entered the foyer. "I hope your trip was well?"

"As well as it could be," Durek Svilas said, his smile like a serpent's forked tongue. Amaria's skin crawled as he surveyed her, his eyes lingering over the neckline of her dress longer than was appropriate. "I see you are no longer pregnant. I hope the child is healthy?"

Amaria despised him. He was fishing for information on how to anger her. He was egging her on. He was good at getting under her skin with a polite word, and she suspected that he knew it too.

"Shall we go to the offices to meet my husband or do you need to rest?" Amaria said, trying her best to not cross her arms.

"Lead the way," Durek said, bowing his head almost mockingly.

"How is Morroek?" Amaria asked, keeping her voice light. She knew how Morroek was: decimated. A famine—induced by her no less—had ended only a few months ago. And with winter coming, the hunger would only become worse due to subpar stores of grain.

It was a method used by the Raulets to protect the empire from the unnecessary death of its fighting men. Morroek would one day be a part of the empire, but there was no point in putting a sword in a soldier's hand and sending him off to kill the enemy when the enemy could be killed by hunger without risk to Thestitiunian lives.

Amaria knew that she shouldn't antagonize Durek before a negotiation. However, Durek also knew this and chose to instigate this fight.

Durek's eyebrows narrowed, pausing momentarily in his gait beside her. She forced back the self-satisfied smirk.

"I had the kitchen prepare a feast," she said, "for your arrival."

She saw his fists curl under his cloak. A swelling of pride welled in her chest. He was agitated. Good. It made him weak. She liked him weak. She liked anybody who wasn't completely in line with her goals to be weakened. It made them less of a threat.

"I hope it isn't too modest; we weren't exactly sure when you would arrive." Amaria beamed widely, the picture of a welcoming host. She was doing her job as the lady of the estate perfectly, with malicious acts hidden behind a feminine swish of her skirt or a warm smile. Durek wouldn't believe it anyways—he saw right through her. He was annoying that way. However, he couldn't prove what he knew—she was perfect in every way. That she egged him on by offering him food, as every married noblewoman would do for a guest in her home? It sounded preposterous, even in her head.

"I'm sure it will be as lovely as you are, Marchioness Chauvignon," Durek said.

He was as good at this game as she was. She didn't like him, but she enjoyed sparring with him. She had done it for a long time as her father's representative in Morroek.

They moved through the white marbled halls silently, Amaria's dress dragging over the long red carpets. Soon, they reached the guest parlors, the guards opening the door. Inside, Theodmon was already sitting on the sofas, stirring his tea.

"Welcome, Your Grace," Theodmon's eyes locked on Durek as the door closed behind them. "Would you like tea?"

"Is your wife serving it?" Durek sat on the couch across from Theodmon, his eye contact unbreaking. Amaria's arms tensed. She did not want to.

"Naturally," she said lightly, walking over to the men, leaning over to pick up the teapot on the table in between them. "Sugar? Honey? Cream?"

"Cream, dear," Durek said, his voice venomously sweet.

"Don't call me that," Amaria snapped. "Have some respect." She breathed heavily. "Your Grace."

He laughed. "Take a joke-"

"I would prefer it if you weren't overly familiar with my wife," Theodmon said coldly.

Amaria placed Durek's tea in front of him, moving to sit next to Theodmon.

"We have a proposition," Theodmon said.

"I gathered that," Durek said dryly. "I didn't travel all this way for the pleasure of your company, my Lord and Lady."

"The Westerlands and Perivina Fluere want to make an alliance with Morroek," Theodmon stated. "Naturally, the other three provinces will align themselves as Thestitiunian provinces do—but you'll find this alliance to your benefit."

"I am a duke, not the king. I'm not the proper person for an alliance."

"You are the presumptive heir, a talented military strategist, and have influence with your father-in-law, the king," Amaria said. "Please, hear what we have to say. Nobody is expecting a formal alliance to be made today. We merely want to know whether Morroek would be interested."

"Are you Perivina Fluere's representative?" Durek's lip curled. "Aaron Raulet couldn't ask me himself? I never knew that what Aaron got from this sham marriage was the ability to hide behind his daughter's skirts."

"My father is otherwise occupied," Amaria said, her nostrils flaring slightly. "We're in the Westerlands, not Perivina Fluere, and the intricacies of how the Chauvignons and Raulets alliance operates doesn't concern you."

"Duke Svilas," Theodmon gently placed his hand on Amaria's lap.

"Tell me your offer, Marquis." Durek curtly said, as though he was not the representative of a starving nation and had an advantage over them.

The very thought caused Amaria to snarl internally, but she maintained an icy smile and prompted, "How much do you detest a female monarch, Duke Svilas?"

His eyebrows shot up, a predatory smirk slowly spreading his blunt face. "Ironic of you to ask me such a question."

"Shame. I must have missed my coronation," Amaria deadpanned.

However, she knew exactly what he meant. Her former fiancé had ties to the Avonnian throne. Anybody with half a brain could see what the benefit of that marriage alliance was for the Raulets and for the empire.

"Answer the question, Duke Svilas," Theodmon ordered. "Do you wish to have something that benefits us both—mainly you—or not?"

"Why, of course," Durek drawled. "The real question is how are you proposing to remove Lynette from the Avonnian throne? She's cemented herself quite thoroughly, amongst nobility and drudges alike."

"Many don't like her," Amaria stated, recalling the information she had gained from her spies over the years. "It won't be too difficult to cause internal instability."

"And, while that occurs," Theodmon added, "Morroek and Thestitiunia's armies and navies will attack and cause chaos."

Durek's eyes narrowed. "And what do you gain from this?"

"We hate Lynette Edrion as much as you do," Theodmon said. "She's been causing issues for Thestitiunia, so we both get what we want in having her off the throne."

"Who are you replacing her with?"

"Not my concern," Theodmon dismissed. "Avondra can follow their chain of succession; it's all male candidates."

"She's a dark mage," Amaria coldly stated, her veins feeling like ice from the hatred. She had done bad things in her life, but it was always for a higher purpose. Something that was good in the end.

Dark magic destroyed everything in its path. It festered in the user, causing them to become less than human.

Dark magic had given her sister that damn disease—it was a miracle she had survived. She wouldn't have survived if not for the expenses her father had spent; if Catalina hadn't been a Raulet, she would have been dead.

Like Amaria's mother.

"Whatever monarch follows her is none of my concern as long as they don't practice dark magic." She looked at Durek directly. "You hate female monarchs and magic more than us, why are you hesitating?"

"I don't trust you," he said. "Either of you. I especially have concerns over her." Durek nodded towards Amaria.

"I want Lynette dead more than you," she said.

"And you've seen a dead body?" he asked her patronizingly. "I doubt you'd kill as much as you did with your forced famines if you actually-"

"I've tortured and killed many," Amaria said. "Did you choose to ignore those rumors? Question my ability again and you may find yourself without air."

"Only someone afraid would wield threats as though that will stop them from sleeping with one eye open." Durek shook his head disapprovingly at Amaria. "No matter how many you may starve, torture, and kill, you will always be looking over your shoulder. Scared."

Amaria stared at him emotionlessly, although her eyes watered as panic bubbled to her throat.

He was right. Until the Raulet Ruby was retrieved and Delphina's killers were dead, she would be looking over her shoulder.

Who was she kidding? She would be looking over her shoulder until she died. Lynette was just the current threat. There would always be another threat in politics.

Durek turned to Theodmon, voice dripping in false sympathy, "Are you certain she should be involved with a difficult ordeal? Surely she'd be better off with your child. I heard you have a son, would you rob him of a mother?"

Amaria wanted to remove the air from his lungs. She forced herself to keep the warm smile on her face.

"You need magic to fight magic," Theodmon said. Amaria saw him clenching his fists under the table, the white knuckles against the black fabric of his trousers. "Hers is as powerful as you could hope for against Lynette."

"Your wife is a witch. Lynette is more likely to recruit her than anything."

"I don't practice dark magic!"

"Until it infects you, corrupts you," Durek hissed. "I've seen it happen to folks wandering too close to the Badlands. Don't deny you already have the seeds to go dark, what with you starving hundreds of thousands of innocent civilians of an entire country."

"This isn't relevant," Amaria pushed the truth of his words out of her mind and away from her heart. His words stung. It was easier to dismiss them than grapple with them.

"Is it?" Durek hissed. "Let me tell you what the Badlands are doing to my people. I don't know if your intelligence networks—and I do know about those—are clear, but people die from magic in Morroek. Unicorns run loose, they kill at least three people a week. Letifolds are along the ice caps near the border, people commit suicide and murder after seeing them. There's new creatures, ones we've never seen before: giant spiders, women with blood running from their eyes and after they touch the land, nothing will grow."

Amaria knew it was bad, but the notion of cheimónas existing was worse than anything she could have ever believed. Cheimónas were supposed to be a myth, a cautionary tale for children, a horror story of one of Ghagyn's—the goddess of magic—experiments gone wrong.

"Cheimónas," Amaria's voice cracked. "That woman—that *creature*—is a cheimóna. I can give you books, research on them—they're evil."

"And you want to help?" Durek scoffed. "These cheimónas are making your starvations more efficient. I would think you would align with them."

Amaria's stomach clenched. "I am not your enemy. Not here, not with dark magic."

"All magic is evil. Unnatural," Durek hissed.

Amaria hated the common Morrian view of magic. That view of magic was unnatural in civilized places such as Thestitiunia. She clenched her fists, pulling the fabric of her dress in her hands.

"The only difference I see between you and a cheimóna is that you dress better and your eyes bleed silver instead of red," Durek continued.

"I'm not your enemy with dark magic," Amaria repeated. "I understand magic better than you. Don't lecture me on it."

"As if I would dare," Durek said sarcastically. "You may understand magic better, but you can't deny that even those most against dark magic can still be corrupted by it. I'm not sure I want an alliance with a witch."

"But to have a Raulet in your debt, could you pass on that opportunity?" Amaria's silver eyes flashed, as if frost on a windowsill.

Durek paused. He looked at Theodmon, nodding at him to continue.

"You'll bring the terms of this alliance to your king," Theodmon said. "Our navies and armies will combine forces. While we attack Avondra, Amaria's intelligence network will be laying seeds for civil strife. Additionally, there are those with strong claims to the throne with no love for Lynette, and we will form alliances with them in removing her."

"Your plan is for me to persuade my king into allying with you against our current Avonnian alliances, knowing you're likely moving against Rindria?"

Amaria froze. How did Durek know they'd move against Rindria?

"Don't look surprised," he laughed. "Anybody with a brain could determine you'd use this as an advantage to destroy Rindria. They've two allies—if you cause one of them to go into civil war and promise a stronger alliance to the other, they'll fall."

"Does it bother you?" Theodmon asked, his face impassive.

"Am I Riam?"

"No," Theodmon answered.

"Then you have my answer," Durek shrugged. "I have a condition."

Amaria's heart thumped, fearing what this condition was.

"Seeing as how Morroek will be risking our lives to help save yours, we'll not aid someone who continues to starve us."

"I'll speak to my father," Amaria genuinely smiled at Durek for the first time. He was correct, Morroek needed aid more than anything after the manufactured famine and the cheimónas destroyed the fertile land they had. Another manufactured famine would be lethal to what was now an essential ally. Aion would be angered at this change of circumstance, but he could be placated with the promise of the collateral damage of Avondra and Rindria with these complex webs they spun. Or so she hoped.

"Write to him immediately." Durek smoothly returned the smile as Theodmon stood. "For efficiency."

"Naturally." Amaria indicated her head before standing. "A maid will be here soon to show you to your chambers. I look forward to seeing you at dinner."

"Thank you, Duke Svilas." Theodmon placed his hand on the back of her waist as he guided her out of the room.

"No, thank you," Durek remained smiling. All three of them understood the unspoken truth—a Raulet was now in debt to the highest ranking nobleman, and heir apparent, of Morroek.

Theodmon nodded curtly towards him, guiding Amaria out of the room and into the corridor. Amaria held her breath as she walked over the stone and carpet, the door shutting behind her with a thud. She remained stiff until they had passed several other doors and were nearly a hundred feet down the corridor.

"Are you alright?"

Amaria leaned against the wall, her wrist locking, as she shook, trying to stop herself from crying. Her head sharply jutted to her side, before she looked down, trying to breath as she studied the intricate weavings on the carpet.

"No," she whispered. "I hate him. I hate her. I hate that we need to work with him."

She was being petulant. She knew this, but she couldn't stop herself from whining about it.

"Theo, this is dangerous. I need you to stay alive."

"I don't plan on dying." He brushed a lock of her hair back. "Morroek would gladly kill both of us, and we know this. What can we do with this knowledge?"

"Plan for it," Amaria gulped, falling into his chest. "I need you to be safe. *Please.*"

"You think I'd die with a beautiful wife waiting at home?" Theodmon chuckled.

She closed her eyes as she pushed her face against his chest, hearing his heartbeat. "I'll write to my father about the demands."

"You know, your father once threatened to kill me if I hurt you." Theodmon chuckled, his breath glossing over Amaria's hair.

"He was that blunt?" Amaria smirked, her cheeks moving against the cotton of Theodmon's shirt.

It seemed that Aaron had gotten territorial after Lyseno Vypren cut her open in front of him. Amaria couldn't even find joy in the irony. It hurt too much. She knew it wasn't fully her father's fault; Aion had ordered it. But she blamed him all the same. How could he sway Aion on everything but the matter of her marriage.

Marriage was something that should have been exclusive to Aaron, but Aion dictated it. And Aaron dictated everything else in the damn empire.

"Of course not," Theodmon placed his hands over her clenched ones. She didn't even realize she had molded her hands into fists. "If I remember correctly, he reminded me that he was an earth mage and that I lived on a mountain and that I should remember that fact if I even had the glimmer of a thought of doing anything that would harm you or tarnish your honor."

"And you wouldn't get your debts forgiven."

"That was implied, wasn't it?" Theodmon chuckled. "Any thoughts I had of acquiring a mistress, or beating you-"

Amaria hit his arm with the back of her hand, indignant.

He continued to laugh. "Ammy, I never once thought of hurting you."

Involuntarily, Amaria smiled, and her smile turned into laughter.

Chapter Eleven

Amaria hated paperwork. She stared at the ever growing pile of it on her desk. Her eyes were sore, and she was tired of reading and compiling information. That's all she had been doing for weeks. She sent out contractors to retrieve Liara Nalaeny. They should be en route on the sea, but it was impossible to know until a letter arrived. And considering Tressidil was on the other end of the continent, it was entirely possible Liara Nalaeny may already be in Thestitiunian waters by the time the letter confirming departure from Tressidil arrived.

There was no use in worrying about it. Amaria couldn't plan for unknowns—and for all she knew, Liara Nalaeny could have jumped overboard and drowned. Amaria looked over at Juliette and Nicoletta, who were playing a card game on the sofas.

"Do you want to go down to the grounds?" Amaria's voice cut through the cozy silence.

"You want to watch Theodmon train without a shirt," Nicoletta laughed.

Yes. She did. She loved looking at Theodmon's body—he was gorgeous. Amaria twisted her face at Nicoletta. "No, I just don't want to look at paperwork."

Nicoletta pursed her lips as she rolled her eyes. "Sure. Let's avoid paperwork by going to look at your likely half-naked husband swinging a sword."

"Polite," Juliette sarcastically scoffed.

"Always," Nicoletta linked her arm through Juliette's. "We're all married adults; we aren't innocent to this. And, it's natural to have desires."

"Like you desire your husband?" Amaria lightly bumped against Nicoletta's shoulder, smiling.

"He's old." Nicoletta rolled her eyes. "And I have other inclinations with my desires."

Nicoletta and Haerdnor had similar inclinations. Amaria had known that for a while Aaron considered marrying Nicoletta and Haerdnor to protect their reputations and insulate their desires; she supposed it would also make it easier to conceive heirs if all parties were aware of the desires and inclinations of each other.

However, Haerdnor had ended up engaged to Naomi Brassir, a Tressi noblewoman, for similar reasons with the bonus of being more politically advantageous to marry. Nicoletta was married to an earl who would die soon—he wanted to be in Theodmon's court and Nicoletta got him in by being Amaria's lady. As long as Nicoletta provided him a son, when he died, she would not have to remarry. Amaria hoped that would occur. She did not want to lose Nicoletta.

She looked at Nicoletta's flat stomach, quickly averting her eyes as they entered the corridor. Juliette caught a maid's attention, telling her to bring cloaks to the foyer for them.

"I'm working on it." Nicoletta caught Amaria's gaze. Amaria noticed that she stiffened and turned slightly away from her.

"We didn't say anything," Juliette said as they passed a frosted windowpane.

"I don't think the men will be half naked," Amaria joked, shivering.

"They overheat." Juliette shook her head. "Meanwhile, I'm freezing beneath fur-lined cloaks."

"Anything to see Lucas half-naked," Amaria said.

Juliette shrugged. "I suppose."

They soon reached the foyer, waiting for their cloaks to arrive. As they did so, a page ran up to them, a sealed scroll in hand.

"My Lady," he said with a bow. "A letter for you just arrived from Tressidil."

Amaria sighed. More paperwork. She had an inkling of what this one was. "Thank you," she took the scroll from him, dismissing him with a nod. As he departed, she broke open the seal, Juliette and Nicoletta casting furtive glances at it as Amaria read.

It merely confirmed the contractors left Tressidil with Liara nearly a month ago. At that rate, Amaria suspected they'd be in Aionstown in a month.

"I'll tell you later," Amaria whispered to Juliette and Nicoletta as maids shuffled around them with their cloaks.

Nicoletta and Juliette cast each other a short glance, their eyebrows raised. It happened so quickly that if Amaria didn't know better, she might have believed she imagined their glances.

Rubbing her hands together, Nicoletta turned to Amaria with a smile, all traces of her wily glance gone in a breath. "You're lighting us a fire," she said as the frost crunched underneath their boots. Amaria nodded, seeing her breath in the air. A fire would be needed, she could not argue with Nicoletta there. She didn't want to argue with Nicoletta—their relationship had been strained since Delphina's death. But it also felt stronger in some regards. Amaria wasn't quite sure on how to define the complicated mess of their friendship.

She wouldn't push Nicoletta further. Not when they were almost to the grounds; Amaria could see the men around the bend of the outside entrance as she heard the shouts and clanging of swords and shields.

Theodmon, sadly, was wearing a shirt as he sparred with his brother. Aloysius was red faced, and he swung wildly. Amaria could tell he was angry. It appeared that Theodmon had told Aloysius about his engagement.

Lucas and Henri were laying on the ground nearby, breathing heavily.

"Did you fight?" Juliette asked them as they approached.

Lucas nodded, coughing. Juliette sat down next to him, handing him the water pack that was laying near him.

"Who won?" Amaria asked, sitting down on a bench near where Lucas had collapsed, smoothing out her skirts. She had become comfortable with them during her time here. Theodmon, Lucas, and Henri were close, and Amaria had bonded with Lucas slightly over torture techniques, and Henri, well, Henri could read minds.

Juliette, too, was a friend, quickly meshing in with her and Nicoletta in the Delphina-sized hole. Amaria tried to not feel as if she was replacing Delphina. She wasn't replacing Delphina—nobody could do that. Sometimes, Amaria believed Nicoletta and Juliette liked each other more than they liked her.

Amaria rubbed her hands together, summoning the energy and magic needed to spark a flame to life. Next to her, Juliette and Nicoletta leaned closer.

"Why're you out here anyways?" Lucas asked, watching the fire.

"Wanted to see you," Juliette said easily, squeezing Lucas's hand. "And Amaria has something to tell us."

All four pairs of eyes shifted to meet Amaria's. "We have a wedding in Aionstown in a month. We should pack soon," Amaria said, careful to keep the information bland, always wary of eavesdroppers.

"A wedding?" Henri laughed. Amaria felt him press against the barriers of her mind.

"*Yes?*" She said through the mage link..

"*I didn't realize wedding was a synonym for a gilded prison for potential political assets.*"

"*Almost all brides are political prisoners.*" Amaria looked at him darkly. "*And I'm not interested in whether she's an asset; I want information on Delphina.*"

Henri looked at her skeptically. She shook her head sharply. Not here. Not now. She didn't need him prying into the crevices of her mind.

She felt him withdrawing from the mage link.

"How do you know we're going to a wedding in Aionstown?" Lucas asked lazily, examining his hunting knife.

"Just a hunch," Amaria replied nonchalantly.

Lucas smirked, placing his knife down. "Anything to do with why Aloysius looks so dour?"

"Dour," Juliette repeated, her eyebrows raised. "I hope you know you're insufferable."

"I have an extensive vocabulary," Lucas said, laughing at his wife's jab.

"And you're still insufferable." Juliette shook her head.

"Don't you want to know who the bride is?" Henri asked. In the distance, Theodmon and Aloysius sparred—Theodmon was easily winning, despite Aloysius's magic. It was easy, Amaria supposed, when Theodmon had trained almost every free waking moment whereas his opponent avoided it.

"You would know," Nicoletta snorted.

"Occupational hazard," Henri said.

It was all Amaria could do to not burst out laughing. That was a mild way to put being a mind reader and the knowledge he gained from it.

"Don't repeat this." Amaria leaned in towards her friends, knowing they would not repeat the information, even without the warning. "But a runaway Riam lady whose mother has a particularly valuable gemstone has been, ah, acquired from her hiding spot in Tressidil."

Lucas laughed. "You engaged in some light kidnapping?"

"She's eighteen; it's not kidnapping," Amaria said dismissively.

"I don't think you have to be a child to be kidnapped." Lucas rolled his eyes.

"Can you two stop playing semantics?" Nicoletta said, crossing her arms. "What about this runaway? What do you have planned?"

Amaria couldn't help but notice a slight increase in the pitch of Nicoletta's voice when she asked what Amaria had planned.

"Nothing concrete," Amaria said. "She ran away the same month that Provincia Palencia was attacked. She might know something about that. We just want to have her if needed so we have access to that information."

And to have access to Rindria. Amaria didn't say it, but she knew everybody here knew. One didn't become a member of the Chauvignon's inner circle without some sort of propensity for violence.

Nicoletta crossed her arms. "On a scale of a normal person to what you do in the Drowning Tombs and Mortensia Labyrinths, what do you have planned?"

The fire crackled in Amaria's hands as she recoiled from Nicoletta's words, her eyes watering. Lucas looked over at them in concern.

Nicoletta took a deep breath. "Sorry, I didn't mean it like that."

Slowly, Amaria forced herself to breathe, the flames extinguishing. "It's alright."

Without warning, the sharp ring of metal scraping came from the center of the grounds. Aloysius grunted. Theodmon had his sword's hilt wedged under Aloysius's and was pushing upwards, forcing Aloysius to drop his sword before he pointed his sword at his brother's neck.

"Good job," Theodmon said, lowering his sword.

"I let you win," Aloysius said as a page entered the training grounds, shivering.

Theodmon laughed. "Sure."

"Marquis," the page approached with a bow, giving Theodmon the note. Theodmon opened it and Amaria saw his face become paler as he read. She extinguished her flames, hastily standing up and running to him.

"What's wrong?" She breathed once she reached him.

He silently handed the note to her, letting her read for herself.

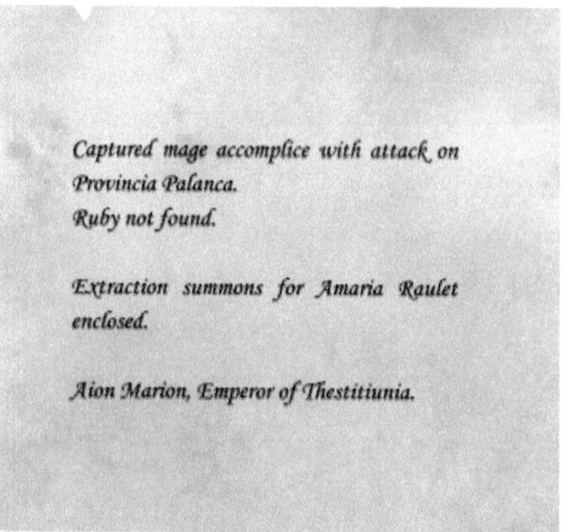

Amaria saw another scroll, tightly bound with purple ribbon, in Theodmon's hands. Her mouth went dry and her heart threatened to explode from her chest. She knew what those were. She dreaded that duty of being an Extractor.

Extractions–pulling magic out of dark mages, was the primary reason Extractors existed. There was a rotation, skipping those who were pregnant or undergoing severe life events as they would be at risk for having their magic corrupted. Now it seemed as if it was Amaria's turn in the rounds.

"Are those...?" She knew those were her formal summons. Still, she found herself asking. She knew Theodmon would confirm they were. She knew he couldn't comfort her, though she wanted him too.

"Unfortunately," Theodmon sighed, pulling her into a hug. "At least we already have to go to Aionstown anyways?"

Amaria closed her eyes, pushing her face against his chest. She could hear his heart beating. She did not want to move. Right now, as he hugged her, even with the cold biting her nose, she was safe. They were secluded. They didn't have politics or dark magic to worry about. She didn't want the false serenity to end.

She wanted the serenity to be real one day. However, although she was ambitious, she knew that was a goal she could never have. The reality of her situation didn't stop her dreams.

Chapter Twelve

To her annoyance, Amaria was up before dawn. She laid in bed, listening to Theodmon breath in his sleep.

The servants were likely packing the carriages now. She couldn't say she was excited for the journey. She'd had to find her Extractor uniform. It was thrown in a chest, bundled up and discarded as if Amaria was trying to forget it existed.

In truth, she was.

She propped herself up, staring at Theodmon. She was surprised he wasn't training, but she was thankful he wasn't. She lay against his chest, trying to time her breathing with his.

It was peaceful for the thirty minutes it lasted.

Theodmon rose early, as was his custom. "You're up early," Theodmon said.

Amaria stretched, kissing him. "Perhaps I wanted to do things with you before we're stuck in a carriage for weeks."

Theodmon kissed her back, pushing her onto her back as he climbed on top of her. "These things?"

"Perhaps," Amaria smirked at him. "Perhaps I wanted to learn how to sword fight."

Theodmon leaned over her, kissing her neck. "This is a type of sword fighting." His breath brushed past her ears, a lock of her hair moving slightly. She wrapped her hands around him, pulling him closer with the embrace.

"Why don't you put it in?" She whispered. She wanted him to put it in. Her lower parts throbbed, and it was starting to hurt below. She needed him in her.

"And if I don't?" He smirked back at her. "Perhaps I'd like to see you this way all morning."

"You'll suffer too," Amaria said, her eyes flashing as they drifted over towards his erect manhood. She could not imagine if he decided to not fuck her after being mounted atop her.

"But to have a beautiful woman lusting after me," Theodmon chuckled, lowering himself down to kiss her breasts, moving his way up to her neck, and then to her lips. She sighed, her eyes closing in anticipation.

She felt him press his hips closer against her, and his cock entered her body. Her hands clawed at his back as he pulsated within her. She felt herself clench around him. "Theo," she moaned.

He was breathing heavily. She lifted her head up, bringing her lips to his. Her silver eyes looked warmly into his hazel. She loved how he had blue flecks, as if they were small dots of the hottest fire. He was fire—passionate, strong, and warm. He was so warm.

She wrapped her arms around his neck, embracing him. "Stay," she whispered. She didn't want to get up. She wanted to stay in this bed forever with him.

He kissed her neck in response. "Always," he said, pulling her closer to him, as he thrust inside of her.

Her mouth opened, small gasps escaping her as her body relaxed. Her hands gripped his back. "More," she commanded.

Theodmon's pace increased, he was pounding her faster and harder than before. Amaria's eyes closed as she tilted her head upwards, pulling Theodmon in for a kiss as he did so. The air around them was hot, as if they were in a sauna.

Her back arched, and she felt a gush come from her at the same time Theodmon moaned, liquid coming from him in unison.

He stayed in her for a moment longer, before pulling out and laying on the bed next to her. "I love you," he breathed.

"I love you too," she replied softly, touching his face gently with her palm. His stubble tickled her and she kissed his cheek. His jawline was sharp. He was handsome. She laid her head on his chest. It was well toned, and she loved using him as a pillow, no matter how uncomfortable.

"Do you ever think about how we did something exceptional?" Theodmon asked.

"How so?" Amaria asked, tracing her fingers over his chest hair.

"We're a political marriage," Theodmon said. "Most political marriages despise each other—look at my mother and father, the gods bless his soul. The fortunate ones are often only friends."

"And we love each other," Amaria sighed. "When do you think we stopped being a political marriage?"

"When I realized you threw card games to let me win when I had a bad day," Theodmon said instantly. Amaria looked at him with her eyebrows raised, surprised at how quickly he answered. She couldn't pinpoint an exact moment she loved him, because it was a culmination of experiences and time together.

She also was upset that he knew she threw games.

"Don't scowl." Theodmon chuckled. "I'll keep pretending not to notice."

Amaria snuggled against him. "I wish I had an exact moment to tell you…I feel like a terrible wife."

"No," Theodmon pulled her closer. "Never."

Amaria wanted to stay here. She never wanted to leave this bed with him. Unfortunately, as soon as she thought it, a knock came at the door. It was time for them to get ready to depart.

Amaria was tired of responsibilities. She still did them with a stiff upper lip. It was what was expected, after all.

And so, they both dressed and went to eat breakfast before departing for Aionstown.

The sun climbed higher and dipped downwards around the edge of the mountains; time moved at such a slothful crawl that the lips of every member in the carriage pressed tightly together. Painfully, near the end of the nineteenth day of traveling, the carriage stopped in front of a pair of sturdy, ironclad gates, imperial guards standing watch just beyond the entrance.

Upon spotting the group, the head guard barked out orders to open the iron bars and approached the carriage, Theodmon opening the door to speak with him.

"Evening," Theodmon said. "May we pass?"

"Yes, of course," the guard said, recognizing Theodmon not only as Marquis Chauvignon, but also as one of the generals of the Thestitiunian army. "Is Marchioness Chauvignon with you? She has summons."

"Yes," Amaria said, cradling Lysander in her arms and moving a wispy lock of brown hair off his forehead. He was small and wriggly, but growing quickly. Amaria couldn't believe he was eleven weeks, almost twelve weeks old.

"My Lord and Lady," the guard bowed his head, stepping out of the way so Theodmon could close the carriage doors and the carriage could pass through the gates. "You should go ahead to the throne room, Marchioness. Emperor Aion wants to address your *civic duty* imminently."

Amaria paled, clasping her hands together under her wide sleeves. She was no stranger to what occurred in dungeons. But using her magic to do these deeds, as an Extraction required, felt as if she was as violated as the prisoner. She hated it. It was her turn on the rotation, so she would do it anyways.

Theodmon banged on the top of the carriage, indicating it should move forward.

Her stomach knotted together and she felt as if she would vomit. She forced herself to focus only on Lysander. He was peacefully sleeping. Amaria lightly traced his cheek with her knuckle.

She wanted to kiss the top of his head but restrained herself out of fear of retching on him. That would be a monstrosity to wake up too. And she did not want to hold him as he screamed, her vomit touching her, until she could hand him off to a nanny.

"Are you alright?" Aloysius asked. "If not, vomit away from me."

"Classy," Celestine scolded.

"It's bad luck to vomit on a groom before his wedding," Aloysius shrugged.

"And who came up with that?" Theodmon said. "You?"

"It seemed implied," Aloysius said. "Perhaps I rediscovered lost ancient wisdom."

"Can you find the pin to deflate your ego?" Amaria shook her head. Still a smile escaped her. Aloysius was easy to like, ego and bad humor included.

"As soon as you look into a mirror," Aloysius responded easily as the carriage rolled to a stop.

Rolling her eyes, Amaria handed Lysander to Theodmon. She pushed her way out through the doors with little regard for how she stepped on the others' toes.

As she reached solid ground, she leaned over, her hands gripping her knees as she tried to breathe only through her nose.

Behind her, Theodmon disembarked, handing their son to a nanny who rode in the other carriage. He approached her, gently rubbing her back. "Take your time."

She would have to rise eventually. She would not be weak when she did so. She loved Theodmon for giving her this. She breathed heavily, and while she was placidly still, her face was proud. She was not weak.

She wished she could bring Lysander with her. But considering she was going to a formal royal announcement and then to a dungeon, she couldn't bring him. Those were no places for a child.

Amaria forced her expression to remain as if she were a painting frozen in time as her feet crunched over the stone paths until she reached the doors from the outer garden to the foyer of the imperial palace.

"You'll be alright," Theodmon held her hand comfortingly as they walked through the palace. Amaria didn't believe it but focused on him as to ground her to reality.

It seemed to work as she didn't vomit or faint before they reached the outside of the throne room. She could see the golden doors now. She could handle this. She repeated that mantra a hundred times.

As they approached, two armed guards opened the doors, revealing a room of golden marble, the last few rays of sunlight pouring through the intricate stained-glass windows. Near the front of the hall, there were two large thrones, carved in the same golden marble as the walls, ceiling, and floor, yet engraved with numerous jewels and carvings. Along the side of the room, there were long benches; the room was large yet, due to it being nearly empty, the silence was tense and deafening.

Standing by the thrones, Theodmon gripped Amaria by her shoulders, whispering fiercely. "You can do this. You can do this."

Seconds later, Amaria smoothed down her dress, the deep red robes draping over an intricately designed underdress—the dress was gray and covered with complex white swirls and fleur de lis, embroidered with a small black outline. She began to pace the room anxiously, her neck cramping from the topaz gems in her tiara. She could do this. She knew she could. She had done it before. She shouldn't feel sick at the thought of an Extraction. She had tortured and killed unflinchingly. She shouldn't be bothered.

But she was.

The tension broke as the doors opened again, this time with the herald blowing a horn. Amaria and Theodmon politely lowered themselves into a curtsy and a bow as a dark-skinned, redheaded man strode into the room, his head set with a crown and a dark purple cape trailing at his feet.

"His Imperial Majesty, Emperor Aion Marion the Second, Ruler of the United Thestitiunian Empire!" The herald announced.

Amaria suppressed the anger and disdain she felt as she saw her cousin. She smiled brightly. Aion had wanted her to be the sun—warm, inviting, and capable of harm. But he had forgotten that the sun was a ball of flame, and those who played with fire tended to be burned.

He was blind to the flames he was standing in, the incompetent fool.

"Your Imperial Majesty," she said sweetly. "It's a pleasure."

Next to her, Theodmon offered similar polite greetings.

"Rise," Aion commanded, and they rose from their reverence. "I assume you've gotten your Extraction summons."

"I have, Your Imperial Majesty," Amaria said. "I'm familiar with her crimes, so please, may we get on with it?"

Aion blinked. "You don't need a debrief?"

"I was there," Amaria said coldly. "Is she in the dungeons?"

"Please wear the uniform before you go," Aion said.

Amaria curtsied once more. "Of course. May I be dismissed? So I can prepare."

Aion nodded.

"I'd like to depart with her," Theodmon said.

Aion waved his hand. "Of course. We'll talk at the party later."

Amaria's blood boiled as she heard that, pausing in her departure, the guards were already opening the doors. He always had a party, a damn feast after the Extractions. As if it wasn't traumatizing to the Extractor and everyone else who watched it—spectator, executioner, Extractor, victim—only Aion seemed to not understand the gravity of the situation.

Aion never understood the gravity of any situation. It was because of him that she had been beaten and then because of him that her uterus had almost been carved from her. Aion had never acknowledged the pain he put her through. He never thought about others or anything other than his vapid, narcissistic parties. Amaria's fist clenched as her eyebrows merged together. Aion was a terrible person and a worse ruler.

And yet he was the emperor.

Theodmon reached Amaria. Hoping that she appeared as a dutiful wife who was waiting for her husband instead of a person who was debating regicide, she forced a smile and squeezed Theodmon's hand.

"Ammy," Theodmon whispered, her pet name escaping easily from his lips. "We can prepare in our own way."

Amaria chuckled. It was perhaps improper, but having sex before an execution was a healthy coping mechanism.

At least, it was healthier than regicide and kin killing.

"You're a terrible influence," Amaria whispered as the doors shut behind them.

"Is it influence if you want it too?" Theodmon said.

Amaria pursed her lips, shaking her head. He was clever and funny. It was a dry banter, but she enjoyed the wit.

"I actually don't need sex as a motivator," she said.

He raised his eyebrows, his mouth twitching in disbelief.

"I'll take it as an award but this Extraction is of one whose attack killed Delphina," Amaria said. "The motivator is her being stripped of her magic and then her dead body."

She didn't kill Delphina by her hand, but if this woman had never stolen the Raulet Ruby, if she had never broken into Provincia Palencia with the other two men, Delphina would still be alive. Amaria hated her because she had as good as killed Delphina.

And she stole from Amaria's family.

"You're startlingly violent," Theodmon said admiringly. "Have I ever told you how much I love that about you?"

Chapter Thirteen

Amaria pushed down the fold of her black dress as she adjusted its collar—it was heavy with the rubies and purple sapphires sewn along it, the gems laden with magical energy. Gems were a good storage unit for magical energy and commonly used for such.

Gems couldn't die—they weren't living after all—still, magic was tied to nature and nature made magic stronger. Energy could be held in gems extremely effectively; the magic never dying, lasting for eternity until it was released.

Shaking her head to clear her thoughts, Amaria looked at herself in the mirror. She looked like a goddess of death, and perhaps, that was the intent of this uniform.

Theodmon sat silently beside her, holding her hand. She wished he would say something, but there was nothing to say.

At least she'd be closer to avenging Delphina. She just wished it wasn't via an Extraction.

Amaria stood up and smoothed her dress down once more before picking up the heavy red sash, embroidered dragons and hydras on the front of it, tying it around her waist, and letting the front of it tumble down her skirt to her ankles.

There was no sense in delaying the inevitable.

"Would you place the veil on my hair?" she asked Theodmon.

He kissed the top of her hair and gently pinned the long black veil in her hair. She could feel the comb stab through the back of her braided bun.

"Thank you," she whispered before departing. The door slammed behind her with a thud. Amaria walked down the stone corridors of the palace, passing the windows with sunlight pouring in from outside.

It was noon, and by the time she was done, it would likely be nightfall. People saw her passing by and they whispered, quickly bowing their heads before scurrying off. It wasn't because she was a noble; it was because she was wearing the uniform of an Extractor. Thestitiunians recognized anyone who was an Extractor to be one of the most powerful mages in the kingdom: someone who could talk to the hydras and dragons, somebody who could help influence battles, and more importantly someone who upheld the Emperor's Justice against wayward mages, destroying their magical identities before their executions. While her status as a noble was powerful, her status as one of the Nine was more feared.

This was her second time wearing this dress, and unfortunately, it would not be the last. With the concerning reports of wayward mages and their activities, Amaria knew she would be performing many Extractions in the years to come. Not all of them, that's why the rotation existed, but enough.

She actually didn't like stripping people of their magic.

"Escort me to the dungeons," Amaria commanded a palace guard.

"My Lady Extractor, you know the way," the guard said quizzically. "You have everything you need and every right to be there—"

"Please," Amaria's voice went soft, "I don't want to walk there alone. Leave me at the entrance but please walk with me."

They walked in silence until they reached the dungeon's entrance. "Thank you," Amaria said. "It's an odd request, but tell me what you would lose if Extractors did not do our duty. What would evil mages take from you?"

"I would lose my son, my wife, my brother. Likely our farm. Stability to the reign."

Amaria choked back her words of wishing to say that natural events or non-mages could also do that. "Have mages ever benefited you? Not lofty ideas about stability, or country, but you, personally."

"Yes. When a drought is approaching, weather mages like you will cause rain to prevent it. I had a healing mage save my leg from infection and amputation. I've had bread made from mages who can influence emotions, and that bread gave me hope after my Pa died. Mages are good, and you, my Lady, are not evil for hurting bad mages."

Amaria opened her mouth in protest. She hadn't ever thought she was evil. At least, she didn't think she ever had that belief.

"My Lady, I'm common, not stupid. I've seen every Extractor and how you react to your duty. It's different reactions every time, but I always see the pain and doubt. But I believe the bad ones deserve it."

"Thank you, you may leave," Amaria said, bracing herself with newfound resolve. She pushed open the entrance to the dungeon and walked past the mostly empty cells, to one at the very end of the hall. It was fortified with magical bonds, and Amaria knew that the guards were mages.

"Let me in," she commanded, pulling a small vial from her sleeve. It was filled with a brilliantly pink liquid—le sedaifa amagida fin.

Made from the rare and magical pink root, amagida fin, the drug was closely guarded by the Extractors. Le sedaifa amagida fin weakened and corrupted a mage's power long enough for another, more powerful mage to be able to alter or remove their magic from them.

Amaria noted it would be a great torture device as well. However, le sedaifa amagida fin was only used for Extractions, and occasionally, a rare Cleansing. Perhaps it was best that way. Imagine if somehow the recipe was widely known?

Or worse, what if there was an immunity built up to the drug?

"Has the prisoner already been drugged?" Amaria directed the guard, pulling herself out of her thoughts.

"Yes, my Lady Extractor," the guard said, causing Amaria to internally grimace. She hated that title. "However, she may need more."

"Understood." Amaria looked at him. "I will inform you if I need more tonic, more herbs, anything. Please be on standby. What is the prisoner's name again?"

It wouldn't matter much by the end of the day, but Amaria worked best with a personal touch.

"Giuliana Vero."

"Open the door," Amaria commanded.

The guards opened the door, and in a dark room, Amaria could sense magic tendrils binding someone. Amaria closed her fist and opened it back up, fire burning in her palm. She used her fire to light the small pyre. In the dim light she saw a ragged woman being bound above the ground by glowing ropes, surely some mages'—another Extractor's perhaps—power.

"Giuliana?" Amaria called out. "Your imprisonment is almost over."

"Is it mercy, Lady Extractor," Giuliana asked mockingly, "to be stripped of my identity and murdered?"

"You committed treason," Amaria said, opening the bottle of tonic. "We must all fulfill our duties to the emperor, and there are punishments for failing."

"Is that why you do a non-mage emperor's bidding? Doesn't it make you sick that non-mages have power over us? You're an Extractor; you have more raw power than Aion can ever dream of—"

It did make her sick. Aion had no power and yet she did his bidding. What made her sick, though, was not that he lacked magic, but that he was an incompetent fool. Many, including herself, were much better suited to ruling the empire. Thinking this, however, was treason.

"Shut up," Amaria hissed, dumping the herbs over Giuliana's still-bound body, burning into her flesh. "There's order in the world, and His Imperial Majesty is the head of it. Magic is a tool; it doesn't make anyone more or less worthy."

"How is it different from your noble birth, *Marchioness Chauvignon*?" Giuliana cackled at Amaria's shocked face. "Oh yes, I know who you are. I stole from your family manor. Those precious jewels you keep-"

Amaria pulled out a needle, pushing it into her bottle. Once the needle was filled, she injected it into Giuliana's neck, her arms, her legs, her chest, her hands, her feet, Giuliana twitching and screaming because of it.

"You can't-" Giuliana screamed.

Amaria injected Giuliana's face with le sedaifa amagida fin. Giuliana was completely paralyzed. Amaria had always been amazed by this drug; the herbs were magical, and it was infused with even more magic when being brewed, thus making it powerful and dangerous.

Efficient though.

Amaria closed her eyes, feeling the mage's bound power. This was Lord Valouis's doing; she knew his magical signature, and so she could readily undo his bonds. Giuliana fell to the ground with a thump.

Although Giuliana was physically immobilized, her mind still had a barrier.

I can't waste precious energy fighting her mind like this. Amaria picked up another herb—this one was to cause pain. Amaria recognized it because she had used it with countless other prisoners before.

She placed the blue leafy herb on Giuliana's forehead, before slowly pouring a murky white liquid over it. Giuliana's skin sizzled, and she screamed. Amaria forced back a gag as Giuliana's face seemed to be eaten away by acid.

Amaria had never enjoyed the smell of burning flesh.

She did enjoy condemning dark mages to Sadthos's Kingdom though. Dark magic had sent her mother there, and Amaria had no issue with returning the favor. Lynette's servants had killed her mother, and Amaria would kill her servants in turn until she could have the chance to wring the life out of Lynette's pathetic existence herself.

Who else could Giuliana be working for?

The pain and shock of the blue herbs caused Giuliana to drop her mental defenses. And Giuliana's mind was powerful. Amaria was more powerful, but even so, she knew this would take a while.

The first shard of magic was small, weak. Amaria decided that she would remove that part first. She reached out her energy and pulled that part towards her. She immediately felt hatred. Hatred towards a father who beat her. Hatred for the nobility who seemed to thrive off the peasants' backs but had little concern for the peasants who suffered under them.

"I'm sorry," Amaria gasped. This was the worst part, sharing the memories that formed the human. She felt what they felt, thought what they thought, if only for a moment.

Still she had to crush the magic and the connection, and she did so, the particle remnant crushed into dust by Amaria's raw power and Giuliana's screams filling the cell. Amaria turned her head away from the fire. She could not let the traitor see she shed a tear for her.

For the next few hours Amaria broke into Giuliana's mind. Taking away her joys of marrying her husband, who had snapped his neck by falling over the banister of the staircase during the burglary. Her ambitions to rise in her station. Her heartbreak of early lovers breaking promises. A wayward mage burning down her home, fueling her hatred again. How Giuliana was caught trying to come back home from Avondra—Aaron had initiated an investigation to identify who her husband was and using that information enacted a manhunt for his wife.

Amaria worked through it all, piece by piece until there were three shards left. Giuliana's body had started twitching, the tonic was wearing off.

It did not matter much—Giuliana was incapacitated, helpless, and sobbing hysterically on the ground. Amaria only had two more shards left before she had to bring Giuliana out to finish the final shard in public. There were three shards, two of a lighter color, and one was pitch black. Amaria braced herself, choosing the larger of the lighter shards.

This part was particularly complex and tedious to extract, clinging onto whatever mental capacity Giuliana had left as if its own life depended on it. As Amaria dug in deeper, her vision started to blur and her surroundings morphed into an entirely new environment until she was left crouching on bare dirt floor in a burned down shack, facing what looked like two ghostly spectrals in front of her.

A fully immersive flashback? That explains why this shard is so large, Amaria thought wearily as she stood up and braced herself for what she was sure to witness next. From where Amaria was standing, she could just make out the words of a conversation that was already underway. As the misty figures turned toward her, she recognized one of them to be Giuliana, slightly younger in years and with a grief-stricken face, her bloodshot eyes filled with rage.

Amaria's eyes narrowed at the other figure who wore a dark cloak that covered her head and left only a pretty but pallid face and sharp green eyes beneath the hood; Amaria did not know who this second woman was, but something about her felt familiar. Amaria moved closer to them so as to better hear.

Giuliana shook her head at the other woman. "I don't know you."

"I'm Queen Lynette Edrion, my dear Giuliana." The woman extended her hand to Giuliana. "I believe we can help each other."

"I can't help a queen," Giuliana spat. "And no nobility would bother to help me. I'm not as ignorant as you believe."

"Would you quiet down?" Lynette snapped at her, all pretense of patience thrown to the wind. There was a sudden cruel edge to her voice that sent a chill down Amaria's spine. "I'm trying to help you."

"You need my help or you wouldn't have come," Giuliana hissed. "Your power is an illusion, and illusions can't truly threaten people."

Lynette smiled wickedly, a lioness in the face of a defiant mouse. "If you think you knew pain before this...."

A moment later, Giuliana abruptly dropped to the ground, hands to her head and convulsing in pain. Amaria frowned as she watched a look of pure terror twist across Giuliana's face, her mouth opened in a silent scream.

"We could have done this the easy way, if you had known your place and listened to me," Lynette murmured, turning her outstretched hand in an invisible swiping motion as

Giuliana's face appeared more and more agonized with each passing moment. "I find no pleasure in haunting your already traumatized mind with your only son's burning corpse. Obey me, and you'll be saved."

"I'll do whatever you want! Please, p-please just stop!" Giuliana cried.

"Good." Lynette smiled, and Giuliana stopped screaming. "I'll give you orders soon."

"Orders on what?"

"A way for mages to rule."

Giuliana gave a harsh laugh. "Oh yes, mages that are nobility. Only nobles can be mages. A much better world. I'll pass, Your Majesty."

"Do you want more pain?" Lynette menacingly drew back her hands.

"No," Giuliana said hastily. "I just don't see how we're helping each other. I'm not a powerful mage. I'm common."

"You aren't a weak mage, either," Lynette countered. "And did I mention the payment, my dear? Fifteen Thestitiunian crowns a month, which I believe was your yearly salary."

Giuliana bit her lip. "I won't have to kill anybody, right? Just take away wealth and steal property and such?"

"Of course," Lynette lied. "Your duties to me won't corrupt your magic. Don't worry."

Giuliana hesitantly nodded.

"Good," Lynette chuckled.

"You'll pay me?" Giuliana asked.

"Fifteen crowns each month." Lynette rolled her eyes, as if payment was an annoyance. "But you must obey my orders and never give up my name. If you fail either of those tasks, the money will stop." Lynette turned her head, and even though Amaria knew it was only a memory, she felt as if Lynette saw her.

At that moment, her vision blurred again as she felt herself falling back into reality. Amaria screamed, her mental fist wrapping tighter around the fragment. As the fragment shattered, Giuliana let loose blood curdling screams, weaving into and continuing with Amaria's. The particle was now collapsing into dust. Amaria gasped, falling backwards. "Guards! Get in here *now*!"

One of the guards swung open the prison door. "Yes, my Lady Extractor?"

"Get the emperor, the prisoner is almost ready to be taken in public." Amaria's nostrils flared. She despised sharing the memories of the prisoners. Extractions were cruel, needlessly so. Magic would die with its vessel, so stripping it was wholly unnecessary.

What kind of depraved person discovered this? And what sort of depraved person made others do it? Aion wasn't a mage—and even if he was, it was probable he wouldn't have the power for this ritual. Yet he made others do it with little remorse.

"My Lady Extractor, are yo-"

"Get the emperor and do not presume to ask me stupid questions or I may extract your tongue." With that Amaria turned back into the cell and faced Giuliana. "Sadthos, Iena, Iyesus, have mercy on her," she quietly prayed to the gods and goddesses of death, funerals, life, and penance in the afterlife.

"I'm not dead yet," Giuliana weakly sobbed. "There's hope-"

"Quiet," Amaria said sternly, her eyes watering. "Please, let me do something...something to show you I'm not as cruel as you believe."

Amaria wasn't like Lynette Edrion. She had to prove she was better than what she was fighting against. She had killed, tortured, and committed horrible actions, but she was better than Lynette Edrion. She had to be.

Why was she determined to help this dark mage? It was stupid. Amaria shouldn't feel pity for this wretched thing.

She moved toward the table with supplies, slipping a handful of poison berries into her pocket. She didn't know what compelled her to do that. It wasn't as if she wanted to sneak some to Giuliana, to give her an easier death than beheading. Would these berries even kill that quickly? They were here for torture.

"You really believe you are nothing like her?" Giuliana gasped weakly. "Whether or not you'll admit it, your magic and your birth encourage cruelty."

I'm not cruel. Amaria told herself, grinding her teeth, and she dove into Giuliana's mind again. How could somebody sobbing in pain inflict something just as painful onto somebody else with mere words? Amaria brought her focus back to the remaining two fragments of Giuliana Vero's mind, picking the lighter one, hoping to have a small breather before tackling the portion that encased the corruption that made Giuliana Vero a dark mage.

"I want another child," Giuliana said to a dark-haired man as they sat in a daisy field. Amaria knew this was her husband, her co-conspirator. Amaria had seen his neck snap as he fell from the top of the grand staircase.

"We can't. Not until the oppressive monarchy and nobility are abolished. It should be mages ruling non-mages, not the other way-"

"Pierre, I don't want to be a radical. I want a family. With you." Giuliana seemed to almost be pleading. "I'll regret not being a mother. We already lost Piero."

"Help me make a better world, then we'll have children," Pierre grabbed her face. "I promise."

Amaria realized all Giuliana wanted was a family with this man, this criminal, this radical. He bewitched her with tales of a family. Giuliana may not have had ill intentions, but Amaria reminded herself that Giuliana deserved this.

Treason, especially from a mage who was entrusted with extra responsibilities around their abilities, was unforgivable. Amaria's power flowed from the energy in the jewels, wrapped around the fragment of Giuliana Vero's mind, and crushed it. Giuliana let loose an animal-like scream, and Amaria could not stop herself from joining her, blacking out in her pain.

"Amaria!"

Amaria blinked, and found herself looking up at Aion.

"Are you okay?" Aion asked.

"There's a fragment left," Amaria dazedly said, coming back to the present. "She's ready for the public."

"Drink," Aion shoved a bag of water to Amaria's mouth, before nodding at the guards to bind Giuliana's hands and feet. "You must look strong for this. I know it's hard—"

"You don't know," Amaria snapped, pushing the water away from her. "You aren't an Extractor; you can *never* know."

Aion recoiled slightly, and almost as soon as the words left Amaria's mouth, she regretted it, hanging her head. She had forgotten to play the delicate game with his ego. She needed that game to hide her true intent, her true feelings. "I apologize, Your Imperial Majesty. I'm stressed and fatigued from the process." She should beg for mercy, but she couldn't find that in her.

"Let's finish this nasty business," Aion said softly. "Are you ready?"

Amaria shakily stood up, nodding.

"Then lead the way, Lady Extractor."

Amaria bowed her head. "As you command." With that she stepped out of the cell, Aion in step with her. She made her way up to the main castle, where she would complete the Extraction outside the castle, by the gates. She saw that dusk had fallen and noted that Giuliana would lose everything as nightfall came. And so, Amaria had to harden her heart against a woman she pitied, a woman she shared a whole life with in a few hours. A traitor.

Giuliana Vero's worst crime wasn't treason, however. And it wasn't even that she had played a part in Delphina's death.

Giuliana Vero's worst crime was that Amaria saw herself in her.

How could Amaria share something in common with someone who used dark magic? She couldn't have anything in common with those who had murdered her mother and had almost killed her sister—only by the grace of the gods was Catalina still alive. It was a cursed, painful existence, but she was alive.

And Lynette, someone Amaria had once known and looked up to, had killed her mother. Lynette had employed Giuliana as well.

Amaria didn't have anything in common with them. Fuck them for making her think it.

Chapter Fourteen

The courtyard was somber, as if death had wrapped its cloak around everyone's voices. Ahead of Amaria, guards dragged Giuliana up to the highest platform. She would die there. Lower members of the court, citizens from outside the walls, and servants and guards stood around. Amaria's eyes drifted over to the second platform. It was not as tall as the one for execution but tall enough to showcase who was deemed important.

She met Theodmon's eyes as he curtly nodded at her, the lump in his throat visible. Theodmon didn't smile.

Amaria didn't blame him—she couldn't smile either. Rolling her shoulders slightly, she picked up the hem of her gown, stepping towards the platform, her dress trailing behind her on the rough wooden stairs.

Aion was already on the platform. He stepped forward to address the crowd.

A young man, a teenager really, came to Aion and touched his throat. Amaria knew he was a mage who could control sound.

"Hello, my loyal subjects!" Aion said, his voice magnified. "We're here today to witness the Extraction and execution of Giuliana Vero for her crimes of murder, larceny of magical gemstones, burglary, conspiracy, espionage, and treason. In these crimes, she utilized her magic as a tool for evil. I authorize the subject's punishment as emperor." Aion nodded and Giuliana was dragged up to the stage.

As Amaria reached the top of the platform, she gazed blandly at Giuliana, whose wrists and ankles were bound in chains. All semblance of her humanity had been stripped away as she crouched in a fetal position on the ground, covered in tears and grime. When a royal guard grabbed her shoulders to pull her into a sitting position, she stared straight ahead at the crowd—a dead stare.

Ghagyn was the goddess of magic, but she was also the goddess of hope. An Extraction stripped Ghagyn's gifts away from a person. For the first time, Amaria realized Extractors did not merely destroy a person's magic—Extractions also shattered hope beyond repair.

That's why it was evil. That's why it felt different than any other activity she had done in a prison. And it was a poor deterrent to future criminals. And it didn't punish them for long—the criminal would die anyway. An Extraction paired with an execution was just a show of the empire's strength—they had Extractors, powerful mages, all in the emperor's collection.

Amaria shuddered, the shivers going through her entire body.

"The Extraction will be completed by the Lady Extractor Amaria Chauvignon," Aion said.

Amaria gave a short curtsy to Aion. An Extraction and its accompanying execution was a show of the emperor's might after all. She wished he would do his own dirty work.

Amaria turned towards the crowd, facing them as she crouched beside Giuliana.

"May you have peace," Amaria whispered. It was no longer her place to judge Giuliana; she was outside Lord Sadthos's gates, and it was the god of death's job to now pass condemnation—a mere human shouldn't usurp the gods' authority.

Slowly, Amaria's eyes fluttered closed, her chest noticeably rising. She stood up and Aion stepped forward, reaching his hand out towards Amaria's shoulders, almost as if he was prepared to keep her upright throughout the Extraction.

Brusquely, she brushed him off as she dug into Giuliana's mind for the last time, focusing on the black shard that remained. Locking her knees, Amaria dove into her mind.

She was thankful for that when she saw the last remaining piece, the core of Giuliana's dark magic, occurred in her childhood home. Amaria was aware of what happened when she had left, however nothing could have prepared her to witness it from the perpetrator's perspective.

"Them!" A servant girl screamed. She was pointing at two men, both of whom Amaria recognized. "They broke into the gemstone hall!"

The girl did not sound fully like herself, and Amaria, in hindsight, knew that Giuliana had hypnotized her with her magic. However, nobody else realized this, as a stampede of servants and guards ran towards the two men. Giuliana was included in this number. And as she did so, Amaria saw her leave a pile of gemstones in Pierre's bag.

She framed him so she could escape. Amaria felt sick at this marital betrayal. Pierre and Giuliana were bonded together for life, by the virtue of Ednar and Colene.

It would be as if Amaria betrayed Theodmon, causing his doom, only to delay her own.

And Giuliana and Pierre were commoners, meaning their marriage was voluntary and lacked all political pretenses or duty because they married purely for love. Or so Amaria had assumed.

Giuliana Vero ran through the commotion, stopping only when she was in the foyer of Provincia Palencia. There she sat down, extending as much of her hypnosis magic as she could bear. She reached out, slowly raising the already tense situation into a frenzy. She would hypnotize as many people as she could into hatred and cause neighbors and friends to turn on each other.

As a result, Provincia Palencia would be left in such a bloodbath, with two scapegoats, and give Giuliana enough time to escape and transfer the gem to Lynette in Avondra. Bile rose to Amaria's throat as her entire body shook.

Amaria saw black in her vision, feeling her own hatred infect her spirit. Amaria had to stop herself from completing the deed, for she could not commit magic with ill-intent without risking her own magic turning dark.

"Duty, duty," Amaria whispered, and she felt Aion grip her shoulder. She thought of her duty, and the reasons she must perform such a horrific act: Theodmon, Lysander, the rest of her family, Juliette, Lucas, Henri, Nicoletta, Delphina, the dead servants and guards who were employed and protected by the Raulet Family, the safety of the realm...there were a million and one reasons to choose from.

Amaria took a deep breath, put forth her final brush of magic, and crushed the dark shard.

Giuliana collapsed back to a lying position on the ground, withering as her shrieks filled the night air. Amaria looked down at the ground, trying to not hurl. A block was brought forward and imperial guards dragged Giuliana onto it.

"Giuliana Vero, you have been stripped of your magic, any direct blood relatives will be punished, and I, Emperor Aion, sentence you to die." Aion called out as Giuliana's head was pushed on the block, her hair moved out of the way.

"It's over, Amaria." Aion moved to hold Amaria from behind, steadying her; all while signaling Theodmon to come over to assist him as the blade came down on Giuliana Vero's neck, her head rolling off the block. "Let's get you some food and drink. You need only stay at dinner to show your face since I've already instructed that your and Theodmon's full dinner be brought to your rooms."

The damn feast. If Amaria wasn't swaying dangerously already, she would have screamed at Aion. He used them all as pawns. He didn't do any of his own dirty work. He didn't understand the toll stripping away someone's magic, their damn humanity, took.

Theodmon was behind her, his hand steady around her waist. "I'm picking you up," he told her before scoping her up in his arms.

She closed her eyes, her head heavy.

Magic was inherent in one's core personality. It could not be depleted. Unless it was stripped from a mage, it would always come back. Giuliana was Thestitiunian, and she knew the consequences. Her magic was corrupted, therefore it had to be taken from her as a deterrent for future wayward mages.

Extractions not only stripped the condemned of their magic, they also lost the second gift Ghagyn had given them and all of humanity. And despite how violent, almost senselessly so, an execution was after an Extraction, Amaria could not help but feel it was mercy.

So why did it feel so evil for Amaria?

"She needs magical energy." A lanky blond nobleman in his forties came to Theodmon. His hands were glowing a dark green.

"Faelyn?" Amaria gasped. The world was spinning. Why was Duke Laurellanza here? Oh, was it because there was a wedding here soon? Or was it because he was an Extractor—though he had healing for his magic—as well? A trickle of blood ran down her nose.

"Set her down," Faelyn Laurellanza commanded Theodmon. "She may need healing magic along with energy."

"What's wrong? Is she okay?" Theodmon panickedly asked, laying Amaria on the stone floor.

"She'll be fine." Faelyn placed his hands on her chest. She felt warm, as if she were drinking hot chocolate on a cold day. And the world around her became clearer. Slowly, she blinked, and she saw Theodmon and Faelyn's concerned faces.

"Thanks," she groaned as she sat up.

"I'll tell Aion you fainted," Faelyn helped her to her feet. "You need rest. It's difficult to argue with a doctor who is an Extractor."

"Thank you," Amaria said as Theodmon picked her up once more, heading towards their rooms.

"Pretend to be unconscious," Faelyn laughed. "In case anybody wants to dispute your story."

Suppressing an eyeroll, Amaria let her head go limp and she laid back in Theodmon's arms. She closed her eyes, praying he didn't hit her head on any doorways.

Chapter Fifteen

Miraculously, Amaria was not bothered by anyone during the days after the Extraction. Perhaps it was because of the upcoming wedding—and the knowledge that the bride did not even know she was traveling to her wedding—that was ample distraction for the court. Still, Amaria was desperately attempting to block out the memory of the Extraction—the simple digressions from everyday life that she normally engaged in were not enough to distract her now. Additionally, her energy was still weakened, despite her resting and recovering throughout the week.

Parties weren't enough of a diversion now. In fact, Amaria hadn't had a satisfactory distraction until yesterday. Yesterday, when the sun was setting but before the moon had risen, Liara Nalaeny had arrived at the imperial palace.

And today Amaria was meeting her. Vaguely, Amaria remembered her from her own wedding, though not much, only that Liara existed, was tall, and did some sort of social faux pas—she had seemed not fully there. Otherwise, Liara Nalaeny was utterly forgettable.

The only thing of note about the Riam noblewoman was she ran away close to the time the Ruby was stolen and her mother was implicated. Still, Liara had to know something. Why else would she have fled her home and everything that was familiar to her.

Amaria and Theodmon briskly passed the open windows in the corridors, a cool breeze wafting through them as the sun rose, illuminating the deep blue sky with pinks and golds. It was still winter, but it was at least warmer in Arbres Dorès than the Westerlands. Then again, that wasn't saying much.

Shivering, Amaria pulled her cloak tighter around herself, hating that they were headed to the gardens. "Must we meet her there?"

Amaria hated being cold.

"She's in the garden a lot," Theodmon said. Amaria supposed winter was milder in Arbres Dorès than Rindria, and the earth mages did make flowers grow year round. "It's not uncommon for couples to court there. It's the best spot, considering the circumstances."

Amaria's shoulders and body loosened slightly as tension ebbed from her muscles. Theodmon was correct—they wanted to stage a meeting that could pass as a natural interaction. Amaria sighed, stuffing her hands further into her fur muff.

As they made their way through the castle to the gardens, she saw mages growing flowers, creating animal shows with fire and water, and servants draping more tapestries and fabrics upon the walls.

There was to be a wedding. And something as trivial as winter would not deter the royal court from decorating with spring flowers for the upcoming ceremony.

"Look," Theodmon pointed out, and Amaria saw a dolphin made from water splash up and down in a bowl.

She immediately wanted to conduct her own water show. She could do one better than these staff mages; she knew she could. She raised her hands, ready to help make brilliant pictures from the water.

"Not now." Theodmon gently moved her hands down.

She rolled her eyes. In that case then, he was going to get a private show in their bathtubs and she'd make the best dolphins he had ever seen.

They moved through the palace and outside to the gardens.

Stones crunched beneath her feet on the pathway, the fragrant smell of lavender and peonies engulfing her. Amaria passed a bronze statue of a woman with flowers springing around her feet as she held a bushel of grain in her arms. Amaria paused, giving her gratitude to Grotuna, the goddess of plenty, wealth, and the harvest.

At the base of the statue, sweet briar rose bushes were neatly planted. The roses had apple-scented leaves, their tart fragrance mixing in with the sweetness of the rose, leaving an obfuscating but pleasant redolence in the air as Amaria passed them. She turned the corner, her hand brushing over the edge of a pool; small frogs croaked on the floating lily pads, with orange flowers blooming and reflecting in the still water.

Next to her, Theodmon held her arm, plucked a rose and handed it to her. To an outsider, they would be the very image of courtly behavior. "Aloysius should be here soon."

Amaria nodded, seeing him enter the gardens, loudly laughing with Henri and Lucas.

In the corner of her eye, she saw a gangly looking blonde slam her book shut behind a bush. Amaria waved over Aloysius, nodding her head slightly towards the scowling girl. Aloysius' shoulders slumped, but he came forward.

Amaria breathed heavily. Liara had seemed simple at Amaria's wedding. Perhaps it was a ruse, an act—much like Amaria's act of being an innocent, delicate flower. If it was a ruse, Amaria could respect that. She may even like Liara more for it. Pretense and manipulation was what Amaria was comfortable with. She could mold people into doing what she wished without them ever knowing and she could spot when others tried to do similarly with her.

"Lady Liara," Amaria said as they approached. "It's a pleasure."

"Stop with the fake politeness," Liara said.

Perhaps Amaria needed to work on her manipulation methods after all.

Theodmon looked over at Liara, his eyes vigilant as if debating on what to say to her. Amaria turned her head, focusing momentarily on the hyacinths and arborvitae blooming around them, the light floral scent wafting through the breeze as fleeting and delicate as spun sugar. Amaria was an aconitum flower, beautiful but poisonous, using her looks to disarm hapless victims. And Liara, while Amaria felt some pity for her, was a victim. She was a pawn—whether it was with, well, whatever she ran away from in Rindria, or now in Thestitiunia.

"I wanted to welcome you," Amaria brushed her hands over her pale yellow dress. She had specifically chosen it to look girlish, harmless, and innocent. Amaria tried to ignore that Liara was wearing trousers. Women in Thestitiunia didn't wear trousers—not unless they were war mages. Come to think of it, Amaria hadn't seen Riam women in anything but a dress. Amaria tried to keep her face neutral, however, she couldn't help her lips momentarily pursing at Liara's blatant disregard for societal custom.

"Why are you here?" Liara's elbows were wide from her body and her chest was thrust out. Amaria suppressed a smirk; it was adorable when prisoners showed anger. "I spent the past few months trapped on your ship."

"I apologize," Amaria lied. "We wanted to ensure you were safe."

"I'm safe," Liara stated. "May I read my book?"

"We have to tell you something," Theodmon interrupted, grabbing Aloysius's arm and pulling him in front of Liara.

"You're to be married," Amaria whispered to her. "I'm sorry to tell you this so early into your visit but-"

"To who?" Liara snarled.

"Aloysius Chauvignon," Theodmon said. "Don't get thoughts about running away, I have chains."

"*You*," Liara hissed towards Theodmon. "You'd really kidnap me and marry me off? I would have thought you'd ask me!"

Amaria would have burst out laughing if she had not been so shocked by the sheer level of stupidity someone had to have to believe their kidnapper cared about their opinion. And the fact that she was acting this way *in public*. Liara had lived at Bria Hall—surely the Riam court was not so different in how courtiers acted. In politics, and court was living in the center of it, people hid their emotions, never revealing more than what was necessary. Yelling in public was something that just wasn't done if someone was going to survive in court.

Amaria cast a glance towards Theodmon, the only emotions conveyed coming from her eyes. She and Theodmon not only survived at court, they thrived. And they had been not only playing the game, but mastering it, since they were younger than Liara. Amaria knew the Riam girl was eighteen, and she hadn't expected her to scream and wail in public. Amaria was only two years older than Liara: how was there such a chasm between their courtly behaviors?

"You know how these things work," Theodmon said sternly. "I won't refresh you on the common procedure for marital engagements."

Or kidnapping. When have kidnappers cared about the opinion of the person they kidnapped? Amaria thought as she carefully watched Liara. Her face was turning red, and Amaria wondered if she would make a run for it. To where Amaria didn't know as there weren't many options for Liara to hide in the Imperial Palace.

"Theodmon." Amaria placed her hands on top of her husband's, holding the calloused palm softly. It would be easier for everyone involved if they didn't have to search the palace for Liara later. And Amaria did feel bad for Liara—it must be scary to run away from home and then to cross the continent to end up with an arguably hostile nation. "This must be shocking news; she's only just arrived in Thestitiunia. I'm sure she is merely processing-"

"How two-faced are you?" Liara snapped. "Just because you're fine with being an obedient doll doesn't mean other people are shallow enough to enjoy it. Are you even as good a wife as you pretend? You probably used your magic to lure him in, *witch*."

"Lady Nalaeny!" Theodmon's voice boomed as he stood up, pulling his hand sharply from Amaria's grip.

Amaria felt sparks appearing around her fingertips. She hated how Riam and Morrians viewed all magic users as evil, as witches and warlocks instead of mages. She hated the implication that she had seduced Theodmon with her magic of all things—it wasn't common per se, but it wasn't uncommon. Unlike Morroek and Rindria, the civilized countries knew magic didn't work that way.

Theodmon cast her a warning look. She wouldn't use the wind to cause Liara to fly upside down. That would be improper. As improper as Liara's trousers were.

"You should understand the nature of your situation." Theodmon's chest heaved as he took slow, steady breaths to calm himself. "You're a lady who will marry a lord. Unfortunately, the emperor decided that a match must be made sooner rather than later."

And the emperor wouldn't have power to do this if she wasn't kidnapped, but that wasn't a current issue Amaria was concerned with.

"Unfortunately?" Liara's eyes narrowed so severely that they appeared as slits. "You protested your emperor regarding this?"

No. They had arranged it. Not that they would ever tell her that. She met Theodmon's eyes. She saw they creased slightly and she knew that they were in agreement in that they'd let Liara think whatever she wanted to. Either perception that Liara had regarding the mastermind of her engagement, Amaria knew they could spin to their benefit .

"You'll be married here within the week," Theodmon continued, walking away and taking the other men with him, leaving Amaria and Liara alone on the bench.

"Oh, kidnapping me on a ship wasn't enough?" Liara exploded.

Amaria wanted to pull her hair out. She forced down her discomfort, smoothing over her facial features as if they were creases in a skirt.

Is it that hard to have some decorum? Amaria had expected Liara to be upset, but to act so dramatically in public was unbecoming. *Go to your rooms and cry in private.* She needed to salvage this situation. Now.

"I understand it's difficult news," Amaria said gently, sitting down next to Liara on the bench. "Nobody likes being married off." She sighed, hugging herself as to suppress a shiver.

Scowling, Liara scooted away. "You're marrying me off."

Amaria shrugged. "And I was married off. It's reality. We make do."

"Were you kidnapped, put on a ship?! What do you know of hardship? You're a Raulet. Who would hurt you and risk your father's wrath? You don't understand how it is for the rest of us—we're pawned off for politics with little regard for our feelings!"

"I was initially engaged to a man my father's age," Amaria's blood turned cold. She didn't like thinking about Lyseno Vypren. But Aloysius, in terms of grooms, was far from the worst choice. And did Liara truly think being a Raulet spared her the expectations thrust onto a noblewoman? If anything, being a Raulet gave Amaria *more* expectations. And it didn't spare her from being pawned off for politics. She felt an ache in her stomach and it took all her will power for her to not hug herself, cradling the scars on her stomach. The scars she was apparently too fortunate to not understand.

"Do you want to know what my first fiancé did to me? He beat me during our engagement. I dreaded being his wife." Amaria was shaking, her fists were clenched in her fury. "When the engagement was broken off he cut me open. Aloysius isn't cruel. He won't beat you. He's close to your age. Do you know how many women would kill to have what you think is intolerable?"

Rapidly, Amaria blinked back tears. Now she was the one about to cry in public. Amaria was ready to give Liara a chance, but she couldn't anymore. By bringing up the memories of Vypren, Amaria despised Liara for ripping open the wound. She knew Liara hadn't intended to make some of Amaria's worst memories swim to the surface, but she had. And Amaria couldn't imagine complaining if she were in Liara's situation. Actually, Amaria had once been in Liara's situation. The girl had been engaged, or so Amaria had heard in gossip.

"Why'd you run away to Tressidil anyways?" Amaria asked through a shaky breath. She needed to regain control. Not only over the situation but over herself. But she could no longer use honey to lure Liara into a trap. The memory of Lyseno Vypren had taken that away. And because of the pain of the ghosts of the past, Amaria was losing patience for the one who dug up the grave.

Liara thought she was a monster. So Amaria would be as horrible as Liara expected her to be. She was a witch, a seductress, a violent person with zero remorse for the harm she did others. They could have avoided this if Liara hadn't been so stupid to think any noblewomen was shielded from the shared experience of being married off. Amaria could still smell Vypren's breath as she remembered the past.

Liara tilted her head, her eyebrows raised as her eyes darted over Amaria. "I ran away from a bad marriage."

"It was nothing to do with magic?"

Liara tensed. "How'd you...what?"

"Rindria and Avondra are working with dark magic." Amaria dropped all pretenses, gripping Liara's arms in hers. "I have suspicions your mother-"

"She's not my mother-"

"She bore you, she's your mother. But if it helps you digest that your mother worked with a dark mage set on being queen of a graveyard then, fine, we can call her Clarissa Nalaeny," Amaria dismissed. "As I was saying, we have suspicions that Clarissa Nalaeny was working with Lynette Edrion."

"I don't see what I have to do with that." Liara crossed her arms.

Internally Amaria screamed. Talking with Liara was like negotiating with a toddler. And nobody negotiated with toddlers, they redirected and contained them. If Liara was going to act like a child, then perhaps threatening her would be the most efficient route to redirect her attitude. Most people were less likely to anger someone they believed would kill them.

Amaria needed Liara's compliance—fighting a child in politics was not what Amaria wanted to do with her free time.

"You'll marry Aloysius," Amaria whispered, grabbing Liara's arm, her fingernails digging into Liara's flesh. "How long you survive after that is entirely up to you. Lynette Edrion was there at Bria Hall when you ran away; several credible sources have confirmed it so don't deny it. You know something and we want that information."

What do you know about the attack on my home? Your mother's relationship with Lynette? What do you know about my friend's death? Where is the Raulet Ruby? Amaria internally screamed these questions. Some were unfair, she knew that. Asking any of them would make Liara close up as if she were an oyster protecting a pearl.

Amaria also didn't really need that information. She suspected it was true, and it would just be nice to have her suspicions confirmed. But making Liara squirm, that was worth it. Liara had made her remember Vypren after all.

"You'd kill me for it?" Liara stood up.

"I'd call it a liberation from marriage," Amaria said.

If Liara didn't have information, she was useless to Amaria anyways. Aside from her being compliant in this marriage, scaring her into submission was what Amaria now needed most from Liara.

"Do you care about me?" Liara's eyes watered. "I thought Thestitiunia wanted to help."

Amaria stopped herself from laughing. No. Aion wanted a destabilized Rindria. He, as Thestitiunia's Head of State, wanted a way to subtly force their way into a destabilized Rindria. She did not particularly care about Rindria. It was a small country with scarce resources and an over-inflated ego.

The only thing notable about Rindria was that a Riam princess worked with the queen of Avondra like an idiot. Dark magic increased, harming Rindria in the process as they bordered the Badlands, the area from where dark magic came from. Lynette Edrion's power grew with the increase in dark magic.

And as Lynette's magical power had grown, so had increased unicorn attacks. As her power had grown there was more dark magic. There were more dark mages. There was more disease. There were horrors creeping in through the Badlands. The Badlands were filled with Ghagyn's—the goddess of magic—rejections.

They didn't belong in this world.

Lynette would bring them here, to Thestitiunia, to Amaria's home, if not stopped. She didn't care about the nameless citizens of other countries, but Amaria cared about Thestitiunia. Her country. Her people. Her home. Lynette had already shown a propensity to kill people in Amaria's home. Multiple times.

Liara was a mere building block for both Amaria and Aion's goals. As much as Amaria hated to admit that she and Aion were united, they were.

"You want out of a marriage, I want information." Amaria pulled a handful of berries out of her bag. "These are poison."

She could tell Liara had a sense of self preservation. She wanted to live. Otherwise she wouldn't have run away. She would have thrown herself off the ship. She would have slit her wrists with a knife.

Amaria hoped she was banking on Liara's motives correctly as she held up a berry, letting the sun's rays bounce off it. If needed, she'd pull out three more—enough to make Liara ill but not kill her. Just enough to cause her to fear for her life.

Fear tended to be a sufficient motivator.

"One of us will get what we want today," Amaria said mildly. "Why did you run from Bria Hall? And don't say marriage, I won't believe you."

"I saw a witch," Liara muttered. "She met with my parents multiple times. The king didn't know. I heard her talking about a dual attack; she wanted something from your family. She said she'd attack your husband's lands while Lynette received it. I don't know anymore, I hid when they saw me."

Amaria, despite her bubbling rage, smiled. Rindria and Avondra had worked together to steal the Raulet Ruby. She'd had suspicions ever since the invasion occurred a year ago, however, this confirmed it. She loved being correct because it was validating.

She must talk to her father. Amaria dropped the berries on the ground, stomping them under her feet. "I'm glad we could come to an understanding."

She cast a glance over at Aloysius, making sure Liara saw her looking before she spoke to the girl. "Do get to know your fiancé. You could do worse."

Chapter Sixteen

Theodmon was leaning against the wall as she rejoined him in the corridor. She wanted to go to their rooms. To be warm and safe and happy. Lysander could join them.

"Your family arrived in the night," Theodmon pushed himself off the wall to stand up straight. "Well Haerdnor and Aaron did."

"Where are they?"

"I told a page to tell them to meet us in our chambers when they're ready," he said.

Amaria breathed in. It'd been nearly a year since she had seen her family and she had missed them.

"Is Lysander there?" Amaria asked.

Theodmon nodded. "I'll make sure he's with us."

Amaria walked silently next to him, leaning her head against his arm. The Imperial Palace was vast, but its decorations paled next to Provincia Palencia. Besides, she had found herself falling in love with the simple practicality of white marble and red tapestries of Forteresse les Blanche. The Imperial Palace was Aion's domain, and while he was incompetent, he had the foresight to hire those who were.

Amaria didn't like the unknown. She did not like the Imperial Palace.

She breathed a sigh of relief once they reached their chambers, the door shutting behind them. She wondered how long it would take before her family arrived at her chambers. Aaron would likely talk with Aion, who knows what Haerdnor was doing, and she just wanted her son to arrive.

Amaria paced the room. Her hands were cold and she kept licking her lips. Her heart felt as if it were residing in her stomach. She didn't know why she was scared. She shouldn't be scared.

She still felt as if she were fighting for her life around her father and yet she wanted to make him proud. However, Amaria supposed she would continue to disappoint him and herself. Amaria loved her father. She dreaded being around him.

"Ammy?" Theodmon said, his voice gentle as if he was handling glass.

She shook her head. She was fine.

However, Theodmon knew her better than that. He came to her, silently embracing her. She closed her eyes, smelling his shirt. It was woodsy, a bit floral. It was nice. She focused on that.

There was a sudden light rapping at the door, causing Amaria to jump slightly, feeling as if she were being brought down to earth from the heavens.

"Enter," Theodmon barked as the door opened. Amaria turned her head to watch who came inside.

A nanny came in. Amaria rushed to take her son from the nanny. As she cooed gently at Lysander, Aaron entered as well, dismissing the nanny as if she were his own staff.

The nanny looked over at Theodmon for confirmation of what to do. Theodmon gave her a short nod, affirming Aaron's decision.

"Your son is healthy," Aaron stated as he watched her and Lysander. "Congratulations to you both."

"Thank you, Father," Amaria muttered.

"I have news," Aaron said. "Sit down."

"More than the wedding tomorrow?" Theodmon smirked as he sank onto the sofa. Amaria realized he was enjoying this, this trap that they had laid for Rindria. She supposed she enjoyed it too.

"Is Haerdnor coming?" Amaria asked, moving to sit next to Theodmon.

"He already knows what I'm telling you." Aaron pulled out a piece of parchment from his pocket. "We have additional concrete proof of Avondra and Rindria's alliance. It took a while, but I broke the cipher on this."

Amaria's blood turned cold as she looked over at the parchment. "It's in Avonnian?" Amaria said hesitantly, unable to decipher the words. "Or is it still encoded?"

"It's Avonnian." Theodmon sucked in his breath as he read over her shoulder. Amaria turned to look at him intensely, waiting for a translation.

"This isn't good," Theodmon said.

"I'm aware," Aaron said gravely.

"What does it say?" Amaria peered at both of them. "I'm illiterate in Avonnian."

"You had the resources to learn," Aaron pointed out, raising a critical eyebrow.

"Father, it's a miracle I can *speak* four languages, however rough my Riam may be," Amaria protested. "You know how difficult that was for everyone involved. Literacy would have been a death sentence on my tutors."

Theodmon coughed, bringing the attention to himself. "The note says '*resources at the Badlands growing, our Riam allies grow impatient, centralize and attack.*' We suspected this, and this confirmation does nothing to help us now." Theodmon said, shaking his head at the cruel irony.

He was right. They needed more information at this point. Amaria wanted to scream.

"She also killed several Avonnian priests and priestesses of Dandar," Aaron informed them. "It was quite the tantrum."

"What?" Theodmon questioned. "Did she only kill priests and priestesses in Raeria?" He asked, specifying the province in which Lynette lived.

"Every Priest and Priestess of Dandar she could find in Avondra," Aaron grimly said, causing both Amaria and Theodmon to look up at him in horror, their eyes wide. It was a crime against nature and the gods to intentionally harm a priest or priestess. The gods would curse you and your descendants with plague, bad luck, bankruptcy, ugly daughters, infertility—there was a whole manner of evils they could choose from as punishment.

"Many are being sheltered in Tressidil and Thestitiunia," Aaron reassured them. "The Thestitiunian and Tressi temples are safely harboring them, and no temples are required to release priests and priestesses in their care under any international or domestic laws."

Amaria slumped back in her seat, feeling ill. She lowered her head, thankful she was wearing a veil. "Lord Eteus please grant them hope, Lady Thoxlena grant them mercy, Lady Iena protect their lives, and Lady Gratelia grant them peace," she murmured. Theodmon clenched his fists, his face turning red.

"Fuck her," Theodmon snarled.

"Are you surprised-" Aaron began, only to be interrupted.

"Of course not." Theodmon's jaw clenched as he stood up, his shoulders slightly raised. "Strategically, it makes sense. But you don't harm a priest or priestess!" His hand slammed down on the chair, the loud crack deafening in the otherwise still room.

Lysander began to cry. Amaria bounced him. "Sssh," she whispered. "Hush little one, don't say a word," she sang, her voice creaky. "Mama's going to buy you a silver bird. And if that bird doesn't fly, then you'll get golden feathers."

She brought Lysander closer to her, calming him. She cast Theodmon a short glance. He cringed slightly, mouthing the word 'sorry'.

"It's upsetting news," Aaron continued. "I need you two to talk with your priests and priestesses of Dandar. A high priestess from Avondra is at the Chauvi temple."

Amaria gingerly leaned against Theodmon, making a silly face at Lysander as she spoke. "We'll make large donations to Temples of Dandar both in Thestitiunia and Tressidil." She felt nauseous, disgusted by Lynette's actions. "We can't change the past, so we'll help these holy men and women in the present and future."

"Theodmon," Aaron directed his attention to the warrior. "How's the Rindria border?"

"There are increasing skirmishes with Rindria, though many of them don't have the Riam Royal insignia. The soldiers are well trained, obviously paid for by a wealthy family, and with the information being gathered, I believe it may be Clarissa and Liam Nalaeny. I'm unsure if the king is aware of what his sister is doing."

Amaria leaned back in her chair, closing her eyes. The men could discuss warfare, she had never enjoyed swords and arrows. It was an inelegant death. Crude.

Amaria preferred subtle touches. Life was artwork, brushes of colors and magic splattered in a way only the gods could find order in.

And death should mirror its sibling.

Chapter Seventeen

The castle's artwork was in full glory the next day for the wedding. Everyone seemed joyful, from the servants moving the decorations around, to the nobles excited for a chance to gossip. And the city's poor were looking forward to the charity that always came with large weddings.

It was hard to plan the exact timing, only getting notification when Liara left Tressidil and a hawk from Poigenoux, Avondra when the ship stopped to resupply before heading to Aionstown.

Even if the exact timing of Liara's arrival had been miscalculated, Amaria knew it would be no large concern as nobles loved to gossip. And with a kidnapped bride, her family uninvited to the wedding, well, there was a ton of juicy drama to keep even the most melodramatic satisfied.

And it did seem as if everybody was happy. Well, except for the bride. Amaria had passed by Liara in the outskirts of the hall by the interior chapel of the Imperial Palace and determined that Liara was the most unhappy bride she had ever seen.

Liara's eyes were red, her cheeks puffy, and she glared at anybody who dared pass her. Her nail beds were picked, the open wounds clear even from ten feet away.

Amaria supposed she could understand the sentiment.

Amaria looked over at Theodmon, focusing on her features to morph her initial disgust into something more pleasant as she turned back to Liara. They had to work with this girl now, so they should make it pleasant. More flies were caught with honey than vinegar.

"You look lovely," Amaria said, choosing to ignore the tear stains on Liara's face.

"I ran away to avoid this, you snake!"

Theodmon frowned at her blunt reaction. "Mind your rough edges."

Liara shot him an incredulous glare. "You're one to talk."

"It's expected of me," Theodmon said. "I do have a reputation to uphold." He turned to see Aion approaching. "The emperor is giving you away, be cordial."

Theodmon squeezed Amaria's hand once, before disentangling himself from her grasp and going into the chapel.

She should try to comfort this girl. They'd have to interact for the rest of their lives in some capacity. Perhaps it could be pleasant. Amaria already had to avoid her mother-in-law. Agatha Chauvignon didn't like her very much, and she wasn't anxious to have more family members she had to avoid at the estate.

Amaria turned towards Liara, keeping her expression as pleasant as a summer day.

"That dress doesn't fool anyone," Liara snapped at Amaria before she could speak.

Amaria knew what she was implying. Her satin thulian had golden buckles held together with a chain across the waistline, subtly referencing the style that high-ranking men wore despite the flowy top sleeves, the delicate rose brooch pinned right above the curving chain, and the demure undersleeves hugging the wearer's arms down to her wrists.

"Everyone knows I'm not benign," Amaria said. "I'm a Raulet and the most powerful elemental mage in the world." She gave Liara a soft smile. "I'm glad you are joining my family."

She wasn't. Amaria still couldn't shake the memory Liara had caused to spring up. And how Liara seemed to bring out the worst in her–the hatred, the petty violence, the bloodthirst, how Amaria manipulated others as easily as she breathed–they were the ugly parts that she kept buried. However, Amaria could tolerate Liara as a way to find revenge on Delphina's killers. She could tolerate Liara's presence enough to weaken that pathetic country she called home to bring it into the empire with minimal Thestitiunian deaths. At least, that is what she was telling herself.

"Marchioness." Liara's eyes flashed, hatred and fury were as poignant as the sparks from a blacksmith's anvil when beating a sword into submission.

"On this happy day"—Amaria leaned in towards her—"let me offer you some womanly advice. Nobody cares what you want. Learn to find happiness in what you have before you fling yourself from the highest tower in your misery."

She stepped away from Liara, seeing Aion approach. "Congratulations," she said warmly. She turned, gave Aion a short curtsy, before stepping into the chapel.

Amaria bit her lip. She had enjoyed her wedding, but still, she understood the notion of being dragged into a chapel to marry a man she didn't want. After all, Amaria had once faced that fate. She knew how harsh this situation could be, she just wished Liara had a semblance of stoicism regarding her circumstances. And besides, Aloysius wasn't a bad match. He was young. He was wealthy. He wasn't cruel. Yes, he would never inherit, but Liara didn't seem as if she were the type to care about that sort of practicality.

Amaria's already limited pity for Liara was in short supply. If they hadn't intervened, Liara would have likely been dragged back to Rindria or another country, and different nobles would be doing this same thing to her.

And to live as a peasant? What an absurd notion.

Amaria sat down, an empty chair next to her. Aloysius stood at the front, his demeanor casual even on his wedding day. Amaria wondered how drunk or high he was. She scratched her arms, feeling a sudden and compulsive need to find wine.

Amaria caught Theodmon's eye as he stood near the altar, by Aloysius's side. His hazel eyes stared intensely at her. She smiled, knowing she could not truly communicate how they wanted. Not now anyways.

The music started, and Theodmon's eyes moved towards the doorway. Amaria too, turned to watch Liara walking down the aisle. Liara was crying through her veil.

Amaria's fingers dug into her palm. This was not a marriage most would cry over. A man only three years older than his bride, with no reputation of cruelty was a chance most women would kill for. Liara had to have known, had to have been prepared for marriage—all noblewoman tended to be prepped for that, regardless of the nation.

Amaria's stomach sank. Liara was naïve or a truly stunning actor. Either way, getting information would be improbable at best, impossible at worst. And marriage was for life—did Theodmon and she accidentally dig a clever hole without realizing they were trapping themselves?

She saw Theodmon whisper in Aloysius's ear, and he stood up straighter. Aloysius glared at Theodmon, obviously unamused at being bossed around by his older brother. As Liara reached the platform, Theodmon hugged his brother, inclined his head to Liara, and nodded at the priest before sitting down. Emperor Aion did similarly.

"We are here today to celebrate the union of two great Houses!" the Priest called out. "The Chauvignon line, rich in spirit and brimming with the fires of courage, will intermingle with the Nalaeny line and the Marion's support. The Marion's are a house of prosperity and leadership. Today stands Lord Aloysius Chauvignon," as the priest spoke, a boy handed Aloysius a ring, "and Lady Liara Nalaeny, the youngest daughter of the head of the Nalaeny House, Duke Liam Nalaeny, and Emperor Aion Marion's ward." The boy handed Liara a ring.

Liara looked around, as if searching for help.

"Lord Chauvignon, do you promise to protect, honor, and provide for Lady Liara?" the priest asked.

Aloysius gritted his teeth, casting Theodmon a glare. "I do." He took Liara's hand in his, slipping the tear-drop-shaped ruby onto her ring finger.

"And Lady Nalaeny, do you vow to honor, serve, and obey Lord Chauvignon?"

Liara stood there, saying nothing.

"Lady Nalaeny?" The priest asked.

"Aloysius," Liara addressed her groom directly, turning her impassioned gaze on him.

"Please say I do." Aloysius gritted his teeth behind a fake smile.

"If I'm to be married to you-"

"Lady Nalaeny, do you vow to honor, serve, and obey Lord Chauvignon?" the priest repeated, screaming over her.

Amaria looked at Theodmon, her eyes widened. This was a disaster in the making. This girl would embarrass them all with her tantrums. Gods, were manners that hard to maintain?

Aloysius cleared his throat. "You're making a scene. Please, say your vows."

"I won't obey, but I do."

Amaria's knuckles turned white as she clasped her hands together. As the wife of the head of house, it was her job to manage the women's sector of the estate. And now she was stuck with a rebellious child who had less refinement in her entire body than a baboon had in its fingers. As if Amaria's life wasn't stressful enough.

"My Lord, you may lift the bride's veil, show her off as your wife, and then kiss her for the gods and men to see," the priest directed Aloysius.

Aloysius gently smiled at Liara, his hands reaching for her veil, throwing it over her head, her tiara now plainly visible. Liara was visibly rigid as Aloysius kissed her and then turned her around for the spectators to see.

"We bless this union," the priest said. "May they be blessed with prosperity. May they be blessed with health. May they be blessed with fertility. May they be blessed with peace. May fortunes rain upon them."

As he finished speaking, Theodmon silently turned Amaria to face him, leaning down slightly, as Amaria lifted her head up, meeting her husband's lips. She leaned against him, remembering her own wedding.

She had been lucky with a Chauvignon. And despite her belief that Liara was an idiot girl who needed to grow up, she hoped that Liara too would find joy with a Chauvignon. And if she couldn't find joy, she'd tolerate her miserable existence and not make Amaria's life harder.

Rindria was going to fall, and Liara might just be the key.

Part Three

the ruby

Chapter Eighteen

Three weeks after the disaster of a wedding, the Chauvignons were back at Forteresse les Blanche. In her sitting rooms, Amaria sat near a roaring fire, bouncing Lysander on her lap as she made funny faces at him, her ladies sewing and playing card games around her.

"Caterpillar," Amaria said in a sing-song voice to her son. Lysander brought her a semblance of peace. He had gotten big in the recent months—he was a little over four months now. They hadn't been gone long, only enough for travel to and from the wedding. Lysander had been there with them the whole time; still, she couldn't believe she once had carried this child within her. Her heart swelled as he smiled at her, and she kissed the top of his head.

"He's beautiful," Juliette sighed, watching Lysander. "May I?"

Amaria nodded and handed Lysander off to Juliette. She picked up her embroidery, trusting Lysander with Juliette completely.

She didn't have much chance to sew before the doors were thrown open by guards, throwing in Liara. She was dressed in trousers. They were dirty, as if she had worn them for months on end. She probably had. Amaria had ordered all of her male clothing destroyed as soon as she had seen Liara in her trousers at Aionstown. It seemed as if a few garments had survived the purge.

"What are you wearing?" Amaira asked, her nose wrinkling. She despised the blatant deviation from societal rules. If you had to do something outside the boundaries of acceptable society, it shouldn't be flaunted. And to have someone obviously breaking the customs in Forteresse les Blanche, it made Amaria and Theodmon look as if they didn't have their household under control.

Perceptions could be deadly. And Amaria wanted to make sure the scale of what people thought was true was tipped in favor of herself–and the perception of mutiny always brought issues. Issues that were often bloody.

"Trousers," Liara said.

"Obviously," Amaria scoffed, looking at the guards. "What happened?"

"She was caught trying to sneak into a sword fight," one told her. "She's not a war mage."

And so it wasn't proper for her to learn. Women didn't learn how to fight unless they were mages. That was only because magic needed to be used or it would consume its user. The more powerful the magic, or depending on the type of magic—war and fire were notorious for this—there would be collateral damage around the mage when it occurred.

Liara wasn't a mage. But she was the wife of Aloysius Chauvignon and should act like a damn lady.

"Do you have a dress?" Amaria asked. She knew Liara had them; she had ordered them to be sewn herself.

"I prefer trousers," Liara crossed her arms.

"And I prefer to not be around someone who smells like pig shit," Amaria snapped. "Guards, find a maid to bathe and dress Lady Chauvignon. And bring me any of her male clothes."

And figure out how in the gods' names she got them in the first place. Amaria suppressed a scowl, forcing her shoulders to remain relaxed. Someone either gave the clothes to Liara or she stole them. Both were unacceptable.

"Why?" Liara asked as the guards pulled her away.

"I'm destroying them," Amaria said emotionlessly as she picked up her sewing once more. She hoped it would be the last time.

Liara gasped, her face turning red as the door shut, separating the two women.

"It's a miracle she lived this long," Nicoletta scoffed.

Amaria agreed. What possessed Liara to do such a thing? Rindria had no female soldiers, so it wasn't a cultural thing. Rather, it seemed as if Liara just didn't like rules and customs. She sighed heavily, her shoulders slouching. Being the lady of Forteresse les Blanche required maintaining the women's spheres. Unfortunately, that seemed to now mean policing Liara's behavior.

"Do you want to hold Lysander?" Juliette asked.

Amaria shook her head, focusing on her stitching. She needed to focus on something with her hands before her anger overtook her. She didn't need to catch herself on fire. She liked the dress she was wearing too much.

Silently, she sewed, piercing the fabric with her needle and weaving the threads through it to make a picture. The fire crackled. She was calm. Liara was a minor annoyance. And Amaria repeated this mantra for thirty minutes until she started to believe it.

She pulled a white thread through her blue fabric, the duck diving into water halfway done. As she pulled the thread through the hoop, her heart stopped, and she found herself on the floor shaking.

Something felt as if it was attacking her. Her body was glowing silver. All around her the room spun, and she dug her hands into the carpet, waiting for the energy surge to pass. It was common for powerful mages to be extremely sensitive to changes in magic, especially dark magic, but this was more intense than anything she could have imagined.

"Amaria!" Nicoletta's voice sounded muffled. "Call a healer!"

"Move!" Juliette pushed Nicoletta away from Amaria, her body glowing turquoise. Juliette placed her hands on Amaria, pulsating her own energy into Amaria's. "Nicoletta, go check on Henri and Earl Belamy!"

Amaria barely registered that Juliette listed the names of the two other Westanni Extractors as she coughed violently, the attack around her passing as soon as it came.

"I'm fine," she sat up, forcing Juliette off her, aware that her other ladies were likely searching for weakness. "Thank you."

"What happened?" Juliette narrowed her eyes.

"Where's Lysander?" Amaria blinked, noticing her son wasn't with Juliette anymore.

"I handed him to another lady when you collapsed. You needed my magic. Amaria," Juliette said sternly. "What happened?"

"There's...there was a surge of dark magic...I think, I think it was from the Raulet Ruby." Amaria's heart dropped; she remembered she had cut herself on the gem when she was fourteen, and ever since then, she had been oddly in tune with its pulsations. "Oh, by Ghagyn."

She sprang to her feet, picking up her skirts, running out of the room and through the labyrinth hallways of Forteresse les Blanche. She did not stop until she reached Theodmon's offices, panting and doubled over for air. Still, she stood up, and pushed open the doors to his office, ignoring the guard posted out front.

"We need to get the Raulet Ruby, *now*." Amaria quickly latched the door behind her, Theodmon looking up in surprise.

"What?" Black blots fell from Theodmon's feathered quill as it hovered over the parchment. "It's winter; we just got back. What happened?"

"Clarissa Nalaeny tried to use it," Amaria hissed, pacing the room. "I felt...I felt a disruption. I can't explain it, but I know she used it." She looked upwards at Theodmon, her eyes widening as she pleaded with him. "That gemstone has centuries of dark magic trapped in it! If it even became chipped it could cause irreversible destruction!"

"What else have you heard?"

"It's hard to figure out what exactly she wants to do with Ruby." Amaria perched herself on Theodmon's lap. "Magic's illegal in Rindria, and she isn't conveying anything about it to anybody. Some of the birds have magic, and they can only relay disturbances they feel." She breathed heavily, trying to calm her nerves. "She's so stupid! That gem isn't a toy; it's not even a tool! She's going to be the queen of a continental grave."

Theodmon placed his quill into its inkwell. "Clarissa Nalaeny isn't a mage. It's snowing. I understand it's bad that she has the gemstone, but what can she do as a non-mage?"

"Every time I had to touch that gem, it screeched at me—in my head I heard tormented screams, I was beckoned by some of the magic—I was going insane.... You don't understand how dangerous it is!" Amaria's hands wove through the top of her hair. "Remember every dark mage you've heard of or actually encountered, then multiply that by a thousand. And this magic has had centuries to fester!"

"My love, we can handle this," Theodmon soothed her, despite his eyes widening. "We *could* flip Rindria against her and get the gem with a small team. Is that what you're asking of me?"

"Please." Amaria's eyes watered. "I don't care how, but I *need* that gem as soon as possible. And I don't trust anybody but myself or another Extractor to transport it."

"Henri and Lucas will join us," Theodmon decided. "Aloysius and Liara will also come, I think it's time we meet our new family members."

"Haerdnor," Amaria said. "Bring Haerdnor. Have him go before us, loudly. They'll be distracted by the fact of a Raulet coming to starve them. It may cover our tracks."

"You want to go undercover?"

"I want to see the layout of the land—magic, attacks, whatever, without others knowing who we are."

"Yes, that can limit perception," Theodmon agreed, pulling her into him. "Alright, we'll bring Haerdnor. Write to him. It'll take us a while to prepare for this anyways."

Amaria hadn't gotten to see her brother at Liara's wedding. There was so much going on she hadn't had the chance. That and he was too busy fucking Oliver Neremoux in a corner of the imperial palace.

Liara was a bigger problem than her brother's sexual activities anyways. And she was determined to not be a lady, as Amaria learned clearly from the girl's jejune behavior this morning.

"Let Liara sword fight," Amaria blurted out. "I hate it as much as anybody but she will let her guard down. She wants human connection–if we show we trust her, she'll be easier to manipulate. Why else would we give her a weapon?" Amaria shrugged. "If we're lucky she'll get herself killed and our hands will be clean—after she gives Aloysius a child."

A child that, if they were lucky, would be the next provincial duke of a new Thestitiunian province.

Theodmon stared at her.

"What?" she asked. Why was he staring at her in that way? As if he wanted to fuck her? She had merely proposed a solution—if you could even call her proposition that.

"You're ruthless," he said, as he pulled her in for a kiss. Slowly, he devoured her, only to break away and leave her breathless. It was such a little action, but it left her yearning for more. "Did I ever tell you how much I loved that about you?"

She kissed him back, nibbling on his lower lip before she broke away. "We're good for each other," she said gently. Her body collapsed against his, his muscles hard against her chest, his heartbeat steady in her ear. Being around him changed everything. Fixed everything. With him, she no longer felt like she was holding her breath underwater—she could finally *breathe*. She barely heard what he said as she closed her eyes, letting his words wash over her. His unique scent, frankincense and cedarwood and something that was distinctly *him*. If only this moment would last for an eternity. But that was a dream. And reality called.

Amaria coughed, clearing her throat. "I'll make the arrangements. With this trip, I can make us peasant garb. If anybody sees it in my belongings I'll say it's charity work for orphans and widows."

"We'll be alright." Theodmon pulled her even closer to him, laying his chin on her head. "I'll protect our family with my life."

Amaria sniffed, giving a small smile, ignoring his hardness pressed against her stomach, as difficult as it was. Theodmon, even the thought of battle always stirred him to lust. "Before you gallivant off to war, make sure you fill me," she told him, her meaning serious despite the lightheartedness in her tone. "We only have one heir, and..."

She wouldn't finish the sentence. Heir and spares. Heir and political marriages. She knew the reality but she would not so crassly call her children that.

"Naughty, you," Theodmon playfully chastised, kissing her passionately as his hand rode up her skirts momentarily. His fingers rubbed against her skin, going ever upward. Dangerously upward. "After we handle this, I promise."

"Good," Amaria breathed, her nose still touching him. Heat pooled in her core. If he kept this up, she wouldn't be able to resist him for long.

Theodmon chuckled, pulling away, leaving a cold emptiness where his hands had been. "I think we should also bring Lucas. He's an excellent tracker."

Lucas. She didn't want to think about Lucas. But that was the difficulty of being responsible—duty had to come first. The ruby mattered more than her desire.

Amaria kissed him on the cheek. "I'll be in our rooms afterwards."

"And I'll make sure to visit you in those rooms," Theodmon said, his gaze darkening as his eyes took in her body, as if he was imagining what she looked like under all those layers.

She shivered, and not from the cold. "I'll be expecting you." A wish and a promise.

"Good." With a smile, Theodmon offered Amaria his arm. "Grab your cloak. We need to go to the Temple of Dandar in Chauvi."

Chapter Nineteen

"I want to know what this prophecy said," Theodmon said as they departed down the mountainous path of Chauvi. Amaria had found this path an enigma. Forteresse les Blanche was built into the mountain, and it was fortified furthermore by earth mages on staff with supplies getting into the castle via a pulley system.

Somehow it was the most inefficient and most efficient system Amaria had ever seen.

Next to her, Theodmon continued explaining his battle plans for the temple. "We need to know why Lynette reacted so harshly. She's many things, but stupid isn't one of them."

"The priests and priestesses of Dandar probably won't tell us," Amaria said. The servants of the god of prophecy were notoriously secretive—everyone who followed the Faith of the Divine knew that. Still, perhaps stupidly, Amaria hoped the priest and priestess would drop their cloud of secrecy just this once. After all, Aaron had told them that Lynette had killed Avonnian priests over a prophecy, so it'd be helpful to know what it was.

Theodmon nodded, his jaw now clenched to keep his teeth from chattering. Amaria too felt her jaw clenching from the brutal chill, despite her keeping a swirl of warm air around them. She blinked, pushing more of her energy out, determined to warm herself and Theodmon to make the errand less agonizing.

Rubbing her hands together in their fur mitt, Amaria glanced around Chauvi as she walked with Theodmon through the winding streets. Chauvi was smaller than Raulle, yet it was busier in a way, as if the Westanni air laid a credence of hecticness that the salt and grime of Raulle could not.

Soon they arrived in the center of the temple district, surrounded by temples of white stone. However, a few temples did not comply with the traditional temple structure. Sadthos' the god of death and afterlife, Cleoana the goddess of pleasure, and Dandar the god of prophecy were notable exceptions.

And Dandar's temple loomed ahead; she had never been where the god of prophecy was worshiped. Amaria could see the large black dome even from this distance. Occasionally a few images would filter across its surface, but only for a moment and only long enough to make you question if you had seen anything at all or if it was your imagination.

Dandar scared her. He seemed crueler, more erratic than the other gods. She didn't like prophecies. If someone could predict what she could do before she even knew what she would do–that premise made her entire line of work rather difficult.

Her shoulders rose into her neck as they neared the temple, each step was as ominous as if she were in a funeral march. Her feet locked in front of the looming building, feeling as if she couldn't step forward: she'd do anything to turn and flee.

"Yes?" The door creaked open, a girl, a child and yet ageless as if she had lived a million years, her milky eyes looking at the Chauvignons—well, rather in their general direction.

Amaria took a step backwards. The girl was slight and answering the temple doors—she didn't seem like a novice or initiate, and greeting Marquis and Marchioness Chauvignon wasn't a job that would be given to low-ranking persons in the temple.

Immediately, Amaria dropped to her knees. "High Priestess. Forgive me."

"Lady Extractor." She laughed. "Stand. Marquis Chauvignon, you may come to the outer sanctum of the temple."

"Thank you," Theodmon clipped.

"I'll only speak with the Lady Extractor regarding your questions." The woman only looked at Amaria as she rose from the street. The priestess knew that Theodmon would hear all she was told as soon as they left the temple. It wasn't information the priestess was containing and protecting—it was who could reach and enter her holy and sacred space.

"Thank you," Amaria said. "I appreciate you offering us the chance to enter the temple. Neither of us are seers."

"I'd doubt your lineage if you were." The door flew open at the priestesses' touch.

Amaria said nothing as they stepped into the outer sanctum, short blazers burning blue and green flames. The smoke burned Amaria's eyes.

"Where?" Amaria's heart stopped as she looked back at Theodmon, wondering how necessary this information was and if it could be obtained anywhere else.

"You won't be harmed, Lady Extractor. We must speak in the middle sanctum."

Why? Why this secrecy? Amaria bit her lip and nodded, forcing herself to follow the priestess towards a black door, leaving the outer sanctum.

She instantly regretted her choice as they stepped through the shadowy archway and with the thud of the door they were encompassed in pitch blackness.

Amaria's chest caved in on itself as her breath became erratic. "Light," she gasped. "Let me use my magic for light."

"No, Lady Extractor," the priestess said. "We cannot see without being in darkness."

"I'm not a seer!" Amaria sank to her knees, pulling at her hair, clutching the scalp as if it were a life preserver thrown for an overboard sailor. "Please, I need light."

The priestess reached down and forcefully cupped Amaria's face on her own. "And what will you give the god of seers, fire mage?"

Anything. Amaria gasped, feeling as if an invisible hand were choking her. She would do anything to not be trapped in this darkness. She needed light. It didn't make sense. Why was she special enough that a god would want something from her?

She needed light or she would die.

"What would the god of seers ever want from me?" Amaria gasped. She had to humor the priestess. She would die in this darkness otherwise.

She needed light.

"Your blood, your future is interesting," the priestess said. "You'll be a queen among all mortals, and you will be despised for it. But the power you have will be unprecedented."

Amaria did not want unprecedented power. She wanted light. Unsuccessfully suppressing a sob, she hated herself for how she was acting—she had no decorum. Amaria couldn't stop herself, for the dark terrified her.

"I control all the elements, I am already powerful! I am a Raulet and a Chauvignon who is already despised by many—this isn't the future, any charlatan could have told me this." Her breath was ragged and her body shook.

Her entire face was wet. She was sobbing.

She needed light.

"Lady Extractor, it is the future. Be careful to contain your hatred and darkness in the coming months."

Amaria's cheeks were wet and she coughed, unable to breath. She would do anything for light. The darkness terrified her; it always had. Since she was a little girl she couldn't stand being without light.

Closing her eyes, Amaria thrust out her arm towards the priestess, hoping she would be quick. The priestess uncurled Amaria's fist, running a finger over her palm gently before steel slashed through flesh.

Amaria felt a small circular glass be pushed against her palm, and she forced herself to remain still as the priestess collected her blood.

"Good, you can have light."

Amaria, now sitting on the ground, immediately brought her cupped hands to hover in front of her face, a trickle of blood dripping down her wrist, as flames were coaxed to life, illuminating the strange room they were in.

It was filled with paintings and statues of thousands of people. What had they done to have their prophecy be documented in this temple?

"You want to ask why Lynette Edrion killed us in Avondra."

Amaria nodded, staring at the priestess. She was unnerving. Perhaps the priestess was more unnerving to Amaria than Amaria was to non-mages.

"And why would we tell you?"

"You have my blood."

"For light."

"I am an Extractor," Amaria's nostrils flared. "Lynette Edrion is a magical threat to Thestitiunia, this is entirely my jurisdicti-"

"I was joking," the priestess crackled. "Edrion killed us because of the second half of the prophecy she heard. We saw her future and the prophecy tied to sins she desperately tries to hide."

"What sins?" Amaria gritted her teeth, trying to stop herself from strangling the priestess.

"Kin slaying, opening the gates to the Badlands, human sacrifice," the priestess rattled off as if speaking on what she would be having for dinner.

"The Badlands will be opened?" Amaria jumped to her feet, her hands on top of her hair as she panted. The Badlands were a land to the north, bordering the tops of Tressidil, Rindria, and Morroek. In legend, it was where the goddess of magic placed her failed project—her rejects. The Badlands would have magic leak, letting a few escape out, every now and again. Amaria could not imagine a full breach.

"No." The priestess flicked her wrist, the door opening with a thud. "They're already open. Lynette and Clarissa sacrificed many."

Amaria gagged. "Human sacrifice?" It couldn't be.

"Clarissa Nalaeny sacrificed her first born daughter to open them," she laughed almost manically. "I could almost feel bad for her. But nobody feels pity for wealthy pawns."

"What?" Amaria's eyebrows raised as she tried to piece together what the priestess said. A fog was coming over her mind, she felt sluggish. Perhaps she could sleep here.

"Leave, Lady Extractor. This place will kill non-seers." The priestess held her arm, firmly leading her to the outer sanctum. Amaria was pushed out and the door shut behind her so hastily, the hem of her dress was caught in the hinges, tearing slightly.

"Theodmon," Amaria curtly said he approached her, holding out her hand for support. "Let's go."

"You're bleeding-"

"She required a blood sacrifice. Let's go."

Theodmon's forehead creased, however he held her arm, supporting each other as they walked out of the accursed temple. They walked in silence through Chauvi, Amaria only hastily disclosing what had occurred in hushed tones once they passed the gate to the mountain path.

There was silence afterwards, the only noise was the wind and Amaria huffing as she held her stomach and her heart–feeling discomfort in both places. They, after many stops for Amaria to rest, made it back to Forteresse les Blanche.

"Ammy, you should relax," Theodmon told her as they stepped inside the gates of Forteresse les Blanche, standing in the vast courtyard.

Amaria curtly nodded at him, unable to say more between her wheezing before she departed from him exhausted from their hike and the temple. Her fur and velvet was stained from her blood, and she resisted screaming as she ascended the stairs to find a healer to treat her hand.

"There's one more thing," Theodmon said. "I really do need to meet the faeries before we leave for Rindria."

Chapter Twenty

They traveled through the rocky precipice of the forest. The fir trees were tall and wide, probably hundreds, if not thousands, of years old. Amaria could smell the moist dirt, as if it had just rained before a garden was tilled. Twigs and leaves snapped under the carriage wheels, birds sang through the trees, and rustles would occasionally occur from unknown animals.

Amaria snuggled against Theodmon, her expression softening as she took in the creases on his forehead. Her fingers brushed against his arm as she took in the smell of cedar and frankincense.

She enjoyed being close to him.

Amaria could almost pretend they weren't going to visit the faeries. Her body tensing, she nibbled on her nails. The faeries were dangerous; their magic was powerful. They were given most of Ghagyn's gifts. Amaria was one of the most powerful human mages, and yet, the faeries could easily discard her and her magic.

It was a trifle to them.

How Theodmon, with no magic—only his family name and history of being a liaison to the faeries—could bear to meet with them was a mystery. He was brave, so Amaria hugged him tightly.

What if one day he didn't come back home to her from his duties as liaison?

"Let's play a game," she told Theodmon, her breath catching in her mouth.

"What kind?" he asked, kissing her head as he steered their horse.

"A riddle. I need something to get me out of my thoughts."

"Alright," Theodmon sighed. "What object is blue and doesn't float?"

Amaria blinked. "A book."

"No."

"A bottle of whiskey."

"Is that blue?" Theodmon laughed.

"It can be," Amaria protested.

"Try again."

"Blueberries," Amaria deadpanned.

"Try red."

"That's not fair! You can't change the color in the riddle when I'm halfway through solving it!" Amaria shrieked in amusement, her mind off her previous woes.

Theodmon shook his head with a smile.

"I've been working under the presumption that the object is small, blue, and doesn't float, and now it's *red*?"

"What is it?" Theodmon chortled.

"A painted pebble?" Amaria pouted as Theodmon shook his head. "I hope you know that I am *definitely* giving you a complex arithmetic problem for your riddle."

"It can also be clear," he smirked. "Come on, Ammy. You're close."

"*Again*?" Amaria's eyebrows shot up in disbelief at the change as she brought her hands together. She wrung them and fidgeted with her rings, as the sapphire, rubies, and diamonds sparkled in the sunlight that poured through the carriage windows. As she touched her rings, she looked down at them and then back up at Theodmon, sudden realization setting in her eyes as her husband guffawed.

"That was rude." She wasn't angry, instead, a laugh resonated through her lips.

Theodmon leaned downwards and kissed the top of her head, chuckling.

"How far away are we?" Amaria asked, peering out the window to gaze at the passing evergreens and snow as she leaned closer against him.

"The terrain is getting rockier, and we're starting to border the faerie lands, so maybe a day or two more."

Amaria didn't want to go to the fairies but she didn't want Theodmon to go alone either. She pushed her head against his chest, focusing on his heartbeat. It was fast—perhaps Theodmon was nervous too.

Amaria bit her lip. She wanted to say something, however, she feared saying something would make them both lose their nerve.

For hours, they silently sat together, enjoying each other's company. It was part of why Amaria loved Theodmon—they could just sit. They didn't need to fill their time together with mindless chatter for it to be worthwhile.

She loved him. She would always love him.

"I love you," she whispered as she smiled softly.

"Always." Theodmon pulled her tighter against him. "Nothing can change that."

In the distance, there were shouts.

"What's that noise?" Amaria hissed, sitting up straighter, her shoulders tensing. She could ignore the noise, but it had jarred her out of her peace with Theodmon. She scowled as Theodmon let go of her, reaching for his sword, which was laying on the otherwise empty plush velvet bench in front of them.

"Hopefully nothing," he said, his knuckles whitening around the hilt. "Though, there are bandits in these parts...."

He looked over at her. "You should run when they come."

"Or I can help you," Amaria said pointedly. "I'm a mage, remember?"

Theodmon shook his head, his face turning pink. "Sorry, I was thinking of physical weapons...yes, help. Thanks."

Amaria squeezed his hand. She didn't mean to embarrass him; she knew he didn't mean to discount her either. Theodmon was a warrior, but he did not have magic. His tool was steel, not magical threads of energy. "Keep watch," she instructed. "I'm going to manipulate air strands to see if I can hear them."

There was no sense in attacking if these people weren't bandits. Amaria smirked as she imagined arguing peasants having Theodmon jumping out at them, swinging his sword.

Silently, she pushed out her magic, whooshing past the trees and streams. Amaria wasn't looking for nature. She was looking for humans.

"....closer to the road...rich carriages..."

Amaria pressed her eyes together with more force, as if being blind could help her hear better through the wilderness with her magic.

"There's also more guards," Another man said. *"Rich fucks tend to be paranoid."*

Amaria heard the crude laughter. She pulled her magic back, opening her eyes to look at Theodmon. "Bandits," she said, her voice cracking. "They're close. I heard them with my magic."

"That's useful," Theodmon complimented, his eyebrows raising.

Amaria gave a satisfied smile. She loved when she managed to not only impress Theodmon, but surprise him.

"Let's keep going," he continued decisively. "We're on a tight schedule, but we'll be prepared if they try something with us."

Amaria leaned back in her seat. "If they choose to attack us, let's not let them know who we are until it's too late."

She wanted to see the panicked realization set in the bandits eyes when they realized how drastically they had fucked up.

Theodmon laughed. "I like it. What do we do about your eyes?"

Amaria sighed. Her eyes were rather distinctive—after all, how many people had glowing silver eyes? "I think I have a veil in my bag." Most of their belongings were in the trunks strapped to the outside of the carriage. However, they had their jewels inside the carriage with them, and Amaria usually had a few veils wrapped in with her necklaces.

She reached under the seat, pulling out the small container filled with rubies, emeralds, and sapphires. Inside, there was a burgundy veil. Amaria looked at her deep blue and gold dress—this didn't exactly match but it would do for the purposes she needed it for.

Gingerly, she pinned the organza fabric to her hair, gently pulling the front piece to cover her face as Theodmon pounded on the carriage, warning the guards and coachmen about the potential bandits.

Amaria and Theodmon did not have to wait long for the bandits to make a horrible decision. Within the hour, Amaria heard the screams outside the carriage, the arrows hitting their guards. She flinched.

The guards didn't deserve that death. She stood up in unison with Theodmon, both of them rushing out of the carriage. Immediately, Theodmon met a bandit in hand-to-hand combat and Amaria threw a powerful air blast against another bandit, throwing him forcefully against a tree.

She heard something crack, and she hoped it was the bandit's bones instead of the tree.

A guard yelped, and Amaria heard the blood splatter. Immediately, she threw a blast of fire towards the bandit who had killed him.

"She's dragon blessed!" Another bandit shouted. Dragon blessed was the name for elemental mages who had both air and fire—the only two elements Amaria had shown to them so far. Hydra blessed were elemental mages who had earth and water together.

Being an elemental mage wasn't uncommon, as it was one of the more common magic types. Hydra or dragon blessed was uncommon, however, and they tended to be more powerful in their elements than elemental mages who could only control one.

To have all four, well, Amaria was the only mage currently living to have that. She would let them think she was only a dragon blessed mage. For now.

Theodmon grunted behind her, and she heard him gut another bandit with his sword before he backed up towards her. Amaria surveyed her surroundings, searching for threats. She was very glad Theodmon's back was pressed against hers—it made her feel secure, as if nobody could sneak up on her from behind.

"I have about twenty archers pointed at you," a sneering voice shouted. Theodmon, his back against Amaria's tensed. She breathed, feeling the air around the vicinity. She could feel the air pressure changing, almost as if she could visualize the displacement a human would have on the air around them.

There were only five displacements, not including Amaria and Theodmon. The bandit was bluffing and they could bluff in turn.

Except Amaria really wasn't in the negotiating mood.

Amaria stepped forward, flames leaping up from her wrists to encompass her entire arm, stopping at her shoulders. "Pretend you didn't see us, and I'll extend the same courtesy." An arrow whooshed towards her. She threw a fireball, closing her eyes and hoping she wasn't pierced to death.

Miraculously, the arrow burned, crumbling to ash twenty feet away from her. She pushed out her magic, sensing where that man was standing. And although she couldn't see him, she used her magic to open up a hole in the ground, swallowing him.

"Your man is buried alive. You have four men, including yourself," Amaria said less to the man and more to inform Theodmon of what she knew. This man was also a mage, and she could feel snippets of his power radiating from him.

And by indicating she had earth, Amaria was no longer pretending she was only dragon blessed. She would let the bandit slowly figure out who he had attacked.

This bandit wasn't a particularly powerful mage, but he had enough magic to be dangerous. Amaria would treat him with caution, as underestimating mages could be, and often was, a fatal mistake.

"You'll burn out with that much magic," the man stuttered. "Magic feeds on energy, and you'd have to be ridiculously...you'd have to be an Extractor..."

Magical energy was directly tied to one's life force. This was one of the most basic rules of magic a mage learned. If you burned through it too fast, you could get sick or in extreme cases, die. Mages could build up a higher endurance over time with practice. More powerful mages had an advantage in that, for whatever reason, they had higher energy reserves.

Amaria supposed it was similar in how certain people were naturally better at horseback riding, sewing, or dancing.

Amaria knew she had a higher energy reserve than this man. She just hoped he didn't have a secret reservoir of gems on him. She hadn't felt extra energy storages, but Amaria wasn't going to make bets regarding magical gems—she didn't have a great track record with those recently.

"I'm not tired," Amaria said, sending out a shot of energy towards a man who was attempting to sneak from the outskirts of her and Theodmon's peripheral vision. The energy turned into warmth, which then turned into flames. The man screamed and Amaria twisted her hands, increasing the temperature of the fire.

"Three," Theodmon stated. "I see an archer."

Amaria groaned, her back still against Theodmon. Similar to the last archer, she found his mass disturbing the air pressure nearly four hundred feet away, burying him alive with her magic.

"Two," she said, raising her hands to lift the veil. "And I *am* an Extractor."

The veil fell off her face, her silver eyes glowing.

The man stumbled backwards, his eyes widened. "Peter!" he screamed, presumably towards his fellow bandit.

"Let's fight," Amaria said. "You and me. Peter, when he comes, can fight my husband. A fight for our lives?"

A fight for whether you die in these woods or are later drawn and quartered in my dungeons. Amaria didn't tell the bandit he would die either way. Why would she? She presumed he likely knew he'd not live long now, attacking Amaria and Theodmon *Chauvignon* on Chauvignon lands.

Amaria threw a ball of fire at him, the flames dancing together from her arms, the red hot energy hurling towards his body. Ice shot up from his hands, blocking most of the flames. Amaria grinned; she loved elemental fights, and it had been so long since she had practiced with someone who had water magic.

She turned towards a nearby stream, pulling the water towards her. Behind her, Theodmon ran towards something, his sword drawn. She heard the clashing of metal against metal—it was immaterial as she was fighting with this mage who was attempting to pull the river towards himself.

Amaria could use her water magic from sweat and the moisture in the air—she wasn't sure if this mage could. She wanted to tire him out because it was easier to win against a fatigued opponent. A stream of water shot towards her.

She dodged it, sending a whip of water from the stream towards the mage in retaliation.

Behind her, a man screamed, a sickening squish accompanying the pained yelps.

"One," Theodmon said, his opponent's body falling to the ground with a thud.

Amaria narrowed her eyes, focusing on this mage. He was sweating profusely—he was tired. She looked at his face, he seemed to not break eye contact from the stream.

She looked back to the sweat on his body. Sweat was water, water could be boiled—and only fire mages had some level of burn and high temperature resistance. Amaria breathed, letting her control of the water in the stream drop. As she did so, the man stumbled, a wave of water coming towards him.

Amaria suppressed a chuckle because she forgot that all of the energy would have to go somewhere. She focused on the man's sweat, boiling it. He screamed, momentarily distracted. She forced a stream of fire out from her hands, connecting it with the mage's body.

As the flames engulfed him, he screamed.

His screams echoed for seconds, minutes, and then he was ash. She took a shaky breath, the fire lighting her body spiking upwards with each panicked inhalation.

The silence in their surrounding atmosphere was deafening.

Amaria felt her jaw relaxing as she watched the flames die off. They were safe.

"Let's get back in the carriage," Theodmon gently guided her towards where the doors were still flung open, their guards dead. Amaria was swaying dangerously, the colors around her blurring. She had exerted too much energy, and now she needed a nap.

"I'll drive us there," Theodmon said.

Amaria tried to shake her head, all she accomplished was making herself incredibly nauseous and dizzy. "I'll be with you."

"Sleep," Theodmon commanded, laying her down on the plush seats. "I'll wake you up when we're there."

Amaria's eyes drooped. She wanted to protest that Theodmon was tired too. However, she couldn't form the words, and her eyes closed, engulfing her in the darkness of her dreams.

Chapter Twenty-One

"We're here." Theodmon shook Amaria gently.

Groggily, she blinked open her eyes. Where were they? Oh, the faeries. Why were they here? Theodmon had to engage in the liaison duties that seemed to have been postponed—well, Theodmon had been avoiding them was a more accurate description. Amaria rubbed the sleep out of her eyes, the sunlight pouring in from the open door.

"I can stay," Amaria offered.

She didn't want to meet the faeries. They scared her. Amaria didn't like feeling vulnerable, powerless. And compared to the faeries, she was exactly that.

Theodmon shook his head. "If something happens to me, you'd rule until Lysander comes of age. That includes being a temporary liaison."

"Shouldn't it be Aloysius?" Amaria asked. "He actually has Chauvignon blood; I just have the name."

"If you were like my mother, I'd agree," Theodmon said. Dowager Marchioness Agatha Chauvignon was Morrian by birth and deeply distrusted and hated magic in humans; it didn't take a genius to imagine how catastrophic it would be to have her manage relations with non-humans who looked human, kind of, with magic. "You're not though, and you take ruling and its responsibilities more seriously than Aloysius."

Agatha barely handled being around Amaria well, though that could also be that Amaria had starved her family back home in Morroek. Theodmon was right, she was a better choice—and widows had been liaisons until their son came of age before.

"Fine," Amaria agreed. Groaning, she sat up, swinging her legs to where she could stand and depart from the carriage.

The leaves around her were brighter—a green so vivid it seemed like paint not nature. Birds dove through trees, disappearing only to reappear moments later. Theodmon crouched near the dirt, his fingers digging in it as he muttered something under his breath.

This must be the entrance to the faerie lands. Amaria felt a lightness in her chest. Slowly, she turned, taking in her surroundings.

"Breath," Theodmon whispered as he approached her. "Don't lie. Don't provoke them. They'll likely insult you—faeries have a superiority complex."

Amaria's jaw clenched. Lovely. "I suppose it's no different than court," she said jokingly, her voice cracking.

Theodmon looked over at her in concern. She shook her head; this was unimportant right now. Especially as she could see a figure approaching in the distance, the leaves crunching under his feet.

As the man came closer, Amaria could see he wasn't quite a man. He looked like a man except he seemed to be more still than a normal human. It was almost as if he wasn't breathing. His skin was deathly pale, with almost a blue tinge to it.

However, his hair was beautiful. It was long and shimmering, almost a blue-silver color. Amaria felt her jaw slacken. His hair reminded her of starlight.

"Oberon." Theodmon lowered his head respectfully to the male faerie. "This is my wife, Amaria Chauvignon."

"And the name she was born with?"

"Amaria Raulet," Amaria said.

"You have magic." Oberon's pale eyes met Amaria's. "Strong. For a human at least."

Amaria wet her lips. "I suppose," she said. It would be unwise to be boastful around a faerie. They were unpredictable—everyone knew that.

"If I died before my son came of age, she'd be the temporary liaison," Theodmon continued calmly. "I figured I'd introduce you."

"We're introduced." Oberon curtly nodded towards Amaria's general direction, turning his body away from her without so much a glance at her directly. "Theodmon Chauvignon, let's talk. There's been an increase of unicorns around these parts. Are humans playing with dark magic?"

Amaria's fists clenched against the folds of her skirts. He was dismissing her to ask a non-mage about magic? "Yes," she said, her chest heaving. "Not us, not Thestitiunians, but some humans are. We're trying to fix it."

She shouldn't interrupt. Theodmon wasn't a mage, but he had been managing this relationship for years. Her ears burned.

"What do you know about dark magic?" Oberon asked, the hint of a smirk on his face.

"Enough," Amaria said. "I'm a powerful mage. I've been dealing with the dark magic in the human lands."

"Why isn't it fixed?" Oberon raised a sleek eyebrow.

Amaria forced her baring teeth to become a smile, disguising her agitation with polite niceties. She didn't see why this was any of Oberon's concern, but it was unwise to antagonize or lie to faeries. Her only real option was to answer Oberon as truthfully and vaguely as she could get away with.

"I don't have much say in the affairs of non-Thestitiunian mages," she forced her arms to open wide, exposing her chest. "We suspect the dark magic is primarily from an Avonnian mage."

Who is working with a non-magical Riam princess who lacks a shred of sense. Both which are, unfortunately, independent sovereign nations. Amaria kept her chin high, not diverting eye contact from Oberon.

"You're working on it?" Oberon challenged.

"Human politics are complicated," Theodmon interrupted. "We're taking care of it. I'll update you when we know more." He too did not break eye-contact with Oberon.

Oberon turned on his heel, heading back into the forest. "A sharp tongue isn't indicative of a keen mind. Be careful in dealing with your dark magic issue."

There was a roaring rushing in Amaria's ears, her body turning hot. She stared at Oberon's back with an intense, fevered stare, sparks flashing from her silver eyes. He had insulted her. And she had no response to it.

She looked over at Theodmon, wondering when they could go home, away from these self-righteous pricks and their wicked kingdom.

Chapter Twenty-Two

Theodmon and Amaria did soon leave the faeries and the trip back to Forteresse les Blanche was uneventful—thank the gods, as Amaria was increasingly busy as soon as they had returned home.

Throughout the next three weeks preparations were made for their trip to Rindria. Clothes were sewn, cover stories were devised, and the relevant people were informed of their roles. Liara, surprisingly, agreed to join, although Amaria knew she was anxious and was almost unwillingly joining, as if pulled by an invisible chain. Amaria despised that they needed her to join—it would seem more suspicious to visit their new in-laws without their relative.

The Westerlands too, seemed unwilling to let them leave its borders. The snow lightly fell each night, layering the tundra with more ice day after day. Amaria shivered as she pulled her cloak together around herself, glad that there were numerous tents, blankets, and furs packed in each member's luggage. In her arms, she clutched Lysander.

She had given the wetnurses, maids, and nannies detailed instructions, as if they hadn't been following those procedures since he was born. She cradled him close to her chest, swaying slightly with her eyes closed. Lysander nestled closer against his mother, his face hitting the white furs draped over her shoulder.

"He'll be alright," Theodmon whispered to her as they descended the main staircase into the entranceway. "You'll be fine as well."

In the entranceway, Lucas was quietly whispering to Juliette, her abdominal bulge larger.

Henri was drinking tea, the steam still visible from his cup as he looked mournfully at the bitter weather outside through the windows. Next to him, Aloysius was draping a fur coat around Liara, clearly attempting to comfort her as she stood, her face taut with worry.

Haerdnor, who had arrived two days ago, held fire in his hands, staring blankly ahead of him, clearly dreading the upcoming chill. Amaria pulled Lysander closer to her. She didn't want to abandon him again. She'd be back soon. They were going to Rindria to greet their relatives, after going in under a disguise to see an unbiased layout of the land and systems. Haerdnor and Henri would go themselves, Liara would be the second distraction.

Somehow, they'd find the Ruby.

Amaria knew she was being more attached than most women of her station were to their infants. However, despite that, she felt no shame in breaking this convention—why wouldn't she be attached to her firstborn?

"It's time to go," Theodmon told Amaria softly.

Amaria would have rather eaten glass than hand Lysander over to a nanny. Still, she forced her muscles to move, forcing herself to ignore that Lysander immediately burst into tears as he was removed from her arms. Still, her hands moved towards Lysander, wanting to hold him again.

"I'm sorry," Theodmon whispered as he guided Amaria toward the carriage. "We have to get this gem. Hopefully you won't have to leave here once we get it."

Amaria shakily nodded, looking back at Lysander as they exited the castle. She had to leave him—this was all to protect him. Dark magic would ravage the lands that bordered them first, but Morroek, Rindria, and Tressidil wouldn't be the only casualties. Soon enough, the Badlands denizenry would move south towards Thestitiunia.

Behind her, Aloysius walked with Liara, followed by Henri and Lucas. Haerdnor trailed along last, dragging his feet begrudgingly through the snow, down the mountain to where a carriage was waiting halfway below where it wasn't as steep.

Amaria pushed her hands under her armpits, scowling. She hated being cold and trudging down a mountain in snow was a special type of torture.

"You alright?" Theodmon whispered.

Amaria shook her head shortly, focused on not slipping on the icy patches near her feet.

Miraculously, nobody fell off a mountain as they reached the carriage. Amaria and Haerdnor went in first, shivering with cold. Liara and Aloysius climbed in second. Henri was third, and Lucas jumped in afterwards. Theodmon cast a final glance around them, and their coachman, to ensure all was well before he joined them, sitting next to Amaria, throwing his arm over her.

Inside the burgundy, richly velvet cabin, Henri was passing blankets around to each of them as the wheels rolled down the mountain path on the dirt-packed road outside of Chauvi, heading into the woods. Theodmon took two more fur-lined blankets for Amaria, cocooning her in them and snuggling his arm around her. She pressed her body closer to his, her entire body going limp. Across from them, Aloysius handed Liara some blankets, his hand brushing against hers, where they lingered, their hands touching each other.

"Thank you," Liara told him, draping the furs across her lap. Next to her, Henri smirked and Amaria made a mental note to ask him what he heard in Aloysius and Liara's thoughts.

"It should take about four days to reach the mountains," Lucas informed them.

"In this snow?" Haerdnor questioned.

Liara snorted under her breath.

"What?" Haerdnor said.

"Nothing," Liara muttered, sullenly crossing her arms. Amaria noticed she avoided looking at Haerdnor.

What's her deal? Amaria thought ill-temperedly. *She shouldn't bite the hand that saved her from...living as a peasant.* She knew nobody saved Liara, but the girl's attitude was grating to Amaria.

Yes, the famines were bad. Yes, Haerdnor tended to be the face behind the Riam famines. It was just business. Surely Liara could understand that.

But Liara seems to especially hate Haer...oh, fuck.

Amaria slumped in her seat, a wave of fatigue hitting her. Clarissa had allegedly abused Liara. And now, Amaria remembered that Clarissa had proposed a marriage between Liara and Haerdnor, despite his existing engagement and that a marriage between her family and the Raulets offered no benefit to the Raulets.

Surely Liara wouldn't be upset about that though? Amaria had forgotten about it, rejecting a marriage proposal while already engaged was normal. Did Amaria make a critical error in underestimating how idealistic this Riam was?

"Can you not be a petulant child?" Lucas said, looking at Liara unblinkingly. "If you're going to be a liability, get out."

"Lucas," Theodmon said warningly.

"No," Lucas said. "I understand why you want her to come—she's a built-in alibi. But we can leave her behind. Claim she's pregnant and can't handle the journey. If she's going to act like a child, she should be treated as one."

"He rejected a marriage proposal *by laughing*." Liara crossed her arms. "He ruined my life!"

Amaria glanced worriedly at Theodmon. Amaria bit her lip. She didn't disagree with Lucas's statement, but they were all crammed together and she didn't want to deal with a fight right now.

"I had no way of knowing, alright?" Haerdnor said, red flashing across his brown eyes. He was angry and was likely suppressing his magic. Amaria was glad he was controlling it—fire in close quarters could be catastrophic. However, fire magic could be difficult to control when angry, and so Amaria tensed, wondering when the carriage would go up in flames.

"You laughed," Liara hissed, seemingly unaware of the danger. Perhaps she was suicidal and wanted to bring down as many Thestitiunians as she could in a firefly blaze?

"I was, still am actually, engaged to another woman when they proposed a marriage to you!" Haerdnor hands slapped his thighs. "How could that ever be seen as a reasonable request?"

"You didn't have to laugh!"

"Breaking off an engagement is an act of war. I'm sorry if I laughed at your mother's *delusional* request."

"And yet, I was left to deal with the actions of *both* of you," Liara said. "You don't care how much she made me bleed!"

"Can you shut up?" Amaria snapped. "You seem to hate your mother, yet from what I've seen, you and Clarissa are the same person. You're delusional, self-centered, and an idiot who thinks they're more important than they actually are."

"At least I'm n-"

"We need you alive, not speaking," Amaria interrupted. Liara's voice was an irritating scratch in her ears—everyone had a sob story. Amaria had a sob story; the difference was that she wasn't screaming at everyone for perceived slights. "Keep this up and I'll cut your tongue out."

Amaria didn't need this tensity right now; there was a mutual concern radiating from everyone in the carriage, except for perhaps the concern herself. Would Liara be able to conduct herself appropriately? Would she sabotage the operation?

Liara glared at her. "Do you even have a knife? You don't seem like the type."

Amaria jutted her leg out, pulling up her skirts to reveal a small jeweled dagger strapped to her leg. "I torture people. You should remember that."

Liara crossed her arms, sliding beneath her quilts. Thankfully, she stayed silent.

"Was that necessary?" Aloysius said to Amaria, reaching out to comfort Liara. Liara pushed him away.

"Yes," Amaria said. "She lacks self control. It's a liability. We mitigate liabilities, in case you've forgotten."

"Can you not talk about me as if I'm not here?" Liara said.

Amaria turned to Haerdnor, gripping his hand. It was unfair that Liara blamed him for things outside of his control. What Clarissa seemed to do, and from what Amaria could gather, it seemed that Clarissa punished Liara for the denial of the engagement. It was unfair for Clarissa to do that.

But life wasn't fair. Fairness was idealistic. Fairness was a child's fantasy. And if you believed in fairy tales beyond the age of six, you were setting yourself up for a long, painful life. Amaria had learned that years ago. Why was it so hard for Liara to process that lesson?

Amaria smiled, the expression of warmth not quite reaching her eyes as she stared at her twin's face, trying to survey how he was.

Haerdnor had also learned the lesson of life not being fair. Both of them had grown up at their father's knee learning the craft of ruling. They also learned lying, torture, and generally unscrupulous behaviors.

The biggest lesson was to follow expectations. It didn't matter what Amaria wanted; she'd marry and bear children. While she enjoyed and loved this with Theodmon, she knew it would be different with Lyseno Vypren. She may have enjoyed her children with him—Amaria loved children—but the marriage itself would have been miserable.

It didn't matter she despised her fiance then, that she would rather be anywhere but with Lyseno Vypren. It didn't matter Haerdnor would rather skin himself alive than be sexually intimate with a woman; he would still marry and have a wife give him Raulet children. Was it a perfect ideal or what either wanted in life?

It was ideal to them as much as turtles enjoyed being eaten by alligators.

Amaria sighed, leaning her head against Theodmon. She enjoyed being with him though. She loved being his wife. It seemed that some turtles enjoyed being eaten by the right alligator.

Amaria felt a fire, flickering and wild flames, pressing against the barriers of her mind. She slowly lowered her mental barriers, as if she were a sea anemone allowing a fish to enter into safety.

"I hate her," Haerdnor said.

"Stating the obvious," Amaria said dryly.

"Why is she even here?" Haerdnor grumbled, casting a dark look over at Liara. *"She has no political grace, no skills with hunting or fighting, no magic; she just bitches about everything that displeases her stupid, turned-up, snotty nose."*

"Rich." Amaria rolled her eyes. *"You're bitching now."*

"Justifiably," Haerdnor said. Amaria did have to agree, it was justified to bitch about Liara.

"Alright," Amaria said through the mage link, Haerdnor and Amaria's magic working together to give them a secret channel to communicate—it wasn't hard magic, any mage could do it with another mage they trusted. *"She's insufferable. But she's a distraction. If we get the Raulet Ruby, I can tolerate her."*

"And after?" Haerdnor said.

"If Thestitiunia gets Rindria, I'll tolerate her," Amaria slouched in her seat slightly, forcing back a groan. She would have to deal with this small-minded shrew until she was no longer needed.

Gods, Amaria was looking forward to the day she could discard Liara.

She met Haerdnor eyes. *"We have to play nice for now,"* she said, slowly pulling away from the mage link.

They could handle this. They were Raulets. Manipulating someone like Liara was child's play.

Amaria didn't acknowledge how being kind to someone who lashed out against you for breathing was taxing on the soul.

Theodmon and Aloysius stared at each other, as if having a secret conversation themselves. However, they weren't communicating in words—only Aloysius was a mage. Theodmon couldn't share in any mage link. A pity. She would love to secretly communicate in more than just looks and half smiles. Even now, she stifled a blush at the things Theodmon would whisper to her.

She didn't need all that now though. It was apparent what the mutual concern was. Sighing, Amaria pushed out her energy through her mage link until she collided with Aloysius's wavelength, Henri's eyes turning sharply to her.

Henri could back off. She somewhat hated that he could hear every secret conversation and thought. Mind readers could be infuriating. Even ones she liked.

"Aloysius," Amaria said, ignoring Henri.

"Hmm?" Aloysius answered.

"Watch her," Amaria commanded. *"Make sure she has a semblance of self control. I meant it, I'll cut her tongue out if she doesn't."*

"You're also a concern, Amaria," Aloysius said tiredly.

"A concern?" Amaria scoffed.

"You have a temper. Especially when someone insults your family," Aloysius said. *"Is cutting her tongue out the best way to handle this situation?"*

"She doesn't need a tongue to get pregnant. It's clear she has no information for us, so unless she can pop out a child with Riam blood to get us a claim to the throne after a civil war breaks out, yes, cutting out her tongue will help us."

"I want to like my wife," Aloysius argued with her.

"With luck she'll die in childbirth and you'll get a better one."

Aloysius looked at her in horror as she pulled out of the mage link. She didn't want to hear his scolding. It was unfortunate he married such a liability. Amaria hated that she had the idea to do this anyways.

Amaria nodded towards Theodmon. They needed to get out of this carriage before weapons were drawn.

Immediately, Theodmon knocked on the top of the carriage. "I think we should go on that hunt, get some fresh air."

Amaria sighed, her shoulders relaxing as she held Theodmon's hand. Their eyes met. She wasn't a mind reader, but she knew him. He knew her. They were both stressed. She gave a soft smile. They'd be alright. His mouth twitched, but he looked pained.

"I'll stay with Henri and Liara," Amaria rubbed her hands over his. "Everyone else should go on the hunt."

"I want to go on the hunt," Liara protested.

"If you think anybody is stupid enough to give you a weapon," Lucas grumbled.

"Because I'm a woman?" Liara challenged.

"Because you're a political prisoner," Theodmon corrected.

"I'm surprised you admitted it," Liara said.

Theodmon shrugged. "A bird is a bird whether or not I call it a bird."

Theodmon met Amaria's eyes as they moved out of the carriage. Amaria sniffed, inhaling deeply to calm herself as the frosty air nipped her nose and ears. She tilted her head forward as she smiled, her forehead scrunching with worry.

Theodmon's eyebrows rose and she shook her head softly in response. They had supplies, but they should go hunt still. Or hike. Anything to separate Haerdnor and Liara.

"Go," she encouraged. "We will start a fire so we can cook whatever you bring back."

"Be safe, my love," Theodmon instructed. "We'll return at nightfall." Amaria watched as they departed, bundling the cloak around herself.

As soon as they left, Liara blew air out of her nose, glaring at Amaria and Henri.

"What's your problem?" Amaria crossed her arms as Henri gathered firewood from the trees around them.

"No problem," Liara clipped.

"Then act like it," Amaria snapped.

Henri scowled, dropping the wood in a pile. Amaria came over, lighting her hands and then the wood on fire.

Liara snorted, tossing her hair back.

Henri cracked his knuckles. "You're the one who needs an attitude adjustment," he told Liara. Amaria made a mental note to ask Henri what Liara was thinking.

Liara blinked at him.

"I can read minds," Henri said dryly. "Don't try anything cute like running away. I'll know as soon as you think of it."

"Well then, since you're going to find out my thoughts anyways," Liara glared at them, "I hope you both get what's coming for you. How many did you hurt to get your magic? You're depraved! All magic users are-"

"Beautiful, bravado," Amaria said sarcastically. "Keep talking and I'll cut your tongue out. Remember? We don't need all of you whole, only certain parts," she sneered, looking Liara up and down her nose.

"You expect me to be nice to you after-"

"I expect you to have decorum," Amaria hissed, hating how much she sounded like her father. Gods, how far she had fallen to be exactly like Aaron. Though, she could not deny the swelling of pride she felt in her chest from being just like her father. Aaron was smart, cunning, capable, and astute. Why was she upset that she was seen as just like her father?

Because he's my father. Amaria thought, rolling her eyes. *Idiot.*

"I have decorum," Liara pouted, her chin jutting forward.

Liara had as much decorum as a milkmaid caught with a stablehand at night. Amaria looked at her, forcing her face to melt into a kind façade. Antagonizing this girl would achieve nothing. Amaria may not be able to convince Liara to trust them. To be fair Amaria wouldn't trust herself either. However, Amaria could try to placate Liara.

"Yes, you must have," Amaria lied. "With a mother like Clarissa Nalaeny."

"What do you mean?" Liara's eyes narrowed. Perhaps she wasn't as stupid as Amaria thought. No matter, Amaria knew what she was doing.

"She always seemed self-centered, petty, vain, cruel," Amaria said. "I'm sorry you had to put up with her worst impulses. What did she do when my family rejected the engagement—never mind. That's none of my business."

Amaria turned away from Liara, as if embarrassed for her foolhardy attempt to intrude on Liara's privacy. She didn't care, truly. Amaria could guess what happened, it wasn't like Liara hadn't essentially told them all already.

"She hit me," Liara snarled. "I ran away to escape this prison of engaged marriages and politics and frivolous, empty heads."

You're one to speak. Amaria thought, pushing her anger down as she kept her face forlorn as if Liara's story was a tragedy.

"It's unfortunate society is that way," Amaria agreed. "But we make do with what we have."

Liara snorted. "How could you say that?"

"You think I'm an empty minded fool content to be ordered around by my husband and father," Amaria said. "I am a survivor. You are a fighter. They are not mutually exclusive, and you're digging your own grave by rejecting every expectation."

"Is that a threat?" Liara snarled.

Henri. Amaria thought, not bothering with the mage link. He couldn't reply to her, but she knew he'd hear. *I'd like to threaten her. Would pulling out the knife ruin everything?*

Henri met her eyes, his lips twitching.

"An observation," Amaria said lightly. "We're forced to find happiness in what we can as women. Finding the negative in everything will rob you of any change of happiness. I am genuine in this advice. Make do with the positives you have."

Amaria hated how sweet she was talking to her but she had to do something to mitigate the chance of Liara destroying everything.

"I don't want to be like you," Liara said. "I want freedom."

Amaria almost burst out into giggles. This girl thought she could have freedom as she went from sheltered noble to protected political prisoner—the Tressi were not risking their necks to be kind, anybody in politics knew that—and then to a Thestitiunian wife, existing to produce a few heirs to sit on the Riam throne.

Amaria remembered her history lessons in which an Avonnian knight united the kingdoms by overthrowing the crown. He had done it guilefully. This clever knight had gifted the holdout nobles ink in stunning gemstone inkwells. Ink that was actually poison acid. The holdout nobles died. The knight became a king. Avondra wasn't a province anymore, but a united kingdom.

Avondra had never been as cohesive as Thestitiunia, and they had always maintained fierce independence in provincial cultures and customs, but the kingdom was destroyed and rebuilt with poisoned ink.

Amaria was as guileful as this Avonnian knight. She was a rose instead of a sword.

And Liara was the Thestitiunian's poisoned ink.

Somehow, Liara didn't see this. Somehow, Liara thought she could get freedom. The best freedom she could get was to make her in-laws not hate her. Amaria had freedom as a powerful noblewoman married to a powerful nobleman. Liara could have had that too, in time, if she behaved.

At this rate, Amaria doubted Liara could behave in a mature and rational fashion. Gods, why was she cursed to put up with this whining girl focused on idealistic impossibilities? Amaria stood up, wrapping her cloak around her as the frost bit her nose. "Excuse me, I'm going to the carriage until the men arrive; it's frigid."

Amaria made her way back to the carriage, suppressing a scream. She needed to be anywhere where that girl wasn't. Henri could handle it. She'd let him handle Liara. She was going to lie under five blankets and try to sink her body into the void, as if the carriage seats could bring her there.

"We're close to the border," Theodmon said.

"We should just go as ourselves," Amaria whispered, watching Liara. "I know the plan was to gather intel dressed as commoners...but..."

"She'll blow our covers," Theodmon finished. His shoulders dropped. "Alright."

He turned to the rest in the carriage, announcing the change in plan. Amaria didn't want to change the plan, if only because she was ready to escape this carriage in any way she could. She felt as if she was overly constrained with the tension in the carriage—perhaps holding people in a confined space for days with someone they hated and a fire mage ready to explode would be a new form of torture Amaria would try.

"Couldn't handle the peasant dress?" Haerdnor smirked in Amaria's direction.

Amaria rolled her eyes.

Haerdnor gave Amaria a genuine smile. "Be safe. Who else would I tease?"

"Try Oliver for once," Amaria twitched her nose at him.

"Get out of your thoughts," Haerdnor told her. "Compartmentalize, remember."

Amaria crossed her arms, scowling at Haerdnor. It wasn't exactly easy to *get out of her thoughts* when she was engaged in twelve deadly games of chess at once.

"Are you ready to get your gem back?" Henri asked, his eyes darting between the twins.

Hesitantly, Amaria looked over at Liara. She was married to Aloysius, and therefore she was solidly Thestitiunian. If Liara ran away, Aloysius could and would exercise husband's rights to have her returned.

Bringing Liara to Rindria would distract the court, hopefully long enough that they could find the Raulet Ruby. But Amaria feared Liara would ruin the plan. That's why the plan was changed—and it was too late to turn back. Amaria nodded, forcing back the vomit bubbling in the back of her throat.

Chapter Twenty-Three

On this side of the mountain there were significantly less trees. Instead, the landscape was mostly never ending fields. Amaria looked upwards, seeing birds flying overhead as the sky started to turn from navy to orange and pink as she breathed in heavily.

They had made it into Rindria.

The carriage pulled to a stop at a border checkpoint.

"I thought we were sneaking in," Liara said accusingly.

"Plans change," Theodmon said gruffly, moving to open the door to speak with the guard knocking on the door.

"But we had a plan—"

"That became more dangerous and suspicious," Lucas snapped. "I'm not trying to end up in a Riam prison. Keep your head down, Lady Chauvignon."

Amaria chuckled. Lucas was a skilled torturer, and hearing him wanting to avoid a prison was a certain type of irony. Liara glared at her. Amaria supposed she thought she was laughing at the name 'Lady Chauvignon'.

Liara's new name was the last thing Amaria found amusing. She would have to babysit this petulant child for the rest of her life. Amaria suspected that Liara thought she was the only one being punished with her marriage to Aloysius. She would be incorrect if that was the case—Amaria had her own children to raise. She did not need an adult masquerading as an unintelligent child.

Perhaps Liara would get the plague. The plague was entirely curable with magic and antibiotics, and Thestitiunia hadn't had issues with the disease for generations. However,

Rindria, a backwards, backwater country, despised magic and suffered for it. Amaria sighed, pushing the thoughts from her head. It would be too easy if all her issues disappeared.

"Names, nationality, and business," a guard barked.

"I'm Marquis Theodmon Chauvignon, I assume you know my nationality with that name. I'm headed to Bria Hall."

"What business?"

"Politics," Theodmon said curtly. "That's my wife, Amaria Chauvignon."

"Who are they?" The second guard tilted his chin towards Haerdnor, Henri, Liara, Lucas, and Aloysius.

Theodmon nodded at Lucas and Aloysius. "My bannerman, Lord Lucas Bécharil and my brother, Aloysius." He turned to Henri and Haerdnor: "Lord Henri Delaluna, and Lord Haerdnor Raulet."

"And their business?"

"Same as mine." Theodmon crossed his arms. "Politics."

"And who is she?" The guard indicated his head towards Liara.

"My wife," Aloysius responded coolly.

If only Liara hadn't married Aloysius. Amaria had planned this, yes. But she hadn't thought Liara would be so naïve. And now she wanted Liara gone, but the Chauvignons being implicated was not a goal desired. It was bad form to betray or murder a family member. If they were related by blood, they were cursed by the gods.

"Nobody else?" the guard asked suspiciously.

Amaria cursed internally. It was odd they didn't have servants or courtiers for a political trip.

"We wanted to make this a quick trip," Theodmon said coolly. "Nobody here enjoys Riam hospitality and my wife is rather anxious to get back to our son. Courtiers tend to slow this process down."

Amaria missed Lysander. How was he doing? Was he happy? Healthy? What if while she was gone, he drowned in the bathtub?

She felt panic rise to her throat as she imagined Lysander dead, seeing his little body floating facedown in a bath. She closed her eyes, trying to banish that thought; instead, she saw a version of Lysander being torn limb from limb. She saw him suffocated.

Her eyes flew open. She didn't need to see this. It wasn't necessary to what they needed to do currently. Lysander was alive. And she didn't know why she was imagining him dead; her nerves were bad but Lysander and his mortality had nothing to do with the current situation.

The guards were telling Theodmon that they would escort them from the border to the heart of the country where Bria Hall—the Riam Court—was. Theodmon was annoyed, cracking his knuckles.

"Theo," Amaria whispered, rubbing his arm. They didn't need to instigate the guards. She hoped he wouldn't do this right now, despite understanding the loss of being escorted. They had wanted Riam intel, and with this change of plan, the chance of getting that had been discarded. She smiled upwards at him, as if prompting him to similarly soften his demeanor.

She hoped he would listen to her silent message. They were a team. She loved him. She knew he loved her. Together, they could do most things.

Including dealing with small annoyances such as Riam guards.

Theodmon looked down at her, his eyebrows bushing together, as he laid his hand over hers. Silently, his mouth twitched, and through his unblinking stare, Amaria knew he was asking her if she was alright. She brought her head down to nod, as if to reassure him with a beguiling falsehood to avoid the calamity of truth, but at the last minute shook her head instead, the long dark braid falling over her shoulder. Amaria could not find it in herself to deceive Theodmon, though anybody else would be unsaved from her prevarications. However, she found tranquility in their partnership for it was based on certain roles and expectations, but a partnership where they were equals, with equally important assignments and information to produce.

Marquis and Marchioness Chauvignon. A match made in hell.

Theodmon squeezed her hand, trying to ease her anxiety with his presence. Amaria knew how certain people, many in the Riam court, described their marriage. Many were unhappy with the match, believing it to be one with disastrous political consequences for them. They weren't wrong; in all fairness, giving one of the most powerful armies in the world access to the coffers of the richest man in the world was dangerous. And Amaria took over running Theodmon's intelligence networks, streamlining it into hers so it would run more efficiently. Neither of these were exactly a good outcome for their enemies. Still, Amaria couldn't agree with the sentiment that they were a match made in hell—it felt too natural and relaxed for that assertation to be true.

They could handle this together.

"Fine," Theodmon voiced loudly to the guards, rolling his neck impatiently. "Let's get this over with."

Amaria took a deep breath and squeezed Theodmon's hand. "We can do this," she whispered so low only he could hear. "This is only for a few days until we reach Weorren City."

The door shut and the carriage rolled forward. Liara was scowling at them.

"What?" Amaria's nostrils flared.

"Can you quit looking like a frozen-over rock for just one day?" Liara retorted exasperatedly. "I thought that guard was going to kill you."

Amaria turned her head, an eyebrow arched sharply in inquisition, looking as haughty and unimpressed as a statute in a temple. What was the purpose of this critique?

Similarly, Theodmon's brows jutted together, looking as if he were scowling at Liara only with his eyes. Amaria was glad they seemed to both be in agreement about the situation.

"Foreign dignitaries," Aloysius clipped, casting a warning glance towards Amaria and Theodmon before focusing on Liara. "Whatever they looked like, they wouldn't be murdered."

Her jaw tightened as she turned her head slightly upwards to look at Theodmon. Staring into his hazel eyes, Amaria took a deep breath. Next to her, Theodmon's hand slipped into hers, squeezing it tightly. She took in his long, dark lashes, and the long bridge of his nose—she felt calmer with each moment she surveyed her husband's appearance.

Theodmon wrapped his arms around her, pulling her into his chest. Amaria leaned into him, hugging his arms with her own. Theodmon was a fortress, and she always felt safe with him. Which she was anticipating she would need soon. She didn't feel safe being surrounded by Riam guards.

She wished they had brought Thestitiunian guards, that they hadn't changed the plan, or that they had left Liara home—any of these would've done. Hindsight truly was a bitch.

"You don't trust me," Liara said.

Amaria twisted her rings with a scowl. Liara couldn't be silent, could she? She was correct because nobody in this carriage trusted her, let alone Amaria. However, what was the purpose of stating this? Was she edging on a fight? Nobody in the carriage said anything, collectively deciding that they wouldn't give Liara the satisfaction.

Chapter Twenty-Four

As they traveled through the Riam countryside, Theodmon and Aloysius played cards to pass the time. Amaria supposed it was a better use of time than compulsively going over what could go wrong in the upcoming plan. Amaria dreaded the future—she feared what would happen if the Ruby wasn't here and they did all of this, for what? Angering Rindria?

It was bad enough that no Riams were invited to Liara's wedding; that slight would be hard to overcome. Amaria would have to direct the conversation as far away from that as she could.

"We should tell them we're sending money and jewels," Amaria sighed, "as an engagement gift." And to mitigate the social faux pas between the nations on this continent from the empire failing to invite any Riam to Liara's wedding to a Thestitiunian lord.

Before anyone could respond, shouts erupted outside the carriage.

"What's going on?" Lucas said.

"Probably you," Liara scowled. "Chauvignons and Raulets and mages aren't popular."

"I'm not a Chauvignon, mage, or Raulet," Lucas smirked. "You're more a Chauvignon—"

"Don't antagonize her," Henri whispered, his face paling.

"Burn the witch!"

Amaria's head snapped around from where they heard this as she pounded on the carriage overhead for them to stop. As the carriage lurched to a sudden stop, Amaria threw open the doors, witnessing the scene before her.

"No, please, I beg you, please, I'm not a witch!" A young woman was pinned against a wall by armored men, tears in her eyes.

"Shut your filthy mouth, stupid girl. We caught you red-handed! You thought nobody would notice your magic? You changed that cat's color!"

Amaria's body tensed, and she instinctively reached out her energy towards the girl. Surprisingly, there was a soft lapping of magical energy coming from the Riam.

"Is that a real mage or just another mistake?" Lucas asked dully.

Amaria's mouth felt as dry as sand. "Real. She doesn't feel powerful, but there's definitely magic.

"If she's a real mage, it's not wise to save her," Aloysius said warningly.

"I don't want to keep hearing about mages being murdered for the stupid crime of having magic," Amaria hissed. "I'm not watching it happen."

Amaria could not imagine being murdered for her magic. It was a part of her, and the concept of her being killed for it was asinine, as if she would be murdered for having brown hair or being right handed. It was just who she was.

She hated Morroek and Rindria for their small-minded superstitions. They had harmed more people than she ever had with their ignorance.

"It's a bad idea," Liara said.

Amaria whirled on her, eyes flaming. How could this girl talk of good and bad ideas? She had never made a prudent decision in her life.

"What did I do?" The peasant girl could be heard pleading.

"You're a witch! The witch we are looking for is dark-haired with light eyes. Pretty. Unfortunately for you, you match that description." The guard sneered as he dragged her past the walls, undoubtedly bringing her towards a pyre.

"Stop!" Amaria straightened her spine, elongating her neck as she called out to the guards. Behind her, she could feel the others' stares boring into the back of her skull, but she ignored them and pressed on with her new plan, striding towards them, storming forward with the rashness of a fire mage. Her face was as chiseled as a statue as if she was embodying the god of rage.

"And who are you?" the second guard said.

"Unhand her," Amaria commanded. "You said the witch you were looking for was dark haired, with light eyes. Are you positive that it was this woman?" she spat, looking him dead in the face. "I'm Amaria Raulet, a notorious witch with dark hair and light eyes."

The guards took in Amaria's enraged face, the silver in her eyes sparking as if melted flames. They took in her elaborate dress and jewelry. Amaria's body was starting to shake and her face felt flushed. Behind her, Theodmon exited the carriage and was standing next to her, his hand resting lightly on the hilt of his sword. Slowly, the guards' eyes widened into shock and horror. Good, they recognized her. Or Theodmon. Either way.

"Release her." Amaria nodded towards the girl, who was cowering against the wall, almost trying to blend into the stone structure. "I'm the one you want, not this unfortunate girl who was stupid enough to share a physical description with me."

"Come closer. I need to see if you actually match the description."

Amaria did not move. However, the guard leaned forward, peering closely at Amaria's silver eyes, brunette hair, and facial features. After what felt like an infinity, he nodded his head, satisfied. "Yes, you match. We'll release the girl. Thank you for your cooperation, Marchioness."

Amaria stepped back, the band around her chest loosening as she nearly fell against Theodmon. Liara stepped up next to them, her eyebrows raised.

The young woman jumped in fear as the guards approached her once more, and she flinched away from their hands on her arm. "No, no, no, please. Please! I'm innocent, I don't want to die."

"You're not going to die," Amaria reassured her, walking up to her and swatting the guard's hands away with a flick of air magic. It was subtler than fire magic at least—still within the plausible grounds of diplomatic relations. "Get in the carriage."

"We're still escorting you," their escort protested as he appeared. Amaria rolled her eyes. Perfect timing, perhaps they were hoping for some fight to break out; it would make their job harder but Amaria and Theodmon were perhaps hated enough that it would be worth it.

"That's why we're getting back in the carriage," Theodmon dismissed. Amaria pushed the terrified woman in front of her, who cowered in the corner of the carriage. Amaria would drop her off somewhere—she just didn't want a mage to die.

"That was kind of you," Liara said, her mouth agape. "Protecting a peasant."

"I didn't protect her out of kindness, I hate people villainizing magic." Amaria threw a glance back at the girl as the rest of their party entered the carriage, the door shutting behind them with a snap. "What's your name?"

The girl stared at her apprehensively. "You're a witch."

"And so are you," Amaria said. "Don't deny it, I can sense magic and you were conducting magic earlier. How've you survived this long in Rindria? What's your magic anyways?"

"I don't know," the girl sighed, her blue eyes cast downwards. "People can see things differently when I want them to. Not large things: a black cat instead of an orange one, that I never walked across the hall but am still sitting in my chair, those sorts of things."

An illusionist. Amaria sucked in her breath.

"Your name?" Amaria said.

"Charlotte, my Lady." The girl wet her lips nervously.

"A surname?" Amaria questioned, causing the girl to slowly shake her head. Amaria looked sharply at her, her eyebrows furrowing.

"In Rindria, commoners do not have last names except for select professions," Liara said. "Greenfield for wheat farmers, Smith for blacksmiths, Tanner for tanners, and so forth. Many commoners don't have surnames."

"They come up with their own surnames, they just aren't state-given." Amaria rolled her eyes. How did she know more than Liara about her own country?

"Petersdaughter," Charlotte whispered.

Amaria nodded. Charlotte Petersdaughter. The girl was too overwhelmed to be much help now, but that didn't mean she couldn't be recruited as an asset in the future.

"What do you do for work, Charlotte?" Amaria asked.

"I'm a cleaning maid at Bria Hall." Charlotte smiled slightly, as if to seem unthreatening.

Amaria nodded again. She looked over at Theodmon and he gave her a small nod. They would recruit Charlotte later. An illusionist was an invaluable tool—to be able to change perceptions, even short term could be the difference between a successful or unsuccessful intelligence mission.

"Do you live in the city?" Theodmon asked.

Charlotte nodded, not meeting his eyes.

"Good," he said, "we'll drop you off outside Bria Hall."

Wordlessly, they sat in the rolling carriage. The shades were pulled down and good riddance. Amaria had no desire to see the lower markets and the city as a whole. She barely had a desire to see Bria Hall; if not for the Ruby, she'd be content to have never entered this miserable town.

She met Henri's eyes, her stomach sinking as she did so. How could they find the Ruby now with them all together—they'd needed someone to search the castle while the rest were distractions.

"Burn me," Henri hissed, looking at Amaria and Haerdnor. "Start arguing loud enough to where our escort thinks it's legitimate and I'm the idiot who got caught in between two fire mages. Haerdnor will be bringing me to aid my burns...we will search then."

"You'll be in pain," Amaria gasped. "We don't have a healing mage...even a healer around."

"We do know basic first aid," Lucas laughed, pointing at himself, Theodmon, and Aloysius.

"I don't want to hurt you," Amaria's voice cracked, her eyes watering as she looked at Henri. She didn't like her loved ones feeling pain.

"For the Ruby," Henri encouraged, looking at the twins.

"Oh, like you're not insufferable," Haerdnor loudly said.

"Less than you," Amaria shot back, forcing herself to look away from Henri. She was glad nobody could see them, she felt as if she were about to cry over what she was about to do to him. She had done worse to other people before. But that was different; she didn't care about them. "You burned all my dolls."

"That was years ago. Are you still upset over that?"

"They were nice dolls," Amaria said.

"Buy new ones," Haerdnor said, snorting. "You'd think you were poor."

Carefully, Amaria sent a stream of fire up Henri's arm and torso, letting it burn for fifteen seconds before extinguishing it. Haerdnor sent a stream of fire from the carriage, just enough to indicate fire magic was being used in the carriage to the people outside.

"Look at what you've done!" Amaria shouted, forcing herself to sound enraged. "He needs medical aid."

Chapter Twenty-Five

T he doors to the carriage flung open. "Witches! You dare use magic?"

"He needs medical aid," Lucas said, ignoring the guards. "One of us needs to bring Henri to an infirmary at Bria Hall." He glanced over at the burnt flesh, scrunching his nose.

"Do you use magic?" A guard demanded.

"No," Lucas answered.

"You bring him."

Amaria met Theodmon's eyes. They wanted Haerdnor to go with Henri—two mages were better than one, especially a hurt one, if the Ruby was found. But they couldn't argue with the Riam guards without raising too much suspicion, and so Lucas would have to do.

"How far away are we?" Theodmon asked.

"We're here," a guard answered. "Get out."

Traffic stopped instantly and a commotion arose as they stepped outside of the carriage. The Riam guards, soldiers, faculty, and market attendees all stopped abruptly in their tracks, gawking at the lavishly dressed Thestitiunians.

"My Lords and Lady." A commander of the wall stepped forth. "I'm Commander Arthur Steele, of the city guard. I'll proceed with your escort to Bria Hall per his Majesty's law. As esteemed guests of our Court, we ask you to speak Riam henceforth."

Theodmon snorted back a chortle, clearing his throat as his mouth muscles twitched. Next to him, Lucas smirked unsympathetically. Aloysius whispered something to Liara who seemed as if she were swallowing a frog.

"Apologies, my wife's Riam is weak," Theodmon stated. Amaria forced back a smile. She would gladly use her poor language skills as a cover for whatever caused Theodmon to react that way. Perhaps it was because this man's accent was common and yet he was a knight, speaking in a way that seemed foreign.

The city guard had risen in rank. Amaria could respect that. She respected ambition.

The commander narrowed his eyes for a split second before politely replying, "A translator will be provided for the Marchioness."

"There's no need for that," Theodmon replied icily. "I'll translate for her. We need medical care for Lord Delaluna."

"How was he burned?"

Amaria's nostrils flared. She wasn't going to explicitly admit to magic—she was smarter than that. "An argument between my brother and I got out of hand. Please, bring us to court."

Amaria held her breath, forcing her eyes to remain still. This could end badly. Everything was going wrong. They had to salvage this. This was—

"Right this way, Marquis and Marchioness," Commander Steele said.

Amaria's chest deflated, her shoulders relaxing. She breathed a small sigh of relief as she looked over at Theodmon as Steele led them inside the palace and to the throne room.

Theodmon's eyes were unbreaking from hers. She saw the creases forming at the top of his forehead. She gave him a tight-lipped smile, knowing that any comfort they may give to each other would be moot. So much depended on other people playing their part. Liara didn't know why they were here. Nobody had told her the full specifics. Amaria wondered how much she suspected.

She glanced over at Liara; she was a wall of ice, frozen over with stiffness and a cold anger radiating from her every gaze, every movement. She had more of a backbone than Amaria had ever seen.

Amaria still didn't like her.

However, sensing that Liara may need some encouragement, Amaria gave her the same tight-lipped smile she had given Theodmon earlier. Inhaling deeply, Amaria brushed down the imaginary folds of her dress. There was nothing to smooth down, but she needed something to do with her hands. She felt the heavy train drag behind her, the skirts billowing with each step, showing off the intricate gold beading and stitching over the scarlet and ivory fabric.

The doors opened wide, and a voice called out, "His Majesty, King Tristan Riarl, and Their Graces, Princess Clarissa Nalaeny and Duke Liam Nalaeny, may I cordially present the ambassadors from Thestitiunia. Representing their provinces, may I welcome the Marquis Theodmon Chauvignon, the Marchioness Amaria Chauvignon, and members of their respective households."

Amaria tilted her head towards Theodmon, her mouth twisting into a wry smirk. He held out his hand for her to walk in front of him, his mouth twitching. She turned her gaze towards the throne several feet ahead of her and took the first step to walk down the aisle. She did not blink, her face morphing into an empty stare.

A collective gasp arose from the onlookers of court as all eyes fell on Amaria's outstanding gown—brilliantly crimson with all the right curves, loaded to the brim with intensely detailed stitching, ladened with meticulously handpicked jewelry and accessories, and above all, fantastically outshining every other woman's fashion in the throne room, including Clarissa. Behind her train, Theodmon had started his walk, giving her dress space to have its desired effect.

Amaria allowed herself one brief moment of expressed pleasure as Clarissa's lips curled into a disgusted, yet almost jealous, snarl.

"Your Majesties," Amaria said graciously, dipping herself into a small curtsy. "It is wonderful to be in Rindria again. Princess Clarissa, I love the designs on your sleeves; it's ingenious how the seamstresses incorporated such a busy pattern onto such a bright color."

"Why, of course." Clarissa smiled, false honey dripping venomously from her tone. "I designed the patterns myself, you know."

"How talented," Amaria remarked dryly as Theodmon stepped next to her, in turn giving the king, princess, and duke a short bow.

"A pleasure to meet you again." Theodmon delivered the greetings politely, but his tone remained cool. "How friendly the Riam people are when they are not attacking my borders."

"Not under this roof, if you'd please, Marquis," King Tristan spoke for the first time since the guests entered. He had gotten old since Amaria last saw him at her wedding—how many gray hairs had he gained in these two years? And what stress was causing him to deteriorate so rapidly?

"Why are you here?" Tristan continued.

"I'm here to show goodwill to my new in-laws," Theodmon said, his shoulders tensing.

"In laws?" Clarissa screeched. She sounded like an ostrich. She looked like one too. Amaria's mouth twitched.

"You think that's funny?" Liam Nalaeny directed.

"Never, cousin," Amaria said smoothly. She needed to buy time. She needed to reach out and see where Henri and Lucas were at. Edging on Liam with the acknowledgment that his mother was a Raulet seemed dramatic enough. It was a distant cousin, far enough from the main line, and yet, she knew Liam tried to hide his connections.

It made sense when the Raulets often manufactured famines, she supposed. The wealth Liam's mother brought the Nalaeny's did allow him to marry a princess. Amaria wondered how he balanced all of these political implications—her father never seemed to like him, calling him a dull blade.

"Explain this marriage," Tristan commanded, cutting off any of the anticipated drama.

Amaria was only slightly disappointed, deciding that this marriage announcement would likely be dramatic enough to satisfy her need for entertainment. Smirking, Theodmon and Amaria stepped to the side, allowing Liara and Aloysius to be in center view.

Aloysius stepped forward, giving a bow. "I'm Aloysius Chauvignon. I recently married Liara Nalaeny."

"You mean kidnapped!" Clarissa gave a false wail.

"She ran away," Theodmon said. "To us."

That was a stretch of the truth. However, Amaria trusted Theodmon. If anybody else went off script, she'd fear the results of the deviation. With him, she knew they would be alright.

"Why would my daughter run to you?" Clarissa said.

"I don't believe you'd want that information public, Princess," Amaria said emotionlessly. "Your actions are illegal under Riam law."

"That's a heavy accusation-" Tristan began.

Clarissa interrupted with, "*Excuse me?!* Is it illegal in *my own home* to ask why my child is affiliated with foreigners who have starved and attacked Riam lands?"

Theodmon squeezed Amaria's hand. It was time to be dramatic. Theodmon would stall. She would determine how the gem retrieval was going through her mage link.

"You've attacked my lands and made no progress in ten years," Theodmon breathed heavily, and Amaria knew he was stopping his voice from shaking and his face from turning red. "You've lost land to conquest, your countrymen have died *for nothing*, because of your stupidity and you want to blame me?"

"You're not answering the question as to why Lady Liara ran to you," Tristan said.

Amaria glared, pulling her magic back into her from where she was slightly extending it to search for Henri and Lucas.

"Dark magic," Amaria spat. "You're working with dark magic. That's illegal under Riam law, is it not? Any magic is illegal, correct?" She looked directly at Tristan. "I believe you are aware of my reputation, magical and otherwise. Before they try to weasel their way out of that one, remember that not only do I have several credible sources, but as one of the most powerful magical users in the world, I can sense magic and am sensitive to dark magic disturbances. And I believe you have had your own suspicions for a while, Your Majesty." Amaria breathed heavily, trying to keep the disdain from dripping off her tongue. She shifted her gaze to Clarissa. "Dark magic takes more than it gives, and you're a fool for thinking you are the exception."

Clarissa's eyes widened, stuttering as Tristan rounded on her, "I always felt suspicious when Liara and Tesden ran away, and Ledora was brutally killed by 'dark forces.' Tell me, how *did* that happen? Our laws against magic are strictly enforced, punishable by death on sight, so who would even possess the means and resources to even bring in dark forces, much less direct it to a designated location where Ledora just happened to be at?"

Amaria gasped. That was one of the human sacrifices that opened the Badlands that the priestess of Dandar had told her about. It had to be.

"Th-they're lying!" Clarissa blurted out. "You know their reputation, their methods. They were trained to destabilize countries from the inside and to bring us to our knees."

"If that's true, then why did your children leave?" Tristan asked.

Amaria squeezed Theodmon's hand. Chaos achieved.

"Do you know where Tesden is? Do you care?" Tristan continued.

Amaria closed her eyes, reaching out for Henri and Lucas. She knew their energy had to be somewhere. She silently pushed her magic around Bria Hall.

"I do care," Clarissa pleaded, her face suddenly heartbroken and her eyes watering. "Please, Tristan."

Amaria's magic recoiled, she had hit what seemed to be a wall made of glass shards. *"Henri."* Amaria tentatively reached out, weaving a small silver strand through a cut in the wall, knowing Henri well enough. *"Henri. Can you hear me?"*

Tristan shook his head, rubbing the bridge of his nose. Ignoring his sister's puppy eyes, he directed his gaze stoically at the Chauvignon couple. "My apologies, Marquis and Marchioness Chauvignon. As this is a conflict directly between your families and Princess Clarissa, a conflict that I was in no way privy to beforehand, I'll allow you to dedicate your investigation into whomever they possess evidence against."

"Do you want to confess?" Theodmon asked Clarissa.

"Confess what?" Clarissa feigned innocence. "I must admit, I've no clue what you're going on about, Lord Chauvignon. What are you even looking for?"

"Yes." Henri's walls became smooth and gossamer, a few leaves, flowers, and fish all floating, or maybe flying, in it. The more you trusted another mage, the more visible their magical energy protecting their mind became in the mage link. It seemed as if Amaria and Henri trusted each other indiscriminately—a good thing, Amaria supposed, considering the situation.

"What's happening?" Henri asked in the link.

"I never said a word about us looking for anything. How did you know we were looking for something?" Theodmon's eyes glinted dangerously as he homed in on her guilt, trapping her in her lies.

"Have you found the gem?" Amaria asked.

"You *are* looking for something," Clarissa recovered smoothly. "Otherwise, you would not have personally come to Rindria. Otherwise, *she* would not have abandoned her first child, a son no less, at home like the awful mother she is."

"No." Henri sounded fatigued in the mage link. *"Neither have the others."*

"An awful mother?" An enraged female voice jumped in.

Amaria's eyes fluttered open in shock, as a feral Liara, emboldened by her indignation, stepped forward, putting herself into clear view of Clarissa. "You really want to accuse somebody of that? Amaria Raulet may be a conniving, manipulative, monster but at least she's not that way to her child."

Amaria resisted rolling her eyes as she reached into the mage link once more. Such kind words.

"Do *not* speak to me with disrespect!" Clarissa reprimanded.

"Tristan will let us search Clarissa," Amaria tiredly told Henri.

Amaria felt Henri recoil, and she could imagine his eyes widening as he ran a hand through his hair. *"How? How did you manage to convince him of that?"*

"It's not disrespectful if it's true, my Lady," Theodmon stated. "Respectfully."

"I told him the truth of Clarissa's meddling in dark magic. Apparently the Raulets are much more trustworthy than anybody could have predicted." Amaria opened her eyes. *"Meet us at the throne room."*

"Respectfully, stay *out* of relations between me and Liara," Clarissa whined. Amaria saw where Liara got her attitude from.

"Respectfully, I can't," Theodmon said, his arms crossed. "She's my brother's wife and part of my house."

"As interesting as this is, we're here to talk about your ventures into dark magic." Amaria stepped forward, nodding at Theodmon. "Including your possession of the Raulet Ruby. Give it back to me."

"I don't have it," Clarissa said. "How can I give it to you when I don't know where it is?"

Amaria wanted to rip her throat out. She had the gem. She had killed Delphina with her stupidity. She couldn't even have the decency to give back stolen property after all that.

"You are as intelligent as you're beautiful," Amaria said calmly. "Nobody's truly loyal to you, and most of your captured spies talk without torture. Give me my family's gem back."

An intense silence dropped harshly over everyone in the throne room. Every pair of eyes stared questioningly, punishingly, at the princess. All awaited Clarissa's actions, holding their breath as she appeared rooted to the granite floor, her face ironclad.

The doors abruptly burst open. Caught unaware, the announcer hastily sprung to his feet as he caught sight of Lucas and Henri. "Your Majesties-"

"It's fine," Tristan dismissed. "Come down," he commanded Lucas and Henri.

Amaria turned sharply to glare at Henri as he made his way towards her. He was bandaged up—she supposed they had to do that as that was the presumed reason Lucas and Henri didn't join the group in the throne room to begin with.

"You had to have the worst timing in the world didn't you." She sourly told Henri through the mage link.

"I was supposed to know?" He replied as he stood on the other side of her, Theodmon flanking her other side. Aloysius stood next to Liara. She was similarly flanked by Theodmon on her other side. Lucas and Haerdnor stood nearby.

"Welcome, my Lords," Tristan's voice boomed once more, leaning forward with definitive fascination.

Amaria, feeling more confident, smiled dangerously as she stared down Clarissa—a lioness facing a gazelle. "Your list of defenses runs thin. Return the Raulet Ruby to me."

"At the very least then, return her to us," Clarissa hissed, dropping all façade of innocence and self-pity. Out of the corner of her eyes, Amaria saw Liara bristle, her jawline jutting out obtusely as she clenched her teeth together.

What was with the Nalaeny's apparent inability to understand marriage customs and laws? While not every country had the same laws regarding property, dowries, or marital rights, all of the nations on the continent shared one thing in common: once it was consummated, the marriage could only be dissolved by death. The option of divorce was destabilizing—marriage essentially served as a permanent alliance. Severing that permanency due to a whim would be catastrophic politically.

No noble, whether they were Thestitiunian, Morrian, Tressi, Avonnian, or Riam would want that, or so Amaria had believed before Clarissa. Amaria was beginning to understand Liara's delusional behavior now—it was a fucking family trait.

"No," Aloysius stated, stepping in front of Liara. "I'm her husband."

Theodmon's hand rested on his sword's hilt on his hip, and Amaria could tell he was analyzing a potential strategy if it came down to a physical confrontation.

"As her mother, I don't approve of this marriage."

"Oh well," Aloysius scoffed. "It was consummated. Disapprove all you want."

Simultaneously, Haerdnor snorted. "We both know that this was the best match she was going to get. You are only upset that she is marrying a Chauvignon because you didn't arrange it."

Suddenly, there was a spike of energy, causing both Amaria and Henri to clutch their ears, hearing tormented screams in their eardrums. Amaria fell to the ground, completely on her knees as she felt a wave of nausea join the pain, as if a million swords were cutting her open. Similarly, Henri's knees buckled, however, he managed to remain upright. Haerdnor and Aloysius flinched, however, they did not seem to have as severe a reaction as the other two mages.

"The gem's in this room," Amaria muttered, standing up, Theodmon helping her, holding her by the crook of her arm. "The Raulet Ruby is in this room." She looked at King Tristan. "I know my gem is in this room."

"I presume that was your magic detecting the Ruby?" Tristan asked.

Amaria and Henri, still breathing heavily, nodded.

"Go ahead," Tristan sighed. "Search Bria Hall and be done with it. I'm tired of hearing about magic. If you leave and take your magic with you, you can search every person here."

"Can you keep everyone in this room here until we finish searching?" Theodmon asked before turning to Amaria. "You think it's here?"

Henri nodded. "It's definitely in the throne room..." he trailed off, turning towards Clarissa. "Why are you so scared, Princess? You have nothing to hide, correct?"

"Nothing to hide because I've done nothing wrong," Clarissa continued stubbornly, pressing her mouth into a fraught white line.

"Then you won't mind being the first to be searched." Amaria smiled sweetly, holding out her hand for Clarissa to step forward. She turned to the king. "You did say it was alright for us to search everyone?"

"Yes, search her," Liara agreed. "Where do you think one of Amaria's credible sources came from? I witnessed you the week before I left, with that deadly mage dressed in all black. We know she gave you the Raulet Ruby for safekeeping, so give it up. You cannot win this."

Amaria forced herself not to scowl. Liara didn't give her that information, nor did Amaria need her too—she had figured that much out on her own before Liara had ever stepped foot in Thestitiunia.

"My Lady." Amaria's hand was unwavering, her sleeves hanging downwards heavily as she stepped closer to Clarissa. "If you have nothing to hide, then this search will be quick, and you will have our deepest apologies."

"I'll not be searched in such a crude manner, especially not in public!"

"Of course not," Amaria said as she forced down her rage. "We will have everyone turn and face the wall as I search you." Next to her, she heard Theodmon crack his jaw, and she knew he likely imagined breaking her neck.

Amaria imagined it too but maintained her smile. "Your Majesty, with your leave?"

"Ladies and Gentlemen of the Court, face the wall," Tristan commanded. Grumbling, the court members shuffled as they turned around, facing the wall. Theodmon squeezed Amaria's hand, as he too, complied with Tristan's directive. Only Amaria, Tristan, and Clarissa remained still.

Once the court members were all facing the wall, Amaria stepped closer to Clarissa. "You're innocent, right? This should be over soon and you'll have my deepest apologies." She grabbed Clarissa, despite the woman being nearly twice her height.

"No, no, absolutely not. Stop it!" Clarissa screamed, backing away from Amaria, her hands raised defensively.

Tristan sighed and stood up, holding his sister in place. "Make it quick, my Lady."

Amaria patted Clarissa down, pressing her hands forcefully against the skirts, searching for hidden pockets or lumps indicating she sewed something into her skirt. Amaria had hidden many things in her skirts. Amaria's hands made it to Clarissa's corset, and as she looked up, she saw a glint of gold poking from under Clarissa's neckline.

"Princess, why is your necklace tucked in?" Amaria asked innocently. "Wouldn't you want to show the world your riches?"

"My family heirlooms are mine to wear however I want." Clarissa attempted to push away from Amaria but to no avail.

"What a fascinating lie. Show me it." Amaria said. "I can forcefully tear it off, but we don't want to risk harming an heirloom, do we?"

"Fine." Clarissa reached her hands up to unclasp the hooked chain, then suddenly threw it against the tiles with all her might.

"Run!" Amaria screamed into the room at large as she ran towards the gem, pulling her energy into a ball at the center of her chest, preparing for the worst.

The court collectively spun around to several things happening at once: Tristan let go of Clarissa, who appeared grimly triumphant, and a spherical, scarlet stone falling onto the smooth granite as Amaria dove after it at full speed, her blood turning cold.

Magical gems were incredibly fragile; what wouldn't harm a diamond without magic could shatter one holding magic. And this gem, a gem older than the entire history of her family, and older than some countries, it was as fragile as sandstone. The Ruby hit the marble floor and chipped, black smoky tendrils snaking out of the break as fast as a shark chasing prey.

The inky tendons were running towards people, who backed away, screaming in panic. Amaria threw herself onto the gem, releasing a blast of her silver magical energy as she did so. The gem and Amaria herself became encased in a silver glow. However, the energy from the gem broke through her magic, and the ancient energy was clearly choking Amaria, tightening around her throat as she screamed for Henri to help her. The magic was going into her lungs, into her blood, and she couldn't think, she couldn't breathe.

A deep blue magical glow joined her as Henri used his magic to help stabilize it. Haerdnor ran towards the throne, Tristan flinching in shock as Haerdnor hurdled over it to reach the gilded box that held Tristan's crown when he wasn't wearing it. He himself was using his own magic to start the process of securing the box as he ran, and thrust the box towards Henri, who immediately used a surge of his power to complete the process. Theodmon threw Henri his cloak, which Henri used to wrap his hands in so he might grab the gem without touching it.

Henri did so, and as he pulled the gem from Amaria, it seemed as if the gem was fused to her. Amaria's hands burned as she touched it. She wanted to pull her hands off, because she had never been burned before.

But she couldn't remove her hands. She screamed wordlessly. She would die. She didn't fully say goodbye to Lysander. She didn't have enough time with him. She didn't have enough time with Theodmon.

Haerdnor shot an aggressive wave of his energy towards Amaria and the gem.

She was screaming. The dark magic was pouring into her, choking her. And then she saw nothing as she collapsed onto the floor.

Part Four

the alliance

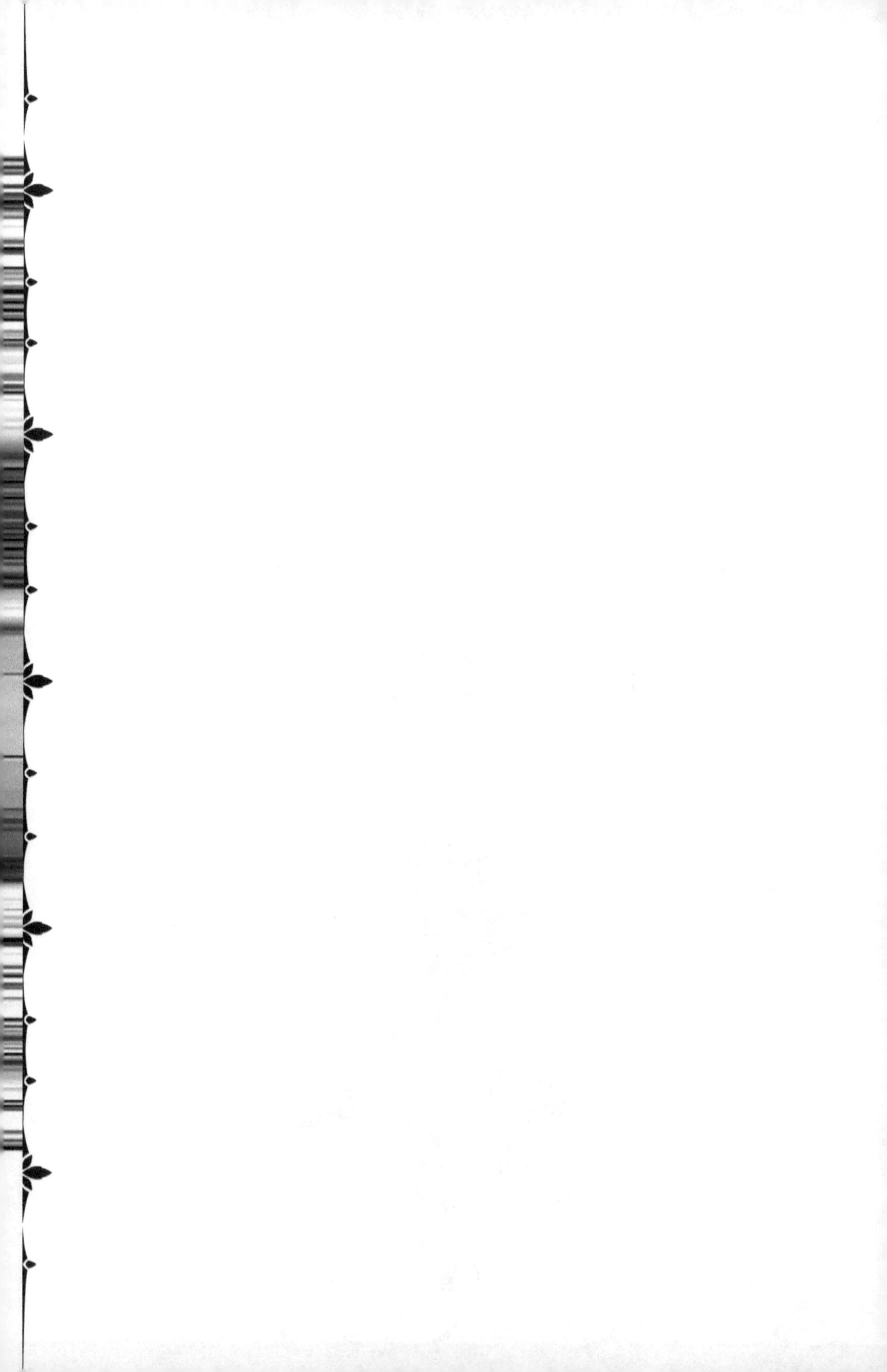

Chapter Twenty-Six

Everything was dark.

Amaria tried to scream. No noise came out. Panic rose as if it were magma and she was the volcano. She was going to die. The darkness would eat her alive. She would die— there was no way she could survive this.

And she desperately needed light.

Panicking, Amaria tried to scream again but found that she was mute. Why was she mute?

Tears now fully falling down her face, Amaria tried to summon flames. The energy sputtered at her fingertips. Amaria slammed her hand down on something in frustration. She wasn't sure what she slammed it down on, as she couldn't piece together the objects around her.

Fire summoning was a basic skill. Why was she failing?

She smelled smoke. She whirled around, being suddenly engulfed by a smoky forest, burning in black fire. How could a fire be without light? There was black smoke around the dark flames.

The black smoke parted for Amaria. Black smoke clung to her skin. She tried to brush the smoke away. The smoke hardened against her skin. Amaria summoned water. At least that skill worked.

The water bounced off the black coating.

"It's part of you," a beautiful woman said. Except, she wasn't quite beautiful. Her eyes were bleeding black blood. She felt familiar, but Amaria didn't know why. The woman held out her hand.

Amaria recoiled. She didn't want to be near her.

"Don't you recognize me?" The woman smirked. "You're one of my most devoted servants."

Amaria's stomach clenched into a knot. It couldn't be. Her mouth opened in horror. And yet, she knew it was true. The goddess of magic had made all magic, not just the magic that was good.

Ghagyn had a dark side.

"You'll wake soon," Ghagyn said. "This is a part of you. Enjoy it and your power will thrive."

"I don't want dark magic," Amaria's chest hurt, as if something was stabbing her heart. Around her, the forest faded away. She felt something warm enter her heart.

Her skin itched. She heard people shouting. There was something metallic being pulled out of her chest. Her eyes opened.

She screamed. She felt as if every bone was breaking. She felt as if her insides were melting. She wanted it to end.

Was the gem still melded to her? She realized she was on a bed. When was she moved? Above her, painted in the wood was a golden griffin. He was holding a rose in his mouth—that was odd. They had that same painting at home. A secret symbol of her and Theodmon's union. It was virtually undiscoverable unless you lay in the bed.

Why would a bed in Rindria have that?

"Amaria." Theodmon's voice became clear. She felt a rough hand press down on her hair, the other cradling her back. "Is she alright?"

"She's waking," Katerina said. "The blood worked."

The pain slowly died down. Amaria couldn't have heard that correctly. What blood worked? How could blood work?

"She's confused," Henri said. He probably read her mind. Amaria blinked rapidly. The light was bright. Too bright. She felt blinded. "We should leave her with Theodmon," Henri continued. "He can explain what happened."

Amaria's body stopped convulsing, and she collapsed on the bed. What happened? What was there to explain.

"Gem?" She said, her voice cracking. It hurt to speak. She needed water.

"Safely contained," Theodmon said. "You're alright." He hugged her tightly, his face pressed against hers. Amaria realized her face had wet spots on it. But she wasn't crying.

"Theo," she said, her throat feeling dry and scratchy.

"Get her water," he commanded. "Food too. She hasn't eaten in weeks."

Weeks? Amaria looked over at Theodmon, her eyes widened. What did he mean by weeks?

"Here." Juliette thrust a goblet into Theodmon's hands. Where did she come from? Theodmon supported Amaria's head, raising the water to her lips. She cringed at first, however, as soon as the first droplets of water rolled down her throat she gulped it down, desperate for more.

"You're safe," Theodmon told her. "We're at Fortresses les Blanche."

"Impossible," Amaria said. "We were just in Rindria."

Theodmon sighed. "Do you need help sitting up?"

"No," Amaria said, trying to force herself out of bed. She was shaking. She collapsed against the pillows. Why was she so weak?

"Yes," she amended.

Theodmon helped prop her against the pillows to have her sit up as the others in the room left. She met his hazel eyes.

"Your eyes seem gray," he said.

"What?" Amaria asked.

"They're usually a light silver," he stared at her. "It's probably a trick of the light." Theodmon shook his head. "Ammy, you've been unconscious for weeks...over a month actually."

"That's..." Amaria's heart thudded loudly. She wanted to say that was absurd, impossible even. However, how else could she be in her rooms now when the last thing she remembered was diving for the Raulet Ruby?

"Is the Ruby contained?" she repeated. She felt as if a haze was strangling her mind. Theodmon had said something about the Ruby being contained earlier, hadn't he?

"As much as it can be," he said. "Amaria, you almost died. I was convinced you were dead."

"But I'm not," she said, blinking slowly. "How? What happened?"

Theodmon's chest heaved. "After you dove for the gem, you died. Haerdnor did chest compressions on you with his fire magic, and you were able to breathe after that. Henri contained it. The Riam king has given us permission to punish Clarissa. It was chaos. Rindria is fully fracturing now." Theodmon sighed. "The prince was hit with a blast of magical energy, likely from the gem. The heir to the Riam throne is dead."

Amaria tried to swing her legs off the bed. She felt dizzy and laid down. "We should finish it then. Rindria is weak; let's take them down."

"You need to recover," Theodmon told her firmly, moving her back to the center of the bed, tucking her under blankets.

"My body is sore," she said. Her sides hurt. She was wrapped in gauze. When she breathed, it felt as if a million needles were piercing her. "Did I break my ribs?"

"Haerdnor did when trying to revive you," Theodmon hugged her, careful to avoid her healing ribs. He took a shaky breath, his tears soaking Amaria's clothing. She noticed that the front of her nightgown had been slashed open, and that her breasts were exposed, a splotch of blood on the bone in between them.

"How'd I wake up?" Amaria asked, her head splitting in two. "If Haerdnor revived me in Rindria, how didn't I...?"

"He got you breathing," Theodmon corrected. "You were dying. Nobody could save you; I even brought in Faelyn, *a healing Extractor*, but nobody could save you until a priestess of Dandar came in with your blood."

"That's good, right?" Amaria asked.

Theodmon's shoulders slumped. "No. She demanded..."

"Money isn't that bad," Amaria said. "How much?"

"She didn't demand money," Theodmon walked over to his desk, picking up a few pages of parchment that were clipped together.

Amaria's blood froze as she remembered the priestess when she had visited Dandar's Temples. "What did you agree to?"

"Unconditional protection. A signed contract with witnesses."

"No!" Amaria gasped, pulling away from Theodmon. "That was stupid! I'm not worth that. If she was asking for that, she's-"

"You are worth that!" Theodmon firmly held her by the shoulders. "We can deal with her later. You're alive."

"Will you have my father look at it later?"

Aaron had originally trained as a lawyer. He was a fourth son, so he was never set to inherit dukehood. That is, until his three older brothers died in a bloody war—the war in which Lynette became queen of Avondra. Thestitiunia only involved themselves for their sisters who were married into high ranking families as ladies, duchesses, and queens.

And Aaron had given away the robe to inherit his new place in the family.

Amaria had never asked more about what occurred. Perhaps she should have.

Theodmon nodded. "That's my plan."

Amaria sighed, sinking back in the bed. "Thank you," she gingerly said, clutching his hands. "Where's Lysander? I want to see him."

"He's in the nursery," Theodmon informed her. "I'll send for him, as well as food. Please eat first."

Amaria nodded, realizing that he had a point. She had been unconscious for three weeks, her nutritional needs surely couldn't have been met. "Can you help me to the dining table?"

"No," Theodmon shook his head. "Eat in bed. You're too weak."

She wasn't weak. She wanted to protest his words. But she couldn't. Her and Theodmon didn't lie to each other and she knew that she looked weak. She looked easily disposable. As she was now, Amaria knew she was a liability.

"Rest," Theodmon kissed her hair, gently cradling her.

Amaria tilted her head upwards, her hand moving to cup Theodmon's jawline. He moved his head downwards, his hand wrapped around the back of her head as his lips connected with hers. Her eyes closed as she returned the kiss, pushing away the feeling of her damaged, chapped lips, instead focusing on how Theodmon was gently pressing his mouth against her own. Amaria wondered how he wasn't gagging, her teeth likely haven't been brushed in weeks.

The doors opened. Perhaps Theodmon had told those he summoned to not bother with knocking. They broke away from their kiss to see servants coming in with food. Amaria immediately brought the blankets over herself, hiding beneath them as the servants laid the food on the table and a nanny entered holding a small wriggling baby.

"Bring my son to his mother," Theodmon directed. "Have a cradle brought for him immediately."

Ignoring that the blankets fell off of her, Amaria reached out her arms, awaiting the nanny to place Lysander in her arms. The nanny did so, looking at Amaria hesitantly.

"Give him to me," Amaria commanded.

The nanny paused. However she moved towards Amaria, gently lowering Lysander in Amaria's arms. He was big now.

"How old?" She asked.

"Eight months," the nanny said, handing Amaria Lysander's light blue blanket with bears and swans embroidered upon it. Amaria recognized this one—she had made it. It felt so long ago she had been sewing and knitting for her expectant pregnancy.

Everything felt more dangerous now.

She kissed the top of her son's head. "I want the world to be a safe place for you. I'm so sorry it isn't." Lysander looked at her with wide eyes.

Amaria's eyes welled with tears. "I don't think he remembers me."

"Don't be ridiculous," Theodmon said. Lysander turned his head towards the sound of Theodmon's voice, giving him a smile. "You know your mother, don't you buddy?"

Lysander maintained his semi-toothless grin. Amaria, against her better instincts, started to relax her mental barriers—she ignored a nagging feeling that something awful would occur. It felt so simple, so easy that the gem was retrieved, Clarissa was exposed, and that there was no evidence that Theodmon and Amaria had intended to destabilize Rindria to be found.

She had always been an anxious person. Paranoia wasn't always reflective of reality. Amaria tried to ignore that paranoia was the only reason she was alive. Her father had taught her how to look for hidden clues, for body language and other signs that indicated ulterior motives or nefarious purposes. She had once felt absurd in searching for hidden signs, convinced they were only there because she imagined it.

She grew up. She became skilled at her trade. She wasn't imagining threats.

Perhaps she was missing potential threats instead.

Chapter Twenty-Seven

Amaria sat at the window seat in her office, staring outside at the grounds below. Even though it was early April, there was still snow on the ground and her breath was fogging up the glass.

"Amaria?" Nicoletta sat down next to her, brushing back a lock of Amaria's hair. "Are you alright?"

Tensely, Amaria gave her a forced smile, wanting to reassure her friend that she was fine and that nothing was wrong, yet knowing she couldn't do so without it being a blatant lie.

Ever since Amaria had been revived, she felt as if there was something bubbling within her. She wanted to lash out at people. She wanted to scream at Nicoletta to go away. She was an unwelcome reminder of the past. Why couldn't Nicoletta have died instead of Delphina?

Did Amaria actually like Nicoletta? She was irritating. Of course she wasn't alright. She had died. Nicoletta should know better than to ask such a stupid question. Amaria wanted to scream at her. She wanted to hurt Nicoletta so that she would feel the pain Amaria felt. How was it fair that Amaria was dealing with so much? It would be nice to have a simple, unexciting life where her biggest concern was what she'd have for breakfast and who she would marry.

Nicoletta should have gotten herself and Delphina to safety instead of gawking.

Amaria knew she was being unfair. None of this was Nicoletta's fault. Amaria didn't want to hurt Nicoletta. She loved Nicoletta. Amaria did not want her friends to feel pain, let alone for her to be the cause of their pain.

These two feelings battled inside of her, and Amaria withdrew into herself.

"No," she sighed. "I don't know what is wrong, but I don't feel...it's not great."

"You did die," Nicoletta whispered, casting a small glance at the other ladies still playing cards.

"And you would know about death," Amaria snapped. "You watched as Delphina died. She was your friend too, I bet you didn't care."

Nicoletta pulled her hand away, her eyes welling with tears.

Amaria felt as if she had run headfirst into a tree. "Oh no," she whispered. How could she lash out this way? "It's not that," Amaria said, staring out the window again so she wouldn't cry. "It's not physical, it's not mental either. I don't know, I feel as if there's a second person inside of me. She's not a good person and I am battling intrusive thoughts, desires to hurt those I care about—and despite what I've done, I've never had any desire to hurt children or my loved ones."

A shrieking giggle sounded from behind Amaria and Nicoletta. Nicoletta's head whipped around, a frown plastered on her face. She stared at the scene of the women playing cards, giggling together. Juliette met Nicoletta's gaze, and she placed down her own cards to join them at the window.

"My magic...it feels weak, but also it feels so strong it may overpower me," Amaria whispered, a tear falling on her cheek. "I have terrible nightmares-"

Amaria cut herself off, not wanting to admit the truth. She had dreamed of Ghagyn.

Amaria could never bring herself to feel anything but respect and awe of the goddess. Ghagyn was who Amaria had chosen as a patron; it felt natural for the goddess of magic to be her patron. And Amaria valued the other staff the goddess carried: hope. Despite the world being cruel and dark and despite knowing she had caused many of the evils within it, Amaria cherished the small drop of hope that flowed within herself.

Without hope there was no humanity.

But the Ghagyn she had seen was deformed, with bleeding eyes and black veins poking through her skin. She was the version of the goddess who had made the Badlands. Amaria pushed back the thoughts she had of why she may be seeing this version of the goddess. It likely was nothing. There was no sense in becoming anxious over something so trivial.

Juliette hugged her. "It's alright. You've stood outside Lord Sadthos's gates-"

"None of this is because I died!" Amaria screamed as she pushed Juliette away from her.

She didn't need Juliette's false comforts. How could she know? She knew less than Nicoletta—at least Nicoletta had watched Delphina die with her. What did Juliette know of loss?

Immediately, the room fell silent, everyone turning to look at her. "You're dismissed," Amaria barked at the other ladies. Some ladies hesitantly started to move, looking at each other questioningly.

Amaria reached out to grab Juliette and Nicoletta's hands. Why was she hurting them? It felt compulsive, as if she had to make them feel bad about themselves in order to make herself feel better.

She knew she shouldn't feel irate with them. She knew they were trying to help. So why was she trying to hurt them?

She didn't want to hurt them.

"Stay," she said hoarsely to her friends. "I apologize…I shouldn't be cruel to you."

"We can talk after they leave." Juliette smiled at Amaria. "Some of those simpering idiots would view anything said as trivial court gossip."

"Get out," Nicoletta prompted, releasing Amaria's hand and moving to usher the other ladies out. "You're a lady-in-*waiting*, wait for further duties anywhere but this room."

The ladies sent them curious glances, yet they departed. Nicoletta coldly watched them leave.

Juliette played with Amaria's hair, talking about one braid or another hairstyle, anything to keep Amaria's mind off of what was occurring. Nicoletta watched the door shut. She turned on her heel to rush to Amaria, embracing her in a hug.

Nicoletta squeezed Amaria, pulling her closer to her. "I don't know how to support you in this, but I'm here for you. Let me know what I can do."

Amaria didn't know how she could be supported either. She wasn't even sure if she actually needed support. She was alive. The Raulet Ruby was back—chained in a gem room and bonded with magic. Rindria was weakening, and within a decade they would be a territory—that was a conservative estimate.

She was home with Theodmon and Lysander. She was safe. Protected.

She could go down to the kitchen and eat cake. Or she could find some fish or honey bear meat. Perhaps she'd eat an apple.

Life was good. She had nothing to complain about.

But she felt a sense of dread choking her. It was as if a storm cloud of poison came in the night and suffocated everyone who slept in their beds. She was scared. She was angry.

And she didn't know why.

Amaria's breath shortened as she clenched her fists. She didn't know why she felt this way. She didn't know why she was suppressing the urge to scream, to smash something breakable, to do something rash and violent. This, whatever this was, wasn't her fault.

It wasn't Nicoletta or Juliette's fault either.

Amaria returned the embrace, her face becoming wet against Nicoletta's shoulder.

"Have you talked to Katerina? Duke Laurellanza is here too, is he not?" Nicoletta suggested.

Faelyn had arrived as she had woken up. He had fretted over her but determined that there was not much to do other than rest.

"Have you talked to Henri?" Juliette asked.

Amaria's throat constricted. Henri's true magic wasn't reading minds, just as her true magic wasn't being heat resistant. He could alter thoughts, change memories, and even control someone's actions through their mind. Henri rarely used his magic. Amaria knew he wouldn't harm her with it, but she could not ask him to change her mind especially when she couldn't pinpoint the exact issue.

"No. I don't want that."

Juliette nodded, squeezing Amaria's hand once more. "It should be spring soon. We should plan an outing."

"We can go to the lake. Or what about Theodmon's hunting lodge near the waterfalls?" Nicoletta said.

"Lysander would like the waterfalls," Amaria said. "I wouldn't mind an intimate gathering there."

"I'll give your other ladies the invite," Juliette said dryly. "Nosy idiots."

Amaria gave a watery smile, chuckling genuinely. "Thank you. Thank you both." She moved over to give room in the window seat. However, it was narrow, and while Nicoletta or Juliette could have sat there with Amaria, albeit with a tight fit, it was insufficient to host all three of them.

Amaria didn't want to be alone, despite the discomfort. She shifted, tilting her hips slightly to give the others more room.

"Why don't we go to the couches?" Nicoletta suggested. "I can braid your hair if you would like?"

"I'll heat the tea," Juliette helped Amaria stand up, guiding her to the couches. "Water magic is useful." She winked at Amaria, obviously trying to cheer her up. It didn't work, but Amaria appreciated the effort.

She wished she knew why there was a herculean effort needed to cheer her up. Nothing should be wrong, nothing was wrong. And yet, she felt stifled, as if she were trapped and bound in an ever shrinking cage.

She was a pig for slaughter, and she didn't know it. Amaria felt stupid for believing this; it was a paranoid and asinine thought. Nothing was wrong, and she needed to relax.

"I'd appreciate that," Amaria told them both sincerely. "I can also braid your hair, or Juliette can braid yours and I braid hers?"

She needed to make amends for earlier. Amaria didn't want new friends but that didn't mean she needed to destroy her already existing relationships. Nobles were all interwoven, and the last thing she needed was a negative reputation. Anyways, she liked Juliette and Nicoletta.

"I'm sorry...I don't know why I'm acting this way," Amaria sighed, hugging her knees as she sat on the couch.

"We'll figure that out later," Nicoletta said gently, sitting on the couch. Amaria sighed, gently laying her head on Nicoletta's lap.

So much of Amaria's relationships had felt shallow, surface level politeness at best. She supposed it was best, there was no need for vipers and foxes to marry. She knew that perhaps her relationship with Nicoletta could appear shallow—it once had been. Nicoletta was an assigned lady-in-waiting, for what five year old was given a choice on her ladies? It was made to appease important families and whatnot.

Amaria sighed, relaxing as Nicoletta's hands wove through her hair. They had eventually grown closer. Amaria appreciated Nicoletta's dry wit and her fierce loyalty. Amaria was loyal too. She loved Nicoletta.

She didn't know why she was having intrusive thoughts to the contrary.

And Juliette. Amaria's eyes drifted over towards where Juliette crouched at the coffee table, meticulously heating the water to a boil as she dropped a pack of mint, hibiscus, and orange in a cup. Juliette was like a hummingbird: fragile looking but fiercely strong in her own way. Amaria respected that. And Juliette was likable. Funny. Amaria had grown to consider her a friend over these past two years.

Amaria did not wish ill on her friends. Or so she had thought until today. She would need to speak to a healer, perhaps dying and being revived had affected her more than she would have liked to admit.

Amaria closed her eyes as Nicoletta ran her fingers through her hair. It felt nice, comforting even, but she couldn't relax. Her muscles felt tense, wired, as if ready to run.

"Thanks," Amaria said after a few minutes. She sat up to drink her tea. Perhaps that would calm her. Juliette had pulled out a book, and was curled in a chair reading.

Juliette looked upwards. "Are you okay?" She asked.

Amaria shook her head. There was no sense in worrying them with the truth. She didn't know if she was okay. Amaria wasn't sure she had ever been alright, nor if she ever would be.

"I'm fine," she lied, laying back down on Nicoletta's lap. "The tea is good, thanks."

Amaria heard Nicoletta blow air out of her nose, and Amaria knew she was scoffing at the obvious lie. Thankfully, she said nothing more as she spread out Amaria's hair over her lap and began adding a multitude of intricate braids to it.

Amaria wished she could pause this moment in time. She wished she could fast forward time to where she no longer felt as if a hurricane was whirling in her. She wished she could go back in time to prevent the Raulet Ruby killing her. She wished she could have prevented it from being stolen. She wished she could go and change so many things.

Unfortunately, she was rather useless in that regard.

Chapter Twenty-Eight

The scent of burning forests filled Amaria's nostrils. Around her, the Westerlands were on fire, as were Perivina Fluere, Morroek, the Faerie Lands, and even the Hydras and Dragons Isles.

She was seeing everything and nothing all at once.

A smoky black tendril circled her. Her breathing became shallow and she tried to burn the black tendril off herself.

It failed.

She tried to use air to push it away from her.

That failed.

Screaming, she forced a vine to grow, hoping to wrap the plant around the shadow and to thrust it away from her. The shadow seemed to taunt her as if she was stupid for thinking she could fight ancient dark magic as a puny human.

"Amaria," a powerful and booming, yet soft and musical voice said, breaking across the stormy sky. Amaria's heart stopped, the black magic was pushing itself down her throat and nostrils.

"Wake up!" Lightning crashed in the sky, and in the brief illumination she saw the star covered face and glowing eyes that were illuminated with every color imaginable staring at her. Amaria did not have time to wonder why she was seeing the goddess Ghagyn again—this time in her kind and beautiful form—before her eyes flew open. revealing Amaria to be in her chambers.

Next to her, a flame from the candle on her bedside table flickered. Amaria breathed heavily, her heart still pounding. She was in her chambers. She was safe.

Amaria turned her head to her other side and saw that the bed was empty, its sheets tousled and thrown off. Swinging her legs off the edge of the bed, Amaria's feet shakily hit the fur rug on the floor. Something must have happened. What was happening?

Her legs wobbling under her, Amaria slipped on her slippers and pulled on a robe, holding the candlestick in her hand as she moved towards the entrance of her room. Cautiously, she slowly pushed open the doors, fearing she would see what had occurred when the Raulet Ruby was taken from Provincia Palencia. She had few friends, and she didn't need another dead one.

"Marchioness?" A guard stated, jolting Amaria into reality as a draft from the hallway hit her.

"Where's my husband?"

"There were scouts that came back late in the night. They had information," the guard's eyes darted around the hallway, before leaning towards Amaria. "If you asked me, they seemed possessed, almost as if they were under some sort of mental haze or spell."

"Henri is with Theodmon?"

"Yes," the guard said. "It will be alright, my Lady. Go back to bed."

Amaria turned her head to look back into the dark but warm chambers. It seemed so welcoming, but if this was a trap, perhaps she should help Theodmon. She had magic, it was as powerful as it could get from any human. If these scouts were possessed or controlled by another mage, it would be her responsibility to deduce who the controlling mage was and to save the scouts from their prison if possible. She looked into the hallway once more.

She sighed, turning around, nodding towards the guard. Lysander was sleeping in here, and she would not leave him alone in a dark room.

Slowly, she made her way to Lysander's cradle. In the soft glow of the candle, she stared down at him. There was drool crusting around his mouth, his tiny arms were thrown above his head, and one foot was peeking out from under the blanket.

Lysander. The thought felt like a warm summer breeze embraced her. He was perfect. Innocent. Pure. Everything she was not. Everything she had wished to be once. Her hand lightly brushed over his head, her fingers dancing over his wispy brown hair. She hoped that he would be like his father in personality. She hoped he would gain her magical ability.

She leaned down to kiss Lysander's head, her lips lightly brushing against his forehead.

Amaria would burn down the entire world for him.

"How sweet."

Bristling, Amaria's hands instantly summoned flames as her spine went rigid, her head snapping towards the unfamiliar male voice. She wasn't dreaming anymore. Her body was too tense, her skin too cold. That never happened in her dreams.

"Who are you?" Amaria asked, her voice shaking. The fear encompassed her and her skin prickled.

She wished this was a dream. She wished she could believe it was a dream—it would be easier to push through the fear if it was.

"Marchioness," the man said mockingly as he evaporated in the shadows, appearing next to her.

Immediately, Amaria extinguished her hands, knowing the light would give him more shadows. He was a shadow mage—a shadow shifter—and shadows were his weapon. He worked in the darkness, but he needed some light to be effective.

Her throat constricted as she stood in the pitch black room. Her stomach was in knotts; she wanted to vomit, she wanted to scream. She couldn't afford to show her fear now. Not with Lysander in danger.

"Leave," she snarled, pulling the moisture in the air towards herself, turning it into water.

The man laughed.

Amaria threw a shot of ice towards the sound. Her bedpost was covered in frost.

"I was told you would be weakened," the man said. "Perhaps I should take this child instead. Lysander Chauvignon may be a more valuable hostage anyways."

"I'll kill you." Air circled around Amaria.

"You'd have to find me." The man was now behind Amaria, grabbing her by the neck. She thrashed against him, attempting to call for help. She used the force of the air accumulating to come upwards and separate him from her, and to then fling his body across the room from Lysander.

Stupidly, desperately, she ran towards the shadow shifter, wanting him to be closer to her. Anywhere was better than near her son. "Help!"

These doors are thick, but they weren't thick to where the guards couldn't hear her screaming. Where were they?

She directed her focus on the shadow shifter, planning to extinguish the life from his lungs. She watched him choke. He smiled as hatred flared in her eyes. And then he disappeared in a single breath.

"What?" Amaria gasped, her magic faltering. Her head whipped around the room, locking her eyes on Lysander's cradle. He should have died—how did he escape?

Behind her, a calloused hand wrapped over her mouth and she was pulled against the shadow shifter with an adamantine grasp. "Mhmm, you're clever," he hissed in her ear. "I see why the queen wants you."

Lynette. That was the only queen who would have the power, resources, and motive to do this. Amaria tried to bring her foot up to kick him. He thrashed, perhaps the most she did was stomp on his toe. She knew that she would die if he took her out of this room. Perhaps he will kidnap Lysander too.

Amaria screamed. Her throat was raw as she bit down on the shadow shifter's hand. She tore at his flesh with her teeth, using summoned fire to burn his other hand, and he momentarily let go of her. She ran, trying to reach the decorative spear that was against the wall near the fireplace. She did not know how to use it, but she had been feeling drained, as if there was a black cloud of mage fatigue waiting to take her.

Behind her, the shadow shifter cursed, before lunging after her again. She had almost reached the spear when he caught her, blood dripping from his hands.

Shadows. Shadows. Amaria thrashed against his hold, screaming. Where were the guards? Why weren't they coming to help her? He moved in the shadows. Light sources themselves don't have shadows. It's only the area around them that does!

Amaria moved her energy to the center of her chest, releasing it in a ball of explosion as she set herself on fire. Now it was her turn to grab onto the shadow shifter, holding him tightly so the flames would remain on him. The smell of burning flesh filled the room as he screamed and withered in pain.

She heard shouts and clangs in the hallway. She narrowed her eyes on the pathetic, withering, burning man in front of her. She felt a surge of power come over her—it felt...different than her normal magic. But it was powerful. Amaria liked power. Power would let her protect herself and her family. This man, this swine, had threatened Lysander.

Anger coursing through her, she increased the intensity of her magic and the heat of her flames. The man was dead; this was entirely unnecessary. However, it felt good.

Amaria threw her head back, laughing. She would burn the world down to protect Lysander. This man was the first one. Nobody would hurt her child.

As she manically laughed, the doors burst open, Theodmon and Aloysius stepped over the guards. Amaria briefly saw the red stains on the floor of the hallway as she turned to face them, still holding onto the blackened skeleton of the shadow shifter. She was naked, her dress was ashes at her feet, and yet she didn't feel exposed.

Exposure was vulnerability. How could she be vulnerable now when she felt power running through her veins?

Her eyes unblinking, still laughing uncontrollably, Amaria met Aloysius's eyes. Immediately, his eyes widened as he met hers, stepping away from her. Aloysius's hands raised slightly in front of his chest as he looked at Theodmon hesitantly, as if waiting for instructions. Theodmon's face dropped as he stared at Amaria's face.

"What?" The fire ceased, and Amaria stood naked with nothing to shield her from the horrified looks of her husband and brother-in-law.

"Your eyes," Theodmon muttered as he rushed forward to Amaria. "I know it's not your fault, and I love you-"

"What?" Amaria's voice shook. "What's wrong?"

"Amaria," Theodmon sounded as if he were delivering a eulogy. "Your eyes are black."

As if an invisible fist punched Amaria in the chest, she doubled over herself, sobbing, before her knees hit the ground. That's where the sudden and unfamiliar surge of power came from—dark magic.

Her body shook as she curled up in a ball, Theodmon sank down to the ground next to her. He embraced her, kissing the top of her hair, saying something Amaria could not understand through her wailing. All she could process was that if her eyes were black, then she was not a mage. Not anymore. For the first time in her life, the slur used against all mages by Riams and Morrians was true.

She was a dark mage. Her magic was dark.

Theodmon told Aloysius to leave, gave him some instruction or another, Amaria did not know. Everything felt as if she were underwater. She could not process anything other than the pain and the knowledge of what occurred.

But the dark magic couldn't be as bad as rumors made it out to be. She had dealt with dark magic—dark magic had killed her mother. But dark magic couldn't be bad. After all, it had helped her save Lysander.

Amaria threw the skeleton of the shadow shifter on the floor as she screamed.

Chapter Twenty-Nine

Amaria paced her chambers, her bare feet sinking into the plush carpet before scratching over bare stone. Outside, there were new guards. There were also mages, some clearly visible and some covert, with the express purpose of protecting her. *Protection.* It was all she could do not to scoff. She was essentially on house arrest—it was for her own protection, but it was still house arrest.

She had dark magic—she hadn't willingly sought it out, but she had it. And since the dark magic came from the Ruby, it was powerful. She was more powerful than she had ever been and she was locked up because of kidnappers and the fact dark magic was a capital offense.

Amaria had been locked in her rooms for weeks; the snow had thawed, and she could hear the pitter-pattering of the April showers outside of her windows.

Rage simmered below the surface of her usually calculated composure, rage that was easily visible now that her irises glowed midnight whenever she dared to use her magic. She hated the color, the dark magic, the sense of control slipping through her fingers like an hourglass full of sand.

Amaria missed Delphina. They used to lock themselves in her rooms for hours and gossip. Amaria's hands shook. She couldn't do this now, not when she was holding on to reality by a singular fraying thread.

She clenched and unclenched her fists, repeating the motion while loudly exhaling to concentrate on her self-control. Amaria would not allow the darkness to consume her. She was who she was, and she was too stubborn to budge against even some of the oldest and most vile magic known to humanity.

The Extractors who could help her and her father found out immediately, of course. Plans for Cleansing were already in motion, which meant Amaria had nothing to fear, or so she told herself. The Cleansing will work, and she'd be herself again.

It *had* to work.

The door opened and she whirled around, a flame flickering from red to black in her palm. Amaria stared at her palm in horror. She had never summoned a black flame before. She hadn't even thought that was possible.

Black was a physical manifestation of dark magic. She knew that.

And ice held black magic.

Amaria paused, wondering where that thought came from. And she knew, even though she didn't know how, that it was a fact.

Was she even in control anymore? The flames grew in her hands, angry and hot as a summer bonfire when oil was thrown on it by a prankster.

"It's me," Theodmon gently said.

Amaria forced herself to breathe, thinking of the sea, calming her heart beat. "I had to make sure," she said as the flames died down.

"I know." Theodmon sat down on the sofa, his chest heaving into itself. "Faelyn and Elena have arrived; they will rest for a day before starting your Cleansing-"

"What if we hid I had dark magic?" Amaria interrupted. "I'm powerful. We can protect Lysander-"

"Faelyn and Elena already know," Theodmon said. "Just…try the Cleansing. If it fails, it fails."

"And if it doesn't? Will the emperor show up to execute me himself or will he just order someone else to?" Amaria's upper lip curled. She quickly turned her head, aghast. She shouldn't show such contempt for Aion, even here it was criminal to outwardly despise the emperor.

Why should she care though? The weak shouldn't rule. That's why they attacked Rindria and Morroek. Aion had sanctioned those attacks. He agreed that those unfit to rule shouldn't. Perhaps they should follow his philosophy and remove him.

It would result in a civil war. These types of things were always bloody. Amaria didn't care. She was tired of Aion's mistakes. Besides, her father did most of the actual ruling anyways. Aion just fucked things up whenever he needed to act on his shallow self-inflated ego.

Like the whole notion of an Extraction for any offense that might hint at dark magic. And then to add an execution on top of it? Amaria's mouth twisted in distaste. Aaron had told Aion this was an inefficient idea, only showcasing cruelty and an inept ruler—this policy of combining the two punishments would only breed anger and strife against the emperor.

Her father was correct. But did Aion listen? Of course not.

"Unfortunately," Theodmon said, a slight hint of annoyance in his tone. Although he concealed his distaste towards Aion better than Amaria did, she knew he felt the same way. She had never dared to admit this to herself before, but deep down she has always understood that the majority of the Thestitiunian Court merely tolerated the emperor because he was emperor. To show weakness would invite civil war.

And it didn't take a genius to figure out who the victor would be.

Amaria wanted this war to happen. She wanted to dispose of Aion. Incompetent fool.

What if Father ruled? Or Theo? The Chauvignons were the first Emperors; they had only stepped down to broker peace between humans and the faeries. He'd have a strong claim. Anyone else besides Aion and the Archambeau's—and that's only because their ruler was a child—would do a much better job at this point.

Amaria took a deep breath, her lungs expanding as if they were a large balloon. Why were they tolerating Aion? Stability was the official argument, but there had to be something else. What if she ruled alongside Theodmon. She turned to tell him her thoughts as he wrapped an arm around her absent-mindedly.

"I have a plan," he said.

"To get rid of this dark magic?" Amaria's slightly tilted away from him. She wasn't sure if she wanted to get rid of the dark magic yet. She wouldn't want to keep it forever, but for now, it could be useful.

"Not exactly." Theodmon sighed. "But a way to weaken Lynette without her being able to pin it on us."

"I'm intrigued." Amaria tilted her head upwards to meet his eyes.

"King Tristan already gave me permission to do with Clarissa what I wished. It would be a shame if someone were to jump the gun, leaving Chauvignon lettering or insignias behind, framing us for the untimely and ghastly assassination of Princess Clarissa Nalaeny."

Amaria tilted her head slightly sideways. "Rindria will likely not take the use of assassins well, especially after the king granted you...they'd take it as a slight that you don't trust them to follow through. That you see Rindria as dishonorable."

"But we were framed," Theodmon repeated. "We would never act in such a dishonorable manner. Remember, Lynette has offered us an alliance in her letter. Before Clarissa dies, let's cement that alliance."

"Rindria will attack." Amaria's mouth twisted upwards.

"The Westerlands will ask our ally for help. If Lynette honors the alliance, well, she's attacking her now-former allies in Rindria."

"And if she doesn't?"

"Then we make our alliance with Morroek public and attack Rindria and later Avondra with the combined might of our two nations. She broke an alliance; it's warranted."

Amaria kissed Theodmon. "That's convoluted," she breathed as she sat on his lap. "Convoluted enough that it may work."

"Lynette's already on her way here." Theodmon pulled her closer on him.

Amaria smiled almost wickedly, savoring the revenge that Lynette was on the cusp of falling for, a revenge that they'd win no matter what choice she made. She wanted to trap Lynette, and she didn't care if she hurt herself in doing so—collateral damage was acceptable as long as Lynette suffered. Amaria remembered stories of how foxes, or maybe it was a bear, chewed off their own paw to escape a hunter's trap.

Amaria would do anything to have Lynette do that. There was a small problem, however.

"She's a seer, have we accounted for that?" Amaria asked.

Theodmon smirked. "Outside this room I have several seers conducting magic, as well as Henri altering their thoughts and visions. Lynette's magic will hopefully be confused to not see this strand or to view it as weak and unlikely."

Amaria hugged him, her heart swelling as she watched her husband. He was clever.

"Do you think that will be enough, letting her own arrogance underestimate this strand?" Amaria still had to ask. Everything had to be accounted for.

"She's shown that pattern," Theodmon said. "There's no reason to believe she would do otherwise."

"And there're plans to hide these strands we're actually planning as we meet her?" Amaria was being neurotic. She knew that. It still was essential to be this way.

"Ammy," Theodmon chuckled. "We're offering to help each other, as she offered in her letter. An alliance, no concrete plans yet. She is a powerful monarch, who wouldn't want an ally in that?"

Amaria smiled, her teeth almost barred. She couldn't wait to watch Lynette Edrion destroy her own life. There was something poetic about it—she destroyed others and so she would continue that modus operandi to her own destruction.

Theodmon kissed Amaria's head lightly. "You should prepare for your Cleansing. I think Faelyn and Elena are ready for you."

Amaria's stomach clenched. She didn't want to prepare for that. She wanted to throw herself on the ground and scream. She could run away. She could attack Elena and Faelyn.

Instead she nodded. She had more manners and sense than to act so childishly.

"I'll send out the assassins," Theodmon said, his lips still brushing the top of her hair. "If all goes well, in a month Clarissa Nalaeny will be dead."

Chapter Thirty

S unlight poured through the stained glass, innocently illuminating the bath house. Amaria couldn't believe it was spring already. She had expected it to be winter still, she didn't understand how she lost months of her life.

Amaria's bare feet touched the chilly stone as she joined Elena and Faelyn, shivering as she approached them, desperately trying to not look at vividly green water as a lump formed at her throat.

A Cleansing was the only way to remove dark magic without completely destroying the person. It was a complex and painful process—or so she had heard. Amaria had never had a Cleansing before. And she wasn't a healing mage or energy manipulation mage—it took extremely powerful mages with those specific powers to be able to do a Cleansing. To her knowledge, only three mages in the known world were capable.

"This will be painful," Faelyn said.

"How long will it take?" Amaria steadied wrapped her arms around herself, cautiously looking over to both Faelyn and Elena.

Faelyn was a healing mage, an Extractor. Elena was another Extractor, but with energy manipulation magic. Amaria hoped they could fix her.

But what if they couldn't?

"Long." Elena's foggy eyes seemed to glance over Amaria. Amaria knew she was imagining that because Elena Marion was blind. "You have an immense amount of raw power. You haven't used your magic since your attempted kidnapping, so it is ready to be used; and your energy, while not fully dark, is heavily corrupted. This will take several sessions over at least a week, potentially longer depending on how weak your body gets."

"You will also be continuously under the influence of le sedaifa amagida fin," Faelyn said apologetically, preparing a vial to insert into Amaria.

Amaria shuddered as she looked at the bright pink liquid that sloshed against the vial. Le sedaifa amagida fin was made to cause immense amounts of pain—it was used in Extractions, for gods' sakes. And Cleansings were a warning to wayward mages to not go any further in corrupting their magic.

Cleansings weren't a favor, Amaria realized. They were a condemnation.

"You're incredibly powerful and your magic will fight back," Elena further explained. "I've fortified this room with my energy so your magic cannot escape. Additionally, only Faelyn and I'll be around you until the procedure is complete."

"So I'll be in pain from the le sedaifa amagida fin for at least a week?" Amaria asked apprehensively as Faelyn wiped her arm off with a small, bitter smelling rag.

"Oh worse," Faelyn gravely spoke as he inserted the concoction in her arm. "The le sedaifa amagida fin is the least painful part of this."

"What?" Amaria's voice rose an octave, shaking. As she did so, Faelyn pushed her roughly into the water below, her face hitting it first. Screaming in pain, Amaria withered, feeling as if her body was being lit on fire and she had lost some of her natural resistance to flames. Her head bobbed in and out of the water, and she felt her energy trying to escape her but being forced back into her by some invisible force. As she fell under the green water again, she choked, her lungs filling up with the liquid. Amaria thrashed, desperately trying to use her magic but feeling her life force beginning pushed back inside her. Her eyes burned worse than her body now, and she felt herself sinking to the bottom of the stone basin, feeling more lightheaded.

She was convinced she would drown. A haze took over her mind, and she knew the le sedaifa amagida fin had hit her system. Her energy was dying down in force, and in the back of her mind, she heard a calling—not a voice but rather an idea—telling her that resisting was fruitless, and she should just give in to the pool's wishes and obey.

Obedience is why she was here. Amaria's mind briefly flashed with the sour thought. She was good at obeying orders. She was a good wife, a good daughter, and a good subject. She—

Pain ground her bones. She felt as if acid was on her skin. She screamed, wanting to pass out. It seemed as if the substance knew this, as the pain stopped only slightly enough to where she was no longer seeing black.

Of course she had to be conscious during a Cleansing. It would be too simple otherwise. Amaria ground her teeth, part in anger and part in pain. Around her, her body glowed green and lavender—Faelyn and Elena's magical auras. She shut her eyes, feeling nauseated. She tried to ignore the forceful feeling of someone pushing aside her internal organs and taking her energy and splitting and twisting it. She was screaming, she knew she was screaming although she felt like a stranger in her own body.

Amaria hated this process. And worse, what if she did this process for nothing? What if her magic was still dark after this? Painful, full body sobs wracked across her entire body.

She smelled mint. "Sleep," Faelyn whispered as a green wave overtook her, forcing her body to be rendered unconscious.

Faelyn reached out his hand to Amaria as she waded out of the pool, the substance clinging to her. "Take my hand."

"Did it work?" Amaria gasped as Faelyn helped her out of the basin, Elena quickly throwing a towel over her.

"Your magic is still dark," Elena said. "It didn't change much, but we'll slowly lighten it with this process."

Dark magic was like dirt. If you scrubbed dirty hands hard enough, they would eventually become lighter, cleaner. That was how Amaria interpreted the Cleansing process. She had asked once, but she didn't fully comprehend the healing magic and energy manipulation magic required. Amaria was good with burning things, using wind, manipulating water and earth, but healing a human being, absolutely not. Still, she knew enough to know the Cleansing failed.

"It didn't work then." Amaria pushed the towel off her, her eyes welling with tears. Why was she crying? She could keep her dark magic, wasn't that what she wanted?

No. She had a choice: she could fight the dark magic or she could accept it. She didn't want this choice; she wanted something to be easy. She wanted to be safe without having to make a hard decision once again.

Her entire life she had made difficult decisions. Was it too much to ask for one hard choice to be made for her?

"There's still a lot left of the process—" Elena said.

Cringing, Amaria shut her eyes. "How often does the first cleansing not lighten the magic significantly the first time?"

Elena and Faelyn were silent, only casting each other a glance. That was the only answer Amaria needed on how this process was going. She knew the answer in her soul, the dream with Ghagyn—both versions of Ghagyn had confirmed it for her.

Faelyn and Elena's reaction only further vindicated the sinking pit in her stomach.

"I'm going to change, please leave," Amaria said.

"Amaria—" Faelyn started.

"Leave!" Amaria screamed at him, her voice cracking. "I want to be alone, please." She clenched her fists as her lower lip shook. Invasively, she heard her father's voice in her mind. *An inability to control your emotions is weakness. Do you know what happens to people like us when we are even perceived as weak?*

Amaria bit her lip, turning her back away from Faelyn and Elena as the tears openly fell down her face.

When you are weak your head ends up on a spike.

And, executions occur for those with dark magic. Whether because of her perceived weakness or her magic, she must die. Perhaps she could hold on, do what she could to help Theodmon and her father to stabilize things, to get them closer to having control over Rindria, the dark magic, Lynette, and the Badlands, but that didn't change the truth.

She must die soon.

Amaria collapsed to her knees, sobbing. Faelyn rushed to her side, cradling her as he sat beside her mummering false comforts. She knew she was not alright. She knew that this situation was not going to correct itself.

She was doomed. And yet, she did not have the heart to correct Faelyn with the reality they both knew. If they didn't acknowledge this ugly truth, perhaps the beautiful lie could be forced into existence.

She would live. She'd grow old with Theodmon. She'd banish the energy from an ancient gem so her magic would not be dark anymore.

The lie was not one of her more believable ones.

But what if she wasn't entirely lying? She would live. But she wouldn't banish the dark magic—she'd keep it, let it grow, and use the dark magic to protect herself and her family.

And if anybody tried to kill her, she'd make them regret their entire miserable life.

Chapter Thirty-One

"A mmy," Theodmon brushed back her hair that was laid over the pillow. Amaria groaned, pulling her arms over her face, shading it from the sunlight pouring in from the windows.

"It's too bright," she grumbled.

"It's two in the afternoon."

"Cleansings take a lot of energy out of you," she turned over to squish her face into the pillow. "Especially when they fail anyways."

Just as Amaria predicted, the entire week-long process was unsuccessful despite Faelyn and Elena's best efforts. Her magic was still dark, and none of it had been successfully lightened; the magic from the Raulet Ruby was too powerful.

"We can try again," Theodmon encouraged gently. "There's another way; there always is."

"Cleansings aren't exactly a safe process." Amaria slightly turned her head, only enough so her speech wouldn't be muffled.

"I understand, my love." Theodmon slowly eased himself off the bed, extending his hand out for Amaria to grasp. "You can't coop yourself in here forever. It's been a week."

"I have dark magic and it's not even my fault!" Amaria screamed into her pillow. "I didn't even make this choice to host this *visitor.*" Disdain dripped from her voice–what an ironic understatement it was to call the dark magic a visitor. "Dark magic takes and takes until you can't give it anything else!"

And I'm not sure if I even want it to leave.

"It won't," Theodmon said. "I swear I'll do *everything* it takes to save you."

"But that's what dark magic does!" Amaria forced herself into a sitting position. "It takes from those who use it. And you have to use it if you are its host, or it'll eat you alive, well, it'll take from you sooner rather than later."

Theodmon shuddered ever so slightly at her words, a shudder that was unnoticeable unless she was paying attention, but his stony expression remained unchanging. "You can't give up, Ammy. We'll find a cure."

"And what if we don't?" She threw the covers off her, her feet hitting the ground. "I had two of the three able people try and they failed. What can we do? You know the law, Aion will have me executed. He'll take my magic!"

"The third one might work. And your father always has a trick up his sleeve."

"The third one is from Tressidil; forgive me if I don't want to let that information potentially go to other countries!"

"We have contacts in Tressidil. Couldn't they put pressure on him to not speak?"

"And if I'm cured? I don't want to walk around with the liability of someone slipping that I was a dark mage once."

"Why is that important?" Theodmon said.

Knowledge was power. Amaria didn't want someone holding that information over her. She couldn't see it impacting her now, but she couldn't see the future. The more intimate details that were known about her, the more blind spots she had.

She could only imagine how the knowledge of her having dark magic could be used against her. But could it—she already did bad things...would being a dark mage actually affect her?

Yes. There's a difference in doing bad things for a good purpose. Dark magic lacks the good purpose.

"The information could get out. Dark mages are killed in Thestitiunia," Amaria said. "I don't want to risk looking over my shoulder—"

"We could kill them and make it look like an accident," Theodmon dismissed.

"We shouldn't kill an innocent mage just because he saved my life!" Spit flew from Amaria's mouth.

"If they're foolish enough to rat us out, we will treat them as a rat." Theodmon shrugged.

"This is why people despise us."

"Then we tell the Extractors you're infected, you're looking for a cure," Theodmon rubbed his temples. "They'd have to be the ones giving punishment. Most of them don't seem to like Aion enough to turn against one of their own."

"Most of them like living," Amaria countered.

"Do you have another suggestion?" Theodmon snapped. "I watched you die. I'm not doing that again."

Amaria sighed, hugging her knees to her chest. No. She didn't have another suggestion. She knew Theodmon had a point—she just didn't know how to handle this situation. She was helpless. She had never been helpless. She had made it a point in life to always be in control of the situation in front of her, or to know and be allied with people who had control.

She had always been wielding the knife. Now she was the prisoner.

"I'm scared," she whispered. She didn't know what to do. She didn't even know what she wanted—she wanted to protect her family, but she didn't know how. Could she protect Lysander better by keeping the dark magic? Or was Lysander's best chance at protection was her separating this foreign power from herself?

"I know," Theodmon hugged her. "I'll write to the Tressi-"

"No," Amaria shook her head. "I don't want to risk that. How am I any better than this thing inside of me if I would murder those who help me?"

"Those who genuinely help you wouldn't betray you. It's business. If he keeps his mouth shut, he'd be safe."

Amaria knew that was a lie. They didn't allow others the chance to betray them when the information was that sensitive. They mitigated the liability early. Dead men couldn't speak.

"What if I don't want to betray myself?" Sparks flew from her eyes as she glared at him.

"You're being inefficient, Ammy. Is risking yourself dying to dark magic or worse not the first act of self-betrayal?"

"Don't." Tears welled in her eyes, yet she maintained her glare. "Don't you dare. You wouldn't be the one suffering."

"You think I wouldn't suffer if you died? You say I won't be the one suffering, but you're lying to yourself."

"You'd find a new wife, you'd get to keep the Raulet alliance because of Lysander, my father would protect his grandchild. You'd get over me in time." Amaria tried to turn her face away as the tears rolled down her face. Theodmon's hand tightened around her chin.

"As if any woman could replace you." Theodmon barked a harsh laugh. "As if any other woman could ever be good enough for me."

"Please," Amaria sobbed, "stop."

"If you fear dying and failing so much, why shouldn't you be able to do what needs to be done?" Theodmon tilted her chin up to look at him.

"Because maybe then I'll know that it's not the dark magic making me an awful person! It'll be confirmed that I am *actually* this depraved. That everything said about me is correct! What if I am soulless? What if I am evil?" She gulped.

"Ammy, stop." Theodmon shook her shoulders. "You're *not* evil."

"You don't know that." She sank down to the ground, her legs shaking underneath her.

"I do know. I knew exactly who you were, knew what I was getting myself into, when I married you, Amaria Chauvignon." Theodmon sat next to her, cradling her in his arms.

She looked at him skeptically, wiping her eyes with the back of her hand. "And what did you get yourself into?"

"A loving wife, a doting mother." Theodmon paused to wipe the tears from her cheeks. "Efficient. Intelligent. I enjoy having you as a spouse and my closest ally."

"You made an alliance with my father, not me," Amaria protested. She couldn't listen to his words. If she listened, she would falter. She would be forced to acknowledge the veracity of his words. She had to poke holes in the statements. "I'm just a pawn, women aren't the alliance, just symbols of it."

Theodmon shook her. "Stop it." He breathed heavily. "That might be true for most but I am willing to bet that Aaron gave you specific tasks. How many of those tasks did you abandon because you loved me?"

She could make this easy for Theodmon. She could tell him she never loved him, that she had never abandoned any task given by her father. She was a good liar.

She met his eyes. She couldn't lie to him.

Tears fell down her face, her chest racking with sobs. The dark magic surge from the Raulet Ruby should have killed her. For some reason, it didn't. The dark magic should have fully engulfed her. It didn't—not yet. She had her old magic still—it was weak and cowering in a corner. It was beaten. It likely wouldn't survive long.

But it existed.

How could any of that occur if Amaria had even been a good person? Dark magic tended to kill its host. It could take years, months, or days. She was scared. Not only of what would happen if the dark magic grew within her, but also of what her hosting it now meant for her present state and her past character.

"Tell the Extractors," Amaria whispered. That seemed to be the best route of survival. "I don't want to die."

"I swear to you, you won't die," Theodmon kissed the top of her forehead. "I'll write to them today. Rest."

"What if we can't get rid of the dark magic?" Amaria's chest tightened. "Dark mages are executed, and I wouldn't want to be trapped in a version of myself I won't know or like."

Before Theodmon could respond, a sharp knock at the door jarred both back into reality. "Marquis and Marchioness, may I make a formal announcement of visitation?"

"Who is it?" Theodmon directed.

"The lady requesting your presence is one Queen Regnant Lynette Edrion, hailing from Vorgosana, Raeria of the Kingdom of Avondra."

Amaria looked at Theodmon, her eyes widening. Lynette had the audacity to appear here? And who was she to make requests in another Lord's house in a foreign nation?

Theodmon sighed. "She did send notice...are her couriers here?"

"Yes, my Lord," the herald said. "They're adjusting to your hospitality currently."

"And the Avonnian queen?" Amaria asked.

"We're bringing her to a sitting room; she insisted she has important state affairs to discuss with the Marquis."

They should throw her in a dungeon and throw away the key. Perhaps Amaria would rob her home and kill her friends while she rotted in prison.

That is if Lynette had any friends. Who would want to be around an old putrid hag anyways? She had killed her brother—Lynette was a kinslayer. The word felt sour even in Amaria's thoughts. The gods should have struck down Lynette where she stood. All her food should have turned to ash as she ate. She should be tortured in lava.

Why did none of these happen? Amaria scowled. She loved the gods, and she respected them. But the gods had a shitty and myopic strategy in human affairs. Amaria hated the gods for that. If they were all powerful, why did they allow suffering?

Amaria closed her eyes, breathing in through her nose to clear her thoughts. This was a dangerous road to go down. There was one thing worse than treason—the worst crime that could be committed in the realm of men.

The crime was heresy.

"Ensure only the highest-ranking lady maids to serve her," Theodmon directed the announcer as Amaria steadied herself.

"Let's get dressed first," Amaria interrupted, looking at her sheer nightgown. She directed her attention back to the guard. "Bring her to the nicer offices on the third floor. Offer her tea or coffee." She sighed heavily. "Lady Juliette Bécharil should be one of the ladies. Find her and tell her purple onions with the message. Countess Nicoletta Astasuel as well."

The guard departed, the door clanging shut.

"Purple onions?" Theodmon raised an eyebrow.

"It's a discrete way to communicate." Amaria shrugged. "I don't like giving Nicoletta and Juliette orders." She forced herself off the ground, moving towards the vanity. "Gods, I look like I've been crying."

Theodmon arched an incredulous eyebrow at her but kept quiet.

"I'm being irrational," Amaria noted as she pulled a brush through her hair. "I shouldn't be, but I'm just so scared. I'm sorry."

"You are," Theodmon admitted. "I get it though."

Amaria forced back the lump in her throat as she braided her hair. "Could you get my indigo dress?"

Amaria knew that Lynette Edrion wanted to be a ruler. That was fine. However, Amaria would not be intimidated in her own harm. If that is what this bitch queen wanted to do, she would be sorely mistaken.

Two could play at power games.

Chapter Thirty-Two

"Good day to the pair of you, Marquis and Marchioness," a deep, clear female voice greeted when the Forteresse les Blanche office guards pushed open the door for Theodmon and Amaria.

"Your Majesty." Theodmon nodded curtly. "It's an honor."

"The honor is mine, Marquis Chauvignon." The Avonnian queen didn't bother to stand up, electing to stir her delicately fine china cup of tea as she eyed him intently. Behind her, Juliette and Nicoletta cast each other a glance.

"Welcome to Forteresse les Blanche, Your Majesty." Amaria smiled sweetly, her voice edged with a hint of irritation.

And why in all of the gods's names was she in Amaria's home? Amaria knew why. Politics.

What a presumptive reason. Why was Lynette actually here? Was there another mother to kill? Was Illyana Raulet not enough for Lynette?

Lynette's vert irises locked sharply with Amaria's, as though absorbing her emotions. Amaria's now dark gray irises met Lynette, and she was unflinching as she stared at the Avonnian. Lynette may be a queen in her nation, but she was not one here in Thestitiunia. She would not intimidate or disrespect Amaria, or Theodmon, in their home.

Lynette finished stirring her tea and slowly stood up, taking her time with each calculated movement. Her long black hair hung loosely down her back. There were no jewels, no elaborate braids—Lynette had power and wealth, she didn't need to insecurely flaunt her status. Unlike Clarissa, she wasn't searching for a scrap of self-importance—Lynette could stop now and still be powerful in her own right.

Despite Amaria's hatred, she could respect Lynette for that.

"We're incredibly busy, as I am sure you are as well," Amaria stared directly at her. "Please tell me why you're here, or we'll eject you. Your employees confessed to invading Provincia Palenca. You killed my friend. You'll have to forgive my lack of hospitality under the circumstances."

Perhaps Amaria shouldn't have accused her of Delphina's death. It was showing her hand too early. Amaria knew this and yet she didn't care. Why would she play nice with someone who played that dirty? Amaria was powerful and the dark magic made her more powerful. She could kill Lynette where she stood—it would save everyone the grief of kissing her ass.

Lynette clasped her hands together, adorning a perfectly practiced expression of sorrow. "Precisely why I cleared my schedule to prioritize apologizing to you in person. My agents were wayward. I would never tell them to steal the Raulet Ruby—"

"Only to spy on us," Amaria said coldly. "Apology not accepted."

Theodmon shot her an incredulous glare. She was going off script, and she knew that. What was anybody going to do about it?

"I'll accept your apology, Your Majesty," Theodmon responded stiffly and gave Lynette a small bow out of respect for royal etiquette.

"Praise be the gods." Lynette held her palm over her heart, feigning a bewitchingly believable façade of pureness. "My sincerest congratulations to your family, once more, for your firstborn. I dare hope the child is a son?"

She knew this. Amaria'a nostrils flared. Lysander was almost a year old now. The time for congratulations was past. Amaria clasped her hands together, hiding how they shook from anger. She wanted to strangle Lynette. Amaria could do it. Her magic was stronger than Lynette's. Even if Lynette saw her coming, she couldn't fight off fire. She couldn't fight off being choked to death by the air in her own lungs.

"Yes," Theodmon said. "His name's Lysander."

"Lysander Chauvignon, what a wonderful name. May he grow strong and healthy." Lynette smiled gently, then nodded to Juliette. "My cup of tea with a scone, thank you, dear."

After Juliette compiled and resumed standing next to Nicoletta, Lynette faced Theodmon and Amaria again, her expression significantly more serious. "In the interest of our children and our love for them, I, in my power as Queen Regnant of Avondra, formally propose an alliance with the House of Chauvignon, as well as Lady Amaria Chauvignon and any affiliated individuals of the House of Raulet she wishes to include in the proposed treaty."

"You'll have to make an alliance with my father for that. Juliette, would you mind bringing me a teacup? You may both sit if you wish."

"Of course, Marchioness. However, would the Marquis be interested in an alliance with Avondra?"

"What does this alliance entail? We received your earlier note, but it was not clear on what the specifics of this offer were." Amaria said, looking at Theodmon. While she hadn't seen the earlier note, it had apparently arrived while she was unconscious, she had more practice with trade deals. Although she did end up threatening most with starvation.

"The usual standard provisions: reduced export tariffs and mutually exclusive imports. Whichever products these imports may contain can be decided in detail after—"

"Now," Amaria interrupted, "if we are signing an alliance, we need the full terms of economies beforehand."

They had to play nice. The last thing Amaria ever wanted to do was negotiate over the economy with the woman who killed her friend, her mother, and had almost killed her sister. Amaria hated politics.

But torturing Lynette would be an unwise decision on several counts.

And they needed at least the presumption of a valid alliance before they manipulated events for Lynette to break the alliance; the empire could just invade, but that would be a pointless waste of Thestitiunian lives. It was better to preserve resources in conquest.

Lynette looked at Amaria and Theodmon with her eyebrows lifted. "Alright," she said. "Let's discuss."

Over the next half-hour they came to terms with trade: the Westerlands would give lumber and gems, Avondra would give steel and wool.

"Is this agreeable?" Lynette asked at the end of the negotiations.

"That's agreeable," Amaria said. "Nicoletta, will you go find a lawyer to draft this contract up?" She turned to look at Lynette. "Are our lawyers suitable?"

"Have your lawyers consult with my scribe and provide copies of each signed contract, treaty, and clause for me to bring home," Lynette instructed with a smile.

"And the military agreements?" Theodmon interjected, Nicoletta pausing at the door.

"We'll be allies-in-arms. If your municipality is threatened, we will aid. If our kingdom requests aid, you will answer. It is only fair, wouldn't you agree?"

"We cannot defend you against other Thestitiunian provinces, I am sure you are aware of the intimate relationship between the Westerlands, Lierre Fideles, Arbres Dorés, Sauvegarde Corolline, and Perivina Fluere share?"

"Of course, Marquis. We'll only call for Westerlands aid if it's a threat not originating from Thestitiunia."

"Then we agree," Theodmon said.

"Now that we are all satisfied with the economic and military details, I'd be happy to add certain bonuses to sweeten the deals. If it pleases you, Lord Vypren would be forced to publicly announce that the Lady Amaria Raulet is lawfully wedded to Marquis Theodmon Chauvignon and that he never consummated the marriage. And—"

"There's no need. My wife is already my wife; we consummated immediately and are now producing heirs together. Duke Vypren's *transaction* with Duke Raulet was legally nullified."

Amaria bit her lower lip, more so in a pretense of emotional pain than anything. Although Theodmon's blunt wording did sting a bit, she understood exactly what he meant and what he was baiting Lynette into doing: be tricked into believing she could sabotage their marriage, only to discover in the end, after everything beneficial for Westerlands was signed, that Amaria and Theodmon would always remain a united and unstoppable front.

She knew many people dreaded the alliance between the Chauvignons and Raulets and those especially well-informed or prudent feared Amaria and Theodmon specifically working together. Amaria, as did Theodmon, had guessed Lynette was in the latter camp. And they knew that Lynette would pounce on any opportunity she saw to cause discord, or better yet, tend for and grow existing seeds.

"Nicoletta, go find a lawyer please," she repeated gently, watching Nicoletta softly curtsy and depart from the room, before facing Theodmon with soft eyes and pouty lips. "My love, if it is possible, won't you reconsider? For my pride?"

"No, love. Your pride is my pride, your name is my name, and you bore a son for me, with more heirs to come. Our marriage is indisputable. Allotting time for a frivolous announcement is wasted time that we barely have enough of."

Amaria turned her face away, batting her lashes furiously to appear tearful. Lynette's eyes widened in shock at Theodmon, then morphed to sympathy at Amaria. In the corner of the office, Juliette sat uncomfortably on a lounge chair and stared hard at the floor, not yet aware that the couple were only feigning a fight to manipulate the queen.

"Marchioness Chauvignon, if I may have a word in private?" Lynette asked delicately, gazing directly at her.

Amaria gazed back at Theodmon, forcing herself to look dismayed. "I suppose," she muttered. "Uh, yes, Your Majesty. Would you like to stay here or walk?"

"Walking off the scone sounds lovely."

"Will your entourage outside the door join us?" Amaria asked. She did not want to be alone with Lynette. She also didn't want to be surrounded by Lynette's allies.

"They'll stay behind," Lynette dismissed. "I said private, didn't I?"

Theodmon puffed up his chest as he inhaled, before loudly exhaling. "Don't dally too long, Amaria."

Lynette nodded quickly to Theodmon on her way out, followed by Amaria, who shared a brief but meaningful look with him.

She could play this game as easily as the next and was twice as deadly.

A wide grin broke across Amaria's face as the door shut behind them. "I may show you the gardens, if you would like Your Majesty?"

"If you'd be so kind. Thank you, Marchioness."

As the fresh spring breeze blew strands of their hair back through the open windows in the corridor, the two ladies walked, falling into pace with each other. It was a long moment before Lynette spoke. "We remain dutiful royals in our own right, always, but right now, I'd love to be a friend to you. We are women in a world of men, and what are we if we don't raise each other up?"

"I'd like that very much."

Lynette smiled warmly at her, but then frowned in concern. "Do you enjoy being a consort, my Lady?"

Amaria blinked in genuine shock. "I'm not sure what you are asking me. Are you asking if I enjoy being Theodmon's wife?"

"Between the two of us, yes, that's precisely what I'm asking. And please don't hesitate to be honest; you are safe here."

"Of course," Amaria said automatically.

Lynette raised an eyebrow, tilting her head slightly.

"He's kind to me, and he doesn't beat me. It could be worse," Amaria shrugged. She needed Lynette to think that their marriage was shaky, but it could not be so heavy handed it was unbelievable. Amaria and Lynette were both well-mannered and trained enough to have immediate suspicion of any woman who easily slandered her husband.

"Does he love you?" Lynette asked. "Do you love him?"

"Does it matter?" Amaria lifted her skirts slightly as they descended the stairs. She knew better than to answer that question. She would not be able to effectively lie.

"You're deflecting the topic. I believe love in a marriage matters, especially in moments when you would otherwise need to hide a part of yourself from your husband because you don't trust him."

"I don't believe or particularly care for love in a marriage. I care about safety. He doesn't beat me, he doesn't stab me," Amaria paused, her eyes unbreaking from Lynette's as they entered the gardens. "I'm safe so my affections are of little concern. We're noblewomen, and despite all our privileges, love is a luxury we don't have the pleasure of when the choice of our partners is made for us."

"I'm sorry for asking about the details of your marriage," Lynette glanced away at the rose bushes in the garden, reaching out a pale finger to brush a crimson petal. "You are a rose: fully capable of protecting yourself, fierce, beautiful, and alluring. But all it takes is a fist around the rose, and you can't live your life anymore." She turned to gaze at Amaria intensely. "How safe are you, truly?"

Amaria kept her face blank as she watched Lynette's hand clenched around the rose petals, suffocating them. Lynette didn't care. Lynette didn't know her. Furthermore, Amaria was offended that Lynette thought she'd be stupid enough to fall for such an obvious trick.

The rose in the fist was such an obvious metaphor. She had hoped for something less trite from a woman said to be as intelligent as Lynette. However, perhaps she shouldn't dismiss her adversary so soon.

That was how fools died.

"All Raulets are roses," Amaria scoffed. "And safer than I would be in Avondra. Do you know what Vypren did to me when my father came to get me?"

Lynette's emerald eyes softened. "That's why I suggested that Duke Vypren apologize to you publicly and renounce his rumors against you. Sadly, your husband rejected that idea."

"My family is rich and powerful enough that those rumors are bug bites," Amaria dismissed.

"But it hurts you."

Amaria coldly looked at Lynette. "So does being stabbed. So does childbirth. Neither instance is worth trying to change. It's not in my best interests to fight against the tide for a gold coin when I have twenty coins in my pocket."

"How well will Marquis Chauvignon's best interests align with yours if it's true that you have dark magic you cannot control?"

Amaria froze, her heart thumping against her chest. Her thoughts swirled as if they were water in a hurricane. How could Lynette know? Of course, she would hear about what happened in Rindria. But she couldn't truly know? It had to be a mere suspicion.

"I don't have dark magic."

"And how long will he believe that lie?"

"It's not a lie." Amaria turned to face the rose bush, her fingers brushing over the petals, careful to avoid the thorns.

"Please, look me in the eyes and tell me the truth. Tell me you don't have dark magic."

"You know I can't do that." The words slipped from Amaria's mouth, the action felt foreign, as if her body was betraying her. She pricked her finger on the rose, bringing her finger to her mouth as she gasped in pain.

"I saw it in your eyes earlier. Your magical aura is pulsing, transforming. I also heard from King Tristan what occurred in his throne room." Lynette paused. "What you did to save everyone there was an incredibly honorable act."

"And look where it got me," Amaria scoffed. "Perhaps I should have fallen into line with the common belief about Raulets."

"Let me help you."

For a moment, Lynette sounded so sincere that Amaria was almost willing to believe her. *Almost.*

"How?" Amaria forced herself to sound guileless as she turned to face Lynette. "I don't want this dark magic. How can you help me? We are both powerful but neither of us has the magic necessary to perform a Cleansing." Amaria breathed, steadying herself for the truth. "I've had a Cleansing fail."

The best lies had truth woven through to where the true story became indistinguishable from fiction.

"Perhaps I'm powerful enough," Lynette said smoothly.

Amaria felt her energy spike—it was hot. She wanted to slap Lynette. How dare she lie? How dare she be so blatant with the lie?

"Don't lie to me," Amaria said. "We both know sheer power isn't enough for a Cleansing, you must have a certain type of magic for that. And I'd rather die than have an Extraction and live without my magic."

"Even if you cannot have a Cleansing, allow me to at least protect you physically and politically. How would the Marquis react if he found out that you, the mother of his son, will succumb to dark magic soon? What would he do? You should be more aware than most of the laws of Thestitiunia."

"Yes, it's my job to enforce those particular laws."

"It doesn't have to be that fate for you. And it shouldn't be. You sacrificed yourself to save the same people who would later be forced to report you to Emperor Aion and watch you die. What about Henri Delaluna? You risked everything to save him. Would he do the same or comply with stripping you of your identity?"

"What do you propose?" Amaria gritted her teeth.

"Return to Avondra with me."

"So you can kill me?" Amaria snapped. "No. I won't."

"You think I'll kill you by offering sanctuary?" Lynette said. "Why would I do that? If I wanted to hurt you, I'd let you die here."

Amaria ground her teeth. It was a good argument, she had used it before. She locked her jaw, reminding herself to stay focused. Lynette was attempting to trap her.

Amaria needed something to justify not leaving Thestitiunia with her. Lynette knew Amaria was intelligent, so she needed an intelligent excuse. Amaria looked down at her feet, scanning the ground, looking for some inspiration. Or perhaps an intelligent excuse and a reason to be irrational. Her hands moved to her stomach.

"I can't," she repeated. "I'd be returned immediately, and not for the dark magic."

"I am the queen, even the High Council listens to me. I assure you nobody there has the authority to return you without my permission."

"I'm pregnant," Amaria said. Her hands were cradling her stomach as if something were growing inside of it.

A horrified look spread across Lynette's face. Amaria was unsure if it was genuine fear for her life or if it was disgust at her staying with Theodmon. "Are you doing alright, Marchioness? Are you eating well? A second baby so soon after Lysander is no small feat."

Amaria resisted rolling her eyes. It was a year gap, nothing that dramatic. Not that she expected an old, childless hag to understand that. She actually wished she was pregnant again—well, she would if not for the dark magic.

Children strengthened the future of her family. And when her family was strengthened, she was too.

Children make you weak. Amaria's lip curled. She flinched. *Where did that thought come from?* She had never thought children were a weakness. She loved Lysander. Why did she just think that?

Pathetic. She thought.

Her stomach dropped when she realized she was thinking that about herself. She didn't recognize this inner voice.

Was it her new dark magic? It felt leering, as if it was a man in a story who would kidnap the maiden. Amaria clenched her jaw. How fantastical.

Shut up. She told it. She was going to use this dark magic, if she used it, to protect Lysander.

Lynette was looking at her expectedly. Amaria was tired. She wanted to lay down and not interact with the world for a month. It was exhausting being so manipulative.

"The nausea hasn't fully set in yet." Amaria chuckled.

She wanted to kill Lynette. That Avonnian bitch had killed Delphina. She had killed her mother.

Amaria despised playing nice to this hag. And she knew she hadn't been doing it well with her previous outbursts. But Lynette could not have expected an easy acceptance, so perhaps Amaria didn't damn them as much as she believed.

Amaria inclined her head toward Lynette. "Do you see my predicament?"

"Oh yes, you're stuck in between a wall and a rock," Lynette concluded wistfully. "It's such a shame; you are still so very young, and you carry impressive potential."

"You have the power of prophecy." Amaria looked at her almost eagerly, hoping this would convince Lynette of her wayward and swaying loyalties. Amaria obviously was blessed with a healthy dosage of self-serving self-preservation. It shouldn't be too unbelievable. Or so she hoped.

"Could you sense my future? If I live?" Amaria continued.

"The...future contains many branches," Lynette answered, for once, she sounded truthful. "From what I could see, there were countless possibilities where you died, often painfully. And the ones where you do survive, I saw an event that made little sense to me, so it's difficult to know what to expect."

Of course she wouldn't tell me. Amaria forced herself to look dejected, not angry.

"Please," Amaria forced her voice to crack. "Let me think about this." She brought her sleeve to her eyes, wiping away fake tears. "I'll write to you if I need your help. Is that alright? I'll have a servant bring you back to Theodmon. I apologize, but I need to be alone."

She turned on her heel, headed towards the kitchens. Theodmon would complete his half of what needed to be done. He would find her. She knew that. They were a pair, and not just as a couple. They worked well together, they were two halves of a whole unit. She had met her match in him, and she was never going to be alone as long as they were married.

She knew this.

So why did she still feel so alone?

Amaria wandered the castle to first clear her mind.

She could guess Lynette would not be weaving her lies and traps with Theodmon, pitting husband and wife against each other. Amaria hated her. She hated that Lynette was trying to turn Theodmon against her. She had something good in her life and Lynette had to ruin it.

It wasn't enough that her thieves stole from Amaria and killed her friend. No, Lynette also had to try and make her husband hate her.

Lynette Edrion was a miserable hag.

Amaria stepped off the staircase at the first level of the fortress. She walked a while before he stepped around the wall of the circular staircase in the foyer, leaning against a plain wooden door.

The door led to another corridor—everything was a maze here, intended to confuse any attackers or invaders unfamiliar with Forteresse les Blanche. As she moved down the narrow stone hall, Amaria heard the clanging of pots and the hurried voices of chefs barking out orders.

She inhaled the sweet and savory aromas as he nudged the double swing doors open to reveal a cavernous hole-in-the-wall bustling with apron-clad chefs, butchers, bakers, sauciers, and servants. As he stepped inside, a few servants noticed and curtsied and bowed. She shook his head slightly, stopping the ineffectiveness of causing the kitchen to come to a standstill amid last-minute preparations for a feast.

"Get me some oysters," she told a servant as she sat at the stone countertop. Amaria missed salt-water oysters from the warm water of the Émeraudes Sea. Freshwater oysters that the Westerlands had tasted almost stale. Amaria couldn't quite place her finger on the exact difference, she just knew it was different and she didn't like it.

The servant came back, giving her a plate of steamed oysters. Amaria nodded her thanks, picking up the lemon slice and squeezing it over the oyster. She wondered what Lynette was telling Theodmon. Maybe she destroyed the roses that he planted so lovingly to her. Probably that she was hiding a pregnancy—that corner Lynette forced Amaria into may turn out to work to her and Theodmon's benefit.

Plans were hard. They had to change consistently, to respond to new information and events, to be successful. To not adapt was to die. Amaria slowly poured the oyster down her throat.

She was adaptable. So was Theodmon.

Lynette, it seemed, was adaptable too.

Amaria had to acknowledge the problematic nature of that fact. And Lynette had powerful magic. She was a queen. This was all knowledge they knew beforehand. However, seeing it always brought reality down harder than mere words on a paper report. And some of these reports from their spies were definitely lackluster. Amaria made a mental note to deal with that deficiency later.

"Ammy." Theodmon laughed behind her, wrapping his arms around her waist, his lips brushing over her ears. "Are you sure you should be eating that, my dear pregnant wife?"

She nearly spat out her half-eaten piece. She hadn't seen him come in as she had been so engrossed in her own thoughts. Sputtering, Amaria jumped up from her seat, throwing her arms around him. "Welcome back, my love."

"How's the whiskey?" he snorted, glancing at her glass of lemonade.

"I'm a problem drinker? I've been busy in death."

Theodmon chuckled. "Apparently you have been drinking extensively since Delphina's death and have been hiding it so well I didn't know about it."

Amaria rolled her eyes. "She's overreaching."

"She's cocky," Theodmon corrected. "She also told me you were hiding news of a second child from me."

"If I am, the baby is hiding from me as well." Amaria laughed.

Theodmon stared at her seriously. "Finish eating, and we'll head back to our chambers together. Too many eyes and ears here to unpack."

Amaria took a gulp of her lemonade, washing the remnants of her meal down. "Let's go. Are we going to be angry and cold with each other as we walk?"

"No holding hands." Theodmon clipped stonily.

Amaria forced back her smile, swinging her legs over the bench. Silently she walked next to Theodmon from the kitchen to their rooms. Along the third floor he suddenly turned on her.

"Walk a few steps behind me," he hissed, loud enough for one of Lynette's attendants, who was sewing in a window still to see. "Must I remind you that you're my wife?"

Amaria's mouth dropped, and she clamped it shut as her face dropped downwards, studying the stone tiles. "Yes, my Lord Husband."

Two more flights of stairs and another hallway later, Theodmon swung open their doors aggressively, stepping in first and not bothering to hold them open for Amaria. The door thudded shut in front of her face before the chamber guards opened the door once again.

Amaria gratefully smiled as she stepped inside the chambers where Theodmon was already taking off his shoes and socks.

"Slamming the door in your pregnant wife's face." Amaria shook her head in mocking disapproval. "What did Lynette tell you for me to get that kind of treatment?"

"You can't eat those oysters at dinner tonight, as you're pregnant." Theodmon pulled off his shirt. "I feel gross after dealing with her. She obviously wanted me to say more."

"She tried to get me to admit to not loving you." Amaria too, sat down and took off her shoes.

She could never not love Theodmon. It sounded silly almost to love your husband. However, she did. And Lynette had tried to get her to betray Theodmon and herself by denying that love. Amaria's nostrils flared in anger.

"And did you tell her I was a monster?"

"I told her you didn't beat me."

"Ah, I was going to ask you to use your makeup to give yourself a black eye, but perhaps she expects the poor emasculated Marquis to have bruises instead." Theodmon smirked.

"Emasculated?" Amaria muffled her laugh behind her palm. "She played the opposite card with me; she thought I wasn't safe with you and obviously wanted to kidnap me back to Avondra."

"Kidnap?" Theodmon questioned. Amaria did suppose it sounded melodramatic.

"It was delivered as a political asylum but yes," Amaria rolled her eyes. "It's why I announced my 'pregnancy' to her, I needed an excuse for why I wouldn't flee, as she was annoyingly rationale towards the situation. Sadly there will be a miscarriage soon. But these things do happen."

Amaria didn't want to do this. She didn't want to placate Lynette. But they needed this alliance—at least they needed Lynette to believe they needed this alliance, and more importantly, that the alliance was valid and entered into with good faith.

Theodmon and Amaria had to let Lynette believe that she had power over them, luring her into making a stupid mistake or ignoring a vision that could show her everything wasn't as it seemed. Lynette thought Amaria feared for her life—in truth, whether or not Amaria kept her dark magic or not was immaterial; she just wanted Lynette dead and better yet, humiliated.

Lynette thought Theodmon was cruel. Amaria's jaw popped as heat rushed to her face. Lynette deserved Amaria's cruelty for even daring to think that, let alone insinuate it in Amaria and Theodmon's home.

"That's why she made all that effort to physically visit us," Theodmon said. "She wanted you."

"Yes, and the other thing." Amaria looked up at him worryingly. "She knew right away I have dark magic, and she'll continue using that against us in every way she can."

"We're announcing our alliance tonight." Theodmon kissed her neck. "We're setting plans in motion for her to break it to the scorn of the international community. Quick, scream something at me."

"I'm sorry!" Amaria screeched on command. "I tried as long as I could, but I can't do this! I can't be the perfect daughter for Aaron and the perfect wife for you every single day!"

"But drinking and drugging yourself while we're actively producing heirs?!" Theodmon roared back. "How could you do this to me?"

"I only had Lysander this year! How was I supposed to know I'd be pregnant again so fast?" She lowered her voice, speaking hurriedly. "I'll have Henri send letters to the other Extractors. I think they'll need to start planning defenses against Lynette sooner rather than later."

"Yes, it appears she's reached the peak of her powers," Theodmon whispered. "Make sure she touches *nothing* and sees *nobody* that we don't want her to be in the same room with." Raising his voice, he yelled, "It's your duty to keep yourself healthy and ready to have children. Didn't your father train you better than that?"

That and other things, Amaria thought. *Looks like I'm using some of his training now. I wonder how my father would feel about these methods. Would he approve?* Amaria blinked, clearing her head. As long as they were getting the job done, her father would eventually approve. Or at least learn how to keep his criticisms to himself.

"Henri will miss the feast tonight. Food poisoning, the flu, some illness will prevent him from leaving his chambers while Lynette is here." Amaria sighed. "I hate that for him, because he enjoys feasts, but I'm sure he'll understand." She raised her voice, forcing it to crack from emotion. "Theodmon," she pleaded, "you must understan-"

"No." Theodmon's chilly voice boomed over the walls. "I don't have to understand. I've been too lenient with you." He placed the back of his hand on her cheek, bringing his other hand as if he were to slap her. His hand hit his hand.

Amaria cried out in an imitation of shock and pain.

"Take every precaution, love. Our friends and allies will understand," Theodmon leaned in towards her, his lips brushing over her ears.

He stood away from her, raising his voice once more. "You exist to make my life easier, not harder."

Amaria recoiled. She knew it was a ruse. She knew he didn't mean it. It still hurt, as if her heart was torn into shreds. She bit her lip, trying to focus on that pain instead of the words she had just heard.

Theodmon cringed slightly as he pulled her in for a hug, petting her hair. "I'm sorry," he whispered before raising his voice once again. "Plan the feast and don't embarrass me further." He stomped his heels in place, still holding her tightly.

"Keep yelling for the bystanders." Amaria nodded, closing her eyes, "I'm reaching out to Henri now. Would it be too unbelievable if we summoned Lysander after this? I...I need him."

She sounded pathetic. Amaria didn't like how weak she sounded. Inside of her, the dark magic purred its agreement. She wished it would shut up.

"Perhaps seeing our first son will remind you of your performance here and motivate you to perfect it!" Theodmon answered her request with a seething shout. "You'll stay here with him tonight to learn your place."

Amaria forced her energy outwards. "Lynette might sense my energy," she whispered. "Yell about my magic or being power hungry or something for our plausible deniability with bystanders relaying what they heard."

"Are your eyes glowing? Really, using magic now, Amaria?"

"I can't control it!" She whined, her magic slowly embracing Henri's as she sensed the library of his mind. Guarded by tall towers and covered in ivy, a slight blue aura tinting everything from the pages to the flowers blooming on the vines.

"Henri," she said.

"I'm on it," he said. Amaria wondered how he knew. She only wondered that for a fleeting moment—Henri was a mind reader after all.

She wasn't sure if she would ever get used to that fact.

"I'll write the letters and send them immediately," Henri continued, *"and I'll burn the quill I used to write it too. Also, those oysters gave me food poisoning."*

Amaria's stomach twisted. What exactly did he hear? *"Henri?"* She questioned.

"I've been listening to the show this whole time," he said lazily.

"Henri!"

"You two are very loud, you know." Henri laughed. Amaria's face burned. *"I'll let Faelyn and the other healers know you aren't pregnant and engaging in risky behavior before he rips your head off. I'm sure he's already heard the rumors flying around the castle."*

"It's been an hour, if that." Amaria scowled.

"As I said, you two are very loud," Henri said before Amaria let her magic dissipate. She opened her eyes to stare at Theodmon's hazel ones. His eyebrows were raised in question.

"What is it? Did you find Henri?" Theodmon whispered.

She nodded, giving him a thumbs up, knowing more yelling should occur now in order to cement their ruse. "Please!" She sobbed. "I'll do better. I swear it."

He raised his voice slightly. "You will. I'll lock you in these rooms until you can act like a proper wife." He picked up the sewing hoop she left on the table. It was empty, only a blank piece of cloth stretched across it. Theodmon met her eyes, shrugging as his eyes dropped.

He flung the embroidery hoop against the wall, the wood cracking against stone. Amaria gasped: in part this was an act. However, she was still surprised that he had thrown something in front of her. He had never been rough with her or her property and had never thrown anything as a form of intimidation.

It was an act. She knew this. It still felt real.

"Go sew, woman," Theodmon snarled as he approached her, his arms outstretched. "I expect you to devote your time to knitting for the baby while I'm conducting business with the queen."

He pulled her into a hug, softly petting her hair.

Amaria buried her face into his chest before pulling away, sniffling loud enough for any eavesdropper to hear. "Yes, my Lord Husband, and thank you for your kindness."

"We'll destroy Lynette," Theodmon whispered, holding her tightly. "Write to your father while you're here. We'll need his help. Sorry about your hoop."

Amaria nodded. Fuck the Avonnian queen.

She would write to her father though. Theodmon had a point in that Aaron was the best help anybody could have in a tricky political situation.

"And gods, if she ever enters my home again, I'll cut her head off myself," Theodmon said.

Amaria looked upwards at him. She almost flinched away as she saw the hatred firing in his eyes. She didn't like him yelling at her—with that expression, she feared he'd hate her. But he didn't hate her. He hated Lynette.

She hated Lynette too. Lynette had made Amaria believe that Theodmon hated her.

Why do you care so much about others' approval? The slick voice of the dark magic criticized. *Those with opinions are irrelevant. You're a zenith above where they can only dream of reaching. Powerful. Beautiful. Ruthless.*

Amaria tried to push the voice from her mind. Powerful, beautiful, and ruthless or otherwise, she still needed and valued the human connection she had with her family and close friends. The dark magic could fuck off.

She cupped her hands over his face. "In due time, my love, in due time," Amaria murmured.

The hardest battle was yet to come.

Chapter Thirty-Three

Amaria wanted to kill someone; she wanted to taste the iron scent of blood pouring out of human flesh. She could go down to the Mortensia Labyrinths, find a prisoner—any prisoner—and cure her bloodlust.

Who cared what they had done? They were in prison so they did something to at least be suspected of a crime. And most of the criminals there were enemy soldiers or spies. They deserved it.

Amaria forced herself to look at her son's smiling face as she bounced him on her leg. She couldn't torture someone right now. Lysander would cry if she set him down. He was the world to her.

He meant more than the idea of using her magic to tear someone limb from limb. She wasn't sure how she could do that with wind, fire, earth, or water magic, but she could find a way. She was creative and resourceful; if anybody could come up with a new idea for torturing with magic, it was her.

Amaria's bloodlust had dramatically increased recently. She knew it was because of the Raulet Ruby, so she tried to suppress those thoughts.

She didn't want dark magic. However, she didn't necessarily want to give up the power it gave her either.

Amaria tightly pulled Lysander to her chest, kissing his soft wispy hair. He babbled happily, blinking upwards at her. His eyes, so light at birth, had darkened to brown. "I love you," she whispered.

"Nobody will ever hurt you." She kissed the top of his head as he tried to grab a nearby wooden toy horse.

Silently, she watched him play with his toy. Beaming, Amaria reached for Lysander, her cheeks flushing. Her heart swelling as if it may burst, she kissed the top of Lysander's head lightly. She would have to make more heirs soon enough—it was her job after all. And she liked children.

Amaria ignored the fact that impregnation would be foolish with the dark magic coursing through her right now. She was a liability, and that meant she would die soon. People with dark magic weren't allowed to live. She wouldn't be an exception, and it would be foolish to wager on a delusion.

But she wasn't going to die without a fight.

She debated summoning a maid, however, she did not want to be bothered. "Ssh," she soothed Lysander, placing him in his crib. Immediately, he started to wail. She picked him up again, his cries ceasing instantly. "Sorry, caterpillar."

He blinked at her. Gingerly she crouched down, placing him on the fur rug near the bed. Lysander voiced his disapproval when Amaria sat five feet away from him. "Walk," she encouraged.

He could walk; she had seen him do it. He just preferred to be carried everywhere.

Lysander forced himself up on his pudgy legs, walking over to her babbling with a grin on his face. Amaria beamed as he reached her, scooping him into her arms. "You're doing well, caterpillar." She brushed back a lock of his hair. "Soon you'll be big and strong. You'll be a ferocious warrior. You'll be a wise scholar. You'll be an astute leader. Whatever you set your mind to, you will accomplish."

The door unlatched. Amaria's head jolted upwards. "Theo."

"How are you?" he asked. "How's my little man?"

"He's well," Amaria brushed off his question about her. She was not alright in any sense of the word. Theodmon likely knew that. And she couldn't lie to him. However, there was no sense in worrying him by confirming what he already knew about her.

"How did it go?" she asked. Knowing about the feast, the false alliance, their trap for Lynette was infinitely more important than how she was.

At the same time, she wanted him to know she was suffering. She didn't want to fight the dark magic alone.

Pathetic. The dark magic scoffed.

Go away. Amaria told it.

"Ammy?"

She shook her head, not breaking her eyes from their son in her arms. "Not now. Look, caterpillar," she cooed. "Say hello to your father."

"Lysander," Theodmon sing-songed, running a palm over Lysander's hair. "You look like your mother."

Amaria chuckled. "That's a lie."

"He has your eye shape."

"And your eye color and your face and your hair and your eyebrows," Amaria scoffed.

"I think he looks like you." Theodmon said. "Art is perception, right?"

She scowled at him. "You aren't funny."

"Love, I'm hilarious."

"Put him in his cradle," Amaria crossed her arms, unable to hide the soft smile breaking across her face.

Theodmon laughed, raising an eyebrow.

"I want to throw a pillow at you." Amaria said.

"But I haven't told you about the feast yet," Theodmon said, smirking. Amaria sat on the bed, looking at him bemusedly. Theodmon would tell her. He just enjoyed his games.

"So what happened?" Amaria asked as Theodmon sat next to her.

"Aloysius called her old," he said.

Amaria snorted, choking on her own saliva. "No he didn't."

"He did. Aloysius was told to act like himself as to ah... 'further the perception I don't have my household under control' and when Lynette tried to announce your pregnancy, well he told her she couldn't understand anything as she never had a kid."

Amaria scrunched her eyebrows together. "I don't see how him calling her old is relevant?"

Theodmon laughed, his chest shaking. "She tried to say that she could have a child, Aloysius refuted it by calling her old."

Amaria burst into laughter again, leaning against Theodmon as her ribs pinched. "I bet she loved that."

"Almost as much as she loved Liara glaring at her. I sat them next to each other," Theodmon said.

"What is Liara's deal with her?" Amaria's nostrils flared. At this point, she wasn't sure who she hated more: Liara or Lynette. Lynette had done terrible things, but she was smart. Amaria respected her intelligence. She made mistakes, but that was the nature of being a human. Lynette was pragmatic, powerful, and an adversary that if there weren't risks like the death or her loved ones involved, Amaria would enjoy the fight with.

Liara hadn't hurt her, or anyone really, but she was painfully stupid. Amaria felt as if she lost brain cells every time she had to share the oxygen of that spoiled brat. She believed that natural consequences were injustices, expected pity for situations others had to endure with grace, and acted as if she were better than everyone else for not conforming.

A shot of black energy escaped from Amaria, hitting the stone wall in a burst of flames.

"Let's get Liara to kill herself," Amaria snarled.

"What?"

"Idiot girl wants to sword fight," Amaria laughed maniacally. "We'd likely have a war with Rindria soon enough, right?"

Theodmon slowly nodded.

"Let her learn. Don't give her the best sword masters—they're preparing for war. The armies will kill her, and if she's captured, well, many will likely think she committed treason by running away. She can't be well liked. Let her die."

Amaria tossed her head back, magic flowing through her veins. Let this girl who brought out the worst in her leave once and for all. Amaria wanted peace, and she couldn't have it when she had to police Liara so she didn't embarrass the family.

"What about Aloysius?" Theodmon said softly.

"Who cares?" Amaria laughed. "She's the most useless political alliance in the history of the Chauvignon House. She has no information, no grace, and her blood ties...why do they matter if we'll destroy Rindria anyways?"

"We need an heir to the throne," Theodmon said. "She, or rather her sons, give her that."

"*If* she can produce sons," Amaria scoffed. "That would require her being able to do something correctly—I'm not betting on an impossible situation." Amaria stood up, leaning over Theodmon with gleaming eyes. "We can kill the entire Riam Royal family. It'll be a power vacuum. They're disorganized, weak—how well would they stand up to the imperial army taking them over?"

Amaria laughed. It all made sense. "You sent assassins to kill Clarissa," she reminded Theodmon. "They'll discover things linking us to the assassin and attack—it's what we've been working towards this whole time. We can kill them all in the siege."

Amaria wanted to taste the blood. She wanted to see it pour over the Riam lands.

Theodmon sighed, looking at her softly. "This is insane."

"It'll work. We get rid of her, and since the enemy killed a member of our house, we have justification to be aggressive."

"Do you feel bad killing a family member?"

"I'm not killing her," Amaria dismissed. "I've given her ample warnings on how her wishes and attitude will get her killed. I'm merely letting her act how she wishes and letting the natural consequences of being dumber than cowshit happen."

"She's related to you by blood," Theodmon pointed out. "Her grandmother was a Raulet—"

"Distant cousin," Amaria said. "And kin slaying curses don't count unless you kill them yourself or set up assassinations. I'm not doing that. Liara could live a long and peaceful life if she didn't sword fight when she can barely walk. She could choose to comply with societal expectations and avoid this. But she wants to sword fight, and she'll fight against trained killers."

If not for the gods cursing me and the political ramifications if I did this, I'd kill her myself. A surge of energy flowed through Amaria. She felt alert, as if she were a hunter before a kill. She needed to attack something.

"Put Lysander down," she commanded Theodmon.

He turned to look at her inquisitively. She couldn't kill something, but she could be fucked. She lifted up her skirts to reveal her upper thighs, quickly dropping them to remain appropriate around her child.

Why do you care? A silky voice muttered in her mind. Amaria froze: it sounded like her inner thoughts. It didn't sound like her.

I'm more powerful than you, the voice purred. Amaria's muscles froze. This was dark magic. She could hear it now; what did that mean for her?

Give in, the voice said. *You'd be a queen among mortals.*

What had the priestess said in the temple of Dandar? That she would be a queen among mortals? Was this her future?

Theodmon placed Lysander in the cradle, coming back to lean over Amaria, pinning her arms to her side as he pushed her on her back. "No," he breathed in her ear. "Let's send Lysander to the nursery for the night."

She wanted to escape these walls. Before they were comforting. Now they were a prison.

"Let's get out of these chambers," she said. "The private gardens?"

"Don't wear anything under your skirts." Theodmon released her arms only to go and bark instructions to the guards and nearby servants in the corridor.

Within minutes, they were walking down the corridors to the interior courtyards and gardens. "What if somebody sees us?"

Why do you care?

She didn't care. Why should she when she could incinerate the world?

But she didn't want to burn the whole world, only certain portions. Perhaps they shouldn't fuck in the gardens.

"I've told guards to redirect others from the garden. I want alone time," Theodmon said.

"What if somebody slips through?" Amaria's face burned at the notion of a courtier seeing her engaging in intercourse.

Weak. The magic scoffed. *You're not half as powerful as I believed. Am I cursed with a weak vessel?*

Amaria ground her teeth. *Shut up.* She told the magic.

"Then I'll shoulder the blame." Theodmon snorted. "You are just an obedient wife following her husband's command and I corrupted you bullshit. Or perhaps I am punishing you for your previous indiscretions." He brushed back a lock of her hair looking at her flat stomach.

She wondered when they would announce her miscarriage. The pregnancy was false, and they would have to build on the lie soon enough to avoid being discovered.

"I'm Marquis Chauvignon, so they'll not publicly question it." Theodmon's voice jarred her out of her thoughts.

"Publicly," Amaria repeated.

"And that's what matters," he whispered. "I'm going to enjoy punishing you."

"How?"

"How do you think?"

Amaria didn't answer. Her heart throbbed, beating loud in her ears as her blood rushed to her core. It was too much. All too much—the magic. Lynette. She needed the silence. She needed something to soothe the rage in her mind.

She needed him.

"We can go back to our rooms," Theodmon suggested.

"No," Amaria said, her voice ringing. "No. Don't you dare."

"Are you sure?"

Amaria met his hazel eyes, concern swirling around those fire blue specks. She nodded, wrapping her arm around Theodmon's. His hand reached down to cup her ass and she playfully swatted it away.

"You'll treat me like a lady as we walk to the gardens."

"When do I not?" Theodmon laughed, kissing the nape of her neck.

Amaria raised her eyebrows at him, as if in a challenge. "I don't believe most ladies accompany their husband to torture prisoners."

"And that's why I thank the gods I have you." Theodmon grinned. "You've always been willing to do what needs to be done. They say that men are the stronger sex, but the fools who say that have never met you."

Amaria blushed and looked downcast. Did she need to do it? Yes. But, worse, she enjoyed it. Even before the dark magic, she had enjoyed violently prying information out of others. She liked knowing what others didn't know.

She liked inflicting pain. It soothed something within her, something that wouldn't let her be the victim again. Her bones became warmed as the magic swirled inside of her. She was strong. Those who weren't strong deserved to be killed, mutilated, and trodden into the ground.

"You have been trained as a torturer and trained to endure those techniques yourself." Theodmon leaned down and kissed her neck. Her skin prickled at each touch, plucking a note deeper within. "I believe we can call that an exceptional circumstance. Besides, I love that about you."

"My torturing abilities? Because I can think of something I would like to torture." Amaria chuckled as they walked down the corridor. She forced herself to feel the fabric of her skirts, to smell her own perfume—was it oranges and vanilla? Roses? She couldn't remember which one she chose this morning.

She needed to be in the present.

"Intelligence, problem solving, ruthlessness, take your pick," Theodmon said.

Amaria smiled. She was glad he didn't say anything about her beauty. That was all most people seem to see. It benefited her, but it still frustrated her.

Silently, they walked past the tapestries on the walls, the suits of armor and weapons standing as if they were exhibits in a mausoleum. Amaria breathed in, smelling rosewood and orange, the sharp but woodsy and almost floral aroma bursting against her senses. Her dress was too tight, and with each step the fabric brushed against her tender skin. How much further was it to the garden? Too far.

Soon the floral scents of their perfume gave way to the scents of poinsettia, snowdrop, and cyclamen as Theodmon led them into the private inner courtyard garden. Nobody was there.

Theodmon led them over to a bench, the water in the stone fountain trickling down. His hands moved to his clasp, and like blood, the red fabric soon covered the gray stones. Without pause, Theodmon began to remove his shirt and tunic.

Amaria's mouth went dry, her breath caught in her mouth. She looked over at her husband, her heart fluttering as she saw his uncovered abs. She bent down, pulling off her heeled shoes and tossed them aside. Slowly, she made her way towards him. He was a god, a statue made of flesh. Battle had hardened his body, a weapon of muscle and brutality. And he was hers.

Theodmon didn't wait: he grabbed her and pulled her in for a kiss, and she felt that she had come home. His tongue pressed against hers in a rhythmic dance, and she bit his lip as she pulled him closer to her. Consuming her. The two broke away, gasping for breath, and Theodmon spun her around, pressing her back to his chest.

"You're beautiful," Theodmon whispered in Amaria's ear, moving her long hair over her shoulder. Alright, sometimes she liked when people complimented her beauty. His rough hand caressed her gown, tugging gently as the decorative laces. "Can I see more?"

"Always."

"Let's get you out of some of these." Theodmon's breath quickly came as a pant as his hands ran over the woven strings of her dress. She supposed he would unlace her. But instead of his hands, there was the unmistakable sound of a dagger being unsheathed. "Strings are replaceable, correct?" He asked, the dagger no doubt in his hand.

"I...yes," Amaria said dazedly, but Theodmon was already carefully cutting open the strings instead of bothering to unlace them. One after another popped, exposing her skin to the night air. "What about going back? Won't someone see me?"

"My cloak can cover you." He pulled off the overdress and cut her corset strings as well before turning to place his dagger on a stone bench.

Let them look. The intrusive thought flashed across Amaria's mind. *What can they do but worship and die for me?*

Amaria removed her clothing, leaving only the chemise covering her top, which was tucked into her skirts. With each movement Theodmon watched, his gaze wolfish, an approving smile lurking on his lips. If only he would touch her, because the hesitation was making the throbbing in her core more insistent and impossible to ignore.

"Pull off that, keep your skirts on," Theodmon commanded. He smirked, as if he knew the torment brewing within her. Though judging from the bulge in his pants, he was fighting the same thing, with much more control than she.

Fine. If that was how he wanted to play the game, she would win.

Amaria nodded and obeyed Theodmon's command, moving to get out of her chemise, however, she only managed to untuck it before Theodmon suddenly ripped it off of her, all but attacking her. The fabric loudly tore, the cool air of the night already hitting her back as Theodmon ripped the dress off of her before picking her up and lightly placing her on the bench, the stone pressing against her ass.

Alright. This was more like it.

Amaria smiled, looking up at Theodmon's face as he kissed her neck. Her face brushed against his chiseled jawline as he kissed her. His light hazel eyes peered down at her, and she could tell that he was surveying her, taking in every part of her. Amaria pushed her body closer to his. She needed him. Now.

Slowly, she spread her legs, inviting him in. He knew what she liked. He knew the little spots that would make her moan and fall apart. She wanted him to kiss her breasts, her stomach, her center, all of her. By the gods, she loved him.

Amaria grabbed his hand, moving it towards her breasts, not turning to face him. She moaned, the heavy and rough hand on her soft skin further inflaming her passions as she turned around, cupping her hands around Theodmon's face. And then Theodmon picked her up, making her stand upright. She stood on her tiptoes as he leaned downwards kissing her.

What if someone came in? What if someone was watching? Somehow, the thought stirred her, and she threw her head back in abandon.

Let them watch.

But Theodmon wasn't done with her. Theodmon lifted her up, wrapping her legs around his waist while not breaking away from their kiss. He was strong enough that her small frame was easy for him to manage. He maneuvered her expertly, placing her over him as he tugged down his breeches. Moments later his member prodded against her opening, insistent.

"I love you," Amaria breathed, her nails digging into Theodmon's back. "Fuck me."

She leaned her head back, Theodmon still holding her, catching her breath as he bit her breasts. "I love you too," he breathed to her, kissing her once more.

"I love you," she sighed looking upwards at Theodmon, spreading her legs apart as he had directed. Amaria tilted her head back, closing her eyes.

"I love you too," Theodmon whispered as he expertly rubbed himself over her wetness. She moaned—this was torture, having him so close and not inside her. As her back arched, Theodmon moved to impale her, his hand brushing under her chin softly, before roughly grabbing it upwards, forcing her to look at him. "I enjoy making love more." He sighed, his breath connecting with his wife's, as their bodies became one.

"Urgh!" Amaria grunted, the discomfort giving away to ecstasy. He filled her, every last bit. Gods, yes. This was what she wanted. Fuck. Her hands gripped his back, her nails digging into his skin as she moaned mindlessly. She stared at Theodmon intensely.

Her arms wrapped around him, holding him tight as he maneuvered inside her. She was lucky, so lucky, that this man was hers. All of her plotting as a Raulet couldn't have given her *this*.

Suddenly, he jolted inside her as his strong steps moved over the garden path and to the stone wall. Gently, he placed her against it, her hands gripping on the ivy and the stone carved designs that jutted out from the walls. Did whoever designed this garden intend for it to be used like this? Probably not. Hopefully they would be proud of their creation.

"We told a guard to not have people intrude, correct?" Amaria asked as Theodmon kissed her neck, his pace inside her a steady rhythm.

Theodmon paused, picking her up to where she was level with him against the wall. "Nobody comes here anyways." He kissed her neck again.

This was typical of her—she needed to be decorous. Always. But it was nice to forget once in a while.

With a free hand, Theodmon reached for her sensitive nub at the apex of her thighs, pinching and flicking it just in that way she liked. She moaned, her entire body buzzing. Every hair on her body was raised in anticipation. She needed him. She wanted him.

Amaria wanted everything and nothing all at once.

"You worry too much." Theodmon adjusted so that he could better reach her. The fire within her burned, growing with each movement. Much more and she wouldn't be able to stop. And he kept going, stroking her into a frenzy as she clenched him as hard as she could.

Amaria moaned, throwing her head back, her hair getting pulled by the wall as it stuck in the stone behind her back. "I love you," she gasped, keeping her eyes closed.

"I love you too." Theodmon pushed his mouth onto hers once more as he continued his rhythmic thrusting. "But you're not done yet."

"What?"

"When you come, I want you to cry out my name." He lightly bit her bottom lip. "Mine."

"Yours."

When Theodmon removed his hand from her it left an ache. She needed more. Fuck him. What was he doing to her?

Yet her moans did not dissuade him. Theodmon dropped Amaria's legs one at a time, letting her safely stand on solid ground before he forcefully guided her near the orchids.

"Smell those while I fuck you," Theodmon commanded, pushing her down onto her hands and knees, careful to ensure she hit the dirt instead of the gravel pathway.

Amaria quickly obeyed, her eyes rolling back with pleasure as she did so.

This time there was no hand on her, teasing her. There was only Theodmon's grip on her hips and his manhood back inside her. Yet she didn't have time to savor that the fullness was back. Instead, Theodmon thrust harder and harder, pushing her onward, making her cry out in pleasure and despair. How was he doing this to her? She was a Marchioness, and she was getting rutted like a peasant in the stables.

And she loved it.

"Now, move," Theodmon whispered, kissing her once more before pulling himself out of her and flipping her over to her front. Not even a breath later he was back inside her, his fingers and cock stirring her once more. Her body was alive, vibrating in a way that only he could do. She spread herself as wide as possible and lifted her hips. Him. She needed him.

"I'm going to impregnate you," he promised lowly, pulling her hair back as he fucked her.

Who cared about the consequences now? There was only *this.*

Nothing else was real.

When her pleasure washed over her, it was with a guttural cry that made her transcend her body, lost in the sensations Theodmon coaxed from her. He followed moments later with a moan. He was so beautiful when he came, a vulnerability that he never showed with anyone. Only her.

The world hated them, but they had each other. And together, there was nothing that they couldn't overcome. While their bodies were interconnected, reality did not—could not—exist outside of their bond.

Chapter Thirty-Four

Aside from the secret war preparations and the unwanted visitor Amaria was hosting inside of her, life was moderately peaceful for the next two weeks. Theodmon was publicly treating her with disdain—Lynette had spies afterall. And for the plan to work, Theodmon had to remain angry with Amaria.

And she had to remain 'pregnant'.

She had gotten very good at using her magic to manipulate water splashing to sound like vomit behind closed doors.

Everything seemed to be going too well.

Amaria knew that it was a trap. Life wasn't that kind. An early lesson Amaria had learned not only about business but also the world as a whole was that if something seemed too good to be true, it likely was.

And she had forgotten that, bought into the trap that perhaps she could pretend to have some semblance of peace as the dark magic surged in her veins. She pushed out the notions of what had occurred this past year; she ignored Theodmon's scheming despite her active participation in it. She ignored that her father was likely planning something worse.

Amaria breathed heavily. Theodmon had a plan. Her father would have a plan. She had plans. But her plans would be cut short.

She couldn't ignore her unwanted visitor for much longer—the dark magic was growing stronger by the day. She knew her dark magic would be a nasty issue soon for Thestitiunian law required the Extraction and subsequent execution of a mage who used dark magic.

She doubted Aion would make an exception for her. He'd likely order someone to Extract her magic, but not execute her. She was a member of a prominent family, and executing her would be politically messy. Aion could rationalize it as "an unwilling host of dark magic doesn't deserve to die," rather than the true reason: Aaron would no longer support him if Amaria was killed. And without Aaron, the empire would collapse on the emperor.

Amaria wouldn't allow that to happen. Not out of love for Aion. No, she would rather die than be without her magic. Was death really preferable in this case? She had seen what Extractions did to their victims—they became empty, devoid of hope or humanity.

Killing those prisoners after an Extraction was a kindness. Amaria would not allow herself to live that way.

But this magic wasn't hers. Her magic was still there, weakened, but fighting against the dark magic from the Raulet Ruby. An Extraction could be more risky for the world—or so Amaria could and would argue if it came down to it. A Cleansing required much less energy and force than an Extraction, and it had failed even with two mages jointly working together. An Extraction would risk the dark magic leaving and spreading into the greater world.

"If the vessel dies, the magic dies," Amaria groaned under her breath. It was one of the most basic rules of magic a mage could learn. It's why magical energy was held in gems. All magic was tied to nature, and nature made magic stronger. And gems were unable to die so the energy and magic stored in them could last for eternity unless it was used or otherwise released.

She didn't know what to do. She couldn't even predict what would happen. Amaria hadn't come to terms with dying. She wasn't planning on dying. Law or not, she'd live. At her core, she was a survivor. And Amaria wasn't going to let something as trite as legality control her ability to live or die.

She wouldn't live without her magic. And she wouldn't let them talk about her magic and death. They had no say in her life. The emperor had no say in her life. Or her magic. She was tired of giving that idiot power over her. Amaria knew she'd be executed if she continued to allow Aion to have power over her. She didn't want to be executed.

Then become the empress. The dark magic purred. *You can't be executed if you are the law.*

Amaria clenched her fists. The magic was treasonous shit. She tried to find the small fragment of her silver magic inside of her.

It was weak. Easily disposed of by the dark magic. Amaria supposed her magic reminded her of Aion.

I don't want to be the empress. She told the dark magic firmly.

I'd have thought a competent ruler would entice you. The dark magic said mockingly. *Isn't that why you're destroying Rindria?*

Being empress was entirely different from wanting to destroy Rindria. Rindira was weak... Aion, he listened to his advisors. He was wise to outsource to competent people, like Aaron Raulet. She missed her father. His knowledge, experience, and resources made these sorts of things easier. Amaria wished he was here now.

Amaria clenched her fists. The dark magic was wrong. She wasn't that power hungry. She wasn't determined to be at the top, no matter what. That would be absurd. The dark magic didn't know anything; it was messing with her mind and emotions. She was loyal. She had never considered treason. She repeated this a million times.

Perhaps one day she would believe it.

She ignored that she wanted to see an entire country burn.

She ignored that she wanted to be the queen of the ashes.

Amaria had a façade of peace. As long as nobody moved the curtains back, she could trick herself into believing everything was alright. It was a fragile façade, so it shattered as soon as a black raven bearing a scroll entwined with yellow wax and the horse seal of Rindria arrived at Forteresse les Blanche.

"I wonder what this is," Amaria said sarcastically. She knew before opening it that it would contain news of an assassination attempt: Theodmon's plan was either successful and Clarissa was dead. But if it was unsuccessful, well, there would be war anyways.

She popped open the seal. It was in Riam. She scowled. She couldn't read in Riam.

She folded up the parchment, slipping it into her sleeves as she exited the halls. She would need Theodmon to translate it. Together they would know what happened. Together they would make a plan based on the information in the letter.

Amaria carefully held the silver tray in her hands as she approached Theodmon's offices. She forced herself to appear pleasant, keeping the hatred from her features. She despised that she had to humiliate herself to keep up with the ruse for all who may relay information back to Lynette. It was impossible to find every spy, but Amaria wanted to string up everyone who even breathed in a manner she found suspicious.

She was a meek wife bringing her husband tea. She would serve him tea in his offices. Theodmon would whisper information and plans to her as he secretly showed her documents in his office. And later, at night, in their chambers, they would flesh out these plans in whispers.

Amaria despised this routine.

She stopped in front of the guards in front of Theodmon's office. "I brought my husband tea," she said.

"Did he summon you?" The corner of the guard's mouth turned upwards. Amaria wanted to throw the hot liquid on him.

"Ask him," she said sweetly.

The guard humped, knocking on the door, announcing her presence to Theodmon. Amaria forced herself to look nervous; she knew that was what an outsider would expect as they looked into her and Theodmon's current relationship.

She wasn't worried.

Theodmon told the guard to let her in. He would always let her in. That hadn't changed. And as soon as Lynette was dead, she'd never appear under the presence of bringing her husband tea. She wouldn't need a ruse. They would be Amaria and Theodmon, a team. Not Marquis Chauvignon and his submissive wife, good only for sexual favors and birthing children.

"Place the tea on my desk," Theodmon commanded as the guard let her in. He barely looked at her. "Sugar."

Amaria nodded softly, forcing herself to look dejected. The door shut. Theodmon stood up, locking the door. He embraced her. "Sorry, love," he whispered. "I'll pour my own cup."

"It's not your fault," she told him softly.

He kissed her gently. "Doesn't make it less shitty."

Amaria couldn't argue with that. She pulled out the parchment from her sleeves, handing Theodmon the parchment.

"It's in Riam," she told him.

Theodmon took the scroll from her hands, his eyes quickly scanning the words "Our assassins failed to kill Clarissa, but they found our crest."

Amaria's chest deflated. They had failed. Perhaps this would be enough to spur a war? No, an actual death was more justified. This failure would ruin everything—

"They reminded us the prince is dead, killed by the Raulet Ruby."

Amaria recoiled, those twelve words enough to pull her out of her thoughts.

"Edward Riarl? We didn't... Are they blaming us for his death when Clarissa threw the gem?"

Amaria couldn't imagine killing a child. Even indirectly.

Theodmon's shoulders sank. "Unfortunately. Paired with the assassination attempt and the general distrust of magic, Raulets, and Chauvignons, they believe we planned this."

The Riams weren't entirely wrong that they had planned to destroy Rindria for a long time. But to blame them for the prince's death when he had been killed by Clarissa being stupid with dark magic?

They didn't kill a child. Perhaps it was a ridiculous distinction. In these larger politics, what was the difference between a child and an adult other than competence?

She still wouldn't kill a child. They were innocent. Harmless. Amaria couldn't bring herself to destroy something so pure.

However, the prince dying, even from dark magic, was fortunate. It was one less person in line to the Riam throne. It was one less person to dispose of to destabilize Rindria from the inside out. Amaria didn't want to ever dispose of a young child for political reasons. Thanks to the gods for taking care of Edward Riarl for them—she hoped the young prince had peace in Sadthos' Kingdom.

"Summon Henri and Lucas," Amaria sighed, rubbing her temples.

"Aloysius too," Theodmon said. "He deserves to know what's coming as he will deal with the brunt of Liara's emotions with it."

Yes, the planned removal of the entire Riam royal family. Amaria wrapped her arms around herself. The planned removal of Liara's entire family.

"And he won't tell her in advance?"

"He can only tell her about the dead prince. My brother knows how to keep his mouth shut and we need them to not despise each other completely now," Theodmon said.

Amaria knew why. It was harder to get a son when the potential parents despised each other. She sighed, opening the door and telling the guard to summon those people at her husband's command. Behind her, Theodmon barked an order at the guard.

The door shut and Amaria walked over to the couch with slumped shoulders, flopping down on the couch as Theodmon wrote a note to Rindria. He would deny their allegations in full. She watched the flames in the fireplace in front of the couch as she listened to Theodmon's quill scratch.

Amaria scratched her arms, red bumps appearing from stress. It felt as if she was sitting in tense silence for a million years before a knock pounded on the door. It swung open, and Aloysius, Lucas, and Henri stepped inside.

Aloysius was red faced and out of breath.

"I heard you needed us?" Henri said.

"Lock the door," Theodmon said.

Amaria wondered where this impatience was coming from.

"Ammy, mind filling them in as I finish this note?"

Amaria shook her head, wetting her lips. "Our assassination attempt on Clarissa Nalaeny failed. Rindria blames us for Edward Riarl's death."

"He was blasted by the Raulet Ruby," Aloysius countered. "After Clarissa threw it."

"We were caught trying to murder a Riam princess," Amaria said. "It's not an entirely irrational presumption."

"It is," Lucas countered. "We all saw him die. It was chaos, but neither you or Theodmon hurt him—Clarissa caused the gem to explode, you tried to stop it and died, and Theodmon was focused on that."

"Anyways, Clarissa Nalaeny's unfortunately still living but very injured body was found with a note from Theodmon, Thestitiunian daggers and coin, and a Chauvignon seal," Amaria continued, ignoring what Lucas had said. "We'd never be so stupid to leave so many clues behind—"

"You were framed?" Aloysius asked his brother skeptically, rolling his eyes.

"That's the *official* story," Theodmon said. "And what I am telling Rindria. I'm horrified they'd insult my honor and we should find this criminal who tried to kill their princess and identified me in the crime. King Tristan already gave me leave to punish her, so why would I disrespect the sanctity of his nation's sovereignty and attack within his borders?"

"You almost sounded sincere," Henri muttered.

"Why?" Aloysius asked.

"We're trapping Lynette Edrion," Amaria said. Quickly, she recounted the main points of the plan, stressing that it must remain secret to all in this room besides Lucas, Juliette, Nicoletta, Haerdnor, and Aaron.

"Aloysius sends this note to Tristan Riarl once we are done." Theodmon came back to the couches, handing his brother a sealed scroll. "Rindria is angry, and they're planning war. I don't want to deal with a siege, nor do I want Riams attacking my lands and countryside."

"You're not saying..." Aloysius stared at Theodmon, his eyes creasing as his eyebrows merged.

"Exactly," Theodmon confirmed. "We'll bring the fight to them, at Bria Hall. Our intel shows us that nobody has a sense of duty to their country, they don't feel a connection as Riams. They feel a connection to their neighbors, their family, their village, but next to nothing for their country."

"They'll fight for their survival," Henri countered. "You're invading."

"I'm counting on that. Rindria is a powder keg. All we need is a few uprisings and revolts; it will disorganize them. A famine and choice assassinations and we can place our own candidate on the throne."

Aloysius looked at Theodmon. "Don't you fucking say the candidate."

Amaria knew that they all knew the candidate was Liara—rather, Liara's future son ruling through Aloysius until he came of age. Not saying the reality out loud didn't make it less true.

"Make preparations," Theodmon dismissed Henri, Lucas, and Aloysius.

Silently, with a few death glares from Aloysius, they departed, leaving Amaria and Theodmon alone. She leaned against Theodmon as the door shut.

"Do you ever tire of the schemes?"

"No," he replied. "Do you?"

"No. I thrive off them. It's a game of chess to me." She met his eyes. "Are we bad people?"

"To some," Theodmon admitted. "To others we are pragmatists and to a few we may even be heroes. Reputation is decided by the winners when the players die."

He kissed the top of her head. "Let me write this letter to Lynette."

Amaria moved off him, watching him stand up and go to the desk, moving papers from it to find a blank parchment.

Theodmon dipped his quill into the inkwell. "And so it begins," he muttered, bringing the quill down, slashing words across the page, the pen his weapon instead of a sword, the blood black instead of red.

> Your Majesty,
> Queen Lynette Edrion of Avondra,
>
> You recently visited me in my home seeking for the Chauvignons and the Edrions to work together, to put the vestiges of the past behind us so we may have a brighter future for both our nations and people.
> Rindria is accusing me of murder. I fear they will start a war soon; they have attacked my borders for years over lesser imagined slights. I did not kill, or order the killing of, Aliandra Nalaeny—frankly, between two intelligent leaders, I am not stupid enough to do so.
> Yet, my sigil was somehow found at the scene. I am being framed, and I will likely need all the allies I can obtain. If you were serious about an alliance, now is the time to secure it.
>
> Marquis Theodmon Chauvignon
> of the Westerlands, Thestitiunia

"A bit heavy handed, don't you think?" Amaria peered over his shoulder, scanning the note.

"I'm direct. It's expected of me."

Amaria sighed, sitting down on his lap as he moved the note over to dry. "Do you think she'll take the bait?"

He kissed the top of her head. "I believe so. She doesn't believe anyone could outsmart her. She's arrogant and she's weak because of it."

"And are we arrogant for believing our plan will work?"

"No. She has no way out. Either she preserves our alliance and shatters hers with Rindria, or she shatters our alliance, and we can publicly announce our Morrian alliance with little scrutiny. There are ways this plan could go wrong, but Lynette's actions aren't one of them."

"Doing nothing isn't even an option for her," Amaria agreed.

"That's what we expect her to do, so it's the safest option. But we believed we were going to be attacked, and in those circumstances a new alliance with Morroek isn't unfounded."

But the true alliance to dethrone Lynette is. At least publicly. Amaria lightly chuckled. They pretended to be horrified at the underhanded actions of their peers all while trying to backstab and cheat themselves.

She looked over at the parchment, the ink now dried. "Let's get this sent out today. I doubt Rindria will wait for long."

Chapter Thirty-Five

Weeks after the letters declaring war on Rindria had been sent, the castle was bustling, as war preparations were in full swing now. If Amaria had thought Forteresse les Blanche was busy before, she had been comparing a river's current to a riptide. Morroek was summoned, per their alliance. Weapons were being made and sharpened. Armor was polished. Grain was stored and loaded into wagons. Horses were treated, making sure they were healthy and ready to fight.

And Amaria felt as if she were a prisoner. They were still playing Lynette and so, except for behind closed doors where it was only her and Theodmon, she was a punished and pregnant wife with little insight or responsibilities other than what colors were needed to knit blankets for the baby.

She bitterly ground her teeth as Theodmon explained to her what she missed in planning sessions. They were alone in his office, and she had gotten in through the usual way: a lie that she was there to serve her husband in any way he deemed appropriate.

Theodmon had recently seemed to develop a fondness for having his cock sucked as he worked.

Or so everyone else thought.

"Durek hates female monarchs," Theodmon told Amaria as she perched on his lap in his offices. "And he's the heir presumptive of Morroek."

"Yes," Amaria snapped. "He has the old king's ear."

She was annoyed at everything recently. And respect for her had decreased when it seemed that Theodmon didn't respect her, instead only seeing her as a receptacle for his semen—for breeding purposes or otherwise. Yes, they still feared her—her magic and previous acts of murder, espionage, and torture made her formidable—but fear wasn't the same as respect.

Amaria despised the disrespect. She hated acknowledging she was only as comfortable as she had been because Theodmon had respected her. When she seemed to have lost that respect from him, she was nothing.

She could give commands, but they couldn't be contrary to what the servant or guard thought Theodmon wanted—as if they knew him better than her. If she was giving a sole magical command, their compliance was based on fear and rank, nothing more.

She had overheard a guard mocking her, insulting her—*glad the Marquis sees through her now, was worried he was blindsided by the pretty face. His wife is like a unicorn, beautiful but bloodthirsty. Gods, the Raulets are fucking insane.*

Anger boiled in her veins as if her blood was fire. They insulted her family. They insulted Theodmon's intelligence. She also wasn't like a unicorn. Unicorns came from the Badlands, entirely crafted from dark magic. They lurked in dark forests on the outskirts of civilization, waiting to lure unsuspecting people in with their beauty—their magic was like a siren's call—where they would then eat their poor victim alive.

Amaria didn't kill innocent people.

However, recently, because of this façade, she had wanted to kill everyone around her. Theodmon had publicly yelled at her, dismissed her, and to outsiders it seemed as if she were only allowed in his offices if she were there to serve him, either with tea or sexual pleasures. Amaria did not want to imagine what others thought was occurring behind these closed doors.

She wanted to be respected again. Without it being dependent on Theodmon.

She was a woman.

She had dark magic.

Perhaps she could join Lynette; perhaps she wasn't as crazy as she had been written off to be. Amaria wouldn't mind watching several of the men inside the castle being eaten alive by unicorns. She wouldn't mind burning them alive. She wouldn't mind boiling or freezing their blood.

"Are you okay?" Theodmon asked her, holding her firmly as his eyes scanned over her. Wrinkles appeared on his forehead.

A knock thudded on the door. Theodmon gently pushed Amaria off of him, unzipping his pants. She ground her teeth as she sat on the ground by his feet.

"Come in," Theodmon barked, his voice slightly breathy. As the door opened, he looked at Amaria. "Wipe off your mouth," he said dismissively, zipping up his pants. "Go sit on the couches and wait."

Her face burned. She hated this. She kept her eyes lowered as she pretended to wipe his cum from her mouth.

She could feel the messenger's mocking smirk as she passed him. "Apologies for the interruption, my Lord," he said, bowing to Theodmon. "A letter from Avondra just arrived."

"Leave it on the desk," Theodmon commanded. "Is there anything else?"

"No, my Lord."

"Leave," Theodmon said. As the messenger departed, Theodmon's eyes slowly moved over to Amaria. "Come here," he told her. It was the last thing the messenger heard as the door shut behind him.

Amaria's face burned. She knew that the perception of what they were showing the world wasn't real. Perceptions sometimes mattered more than reality. Were they damning themselves in the future to bring down a current enemy?

"I'm sorry," Theodmon whispered as he pulled her onto him, bringing her into a tight hug. "If I knew there wasn't a chance of spies reporting everything to Lynette..."

"I understand," Amaria sniffed. She did, as much as it hurt. If she and Theodmon acted how they had before Lynette visited, if they acted how their relationship truly was, then Lynette would know they were playing her.

They were playing with fire already, and they didn't need her to have reports on the health of their marriage.

"As soon as this is over, it'll be how it was before. If anybody tries to disrespect you, I'll give them a sharp warning blow to their neck."

Amaria gave a broken smile. She appreciated that Theodmon acted like there was an afterwards where she was alive. As long as she had dark magic, it would be her head on the chopping block, not anybody else's.

"We do have an issue with bringing you to war," Theodmon continued, rubbing his head. "You're pregnant, you're playing my submissive and downbeat wife...it's hard to explain why you'd be there."

"Extractors helping with magic in wars isn't enough?" Amaria said.

"Not entirely," Theodmon admitted. "It may work for most, but for Lynette, she'd suspect something. If I want a submissive, docile breeding doll, I'm not sending it to a battle while pregnant."

"You'd obey the emperor," Amaria said slowly. "I'll have my father write a note—he writes most of the emperor's decrees anyway. Either him or Aion can back date it so it looks like it arrived this week."

"That may work," Theodmon agreed.

"It's not disputed you love me," Amaria said softly. "Or at least, you still prefer me as a sexual partner." She hated describing herself in this way. She knew it was the reality of how others may view her, but it was dehumanizing. And when she repeated it, she felt as if she were bringing the crude remarks to life.

"So on top of Aion ordering you to perform in Extractor duties, I'm bringing you to warm my bed because I can't survive without sex for months?" Theodmon laughed. "And I prefer having you wet my dick over a whore?"

Amaria's eyes welled with tears. "Please," she sobbed. "Don't." She was tired of the dehumanization. She couldn't bear to hear it come from Theodmon's mouth.

He kissed the top of her head. "I want you there with me. Not for the reason we are giving publicly either. You're talented, intelligent, and I love you."

Amaria pushed her body closer to his. She loved him too.

Disgusting. The dark magic forced itself to the forefront of her mind. *No wonder it was easy for others to treat you as disposable—you're a weak little girl obsessed with pleasing a man. Love doesn't exist—*

It does. Amaria snapped back.

Pathetic. The magic ignored her. *I would have hoped you would have done more with your life than spread your legs—even that you didn't do well. Only one child? Faking a pregnancy? I thought you were raised for that.*

Shut up! Amaria internally screamed.

Accept your power. The magic sneered. *You'll give in eventually; fighting is stupid. Are you stupid?*

No. Amaria was not stupid. The magic knew that—it had to know that. That was why it was egging her on. She didn't want this damn thing inside of her to be right.

She was much more than what the magic said she was. She could do everything the magic said she couldn't.

"Ammy," Theodmon gently held her hands, his palms caressing hers. "Look at this." He handed her the note he had received, its seal opened. In his other hand, he had the written manifestation of the alliance with Avondra.

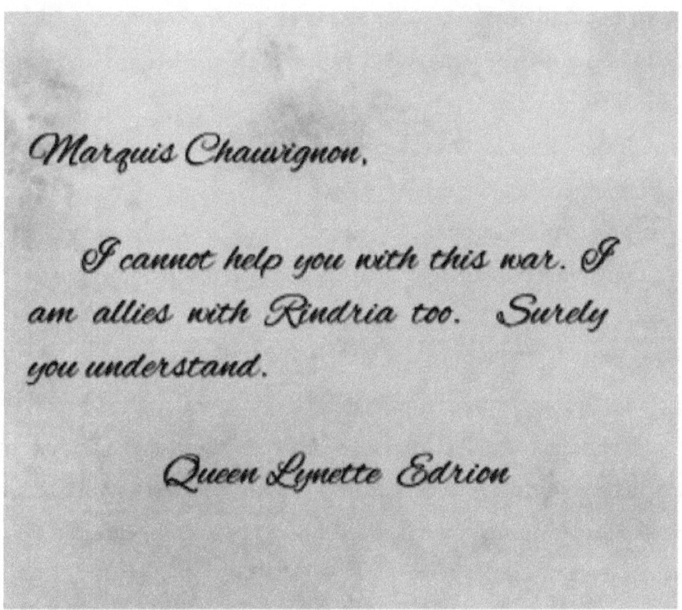

Amaria scoffed. How apt of Lynette to back out last minute. She paused. Why did she scoff? This was what they wanted, for her to betray allies to the scorn of the international community.

Amaria smirked. Revoking an offer of alliance when needed was rarely taken kindly amidst nobles, regardless of nationality. To make matters worse, it was an alliance she initially solicited from the Chauvignons. Lynette was digging her own international grave.

It was working.

Clarissa was alive. However, Amaria couldn't be too angry about that. In fact, she was glad Clarissa was alive. Amaria wanted to kill her. She wanted to watch the panic in Clarissa's eyes as she realized she was dying. She wanted Clarissa's death to be long and painful. Amaria wanted the Riam bitch to be cognizant of her impending doom.

Most importantly, Amaria wanted to be the last thing Clarissa saw. While it wouldn't bring Delphina back or cause the dark magic to abandon her, Clarissa's death would make Amaria feel good.

Amaria liked feeling good.

She looked over at the stack of sealed letters on her desk. She breathed in, running her hands through her hair. "Thestitiunia and Morroek have an alliance in a shocking turn," she muttered sardonically.

"I'll have scribes send out the condemnation of Lynette breaking her alliance," Theodmon said. "They'll copy her letter word for word on the letter. I am also formally announcing our alliance with Morroek."

Amaria nodded. This all sounded rational. She knew she couldn't do anything, and Theodmon was only telling her out of respect.

"You should go to our chambers," he tiredly kissed her hair as she stood up.

"We need to plan my miscarriage," Amaria whispered, looking at her flat stomach. "It has to be soon, or else...."

"The stress of battle," Theodmon said. "It's believable."

Amaria couldn't argue with that.

"We should be prepared to leave in two weeks once these scrolls are sent out," Theodmon said. "It'll be about three weeks before we reach Wéorren City for the siege."

Amaria felt a tear running down her face. She was weak. She shouldn't cry.

She would miss Lysander.

She was weak.

Last time she was in Wéorren City she had almost died. She would die anyway if she didn't find a cure for her dark magic. She would be executed.

You could take over your homeland. The dark magic reminded her.

Amaria scowled, tired of how trifling this magic was. Why was it trying to tell her what to do anyways?

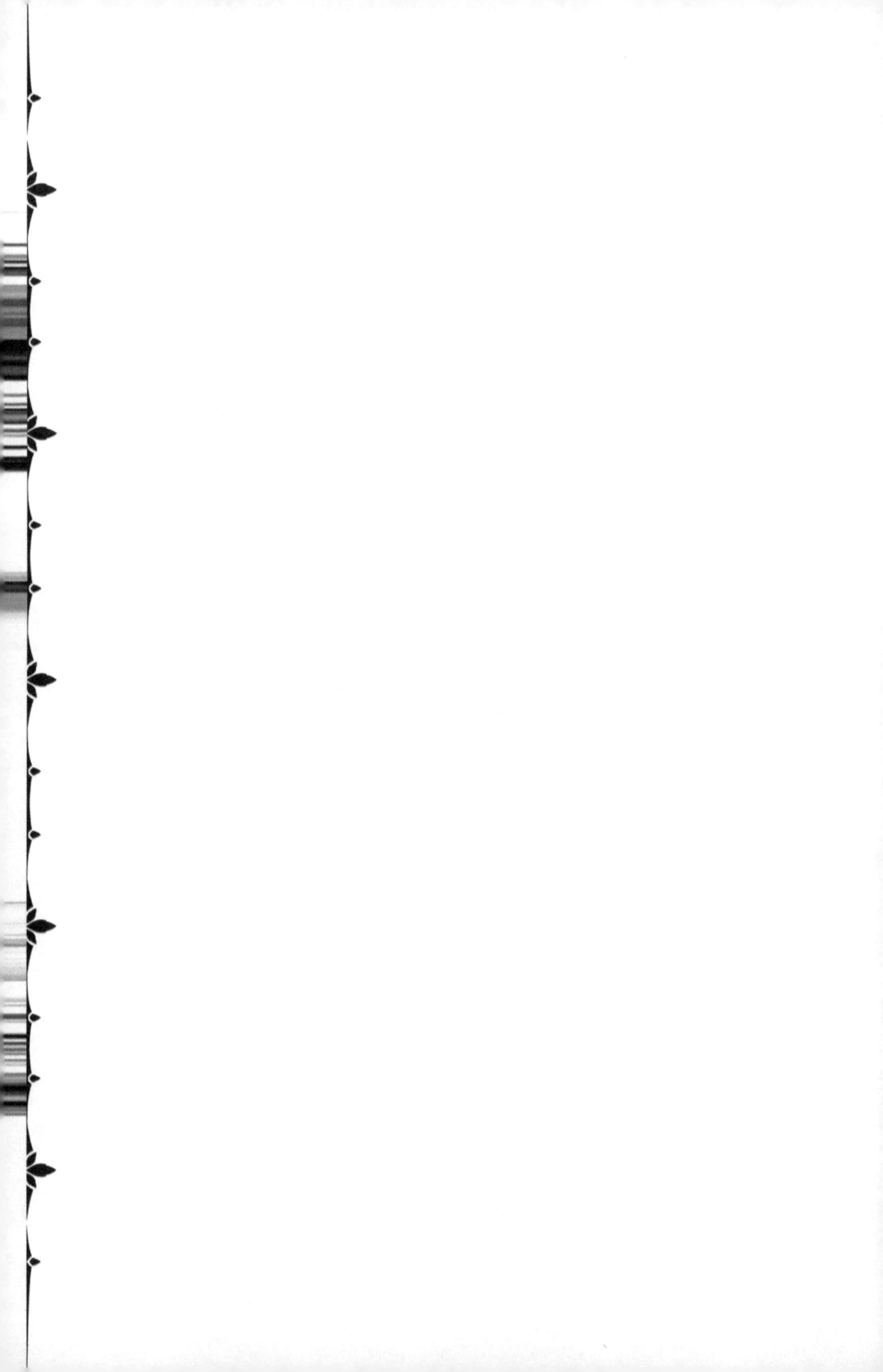

Part Five
the battle

Chapter Thirty-Six

A maria hated the smell of shit.

That's what war camps smelt like. Shit.

Amaria pulled her cloak tighter around herself as she walked from where the latrines were towards the center of the camp where the habitable areas were. It was annoying to have to walk that far to use the bathroom, but she supposed it was preferable than the alternative. It had taken them almost a month and a half to arrive here and then a further few days to set up this monstrosity.

"Amaria." Theodmon was waiting for her only twenty feet away from where she had used the bathroom.

She slipped her hand in his, the large calloused palm engulfing her own tiny, soft one. He had told people off, demanding they respect her again. He blamed Lynette for his sudden change in behavior—she was a seer, but her magic had a sort of psychic control that nobody could explain. It was a believable enough excuse that not only allowed them to continue the pretense that they had always entered into the alliance with Avondra in good faith and also allowed them to blame Lynette for doing unscrupulous things to foreign leaders.

Amaria wouldn't have put what they were blaming Lynette for past the Avonnian queen anyways. While some people likely wouldn't believe the official story Theodmon had spun, it wasn't unbelievable—it was plausible.

That was all they needed. Plausibility.

"I'm alright," she said, smiling at Theodmon reassuringly. Amaria hoped her lips didn't quiver. She hoped she was imagining her clammy hands.

"I don't like having you at a war camp; it's unsafe," Theodmon said. Theodmon glared at a few Morrian men who were staring at her.

Amaria agreed. Still, Theodmon was tense, wound as tightly as a child's wind-up toy. Agreeing with him that she felt unsafe here would likely cause the protruding vein in his neck to explode.

"I'm an Extractor," she said, rubbing his arm with the hand that wasn't holding his. "War is sometimes a place I'll have to go. Nobody on our side will touch me, at least, not with you glaring at them."

"You're scared too," Theodmon looked down at their entwined hands.

"Nerves, not fear," Amaria said. She knew the excuse was pathetic. Still, what could admitting her fear do now? She didn't know the exact answer to that, but she did know that it wouldn't be anything productive.

"The other side will do worse," Theodmon said, his jaw locking.

Amaria sighed, her shoulders slumping. Yes, the other side would do worse if they had the chance. It was the nature of war.

"Not if I kill them first." Her breath caught in her throat, causing her voice to crack.

"We attack tomorrow," Theodmon whispered, as they walked closer to the center of the camp.

The battle was tomorrow, and the smell of shit would merge with blood and sweat, and the screams of panic and pain from both sides would overpower everyone unfortunate enough to be around the battle.

Men went to war and enjoyed it.

And yet women were the irrational ones.

Amaria resisted the urge to scream. What did it matter anyways on who was rational in their desires? They'd all be dead in the morning anyways.

Because while the victors of war were physically alive, the ballads never sang about the weight the soul carried and how the price of victory—*of survival*—could often be higher than the price it took to enter Sadthos's kingdom comfortably.

Chapter Thirty-Seven

The next morning, Amaria woke entirely too early. Groaning, she rolled over in the uncomfortable makeshift bed and saw that Theodmon was already up and was being helped into his armor by a squire. On a nearby table she saw her dress, gems laid out next to it.

"Good morning," Theodmon said as she sat up, her feet hitting the ground.

"Morning." She rubbed the sleep out of her eyes. "Have you eaten?"

"Yes," Theodmon said. "You should too before you get ready."

Amaria nodded, feeling numb as she grabbed her hair brush to brush her hair. She wasn't particularly hungry. Not in the traditional sense at least. She wanted to see Rindria burn so much it felt as if she had an insatiable hunger.

As for food? She felt as if she may vomit if she had to eat any. Her stomach was a bundle of knots. Still, she managed to drink some wine and have a little bread and jerky before she dressed and her attendant appeared to lay the gems across her—almost as if it were armor.

Amaria supposed it was armor in a way because the extra stores of energy would protect her. It would be near useless in stopping swords and arrows, but she didn't defend herself or fight with steel anyways.

Her offensive and defensive methods were her magic.

Amaria was not made for war. Intelligence, detaining prisoners, sure. But the active battlefield was entirely different. Extractors were expected to help in battle for the empire, for their province, and against magical threats. In the brief time she had been an Extractor and unmarried to Theodmon, her father had not had battles. And Theodmon never forced her to join him at a war camp.

"Are you ready?" Theodmon asked her as his squire tightened his breastplate.

"Of course not." Amaria waved her hand, dismissing her helper.

"It'll be over soon." Theodmon too, dismissed his squire, and clanked over towards her.

"Sieges can take months. That's not over soon."

"Relative to the rest of our lives." Theodmon held her hands in his. Her fingers ran over his callouses, the lines deeply etched into his flesh as if he were a stone statute instead of a human.

"It's alright to be nervous before your first battle." Theodmon squeezed her hands. "You weren't exactly prepared for this. I think you should have been. Anybody could have seen you would be an Extractor as a child—"

"It doesn't matter, does it?" Amaria snarled, pulling her hands from his. "The perception of a Raulet bride is more important than reality."

Reality was fragile, like murky glass spit out by the oceans. Reality, like seaglass, was difficult to see through; it was coarse and inelegant. It would not be accepted in the midst of society, rather it was discarded and kept out of sight. So they painted the glass a pretty color, faked it to be a piece of art, and the perception was not only accepted but celebrated. More mosaics could cheaply be made in city squares without the hassle of ceramic. Nobody saw the reality of the glass—they saw its façade.

Until the glass shattered.

Glass hurt more than ceramic. Reality hurt more than ideals.

The concept of openly training a Raulet daughter for war instead of marriage was not a palatable arrangement. So Amaria was trained in secret for intelligence and torture all while remaining the unassuming and beautiful image that was expected of her. And she was more dangerous because of this pragmatism—it wasn't acceptable for her dangerous skills to be known.

And they had made her so much worse by keeping the ugly and nasty parts of her contained. She wasn't interested in suppressing her worst impulses any longer.

"Before they charge, let me kill them," Amaria stood up. "We all need air to breathe; what if the flow of oxygen suddenly became unexplainably obstructed in the Riams?"

"That could help save our people," Theodmon agreed.

"Why even send our people in at all?" Amaria paced. "They'll wall up their castles, thinking they're safe. I can kill each person without touching them. We can launch rats inside the walls—they'll spread disease, eat their food. Why should any of them get the mercy of a quick death?"

Theodmon stood up, grabbing her by the shoulders. "A sword cut isn't exactly a merciful death."

"It's over sooner than starvation," Amaria laughed. "It hurts less than being burned alive. It hurts less than being flayed. And there's no panic, no mystery on why your body failed you. You know why you're dying. Choking to death suddenly, that's where the fear of why you can't breathe comes in. You don't know why—a sword is mercy!"

She breathed heavily, her fists clenching. She was tired of playing nice. She was tired of pretending. Fuck Lynette. Fuck Clarissa. Fuck dark magic. Fuck Rindria. Fuck Morroek. Fuck everyone that wasn't hers.

"They'll suspect you," Theodmon sighed.

"So?" Amaria challenged. "Let them. Let them demand my head. They can't have it; they won't even be a country soon."

It was a war. People died.

They didn't care about her loss, and she didn't care about theirs.

"How far is your range?" Theodmon asked, sitting back down. Amaria closed her eyes, pushing her magic outwards.

She couldn't see with her magic, but she could feel the movements and vibrations in the air. She could hear the voices carrying over the wind as people miles away talked to each other.

She could hear the clattering of shields, swords, and bows. She heard the thumping of boots and the yelling of women for children to finish pulling the wash down and prepare for the siege.

Amaria guessed that she was sensing a scene within Weorren City but not near Bria Hall.

This wasn't ideal; she wanted the head of the dragon cut off so it couldn't lead its army. But she supposed this would be good practice. Nobody cared about the people who lived and worked near the city walls. They were expendable.

Nobody would care about their mysterious death.

"I can feel the outskirts of the city," Amaria said. She imagined that the air around the soldiers she felt was hardening, she imagined the silver glow around the air—she knew her aura was black now, though she wanted to pretend it wasn't. She felt the masses in the air and guessed there were twenty or so sentries on patrol; she twisted the air around five of them, hardening it.

She pulled back as she felt the air give way, the bodies dropping to the ground. She didn't need to risk an exposure of potential magic as they died.

But did it matter? She dove back in, repeating the process with five more. They all would die anyway. They couldn't testify to what they saw.

Corpses didn't speak.

She wondered if she could kill more than five at once. Could she kill ten? She pushed her magic outwards, twisting and hardening the air around the remaining ten bodies. There was a scream, and she felt the disruption in the air.

Nine bodies dropped.

She pushed her magic outwards, the survivor was running—air magic took time to kill. She had no time. The sentry had energy and body heat; he was screaming. She considered trying to burn him alive. It was risky from this distance, and it was risky when she couldn't see the target.

"By Ghagyn's shroud," Amaria cursed. She had to try something before this became an issue. Water. Was water an option? It was dry here in the arid grasslands. Barely inhabitable for civilized life.

Every living thing had water in them; she had learned that blood was mostly water and how to get certain substances to react with water and iron as part of her education. It had always been delightful to hear the screams and begging by the time the true test of practice came in the Drowning Tombs, and later, the Mortensia Labyrinths near Chauvi.

Water could boil.

She shot a burst of her energy out, her heart thumping. She raised the water temperature within the sentry, and pulled out right before every blood vessel in the sentry popped. That would be a horribly messy clean up for whoever found the sentry.

She opened her eyes with a smile. "We have twenty fewer soldiers to worry about."

Theodmon went slack, blinking at her. "Twenty? Amaria, it's not even been twenty minutes. You killed a man in less than a minute...Are you alright?"

Amaria tilted her head. She felt fine. Why would he think she wouldn't be alright?

"Never better," she said.

"Murder...it takes a toll-"

Amaria crossed her arms. She knew what murder was. What did he think occurred when she went to dungeons? Tea parties?

"I've killed plenty before," she interrupted. "So have you, before you get self-righteous."

"Stop," Theodmon told her. "Stop taking out your aggressions on me. I know you're dealing with a lot; please don't make me your tortured prisoner."

Amaria snorted. If she wanted to make Theodmon her tortured prisoner, he'd not be in armor.

He's weak, the dark magic purred. *What do you see in him?*

Amaria recoiled. The dark magic was wrong. Theodmon wasn't weak. He was strong, brave, and honorable. How could the dark magic think he was weak?

Or did *she* think he was weak? She couldn't tell anymore.

Amaria sank down to the ground, clutching her knees as her body shook. "Theo," her voice cracked as if it were a spot in the desert ground. "I don't know...There's something wrong with me."

"It's the magic," Theodmon said, leaning close to her.

Was it? Amaria wasn't sure she could blame the dark magic. She wasn't sure if she wanted to either. It felt good to not hide herself. It felt good to hurt others.

"I'm never pretending to be an innocent, harmless girl again," Amaria met his eyes directly, unblinking. "And I will never pretend to be your suppressed, obedient wife again. We will not continue this farce for Lynette or anybody else."

Theodmon sighed as he hugged her, the armor clanking uncomfortably loud. "Agreed."

"Let's go conquer a country," Amaria said.

"It's only the first step," Theodmon reminded her.

"They'll fall soon enough." Amaria smirked. "It's a siege. They're not protected by walls or armor when I can boil their blood."

She grinned. Her skin tingled, she felt focused, and she felt the air go through her nose. She was alive.

She was most alive when killing others.

Amaria was made to do this and she enjoyed doing these things. Practically, she was good at torture, murder, and gaining leverage over others in any way possible. And she was tired of pretending that she didn't like it. She was tired of pretending that she wasn't gifted at it.

Amaria swore that part of her would die with Rindria.

The world would have to endure the monster they had created.

Chapter Thirty-Eight

The monster was to be with the archers during the siege. Her magic had an extended range, and it was safer for her with the archers.

As Amaria made her way through the camp, people saw the gold, purple, and scarlet dress and moved out of her way. The dress of an Extractor. She had her silver cloak and gloves, made to match the aura of her magic, in her arms. It was too warm to wear them now, but as her energy depleted, she would become cold, needing the cloak and gloves to protect herself from hypothermia.

The archers' commander quickly nodded as she passed him heading up the stairs of the makeshift towers over the otherwise flat plains.

Henri was there already. Durek, the damned Morrian duke, was with the Morrian archers on one of the other platforms. He was talented with a bow, more so than a sword, from what others had told her.

That may be a problem in the future. Amaria didn't like that he was skilled and seemingly preferred a ranged weapon. He could kill her without her seeing it. She wanted to be the only one with the advantage. She would have to find a way to cut off a limb of Durek or some other way to incapacitate him.

"You'd ever think Thestitiunia and Morroek would attack Rindria together?" Henri asked as she stood near him. He was in the gold, purple, and scarlet armor of a male Extractor, his deep blue cloak flapping in the wind.

"You read my thoughts already, so you know that answer," Amaria said. "The world's odd."

"Perhaps," he agreed. "How are you feeling?"

"I'm not as fragile as I look."

"Nobody said that you were. It's alright to not feel invincible in war."

"I've never felt invincible. However, I don't need to be treated like a fragile flower."

"You're as fragile as naphtha."

Amaria resisted rolling her eyes. Naphtha was a dangerous substance—fire that couldn't be suppressed with water and was hotter than most other flames. How apt was it to compare a fire mage on the brink of insanity to naphtha.

"That's not here, is it?" Amaria asked, surveying the grasslands.

Henri laughed. "No. Fire that can't be put out with water or a lack of air and spreads faster than a cheetah can run was universally seen as a bad idea in a grassland. We would hurt our own people."

Amaria nodded. Naphtha was one of the few substances that could burn her. It was a fire that even as a fire mage terrified her.

The dark magic swirled inside of her. That new part of her hissed. It wanted to hold naphtha and to mix magic with it, allowing it to spread and destroy and kill as many as it could.

She looked at her hands. She wondered if she could summon a fire as hot as naphtha. She should try and test the limits of her power more—she was growing more powerful by the day. Had she always been this powerful or had she been too scared to try and test the limits because she needed to be accepted by society.

What a stupid little girl she had been.

"Archers!" She screamed, flames springing to life in her hands. "Who has an unlit brazier for their arrows?"

The Riam war horn blared, the gates shuddering open to reveal a battalion of Riam troops. Their bannerman bore the flag of King Tristan Riarl, whereupon a black horse reared in a sea of golden fabric.

Amaria narrowed her eyes focusing on the ground around his horse. "Aim for the king," she commanded an archer. "Release when I tell you too."

She focused on the ground a hundred feet in front of the king's horse. She breathed, forcing her magic to sink downwards, holding in as gently as embroidery floss as the horse galloped forward.

She released all of the energy she had been holding, tearing the embroidery floss in half as the ground around the king sank. She clapped her hands together, forcing the unspent energy upwards, closing the earth around the king and his horse in her momentum. The horse was almost entirely encased by the ground. The king was stuck from the waist down.

"Now," Amaria said. "Aim to kill."

The archer looked at her in surprise. Kings generally weren't the first to die in battle—they were ransomed.

But this wasn't a war in which prisoners would be taken.

"Now," Amaria commanded. She hoped that her status as an Extractor here carried with this command. She had never held a bow but she needed these archers to enact this plan.

The archer released his arrow. It went through the king of Rindria's face.

Amaria smiled, raising her hands to open the earth, burying the corpse of the Riam king and his horse. Tristan Riarl was dead. His son had died the last time Amaria was in Rindria due to his aunt's misdeeds.

The Riams didn't need to know that there was a succession crisis looming. They didn't need to know their king was dead. Not yet anyways. For now, the official story would be Tristan Riarl had been captured in war.

Before the news of his death came out, she needed to kill the rest of the family to remove any and all claimants to the Riam throne. Either Liara would be alive and the only one with royal blood giving the Chauvignons a claim—she was a puppet, whether she admitted it or not—or there would be no Riam royals left alive, making it a power vacuum.

Power vacuums were amazing when one wanted to conquer the land. With no leadership or central power, Rindria would fall easily to Thestitiunia. And it was best if there was at least semi-arguable deniability that Thestitiunia had anything to do with this looming succession crisis.

Amaria looked over at Henri, knowing he read her thoughts. Sure enough, his mouth was agape, his eyes narrowed.

"You aren't," he said.

Amaria didn't need his judgment. "Tell Theodmon," she told him. "Make sure these archers keep their mouths shut."

Henri grabbed her arm. "Don't do it; this plan is insane. You'll die."

Before she could respond, Amaria felt the ground quake beneath her feet. She looked around wildly—earthquakes didn't happen in Rindira. Not unless there was magic...who was stupid enough in Thestitiunia to start an earthquake? She didn't sanction this use of elemental magic. Not in this way. And Rindria wouldn't work with mages, not knowingly as least—

"Elephants," Henri gasped, letting go of her, turning to yell at the archers. "The elephants are coming. Both towers need to focus on them, now!"

"Where?" Amaria's pitch raised. She had received no intel that Rindria had successfully weaponized elephants for war. Then again, it had been hard to receive intelligence when traveling to the front.

Next to her, the tower commander was already signaling for Durek and his men to concentrate everything they had onto Weorren's front gates, but it was too late.

She could hear a deep, ominous drumming that made the hairs on the back of her neck stand on end. As every archer and ground unit turned to witness the enormous spectacle—armored war elephants sprinted out from the gates, trumpeting deafeningly. These were fully grown savanna elephants large, fast, and strong enough to ignore the flames, which had begun to die down, and to squash any soldier who failed to move out of its way fast enough.

"Shoot them down!" Durek shouted. Although an array of shots from both platforms rained down furiously on the elephants, their hides were far thicker than any arrow could pierce, and several were swirling around to glare at their attackers.

"Stop!" Amaria yelled, watching the elephants become agitated as the arrows bounced from their hides, yet remained otherwise unharmed. "Archers stand down."

"They're angry. They're going to charge," Henri said, his knuckles white against the wooden railing.

"Give me energy. I can use the gems, but it might not be enough," Amaria gripped Henri's hands. She had a plan; it was insane, yes, but it would work.

"Amaria?" Henri gazed down at her in shock. "You're not seriously thinking of *choking* them?"

"Do you have a better suggestion?"

"Don't go dark, please," Henri whispered to her as he pulled her in close, shielding her from Durek's gaze while simultaneously lending her as much of his own magic as he could spare.

Amaria nodded, knowing she couldn't promise what Henri wanted to hear but also knowing that he would despise if she tried to lie to him. She turned her gaze, black pouring from her eyes, as she focused intensely on the middle elephant. She forced all the air around the animal's lungs to divert, slowly hardening the air and blocking its airways. She breathed and the animal fell, its body unmoving.

"What just happened?" Durek's jaw dropped. "What the *fuck* just happened?"

Amaria did not answer, instead moving to the next elephants, focusing on downing as many as possible before the beasts panicked and caused more destruction and flattened Thestitiunian soldiers.

"Anybody want to tell me what is going on here?" Durek yelled across from his tower. "Witc—Marchioness, have you always been able to strangle any living thing you so choose *without touching them*?"

Henri swiveled his head to face Durek irritably. "My Lord, kindly refrain from distracting her while she is saving all of our lives."

"I can see that! I can see that she's killing them. But *how*?"

"She can control wind," Henri said pointedly.

"Wind...so she can control air." Durek deduced the rest for himself, visibly stopping himself from going slack-jawed again.

Amaria blocked them out as if they were background noise. One after another, three elephants keeled over onto the grass, puffing up a cloud of dust as their twitching corpses surrendered to death.

In the middle of the field below, the fighting became thicker and frenzied. Although the towers neutralized the elephants after Amaria strangled the first three that attempted to charge the platforms, amid the distraction, the city gates were left unguarded long enough for more Riam units to pour out, including hundreds of cavalry troops.

She slowly killed elephants. She tried to ignore how her magic felt like a cold, dark, frozen wasteland. She tried to ignore the taste of salt and iron hitting her nose before her blood chilled. She tried to ignore that her magic had once had an airy sea breeze with coastal gulls cawing around.

She wasn't particularly successful.

"Excuse me," she said, stepping back from the railing of the makeshift archer tower. She had another goal.

"Amaria," Henri grabbed her arm once more. "I get it, I do. There's another way. Don't be stupid. You'll die."

Amaria laughed. His concern was sweet, but she didn't plan on dying. She wasn't going to play a game in which the rules were rigged against her. She was going to make her own rules and her own game.

"I'll die if I play by the rules. I go back home and Aion executes me," Amaria removed his hand from her arm. "Perhaps I don't care anymore. I'm powerful—much more than our idiot emperor. Don't try to stop me."

Henri opened his mouth then closed it, stepping away from her. She bundled her cloak around herself, heading towards the main battle in the field.

She looked back towards the Thestitiunian-Morrian side, sighing before she made her way towards the Riam walls. Around her, she used her magic to deflect arrows, boil enemy soldiers in their own blood before they could cut her down, burnt them alive, and buried them and their horses in the ground.

She smiled at the screams.

More would die soon. They would unknowingly welcome death into their castle with open arms.

Amaria was a valuable hostage. And she knew that nobody would expect a hostage to secretly kill while remaining a hostage. She was also weakened—her head was buzzing, she could barely walk straight, and blood was coming from her nose and ears.

Strangling elephants apparently took a lot of magical energy. And nobody would expect her to get herself intentionally captured in this state.

Nobody would know the king was dead.

She turned, placing her hands on the ground in front of her. She brought the dark magic to the center of her chest, and she released it into the ground, causing a crack in the earth reaching several hundred feet in front of her.

A Riam man fell in. Amaria closed the gap. Immediately, the dark magic recoiled, and she felt nauseous, having spent her energy. She placed her hand over the gems in her necklace, slowly moving the energy from the sapphires to herself.

Their camp turned, and she knew they were riding to face her.

She ran to meet them.

Chapter Thirty-Nine

"Witch!"

The horses soon reached her, the men pointing their swords and spears at her.

Amaria raised her hands, knowing what was coming but still feeling fearful seeing the blade pointed at her throat. The man, covered in blood and sweat, leered at her. "I caught myself a witch."

"I'm Marchioness Amaria Chauvignon, daughter of Duke Aaron Raul—"

The guy slapped her across her face, the sword still pointed at her. "I know exactly who you are, bitch. It's why you're a prisoner instead of a corpse. King Tristan will decide your fate." He looked to another soldier with rope in hand. "Bind her."

Amaria's body tensed. She should run. Her legs decided to lock into place.

She was a stupid girl making stupid decisions. She was scared. This was a horrible place for her. She wasn't made for war. She wasn't even made for prison.

She was only good at torturing prisoners because she held the power. Amaria would be powerless here. She could get out of this. She didn't have to do this. She could use her magic to bury them alive in one simple swoop. She could run back behind Thestitiunian lines and stay where it was safe. Rindira would eventually fall.

But the fall would be sour. More Thestitiunian lives would die. And every day that bitch Clarissa drew a fucking breath was a damn waste. Amaria closed her eyes, feeling the blade of the sword against her back, pushing her forward.

She had come this far. She would commit to this plan she had made on a whim. And this plan, as impulsive as it was, would work. Amaria knew this.

Amaria was led away from the battle, deeper into Rindria. She craned her neck, trying to look behind herself for Theodmon. To somehow apologize. To feel his comfort.

She knew he would be livid when he discovered she went rogue, getting herself captured. He was fighting now, however. He wouldn't know what she did until afterwards, and by then it would be too late to stop her.

"Move," the soldier barked at her.

Amaria stared straight ahead coldly, walking where she was led. She opened her mage link, searching for Faelyn. He would be the easiest to reach, as she knew the healing extractor would be healing the injured.

And she didn't want to deal with Henri's disappointment again.

She mentally came across a smooth lake, a stone bouncing across the water. The water had blood in it. She breathed slowly, letting herself touch Faelyn's mind. *"I'm sorry."*

"What?" Faelyn asked. *"What's wrong? Is someone hurt?"*

"No," a tear ran down Amaria's face. *"You need to know something. Henri knows it. Let Theodmon know…in case Henri is killed or injured."* Her hands shook. She was so cold. *"I'm captured. Please, gather my ransom. The Riam King is dead, his body is buried with his horse—the Riams must think he's a prisoner."*

"Amaria!" Faelyn scolded. *"Contain the dark magic! The emperor will kill you—"*

"The emperor will force one of you to kill me," Amaria corrected, her fists clenching. *"Let's not pretend he has any agency of his own. And the Riams may kill me. Does it matter if we get land for the empire and can have a border with Badlands?"*

"Can't you escape? You can easily overpower non-mages." Faelyn argued. *"Think through whatever you're about to do."*

Amaria paused, unsure of how to reply. *"Just get my ransom."*

"What in the gods' names are you doing? Does Theodmon know what you are doing? Does your father?"

Amaria closed her mage link, choosing to no longer talk to Faelyn. It was a distraction.

"Walk faster." A guard hit her with the blunt of his sword.

"Don't touch me!" Amaria snapped.

"Or what?" The guard leered.

That was a good question. Amaria hadn't thought that far. However, there was no time for stalling or for panicking.

"My power is my family name." Amaria spat, looking defiantly up at the guard.

Amaria felt a burning sensation across her face, her mouth filling with warm blood as the guard slapped her, grabbing her up as she fell to the ground.

"Insolent bitch."

Amaria flinched. She felt as if her skin were breaking, as if she was porcelain. It was a slap; she knew they hated her. It was a slap. It wasn't that deep. But she felt as if her entire world was collapsing. Gasping in pain, Amaria was reminded of the disrespect given to her as a result of Lynette's visit.

Amaria wanted to kill them all. She could kill them all.

But if she made that impulsive decision, no matter how good it would feel, Amaria would not get into Bria Hall. She would be unable to murder the royal family where they stood. Clarissa would win. Lynette would win.

Delphina would still be dead. She'll still be dead even if Amaria succeeded. That was unimportant. All Amaria wanted—*needed*—was revenge. Necromancy was outside normal decency.

Amaria had standards after all.

"Move faster!" The guard pushed her forward with his spear, causing Amaria to stumble. She noticed his voice cracked and he stood a distance away from her. He was scared, using pathetic bravado to order her around.

Amaria stared coldly ahead, walking closer to the Riam castle. She wished she could look back at the battlefield to somehow see Theodmon. However, she knew that was not an option. She had a mission, and being seemingly compliant was in her best interests. She was still a Raulet and a Chauvignon, and her apparent compliance ended at stony obedience. She would not beg, especially to men beneath her station.

"Hopefully the king lets us have our way with you," a soldier hissed next to her, his rancid breath wafting over her. "Without those glowing eyes, you're less creepy."

Amaria had almost forgotten, her magic showcased as black. Her eyes appeared normal if one didn't look into them too long.

She missed her silver eyes.

"No." Amaria sucked her breath in. "You will not."

"You aren't the king-"

"Your king will get nothing if that happens!" Amaria's heartbeat rose to her throat.

The man touched her face. "Pretty." He forced his mouth to hers. Amaria screamed, hating the taste of his mouth. She sent her magic towards him, setting him on fire with all of the energy and friction she had within her.

He screamed as she stumbled backwards to get away from him. There were several swords pointed at her neck.

"I don't know how they do things in Thestitiunia, *witch*, but here that's murder," one snarled at her, pressing his sword deep enough against her skin that blood was drawn.

"It's called self-defense. Don't touch me," Amaria said weakly, knowing he could slice her open. She didn't want to die.

"We'll do what we like," he grabbed her by the hair as he dragged her across the ground. Amaria screamed in pain; she needed him to stop. She needed to escape. She shouldn't be doing this.

But don't you want Rindria to burn? You can destroy them. You have the power. Amaria did not know if she or the dark magic said this. It didn't matter, she supposed. Whoever said it was correct. She was powerful and she was effective. Rindria would crumble because of her. She would enjoy watching it be destroyed from within.

"Stop it!" Another man chastised and the first soldier paused, dropping her braid from his hands. Amaria spit grass and rocks out of her mouth. "It's not wise to treat nobility this way. His Majesty won't approve."

"Saved by the king," the first soldier sneered, making sure to slam her face into the dirt one final time. "Born a snake, always a snake."

"I was born a rose," Amaria snapped. "Help me up since you bound my hands and pushed me on the ground."

"I'm not touching her." He spat near her face, turning to the other man. "You do it since you're so keen on saving her skin."

"Not her skin, imbecile," the nobleman scolded. "*Our* skin. Specifically, yours as you aren't noble. Help me stand her up so we can walk her to the cell. She can't get up on her own, thanks to you, and I can't pick her up on my own." He looked over at Amaria, who was lying face first on the grass. "Roll over to your back and tuck your legs up like you're going to do a sit-up, do you know what a sit-up is?"

"I'm aware of the exercise," Amaria said, rolling over to her back, her hands pinned behind her on the ground. She tucked her legs, and behind her, she felt the two men hoist her upwards by her shoulders, the nobleman stabilizing her as she stood.

"Thank you, my Lord," she said more out of habit than actual courtesy.

"See, even the vilest of creatures is still capable of respect if you don't hurt them," the nobleman said pointedly to his subordinates, ignoring Amaria's gratitude.

Involuntarily, Amaria's eyes welled. Why was she crying? She'd been called worse and this *performance* was making her look weak. She tried to turn her head to the side, but with soldiers on all sides of her, the wet spot on her cheek was unmistakable.

"Awww, did he make the vile little witch cry?" One of the soldiers escorting her dawdled, and they all laughed. "Look at you, getting hurt so easily. You're just a pretty face after all."

"I hurt my ankle," Amaria snapped, desperately trying to blame her tears on anything but emotional pain. She could not show weakness. However, physical pain wasn't a weakness for her—she was a woman, so it was an expectation.

One of the soldiers pretended to bump into her leg, kicking her shin in the process. When Amaria didn't instinctively cry out or stumble as much as they expected her to, they laughed again. "Yeah, right, *hurt my ankle*, my ass."

"Don't touch me!" Amaria tried to push the soldier away from her to no avail.

The nobleman glared at the soldiers. "Stop touching her unless you want your head on a spike. And her family *will* come for all our heads if she loses even an inch of her feminine worth."

Amaria hated being talked about as if she were an object. However, she knew better than to protest. If objectification would stop her from being raped, she would tolerate it as stoically as she could.

It didn't stop the rage bubbling within her.

"There are other ways to make the witch cry," the first soldier said gleefully. "Emotions are her weakness. We know it now. Insult her fragile ego and she'll melt."

Amaria internally cursed. She let them know her weakness. She knew better, and yet it still happened. "Fragile ego? Those are big words from a peasant. Do try to make sure you understand all of them." Her voice was as chilly as a Morrian lake in the dead of winter.

"I understand Riam better than you, and I know Thestitiunian too," another soldier retorted. "To think all of daddy's money and fancy tutors couldn't even train you out of your stupidity."

Amaria rolled her eyes, focusing on the looming walls ahead. Bria Hall. What an ugly castle. It wasn't even that secure to make up for its ugliness. Still, she hoped the security issue would work to her advantage. She would be imprisoned after all since she was valuable and wouldn't be killed. And once she killed everyone, she could sneak out of the palace.

It was a simple plan.

And it was time to enact it. Learn faces and names of those she didn't know before. It would help in her escape. Information, even nominal, helped in every intelligence situation. People weren't killed for knowing too much. People were killed for not knowing enough.

Even when killed for sharing information or knowing too much, Amaria held steadfast in the rule that people were killed for a lack of knowledge. They seemed to lack the knowledge on how to keep their mouth shut.

She craned her head to look at the nobleman as they led her down a steep stone stairway. "My Lord, I did not catch your name."

"My Lord will suffice," the nobleman said.

Clever. Amaria clenched her teeth, forcing them into a smile. "Of course, my Lord. Do be cautious where you tread. Thestitiunia is famously as kind a friend as it is a wrathful foe. A trite warning, I am sure."

"Watch your step," he stated as they stepped off the bottom step. Around them, it was dark. Amaria froze and her breathing rapidly increased.

She realized too late that she had not thought this through. She hated darkness. And now she would be surrounded by it. But she was a noble, and a valuable one at that. Why was she here?

"Scared of the dark?" A taunting voice whispered as Amaria was thrown into a cell in the dungeon, her face hitting the stone floor, unable to use her hands to break the fall. Amaria rolled on her side, groaning, as the soldiers locked the gate to her cell.

Her chest tightened as if there was a burning ring around her. The darkness was suffocating her.

Why was she scared of the dark? She had always been scared of the dark. In the dark she was utterly alone. But she was the darkness now—she had a companion of dark magic. It shouldn't scare her.

Amaria was sobbing. She was screaming. She needed light. The shadows had a depth she didn't like. She was going to die alone, in the dark, and her bones would be thrown to dogs.

She shouldn't have done this.

"Let me out!" Her voice broke as she screamed. "I'm Amaria Chauvignon! Let me out of this dungeon!"

She heard laughter from other cells. She screamed wordlessly. She wanted to kill them. She wanted light.

Aren't you a fire mage? The dark magic scoffed. *Grow up.*

Amaria paused in her tears, her throat raw. She was a mage, and she could summon light. She'd be breaking Riam law, but she was imprisoned already and had burned a man alive. What more did she have to lose?

She focused on a spot in front of her, imagining warm yellow flames springing to life from the black hole in front of her.

Chapter Forty

A cool bucket of water was sloshed over Amaria, causing her eyes to open in panic. As soon as her eyes opened, she was kicked in the ribs.

"You summoned fire," Clarissa sneered down at her.

Amaria sucked in her breath, focusing on the light that was coming from a touch that a guard behind Clarissa was holding.

"You will not use magic," Clarissa said. "Guards! Unbind her!"

"What?" Amaria questioned.

"There's no point in letting your clothes and jewels sit here," Clarissa said. "You're changing." She looked at a guard who hadn't moved. "Unbind her."

"But," the guard stuttered, "her magic."

"Point a sword at her then," Clarissa dismissed. "Stab her if she tries anything."

"What?" Amaria's voice shook. "No, I won't be naked in front of men."

"You'll do what you are told," Clarissa hissed as a soldier unbound Amaria's wrists. "You're a *prisoner* and prisoners obey if they want to live."

"I'm a noblewoman!" Amaria shouted, rubbing her wrists. "My modesty means more than your average prisoner!"

"Does it?" Clarissa laughed. "Start taking off your jewelry." Clarissa eyed Amaria's necklace, a diamond set around a halo of rubies. Her eyes shifted to a similar ring on her left hand. "You won't get these back; think of them as a good faith down payment of your safe return."

"No," Amaria snarled. "You're not getting my wedding ring."

"I'm getting everything you have on you," Clarissa smirked.

"Not my wedding ring," Amaria ignored the sword against her spine. She was disgusted that Clarissa would view a wedding band as something to pawn. "The rest of the jewelry is yours."

"Surely it can be replaced?"

Amaria wanted to tear out Clarissa's throat. It was sentimental. While, yes, Theodmon could get her another ring easily, that wasn't the issue. She wanted *that* ring, not a replacement.

"I see where Liara gets her stupidity from," Amaria said. "No."

"Beat her," Clarissa told a guard. "Break her bones, just don't permanently disfigure her or rape her—she needs to have some value for a ransom."

"I'm pregnant!" Amaria screamed. "It's been publicly announced. You think killing my husband's child by hurting me will help you?"

Clarissa paused. "Change her," she ordered the guard.

The guard pulled out a knife, cutting Amaria out of her dress. He roughly pulled her out of it, leaving her only in her undergarments.

He saw the knife strapped to her leg, taking it from her. Amaria glared; she understood the need for disarming prisoners, but Theodmon had given her that dagger the last winter solstice. She knew she wasn't getting it back.

"Jewelry," Clarissa commanded.

Amaria glared at her, not breaking eye contact as she unclasped her necklace. "I'd expect you'd be dead, playing with dark magic and risking every—"

"Your assassination attempt made the king love me," Clarissa interrupted, pulling the rings off Amaria's hands and taking the necklace.

"Give those back!" Amaria knew she was being stupid. But she needed her wedding band. She needed comfort. She was risking everything for a ring and she didn't care.

"You're an insolent, arrogant shrew," Clarissa hit Amaria across the face.

Mortified, Amaria swayed, feeling a sense of vertigo overcome her. She blinked rapidly, trying to force back the hot tears dripping down her cheeks. She was nearly naked in a Riam prison being insulted by a woman who had almost caused her to die.

And it was Amaria's own arrogance and scheming that had landed her here. She could escape—but then the situation would be worse. There would be no arguable deniability of her killing Riams. Eyes narrowing, Amaria's jaw locked as she looked at Clarissa, her chest heaving. She couldn't give Clarissa the satisfaction of thinking she'd won.

She imagined Clarissa in her place, being tortured on a rack, her blonde hair grimy and knotted. In her mind, Amaria let Clarissa keep her clothes—they were a punishment enough as it was, and Amaria didn't hate herself enough to witness Clarissa being naked.

"I think you speak of yourself when you describe an arrogant shrew," Amaria spat. No sooner than the words came out of her mouth did the guard hit her, prompted by a look from Clarissa.

"Beat her," Clarissa smiled, looking at the middle of Amaria's white petticoat. "Seems you're no longer pregnant."

Amaria looked down. She saw red. She cursed. She had forgotten about having a period in the midst of being beaten and dragged. And now, because of her extended lie, it looked as if she was in the early stages of having a miscarriage.

They would physically torture her now. They had nothing to fear as long as her injuries weren't permanent. "Your guards dragged me," Amaria said hurriedly. "They caused the miscarriage. Don't make this worse—"

The guard hit her in the stomach and she doubled over.

"I don't give a shit about Theodmon Chauvignon," Clarissa sneered. "You killed his child; I'm sure the beating my guards give you will prepare you for what he does."

Amaria knew she had heard about how he treated her when they had been spinning a web for Lynette. She knew this, and her entire body was shaking. How dare Clarissa insult her husband? She spat at Clarissa's feet. "You should prepare for the punishment the gods give you."

"Strip her," Clarissa ordered. "Bring her to a darker cell."

"I won't be naked in front of men," Amaria said.

Her mind was whirling as panicked breaths caught in her throat. She was being brought to a darker cell. They were either going to torture her or they were bringing her there because they now knew she was scared of the dark because she had been unable to hide it.

"You'll get a change of clothes—a standard prison gown," Clarissa dismissed.

Amaria's nostrils flared. She would kill her. She would kill them all. That was why she was here after all—to be close enough to the Riam royals to murder them in their own home. She glared at the guards, daring them to step near her. However, it was unnecessary as they all looked about as unwilling to come near her as they would come near a unicorn. Perhaps they saw her as one, bloodthirsty and beautiful. Thinking that about her or unicorns wasn't incorrect.

"Don't touch me," Amaria snapped at a guard.

"You don't have the authority—" The guard began.

"I'm not letting anybody touch me when I'm naked!" Amaria screamed. "You want me to stay valuable? Respect my modesty."

The guard looked at Clarissa, who rolled her eyes. "Let her change on her own. Unbind her hands for it—she's gonna be in metal chains soon anyways."

Amaria felt a lump rise to her throat. They were securing her more than she had assumed they would. She was rich, a Raulet, a wife of a Chauvignon—why was she being treated like a common prisoner?

I'm not. Amaria sucked in her breath as the guards cut her rope bonds. *The only reason I'm not dead for magic and using my magic to kill others is because I'm rich, a Raulet, and married to a Chauvignon.*

She should never have come here. Gulping, she steadied herself. She was here though, and she might as well finish what she came here to do. Amaria had been taught early on the value of following through with commitments and threats, and she wasn't about to abandon those lessons now.

Her hands shaking, Amaria turned her back to the guards, facing the wall, reaching behind her to find the strings of her corset. She was here. She would not leave without the entire Riam royal family dead and with a way to deny her involvement and it be at least halfway believable.

However, she'd save Clarissa for last.

"Hurry up," Clarissa clicked her tongue impatiently as Amaria's hands shook over her petticoat. Once she took this off, she'd be completely naked. Flinching, Amaria moved the dress over her head, tears streaming down her face as her dress fell to the ground, leaving her utterly exposed.

Her magic bubbled up, threatening to overflow, to escape from her. She wanted to lash out, to feel the power run through her veins, and most importantly, she wanted to hurt everyone here.

As soon as the dress hit the ground, a guard grabbed her and forcefully pushed her to her knees, bringing her hands back behind her back, the chains clanking as he bound her. Amaria felt completely exposed kneeling in the cell, stark naked. She hung her head, feeling every pair of eyes in the cell scan her body.

"My Lady," Amaria gritted her teeth, "may I please be clothed?"

She wanted to cover herself. Her hands were bound. Her hair was nominally covering her breasts but was otherwise useless. By the gods, Clarissa should be gutted like a pig. Clarissa looked like a blonde pig. Amaria glared at her. She hated that Clarissa thought she had the power.

And yet she loved that Clarissa thought she had power over her. It would make victory much sweeter when Clarissa's position turned to ash and her venomous words turned to poison.

"Who has a better dress now?" Clarissa sneered before she snapped her fingers at a guard. Amaria blinked. Was Clarissa truly shallow and petty enough to be doing this over her being better dressed? Amaria had upstaged her—intentionally—last time in Rindira, but she expected Clarissa to be more angry about things like assassinations or starving and attacking the country.

The guard stepped forward with a brown smock, placing it over Amaria's head, weaving the back of the dress through her arms before forcefully helping her stand. Amaria felt his hand linger on her backside, and she wished she could burn him alive. The guard walked around, and going underneath her armpits, he tied the strings together to complete the dress. As he was doing so, Amaria stared at the ground, horrified that the dress only stopped at her knees and that the strings still left gaps on the side of the dress.

"Bring her down below," Clarissa ordered. "No light. A cell with heavy objects. Nobody gives her food without my permission. Water once every other day." She leaned down to meet Amaria's eyes. "The Raulets starved this country, and I'm happy to return the favor."

Amaria's eyes flashed. "I'm sure that's the first and last thing you'll ever do for your country."

Clarissa hit her across the face, her multiple gaudy rings giving her blow more force than it would have had otherwise. Amaria closed her eyes, feeling herself swallowing blood.

Smiling, she spat the blood out, looking directly at Clarissa. The Riam princess was provoked and her actions only confirmed to Amaria that Clarissa was meddlesome and easily manipulated.

Amaria didn't want to manipulate her though.

"Sleep well," Clarissa said as Amaria was dragged out of the cell.

Amaria wanted to burn them all alive. She couldn't now because it would ruin her true purpose for being here. Amaria had to successfully kill the Riam royal family to weaken the country so it could easily be taken without expending too many Thestitiunian resources or sacrificing Thestitiunian lives needlessly.

Amaria had a purpose for restraining from murder now. However, she couldn't allow Clarissa to do this to her, to humiliate her in this way.

"I'll be the last face you see before you die," Amaria snarled. It wasn't an empty threat. It was a promise.

Clarissa laughed mockingly. "You're in a dungeon. I think I'll kill you."

As the cell blocks got darker and Amaria was brought into a cell that had only a rack table and a place to chain her to the wall, she thought that perhaps Clarissa was right. Amaria was weak. She couldn't do anything as the guards took turns beating her before chaining her to the wall with her hands over her head.

But Amaria wasn't weak; she was powerful. She just didn't feel that way. Amaria wasn't sure if telling herself that she had power was enough to delude her brain from the fact she was a prisoner.

Chapter Forty-One

Amaria's body was numb, her shoulders were curled over her chest as her arms were chained above her head. She had been imprisoned for days. Or she thought so anyway. It was hard to tell when it was constantly dark.

Choking, she tried to breathe only through her mouth, gagging each time she smelled her surroundings. Amaria was covered in her own urine, sweat, and feces. Being chained to a wall meant that she had limited choice in where she relieved herself.

Her throat was sore. Her face was tear stained. She had finally stopped hyperventilating enough to focus. The dark still terrified her, all of the hairs of her body were standing up on end, but she could function.

She had to function or all of this would be for nothing.

"Brandon Hull, Josef Hull, Andrew Hull, Annalise Hull, Christopher Lyncan, Victoria Lyncan, Anthony Lyncan, Edward Fayley, Gabriel Fayley, Jenna Riarl, Karissa Riarl, Clarissa Nalaeny," Amaria muttered under her breath the names of those she was to kill. She wished she could have added three: Liam, Tesden, Liara. She couldn't because she had distant blood relations she had acknowledged—only to anger Liam—and she would be cursed by the gods for kin slaying. If she hadn't been petty, nobody would care about a fourth cousin or whatever being murdered.

Amaria laid her head against the wall, trying to ignore the grime. She had sat in this prison pathetically allowing herself to be beaten, starved, and humiliated. She had to bide her time because it would be suspicious if as soon as she arrived the royal family started to die. Did it matter? If Rindria was overthrown, they'd kill the royal family anyways.

They're still a sovereign nation, Amaria told herself. Unfortunately, the methods of acceptable murder rested entirely on the timing of the killing.

Throwing her head back, Amaria screamed. Every single person in this gods' damned country, this gods' damned court, all of them were worthless. Amaria couldn't believe she had flung herself on a gem to save them. She had done it to save Theodmon, Henri, Lucas, Aloysius, and Haerdnor, but still, these incompetent fucks benefited from her actions.

She had died to save them and now they were torturing her. She had welcomed Liara into her family, despite her intolerance of magic and stupid, naïve behavior that made life more difficult for Amaria. She had even saved that damn peasant. Amaria had done a lot for Rindria. Things she shouldn't have done.

And they killed her friend and fucking imprisoned her.

They even pulled out a few of Amaria's fingernails.

She'd burn this whole country alive. Amaria leaned her head back, screaming in anger and frustration. She sounded feral, as if she were a banshee instead of a human woman. Perhaps it would be better for Rindria if she was a banshee. There was no wrath like that of a woman who had been slighted and disrespected.

She would kill the entire royal family while she sat in this dungeon. She would wait for a few more days because she knew that any death that occurred suddenly, regardless of how long she waited, would cast suspicion on her. However, she hoped that there would be enough plausible deniability to work with. She didn't want to be in this prison for longer than she needed to be. She hoped Theodmon and her father were working quickly on her ransom.

Amaria had a headache. She had thirteen people to kill. The prince and king were dead. Theodmon could handle Liam. Tesden was exiled, so they could hunt him down with an assassin. Liara, well, hopefully she tripped on her own sword.

Did she forget anyone? Amaria reached her fingertips out, summoning fire. She was risking everything because if someone came in and saw her do magic, she would be punished. However, she felt the warmth on her hands as the flames hugged her, and she could not find it in herself to take away the smallest comfort she had.

Amaria closed her eyes, trying to remember the layout of Bria Hall from Haerdnor's reports from when he conducted business, from spies reports, and from her own times visiting.

"Edward Fayley," she whispered, knowing he lived two floors above the dungeons. It wouldn't be too hard to find him with her magic. "Brandon Hull." He lived a few doors down from the Fayleys. "Christopher and Anthony Lyncan." They were more protected, living in fortified knights' corridors. "Karissa and Jenna Riarl." The princesses would die today as well.

Were five murders of the Riam Royal family too much in a day?

Yes, she supposed it was.

Four sudden deaths would do for now. Christopher would be spared for a few more days.

She closed her eyes, dropping her head so her dark hair draped over her like a creeping plague. She extended her magic, amplifying the air so she could hear the voices of her victims. Once they were discovered, once she knew their exact location, the real work would begin.

Her old magic—the small strand of silver in a black pool—stretched. She felt it fighting against the constraints she placed on it. Her magic, the little that hadn't been tainted, screamed. Amaria didn't know how she still had uncorrupted magic. Amaria didn't acknowledge the still uncorrupted magic, as if that acknowledgment would alert the dark magic to its possible last victim. Perhaps she was too far gone. It was true that she wanted power.

She wanted the dark magic.

However, she didn't want to lose her old magic, wishing it would stay with her. Amaria didn't know why, but she just needed to know the small silver strand would be alright. She didn't want it to be strangled by the more powerful black magic.

Slowly, painstakingly, she manipulated the air. After a half hour she had hit gold. She had found Brandon Hull. He was a strong warrior, so a sudden death would be suspicious. Any death would be suspicious while she was here, though.

Amaria stretched out her magic, feeling the air above her. She felt the vibrations pulsating through the air and faintly heard, though heard wasn't the best description, it was as if her energy *felt* the presence of others disturbing the air. Amaria's emotions, and therefore her magic, were about to explode from her.

It was going to be obvious she killed them.

What were they going to do? Beat her? Starve her? They were already doing that.

Amaria gritted her teeth, gathering the air around Brandon's lungs and body. She hardened it, redirected it away from his lungs. She knew that he was choking; his eyes were likely bulging as he gripped his throat as he enjoyed his horrific last moments alive before his body hit the floor.

Perhaps him enjoying it was a hyperbole...no, rather, it was a straight up lie. Who enjoyed their own death? But Amaria enjoyed his death. She had learned the skills of her current captors as a child. She had never been horrified at her lessons; instead, she had rather been enthralled and neurotic in perfecting her skills.

Amaria could not ignore the irony of someone else practicing those same skills on her while she secretly used her perfected abilities to act as a phantom in murdering others while she lay imprisoned, humiliated, and injured in her victim's dungeon.

Perhaps it showed her competence in contrast to the façade of competence Rindria showed. Rindria was pathetic.

She was pathetic in this dungeon. Amaria breathed, slowly pulling away from the small area of air around Brandon's lungs. She focused intensely at that small area of air, recoiling as he fell to the ground, choking. She knew he would take one more breath and then die, but she didn't want to be there.

It was too risky.

Her dark magic hissed. It wanted to stay. It wanted to taste his death.

Amaria, however, had no desire to experience the aftertaste of Brandon's death; she had other things to do. She knew she would likely be questioned about it soon enough and she had three others to kill today before the questioning began. Again, she closed her eyes, searching for the others on her list, soon finding Edward Fayley.

Her eyes flashed as she heard his laugh. Last time she had heard that laugh, he had tried to force her against a wall—arrogantly offering her father money when he was caught.

Her father had arrived too late. Edward Fayley still had a burn scarred face from that encounter.

He deserved to suffer. Suffocation was too easy, too painless. Amaria flexed her fingers, wondering if she had an alternative. She would love to have his blood fill the halls. She stared at her moving fingers; she knew humans were mostly water and that there was water flowing in the bloodstream. She had used this method in the battle a few days earlier.

Amaria shifted the air again, searching for him. What if she killed him with water? With his own body? She clenched her fist as she pushed out her magic inside of him, quickly raising the temperature of his blood.

She heard the screams in the air as soon as she finished. Amaria smiled as she pulled away from her magic.

Good.

She would be tortured soon. Her smile faltered; she didn't enjoy being in pain. She had been trained in interrogation techniques, of course, both as the interrogator and some as the interrogee. Amaria preferred the role of the interrogator.

Hanging her head and breathing heavily, Amaria paused, the world around her spinning as her stomach pinched in hunger. She was weakened, Clarissa being true to her word in starving her. Amaria would have to recover her energy as best she could before using her magic again. A mage overextending themselves could be deadly.

Besides, the Riams would be running into her cell any moment to punish her. They might call it questioning or whatever else, but it was a punishment.

She would endure. She had to. She needed to get back home.

Amaria missed Theodmon. She missed Lysander. She closed her eyes, trying to imagine their faces. She wanted to be with them. What if she died and never saw Lysander again?

A sob escaped her. She wanted to see her son and to be with him. Fuck Rindria for being a country of asinine fools incapable of governance. Amaria could have been at home, but no, somebody had to play with magic and politics and things for intelligent people when the collective intelligence level of the country was less than a half-feral squirrel.

She screamed. Screaming was better than sobbing. Rage was rage. It wasn't a weakness. Sobbing was a weakness—it could only be a strength when she planned her tears. She wasn't faking at being vulnerable now.

Amaria closed her eyes. She didn't need to think about this. She couldn't afford to have these thoughts. She breathed, the stench of herself causing her to gag. Amaria had time before they figured out what had occurred and suspected her. She could kill a few more. Perhaps a princess and Anthony Lyncan.

Slowly, she wove her magic through the palace. She managed to get into the courtyard and heard two girls talking.

"Jenna!" one squealed. "Stop!"

"You're mad I'm better at lawn games," Princess Jenna laughed.

"You're my insufferable little sister," the other protested. "You're only good because I taught you."

Amaria laughed. Forget Anthony Lyncan. She would kill two princesses. She'd make it gentle—Karissa and Jenna Riarl had never committed any crimes other than being the daughters of an incompetent king.

She gently cradled the air around Jenna, leaving a small residue of her magic before doing the same with Karissa. They would die as instantaneously as Amaria could make it. She would hate to have to see Catalina or Haerdnor die.

Amaria realized that they were innocent girls, merely teenagers. And so she would give them a painless death. It wasn't their fault for being who they were.

However, Amaria couldn't let them live. They were still in the line of succession, and they would die in the Thestitiunian conquest of Rindria anyways. Being strangled to death was kinder than what might happen to girls during a siege when the country fell. Especially royal girls.

Her heartbeat rapidly pounding, Amaria slowly decreased Jenna and Karissa's air flow, alternating from one to another. She breathed, mimicking what she imagined was Karissa's labored breathing. Amaria circled her magic around her, cutting off her lungs.

"Help," Karissa gasped, blood pouring from her eyes. Amaria growled, sending a spike of energy, boiling the blood in Karissa's veins. Like a wave coursing through her body, the girl's skin turned purple and blistered, the popping bumps sending water and blood over her tortured flesh.

There was a pop, and Jenna screamed for help. So much for trying to give them a peaceful death. Riams ruined everything. Amaria shot out her magic towards Jenna, killing her in the same way as her sister.

Amaria pulled away as Jenna fell to the ground. They'd come for her soon. Her magic hadn't been exactly subtle. It was a clever way to kill people. But it wasn't subtle.

She leaned against the wall, listening to the water dripping in the darkness. That noise was maddening. It was more maddening to wait in the darkness, to be sitting chained and unable to do anything but prepare for the impending torture. It truly was her father's fault she was in this situation. If he hadn't trained her in this sort of thing, perhaps she wouldn't have run straight into the lion's jaw.

These sort of thoughts weren't healthy, but Amaria still had them.

"Witch!" The door to the cell flung open.

"Yes?" Amaria stared coldly at them, trying to appear unruffled. She supposed that was hard when one was covered in their own waste. Whatever, it was better than begging for mercy.

"Members of the royal court have died," the guard said, pulling in several guards behind him.

Against her will, Amaria felt her eyes water. She wanted to curse. She was showing weakness. Weakness was what got people killed. She wasn't weak.

Is that so? The dark magic scoffed.

Shut up. Amaria told it.

"Is that so?" Amaria's voice cracked as she lifted her head to look at the guard, the corners of her mouth curled into a sneer.

The guard grabbed her, unlocking her from the wall. "Someone's blood burst from their body as they walked. How do you think that happened?"

"Sounds like he was unhealthy. Was he seeing a doctor?" Amaria said. Her arms collapsed to her sides, shaking. They were sore, tense.

"Tie her to the rack," the guard barked at the others accompanying him.

"No..." Amaria gasped as the guards grabbed her. She thrashed, trying to force them off of her. She enjoyed racking others, not being racked herself.

The guards lifted her up and she started to scream. She was a stupid girl who made impulsive mistakes and was going to be racked because of her stupid arrogance.

"You won't be racked," the guard laughed. "It's just easy to secure you so we can do other things. You don't need unbroken legs to be valuable to your husband and father. They'll heal."

"Please," Amaria begged as she was strapped down. Her face was ashen as she stared ahead, yet not seeing anything in front of her. Things were moving so fast that she couldn't process it. Was she going to die?

"I don't know what's going on. What happened?" Amaria whimpered. Her heartbeat was racing so fast it felt as if it would explode from her chest.

"Three royal family members died, witch," the guard picked up a whip, letting it hit across her chest. Even though she had the prison gown on, it did nothing to protect her. She screamed as black dotted her vision. Her back arches and she screamed, her voice shattering between her sobs.

"How did that happen?" The guard said.

"I don't know," Amaria gasped. She couldn't admit anything. She had to lie. But she had to mix the truth in. She had to endure. "Who died? I've been down here. Why are you torturing me?"

"They obviously died of magic." The guard whipped her again.

Starbursts appeared from behind Amaria's eyes. She wanted this to end. Her mouth had a coppery taste in it, and she felt as if the world was spinning.

"When there's a known witch around, who some of us know is bloodthirsty—Aaron Raulet hid your true nature for years, and he did it well. But some of us aren't easily fooled."

"I'm a prisoner," Amaria said.

"Do you take us for imbeciles?" The guard whipped her again; she felt the blood coming from her chest. She closed her eyes, screaming. It felt as if a million swords were scrapping her skin with acid. She was going to die.

She understood why prisoners would often say anything, even if it wasn't true. They wanted the pain to stop. Amaria wanted the pain to stop.

"I believe you have eyes and are intelligent enough to see I was chained to a wall," Amaria snarled weakly. "How would I kill a royal family member? I think you're giving me more credit than I deserve."

"Give me the mallet," he commanded a bystander.

Amaria felt bile rise to her throat. Whipping her wasn't enough. She'd have to confess something soon. Something that wasn't the true crime. By the gods, she was fucked.

A sharp crash came down on her shin. She screamed as she felt her bone shatter. She was passing out.

Cold water was poured over her face.

"No," the guard said, his face directly over hers. "We aren't done."

"Why?" Tears poured from Amaria's eyes. Her leg was broken. She needed healing. She wouldn't get it; she'd be forced to sit in this filth with her broken legs and open wounds. "I'm an important hostage, why am I being tortured for someone else's death?"

"You've broken the law," the guard said.

"I needed light," Amaria sobbed. This was the silver of truth. "I didn't think anybody would know I summoned fire in here."

The guard slapped her. "We told you not to do magic."

"I'm scared of the dark," Amaria said pathetically.

The guard picked up the whip again. "Turn her on her back," he commanded the other guards. "She's getting ten more lashes."

Amaria screamed as they picked her up and turned her on her front. Pain shot up her leg. Pain shot across her chest. She vomited, laying in her own filth.

She would kill more after they left. Perhaps she would kill these guards as well; they weren't important but they deserved as much hell as the rest.

She felt a lash across her back and saw black spots.

Around the fifth lash she became fully unconscious.

Chapter Forty-Two

Amaria was being beaten again, tears streaming down her dirt stained face. Her bronze skin was covered in a myriad of black and purple bumps and open wounds—a mixture of dried blood and fresh intermingling—at this point, she was convinced her body was more bruises and wounds than healthy flesh. If the injuries weren't offensive enough, she was covered in her own waste.

Clenching her jaw, Amaria cursed Rindria with every god's name she could recall. It had been weeks without food. She was delirious. She had only managed to kill five others. Her energy was faltering, and she needed energy to do magic.

Andrew Hull, Christopher Lyncan, Gabriel Fayley, Clarissa Nalaeny. Amaria thought as the whip cracked down on across her arms. She was so close.

She wanted Clarissa to die in front of her.

"Why're people dying when you're here?" The guard said.

"How's my ransom coming?" Amaria's words were slurred.

"None of your business." He cracked the whip again.

Amaria screamed, tears streaming down her face. She was pathetic. She should lean into it. "I want my father," she whined.

The guard grabbed her face, facing her to look at him. "Aaron Raulet can't help you," he sneered. "Tell us why people are dying and we'll let you rest. Get you salve for your wounds."

Amaria wasn't an idiot and he wasn't a good liar. But why would they care if she confessed? Was this gratuitous punishment under a presumptive guise of needing information?

Obviously. Amaria's chest sank. This was just a way for Rindria to punish someone for the wrongs they believed to have endured because of the Raulets and Thestitiunia. Amaria had done something similar with her own prisoners before.

"I already told you," she said. "I don't know."

The whip hit her face. She gasped in between her tears. They hit her face. If it wasn't treated, she'd have a scar. She'd be ugly.

Another guard pushed the whipper aside. "We weren't to touch her face," he said. "Get her a healer."

"Why should we keep her pretty for a rich fuck?" The guard grumbled.

"Because that rich fuck told Clarissa that he'd pay significantly less for her if she wasn't kept pretty for him to fuck," he said.

Amaria was crying more openly than she had before. Her face. She was beautiful. And she couldn't lose that beauty. She couldn't be scarred. Losing her looks would cause her to lose her efficiency in her manipulation methods–she knew she had disarmed more than a small number of people with her beauty.

"Get her food, salve, and water," the guard commanded. "With luck we can make it so this doesn't scar."

"Princess Clarissa said no food-"

"She's had none for over two weeks," the guard pressed a cloth to her bleeding face. Amaria was shaking on the rack. She felt cold, so cold. "She needs food and medical care; she's cold; she has open wounds; she had a miscarriage from what I heard. She might die before we get the king back and Clarissa gets her money. Who do you think the princess will punish if that happens?"

"She's a prisoner-"

"Who's worth over a million gold pieces," the man said. "Try again. You shouldn't have whipped her face."

Amaria sobbed. She wanted to die. Everything hurt. She was stupid. She shouldn't be here. If she got out of this, she was just going to stay home and have babies where it was safe and she was warm and comfortable.

She was never sleeping in any darkness ever again. Candles wouldn't do anymore. She would have to find a way to have something brighter, perhaps several lanterns.

Amaria rubbed her wrists. She had been unchained as she sat in the infirmary, several guards staring at her warningly as the healer checked over her.

"She has sepsis—blood poisoning," the healer said. "The open wounds and broken bones while covered in filth was a bad choice for a high value prisoner. I was also told she had a miscarriage. What were you thinking?"

"It was on my orders," Clarissa stepped in the infirmary. "She won't be treated by you. I will determine Amaria Raulet's conditions here."

"You'll kill her," the healer said. "I hate the Raulets as much as any Riam, but she can't die. I want the king back, killing her is his death warrant."

"I'm commanding you—" Clarissa started.

"I will not effectively commit regicide," the healer stood firm. "The king can punish me how he sees fit. You're not the king."

"You-"

"Get out, princess," the healer said. "Or explain to the king why Theodmon Chauvignon and Aaron Raulet are burning Rindria."

"They're burning it now."

"And how much worse will it be when they find out you killed Amaria Chauvignon and the child in her? I'm treating her. Once she's better, you can put her back in the dungeons."

Amaria closed her eyes. The world felt cold, dark; it was light in here, but it didn't feel real.

The healer tapped her on the head and she flinched.

"We need to clean you up. Stay awake," he commanded her. He looked over towards a female assistant. "Get some maids to clean up Lady Chauvignon."

"I won't have her treated with dignity!" Clarissa snarled. "She and her husband tried to murder me."

"And they failed," the healer said tiredly. "When she's not a hostage we need to exchange for our king, you can kill her. However, the king gave me authority over all medical decisions in Bria Hall; please don't make me have you dragged out of here."

"He'll whip you!" Clarissa screamed. The healer sighed, asking guards to secure the infirmary and take Clarissa away.

"I'll take whatever punishment the king gives me," he said.

Amaria couldn't understand how someone was so loyal to such an incompetent ruler. However, she wouldn't question it for it was what was saving her life.

Chapter Forty-Three

Amaria touched her cheek, flinching as the healer changed the bandages on her back. She had been fed, given a bath, had her leg set, and given medicine over the past week. The healer was gentle.

She could tell he hated her, but he wasn't cruel and changed her bandages without causing her more harm. She looked away, not wanting to make eye contact with him. She was vulnerable and he was her only saving grace.

And she despised not only herself for showing this weakness, but also the healer for seeing it.

"Thank you," she choked.

He stepped back from her. "Your ransom was agreed on and collected; you'll be leaving soon."

"Thank you," she repeated. She wondered why he was telling her. Good will? He had already saved her life. She laid down on her side, wincing, pulling the blanket over her. "May I sleep?"

The healer shook his head in disbelief, walking away from her. She closed her eyes. With some food, though it was stale and limited—Amaria suspected Clarissa had something to do with that—she had mustered enough energy to kill two more. Now only Gabriel Fayley and Clarissa Nalaeny were left for her to kill.

She wondered how Theodmon would cover the three remaining Nalaenys.

She closed her eyes. She was exhausted. Sleeping would be nice.

"Cut her hair."

Amaria woke up to a hand over her mouth, with several men holding her down. She thrashed.

"Stop fighting," Clarissa leaned over Amaria with a sneer, and Amaria realized she was the one who gave the order to cut her hair. "The agreement was nothing permanent to your looks. Hair grows back."

Amaria bit down on the man's hand. "Help!" She screamed.

She was stupid. Why would anybody rush to her aid?

They could cut her throat. She summoned her energy, panic rising to her throat. Every living thing had warmth in them. Fire was warmth and energy. Amaria thrashed, pain hitting every bone and tendon in her body, as she fought against the men.

A long chunk of brown hair fell onto the ground. Amaria's ears roared with the thumping of her heartbeat. She felt the heat radiating from each human, and she twisted her energy around it, intensifying their warmth. Every guard and Clarissa burst into flames.

"Magic!" One screamed. "The witch!" He couldn't get more words out, the pain of being burned alive took away his power to form words.

Amaria smiled, placing her hand on a burning man's arm, the fire embracing her without harm. "Don't try to kill witches when they're sleeping. We're unpredictable and easily angered."

She loved watching them wither and run around in a panic they created. She loved smelling the burning of their flesh. She loved watching the flesh peel from their bones and their bones turn to ash.

They all died and she laughed maniacally.

Specifically, Amaria watched Clarissa die, the princess withering in pain. Clarissa's makeup combined with her melting and charred flesh, blood spots appearing around her cheeks and eyes.

Not so pretty now. Amaria raised the intensity of the heat on Clarissa, laughing maniacally as more guards rushed inside the infirmary, the healer behind them.

Clarissa's skeleton fell to the ground with the rest as a litany of swords were pointed at Amaria.

"They tried to cut my neck," Amaria said, looking at the knife near one of the charred corpses. "I was sleeping and woke up to almost being murdered. I did what I had to do in self-defense."

She still had most of her hair; they had cut only one chunk out, and it could be hidden with careful styling. Amaria breathed heavily, her eyes welling with tears as her hand touched the spot where she now had a short spot near her scalp.

They cut her face. When that failed to make her ugly, they tried to scalp her. A horrible noise came from her—she sounded like a wailing cat. She was crying in front of Riam soldiers and a Riam healer.

Gods, her father would critique her from the grave for seven generations for this. Raulets didn't show weakness.

That seemed to be all she was good for recently.

The dark magic she had was all that wasn't weak. Perhaps it was time to fully embrace it, to let it crush the small silver magic.

No. Amaria shook her head, bringing her arm upwards to wipe the tears away. She couldn't do that. The silver magic was her old friend. She loved it.

She had it when Delphina was alive. She was doing this for justice. She wasn't murdering because she was evil—she was avenging her friend. She was a good person. She could be a good person and use dark magic.

Amaria was not going to let anyone tell her otherwise. She also wasn't going to admit that maybe she wasn't as good of a person as she would like to believe.

"We're to bring you to Weorren Fields," the healer said, his face twisted as if something had died under his nose. "Your ransom is ready."

A guard sheathed his sword, slowly coming towards her. "You have a broken leg?"

She nodded. She needed to get away from here before she lost even more of her dignity.

"I'm going to carry you to Wéorren," he told her.

She was going to see Theodmon soon. She had killed all but one person on her list. Well, that was four people for Theodmon to handle now: Liara Nalaeny, Tesden Nalaeny, Liam Nalaeny, and Gabriel Fayle

Her eyes were heavy. She had to suppress a smirk all the same. She was successful in killing the royal family, and they would never know she intentionally got herself captured.

Amaria likely wouldn't pull a stunt like this again—her own arrogance and scheming had almost gotten her killed. And she was in excruciating pain because of it.

But Amaria had been successful. And she was going home to recover. They were somebody else's issue now, and she didn't care. She closed her eyes, letting the guard take her from Bria Hall, through Wéorren City, and outside to the Wéorren Fields.

The fields stretched to the horizons, and their otherwise homogeneous patterns were only broken up by the shadows cast by the clouds above. Amaria could smell iron. The grass in Rindria where rain was scarce was spongy from the rivers of blood beneath the boots of the guard who carried her. She could hear it.

She focused on breathing, scanning to see if she could see familiar faces as she trudged through the Riam encampment. There was a ringing in her ears—the sounds around her, even if they were right beside her, felt as if they were coming from far away.

She yawned, picking at her fingernails to stay awake. Her body shook. She was cold. So cold.

Worst of all, Amaria was crying. In a cruel irony, large tears had started falling down her face as she was so close to safety. She was so close to a place where she could break down without being seen as weak, and she didn't have to maintain her composure. Amaira tried to curl into herself as best she could yet she felt the sobs trapped in her throat as she gritted her teeth as she desperately tried to suppress the noise. It was bad enough she was crying as a Riam soldier held her; she would not make that pathetic noise.

A shaky gasp escaped her, snot hitting her lip. No. She was sobbing anyway.

Amaria couldn't stop it. She wiped her nose with her hand, her body shaking as she shut her eyes, trying to block out the guard's look of disdain. She would cry, then focus on her surroundings. She would take into account the banners. Most were unfamiliar now, but she focused on them to ground herself to the present reality.

She was going to be safe with Theodmon. Her father was going to protect her.

After what had to be an hour, the banners became more familiar. A dragon with wheat on an orange background, a silver background with a gold star, bears with a forest behind them.

And on top of a low sloping hill, a scarlet and gold banner with a griffin and swords and a blue banner with a golden money scale and red roses. Lucas held Theodmon's banner as he rode his stallion next to Theodmon. Her father was there too, his bannerman closely flanking behind.

Her face broke into a smile, her heart calming. For the first time in days it did not feel as if it was trying to escape from her chest.

"You have to be one of the only people alive who could look at those two banners and feel relief," the guard muttered under his breath.

Amaria did not care that he meant to insult her. She was safe.

She did not break her gaze from the hill, and she could make out more than the bare features of the four people on the hill now. Theodmon's slope on his nose. Graying hairs on her father. A cut on Lucas's forehead. A burn mark on her father's bannerman's face...

The shred of magic that was uncorrupted by dark magic surged upwards as Theodmon's head turned and her black eyes met his hazel. "Theo!"

She was shouting. It was unrefined.

Her father could keep his mouth shut if he dared critique her.

Theodmon kicked his white stallion and within seconds he was at her side. "Ransom is in chests." He nodded curtly towards the piles near Aaron's feet near the top of the hill. "Amaria," he said more gently as he dismounted. "Let's get you on Phantagero."

She hugged him as soon as his feet hit the ground, her body engulfed in his. She knew she was showing weakness. For the first time in weeks, she did not care. "I lost the dagger." A small tear fell down her face. "I didn't mean to."

"Fuck the dagger." Theodmon pulled her tighter. "I'll get you a better one. Are you alright? Why didn't you escape?" This last part was a whisper.

"I lost my wedding ring," Amaria said numbly, tears running down her face as he helped her onto the horse.

"You have a broken leg. Your hair is cut," Theodmon continued surveying her as he climbed up behind her. "Were you whipped?!"

Amaria gave a slow nod.

"Henri told me you went there on purpose. That the king was buried with his horse. If that's true, I'm—"

"You'll be angry," Amaria whispered. "I did it on purpose. The entire royal family except for Liara, Tesden, Liam Nalaeny, and Gabriel Fayley are dead. Rindria will be ours." A bit louder, as she knew the guards were eavesdropping, she sobbed, "I lost the baby."

"Where's the king?" The guard demanded.

"Talk to Duke Raulet," Theodmon said curtly, kicking his horse into a trot. "Let's get you into a carriage. Faelyn is here; you need to see him."

"Faelyn specifically?" Amaria laughed. The colors were bright. She could smell the fresh air. She was delirious. She was free.

"Amaria," Theodmon told her sternly. She knew why. Faelyn was the most powerful and skilled healer around. Of course she'd have him treat her. "We have a war with Lynette," Theodmon continued. "I need you to heal. Thestitiunia needs you to heal—she's gonna breach the Badlands."

"Dark magic isn't bad," Amaria said. "Why are we fighting so hard against it?"

Theodmon's eyes narrowed. "What happened to you?"

"I was tortured for weeks-"

"No," Theodmon interrupted. "Dark magic is bad. Why do you think it's not?"

"I'm not any worse a person with dark magic," Amaria said. "And I don't intend on listening to self-righteous hypocrites anymore. Lynette has a point."

"Everyone occasionally has moments where they're correct," Theodmon protested as the horse stopped in front of a carriage. He kicked himself off their horse, helping Amaria down before carrying her into the carriage.

She hated how her broken leg made her useless.

Behind them, Lucas had followed and jumped off his horse. "We have to go," he said. "They just found out the king is dead; they're calling for her head. Apparently she killed the entire royal family?"

"Not the entire family," Amaria rolled her eyes. "There's four living."

"Two," Theodmon corrected as the carriage door opened. "I killed Gabriel Fayley, and Liam Nalaeny was found with twenty-two burning arrows in him. Henri apparently commanded it."

Amaria smiled. Henri surprised her, but she was glad he did.

"Liara and Tesden Nalaeny are the only two left alive," Theodmon continued. "Tesden is in exile in Tressidil last I heard. Lucas, go find him."

Lucas jumped back on his horse, understanding the command. Theodmon shouted a command for his squire to ride his horse before climbing into the carriage with Amaria, shutting the door behind him with a slam.

"Fight with me," Theodmon grasped her hands, his eyes watering slightly. He blinked and Amaria saw the tears disappear.

She felt as if a knife twisted at her heart. She had wanted to see him, that was all she wanted, and she had immediately made him cry. Why was she hurting Theodmon? How had she hurt him?

She blinked, her head feeling foggy. "Theo? What...what happened? Are you okay?"

"Fight with me against Lynette and the Badlands. Even if you don't care about dark magic, do it to see Lynette suffer—she tried to turn us against each other, she killed your friend...dark magic may not be bad, but she is."

Amaria sighed, hugging herself. He had a point.

"Fight with me to see Liara die. She's gravely injured—she's useless with a sword. Not as bad as I expected, but it's a miracle she didn't die. She won't last long in another battle."

Amaria shuddered. She hated Liara, yes. But she didn't want her dead. Not actually...actually, Amaria didn't know what she wanted anymore. She didn't know what desires were hers and which were the dark magic's. Amaria's chest heaved. Perhaps dealing with the concept of her family being dead and her being a pawn would be a worse fate. But she'd have to deal with Liara, and that was annoying. Amaria scowled. Why couldn't she have everything she wanted all at once?

"Morroek will no longer align with us," Amaria slumped in her seat. "We're out an ally."

Theodmon shook his head. "No. We're not. If Durek thinks you're dying—which it's known what Thestitiunia does to kill dark mages—and with your death I can marry his daughter, he won't pass up an alliance like that."

"And how will we stop Aion from demanding my head?" Amaria asked.

"I'll cut the damn emperor's head off myself if he demands that," Theodmon growled. "Sleep, Ammy. I'll wake you up when we're further away from Wéorren."

Amaria opened her mouth to protest. She didn't know what to say, but she had the inkling that she should protest something. To be a good subject or some bullshit. What was she protesting?

"Sleep," Theodmon repeated.

She sighed. Perhaps he was right. She hadn't gotten a good night's rest since, well, before she ran into Bria Hall.

"Do you think Lucas will find Tesden?"

Theodmon kissed the top of her head. "I do. He's an excellent tracker. But you need rest. Sleep."

Amaria laid down on the carriage seat, shutting her eyes. She tried to block out the shaking of the carriage, the clumping of the horses hooves. Behind her, Theodmon's arms wrapped around her. She felt as if his muscled body could break hers in half, as if she were a twig.

A salty haze came through her closed eyes. She knew that he could, and would, never hurt her. And she couldn't promise him the same thing anymore.

Amaria turned to face Theodmon. Her chest shaking, Amaria sobbed, pressing her face into Theodmon's chest for what might have been minutes, hours, maybe even days. She had no sense of time because it was unimportant. And her husband, bless the gods, just held her, whispering comforts with his touch.

She would have to become ice soon enough, however, that was unimportant as long as Theodmon's arms gave her a semblance of safety. She was ice and fire. A rose and a griffin. Beautiful and dangerous. She was well-known, and yet she would hide relevant aspects of herself in the shadows. Amaria's entire life was duality or circumstance, and she was a master at the game.

She still felt as if she had missed something. She had gotten her goal, but at what cost? She was brutalized.

"I'm so sorry."

She wasn't sorry for the harm she caused others. She just regretted placing herself in a position to have her leg broken and to be whipped.

"You succeeded," Theodmon said.

"At what cost? I thought I was clever. I'm not. I got beaten because they saw through me. I'm a stupid girl playing stupid games, and I will ruin everything we worked for-"

His lips met hers.

Amaria knew she should say more. She should protest. She should apologize. She should make a plan to dig them out of the shit she had landed them into.

She didn't. What could she say? She was with Theodmon. She was melting as if she were a vapid idiot when he kissed her. She pressed her lips against his. They seemed to merge so well together, as if they were made for each other.

They were two halves of a whole. They could figure this out. It didn't matter.

Amaria closed her eyes, breathing slowly through her nose as she wrapped her arms around Theodmon, feeling his heart beat against her body. She never wanted to break away from this kiss. She never wanted to break away from Theodmon's embrace.

Slowly, they both broke away, staring into each other's eyes—hazel and darkened gray, almost black, meeting each other in a symphonic embrace.

"You're clever," Theodmon said. "This action makes our lives harder, but nobody can prove you did anything. They can suspect, but truly, what proof do they have?"

"The elephants." Amaria hiccuped. She had strangled them with her magic. Everyone had seen her do it.

"And people have heart attacks," Theodmon dismissed. "It's suspicious, but it's not definite. And I'll deny it. Will you?"

Amaria snuggled against him, closing her eyes. She would.

"Sleep," Theodmon commanded.

She would. She needed to sleep—she was exhausted. Amaria hoped that when she woke up there would be food. Her stomach clenched at the thought of the stale and moldy bread she had been fed. Gods, she hated Rindria.

If only they could be exterminated instead of brought into the empire.

Chapter Forty-Four

Amaria's eyes fluttered open. Her entire body hurt and how her head bounced as the carriage rolled over rocks didn't make the situation better.

"Ammy," Theodmon almost sing-songed. He gently brushed her hair back. "We're stopping for food. Do you want fruit? Bread? Meat?"

Amaria rubbed her eyes. "Wine," she groaned. She needed the alcohol to numb the pain firing across her skin and her bones. "I need to relieve myself."

Theodmon gently helped her sit up. "I'll go with you. We need to get you crutches until that leg heals; we'll talk to Faelyn to see where he gets them."

"Where are we?" Amaria asked.

"Near the crossroads of the borders between Rindria, Morroek, and Thestitiunia," Theodmon said. "We'll have to speak with Durek now."

Amaria sighed. They'd have to speak with him to convince him to maintain the alliance. More lies. Convincing him that she was dying and powerless. She hated being seen as weak. She wasn't weak. But they still needed as many allies as possible against Lynette, Avondra, and dark magic. They had ripped away Rindria from Lynette—Rindria would be a useless ally during their success crises and soon-to-be conquest—but Avondra could still be, was still, a problem even without Riam aid.

Besides, Amaria had learned at her father's knee on how to lie, kill, and gain power. She wasn't powerless.

Durek always seemed to see her as such. He treated her like an idiot girl with zero agency or intelligence when she was presented. How would he treat her when she was whipped half to death?

"Fine," Amaria said. "Let's get it over with. Help me to the privy first, please?" She reached her arms upward, as if a child. She needed Theodmon to carry her because of her damned shattered leg.

"We need to keep Liara alive," Theodmon whispered softly into her ear as he picked her up. "Only long enough to have her pop out a son. She's the last living royal family member after Lucas is done with Tesden."

"So play nice?" Amaria said.

"Pretend to have some remorse over your murder spree; deny it of course, but pretend to have empathy for her loss," Theodmon said.

Amaria rolled her eyes. Liara would have to be a special type of daft to fall for that. Still, she understood Theodmon's point: whether or not Liara was stupid enough to fall for her having any genuine condolences for the death of the Riam royal family, gloating about it would cause more damage than needed if they needed Liara alive.

The last thing they needed Liara doing was something rash to get herself killed. She could do that after she had a child.

Amaria didn't care if Liara didn't want a child. Liara was an adult, and it was time she started acting like an adult woman. And if Liara's childishness made claiming Rindria as a territory any harder than what it needed to be, Amaria would ensure Liara died in her childbirth bed herself.

Many more lives would be saved with Rindria being a territory instead of a weakened and ineffective independent nation. What was one life compared to thousands?

"I'll keep my mouth shut," Amaria told Theodmon. "I was just tortured, so having any regrets that those who beat me to the point I got blood poisoning is far-fetched."

Theodmon's eyes swirled as if dark amber and light were mixing. "Fine," he agreed, his chest dropping. "Don't antagonize her."

"As long as she doesn't antagonize me."

Theodmon said nothing as he carried in her arms, stepping outside the carriage. Amaria shivered. She was still in a prison gown. A clean one, but still, she was exposed.

"Is there a dress?" Amaria asked, her eyes welling with tears. Everyone would see the lashes across her body. She was scarred. She wasn't perfect anymore. Although she was already scarred before this, those scars were on her stomach. It was harder to hide the scars on her arms than the ones on her stomach—nobody saw her stomach anyways besides Theodmon.

Forcing the lump in her throat down, she shut her eyes, a tear rolling down her face. She had to be perfect.

"Use the privy," Theodmon whispered, setting her down and stabilizing her behind a bush so she could relieve herself. "I'll bring you back to the carriage, then find your clothes and bring them with Faelyn."

Amaria gritted her teeth as she yelped, pain going down her shin as she accidentally shifted her weight on it when she went to pee. The warm urine hit her skin. She winced. She couldn't stand vomit, feces, or urine anymore. She had sat in her own waste for weeks.

"I need soap," her voice shook. "Now."

Theodmon held her firmly, but she felt his hands clenched. "Did they chain you to a wall?"

Amaria nodded.

"Was there a place to—"

"No," Amaria interrupted, knowing he was going to ask if there was a chamberpot or place for her waste in the cell. Visible tremors coursed through her body as her hands gripped her own elbows, her knuckles white.

"You know what chaining to the wall means." She couldn't meet his eyes. Her chin wobbled and she caught a whimper forming in her throat.

Theodmon cracked his neck, scowling. "Can you remember the guards' faces?"

Amaria would remember those faces and voices for a million years. While some of her captors had died in a fiery blaze, many had escaped her anger–there were rotations, different guards for different times and days. She would remember those guards' faces when she saw them. Amaria's face turned with a stoney resolve, her eyes flashing. Those guards would see her and then they would die.

Theodmon's hand gently cradled her cheek, turning her face towards him, meeting her eyes with the same steely resolve.

"Good," he said. "Once Rindria is a Thestitiunian territory, they'll die first."

Amaria's leg was still broken but set with magic to where it was no longer shattered. Faelyn had told her it would likely take two weeks to heal if he continued to weave healing magic through it every day and she took her potions. She was glad this injury would be gone soon as it was terribly inconvenient. Theodmon had promised to commission the making of crutches for her as soon as they got home, yet she still feared how she would make it up the mountain. Would they place her with the supplies and pulley her upwards?

She pulled her shawl tighter around her as she stared at the flames where a rabbit was being grilled. A dress of hers had been pulled from a trunk; thank the gods she had planned to be at a siege for weeks. She hated that she didn't have a high neck dress, and the scars were visible on her upper chest and neck.

Fuck the Riams.

Theodmon handed her soup. She nodded in thanks. In the distance she saw Aloysius talking with Liara, his face twisted with emotions. She was red faced, screaming.

Why did she care? Liara had run away from her family and had been trying to live like a peasant in Tressidil until Thestitiunia found her. She had abandoned her family. Amaria's lip curled in disgust at Liara's brazen indifference to duties.

"She's not pregnant," Amaria whispered to Theodmon. Amaria wanted Liara to die in the battle, but that hadn't happened. And with her and Tesden being the sole Riam heirs, it seemed as if it may be more prudent to avoid an absolute power vacuum and have Liara pop out a son for Aloysius to rule through while Rindria was conquered and integrated into the empire. "Why isn't she pregnant yet?"

Theodmon sighed, looking over at his brother and Liara. "I'll talk to Aloysius. He's trying to have her warm up to him, but it's essential she provides heirs—he knows this."

"Is it possible he's stalling?" Amaria asked as Aloysius seemed to almost be begging Liara for something. If Liara would be murdered after breeding, perhaps Aloysius was preventing her death by avoiding heirs.

It was smart. Amaria knew Aloysius was intelligent, and it wouldn't surprise her if her suspicions were true. She just wondered what he saw in her. There were hundreds of women, each more tolerable than Liara. Most were more intelligent. A few were easily prettier. All wouldn't be a drain on the Chauvignons finances—not gaining a drowsy had been an annoyance. Truly, if Liara wouldn't soon be the sole heir to the Riam throne, Amaria would strangle her where she stood.

"I'll talk to him," Theodmon said pensively.

"Perhaps we should set an example for them," Amaria placed his hand over her stomach. "It's been so long since I've carried your child," she kept her voice lowered, aware that she had allegedly recently suffered a miscarriage.

Theodmon paused, staring at her. "Shouldn't we wait until after we figure out the magic issue?"

Why? What reason was there to wait? Before Amaria could reply, Durek came and sat beside them, his cloak whooshing under him as he sat on the log.

"She has dark magic," Durek said under his breath. "Why shouldn't I announce it now?"

Amaria crossed her arms, hoping the firelight wasn't strong enough to show the lashes along her neck. Durek wanted something. A pathetic beggar who could ruin everything by talking.

"Why aren't you?" She growled. She had to appease him. Unfortunately, she didn't have the energy to do that anymore.

"Duke Svilas," Theodmon said politely. "Excuse the harshness, she—"

"Let's not lie to each other," Durek said, glowering at them. "She's been using dark magic."

Morrian men always looked so angry. Amaria resisted rolling her eyes. They were angry with nothing to be angry about; they reminded her of small dogs that yipped at people's ankles as if they were anything more than a nuisance.

But Morroek was the third largest kingdom—the kingdom with the largest border with the Badlands—and Durek was the heir to it all. Unfortunately they had to play nice.

That didn't mean they were going to admit to his accusation. Amaria met Theodmon's eyes. In a moment the world stopped—not even the air seemed to move around the trees as their eyebrows slightly listed with a twist of their lips.

It was time to salvage an alliance with pure manipulation.

"What?" Theodmon said, sounding aghast. Amaria stopped herself from smirking. He was a good actor, she had to admit.

"Don't play dumb, boy!" Durek's face turned red. "We aligned against dark magic, but she's had it this whole time! Your little witch killed the entire royal—"

"Hearsay," Theodmon dismissed. "Idiotic hearsay as well."

"Is it hearsay that I heard from one of your men how she strangled elephants with her magic at that same battle?"

"That is the technical definition of hearsay, yes," Theodmon said. "You do realize human beings are different from elephants?"

"I saw her strangle them!" Durek's spit flew around him, his face red.

"But you said you heard—" Theodmon began. He was clearly enjoying toying with Durek. Amaria wished they could prolong playing with their food. Unfortunately, they had work to do.

"Theodmon," Amaria interrupted. She had to seem as if they were being honest now. As if they realized they had no reason to lie as Durek saw the events in Rindria. They had to play to his ego that he knew everything because of what he had seen and that they had no more cards.

What arrogance this man had.

"Stop." Amaria looked at Durek, forcing her eyes to widen as if she were a scared deer. "I did not have dark magic when we made the alliance. I've become...*infected* since Clarissa threw the Raulet Ruby in Rindria."

"I'm cutting off the alliance," Durek moved as if he were about to stand up.

Amaria suppressed a smirk. Good. He was buying it. Now they just had to salvage the damage.

"You can do that," Amaria said calmly. "But before you do, hear me out."

"And why would I do that?" Durek hissed.

"Because, you now have more to gain." Theodmon sighed. "Amaria is dying. She'll die soon—call it a side effect of the dark magic and her being a good person."

Durek opened his mouth to protest. Theodmon held up his hand, silencing Durek.

"I'm Marquis Chauvignon of the Westerlands, the equivalent of a king with only one heir. I'll need to remarry." Theodmon's chest heaved as he looked at Amaria.

She nodded, forcing herself to look forlorn as if she were forcing back tears at her inevitable death. But she wasn't going to die. She was too powerful, too smart, to die.

She would live and thrive. Once it became apparent she wasn't dying, well, they wouldn't need Durek anymore as Lynette would be gone too.

And who could challenge her then? Aion, an incompetent emperor? She'd kill him before she let him order her around again. Her father? Aaron was strict and critical but she doubted he'd send her to the chopping block. Another country? With Rindira in chaos, Avondra without a leader, Tressidil being non-interventionist pacifists, Morroek would be utterly fucked.

And Durek would have no one to blame but himself.

"I'll marry one of your daughters," Theodmon said. "Once Amaria's dead."

"Draft the contract now," Durek snapped. "If we have a binding contract that as soon as she's dead and buried you remarry my daughter, I'll stay in this alliance."

"Of course," Theodmon nodded. "I'll find one of my lawyers—we're limited coming from a war camp. I hope you understand."

Durek stood up. "Draft a temporary pledge at least. We'll determine it more adequately after the battle."

He bowed shortly to them. "Apologies for your loss."

Amaria had never heard anyone sound less insincere. He sounded almost gleeful.

"Goodnight, Duke Svilas," she said. She was tired of men like him. Sighing heavily, Amaria turned towards Theodmon. "Can you help me back to the carriage?"

She needed to go back before she indulged in her darker impulses and killed another royal family member—this time from Morroek instead of Rindria. Dark flashes of anger poured from her eyes, her power bubbling to the surface. Amaria imagined skinning Durek Svilas alive, his blood redder than his hair and that stupid looking beard.

He would squeal like a pig while he was gutted. He would sob and beg and she would call him as weak as a woman, only because it would be the worst way to insult him, before she slit his throat.

She could almost taste the victory from the smoke burning in the night air.

Theodmon picked her up, breaking the image. She would have to deal with reality for now. However, her dream was not merely a dream. It was a plan. It was a promise.

Amaria always did the work needed to reach her goals. So if she needed to embrace dark magic to reach her goal of survival, she would without regret.

Chapter Forty-Five

A maria found it hard to sleep with the bumping of the carriage. Although her leg was healing quickly—thanks to Faelyn's healing magic—the bone still ached. And while she could move it now and it could support her weight in small increments, the dull pain caused by each bump in the carriage was unwelcome. However, Amaria would gladly take this pain over the sharp, shooting pains she had when it was broken and untreated.

Bringing her hands up to her face, she rubbed her eyes with the heel of her hands, flinching as she heard her eyeballs squish. Amaria was exhausted, but she couldn't sleep. Everytime she closed her eyes she was back in the dungeon.

Moonlight crept in through the curtains of the carriage. Next to her, Theodmon sighed in his sleep, and Amaria watched the rhythmic rising and falling of his chest. Her hand brushed over his cheekbones, and she kissed his forehead. He looked peaceful when he slept. Her eyes softened as she looked at him. She wished him all the best in life. Theodmon was good. He was honorable. He was intelligent. He was brutally efficient. And she loved him.

Closing her eyes, Amaria leaned up against him, feeling the heat radiating from his bare chest as she tried to match her breathing with his. Although she knew she needed to rest, Amaria couldn't sleep. It was infuriating—she didn't know why she couldn't sleep. By all metrics and logic, she should be asleep for days after her ordeal in Bria Hall.

But the silver moonlight was too bright.

Amaria looked at her hands. She remembered when she matched the moonlight. Now she was the backdrop of the night.

She loved it.

She hated it.

Amaria truly didn't know what she thought of her dark magic anymore. Did it matter?

Her heart thudding, Amaria shook Theodmon's arm. She couldn't be alone with her thoughts anymore. And more importantly, she needed him. Amaria wanted Theodmon to hold her and comfort her and to allow her to do something else other than lay silently with her own thoughts. Amaria desperately needed to do something else. Whether it was talking or sex, she needed a distraction from herself. If left to her own devices, Amaria would be her own destruction.

"Theo," she whispered urgently.

"Mhmm," he mumbled, turning his face over. Drool came out the side of his mouth.

"Theo," she repeated. "I can't sleep. I need you."

"Wasthematter?" Theodmon said, his voice slurred from sleep.

"I...I don't know. My thoughts are bad," Amaria said. She knew how pathetic she sounded.

Theodmon sat up, groaning as he rubbed his eyes. "I'm here," he said as he pulled her against himself.

Amaria breathed in the scent of cedar, juniper, and sweat, closing her eyes as she pressed her face against his chest. "Can we have sex?"

"Ammy," Theodmon protested. "You're injured."

"I'm healing," Amaria said. "I need this. Please."

Theodmon sighed. The only noise was their breath, the crunching of gravel, dirt, and leaves beneath the wheels of the carriage, and the distant hooting of an owl. Amaria hoped he would say yes. She didn't know what she would do if he said no.

Perhaps they would talk. She just couldn't bear to be alone anymore.

"Alright," Theodmon said softly. "Gently though. I'm not risking hurting you."

Amaria kissed him on the lips before pulling away to pull off her clothes. "Thank you," she said.

He pulled her close to her. "Remember when we had sex in a carriage during our wedding tour?"

Amaria laughed. "I think we conceived Lysander in a carriage."

"No, I think it was one of your family's estates that they loaned us when we were near the islands in the Émeraudes Sea," Theodmon said as he removed his pants. He then sat and pulled her towards him.

Amaria rolled her eyes, still chuckling as she sat on top of him, moving her nightgown out of the way. "Is it important?"

"No," Theodmon kissed her neck. "But I'm still right."

"Now it's important," Amaria playfully pushed against his chest. Theodmon wet his fingers and then himself, and when he was done he worked his way into her. She arched her back with closed eyes. Home. She was home.

"Is it?" Theodmon brushed her hair back, nipping her exposed breast. "What's more important than this?"

She moaned, moving her hips over his pelvis, stirring him inside of her. She pulled his head closer to hers, their mouths meeting while her fingers tangled in his hair. Taking a deep breath, she relished his scent that she missed for so long. She wanted him. She needed him. It was only them in this wobbly carriage in the middle of the woods.

She could forget about the world. About the pain and suffering she had endured. About the trials she would face next as she fought for her life. There would never be another woman where she was—she wouldn't allow it. No, that was a problem for another time. For now there was only Theodmon.

If need be, they would stay just like this the whole way to Forteresse les Blanche.

All that mattered was them.

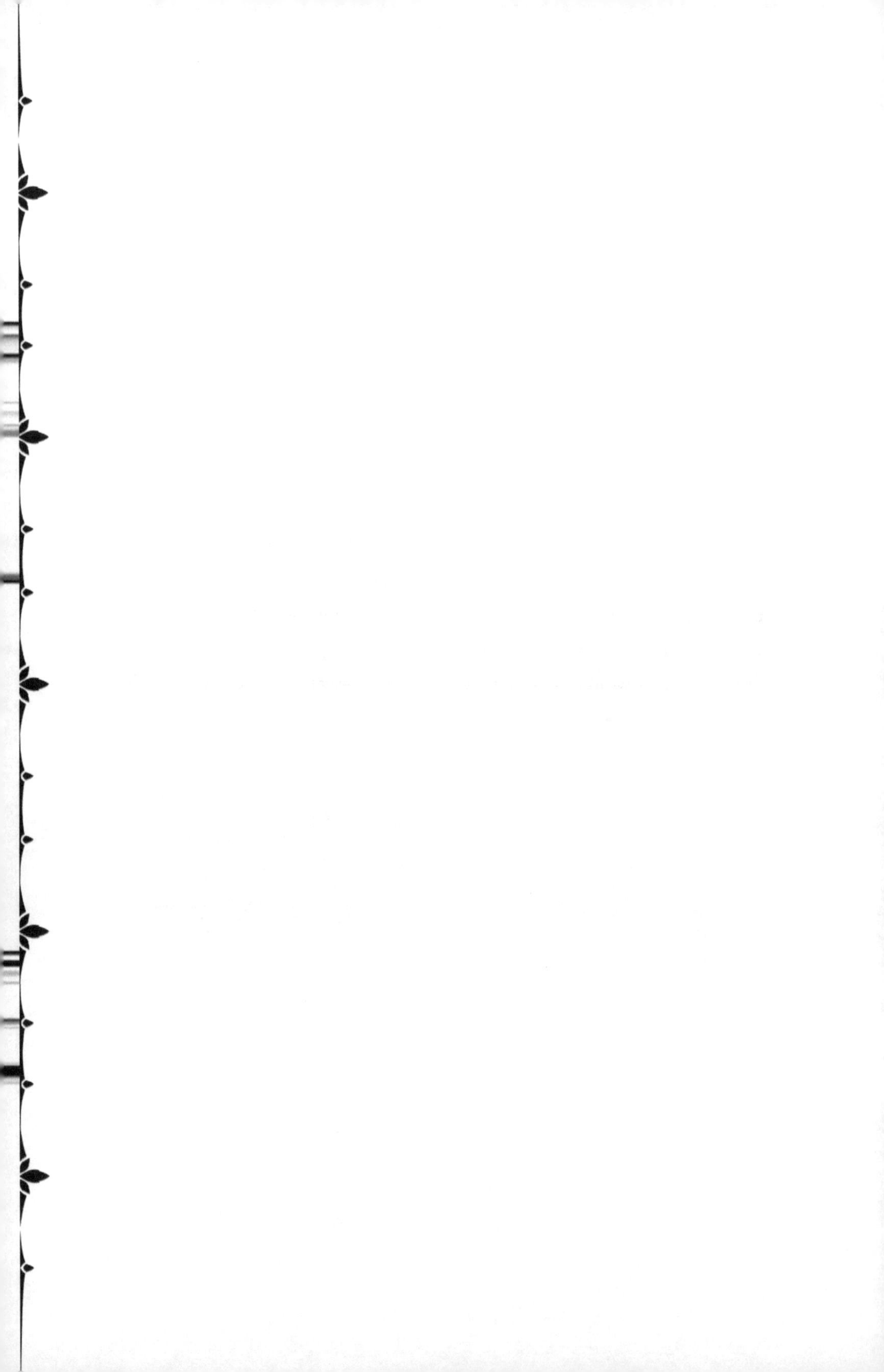

Part Six

the recovery

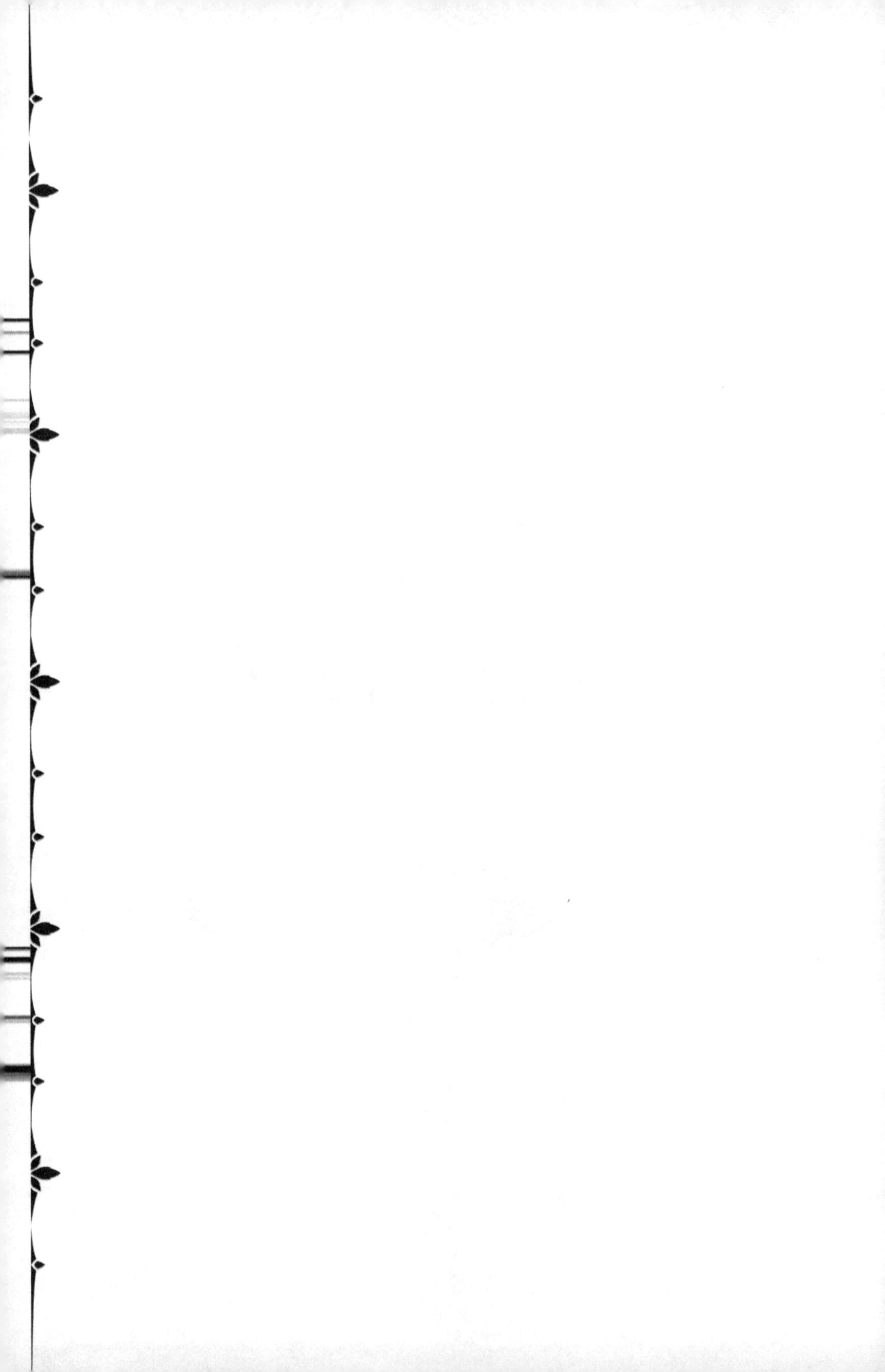

Chapter Forty-Six

Painful weeks passed. But they made it back home.

Amaria walked down the halls of Forteresse les Blanche, slowly breathing in, determined to steady herself before seeing Lysander. They had been at home for hours now, and she had been so overwhelmed with the business of the estate, and worse, the ramifications of her massacre that she had not had any time to settle in.

She had not had time to see her son. Really see him and be present. But he was well cared for by his army of nannies. He would be well-educated by his army of tutors in the future. All standard noble procedures were being followed, as noble parents didn't raise their infants. Once the child was older, five or six or so, then they would gain more interaction with their parents.

So why did Amaria feel neglectful of Lysander?

Perhaps it was because she wasn't pregnant—the reason for this system was to facilitate more babies. It was hard to breed if she had to take care of the children already existing.

Amaria wanted to interact with her son more and she didn't want to wait until he was older. She pushed her way through the corridor, her skirts swirling around her. It felt odd to not have the pressure of a knife strapped to her leg anymore as she hadn't yet replaced the one that had been taken in Rindria. But she didn't want to replace the knife. Amaria wanted her knife back.

Amaria wanted her wedding ring back. Theodmon said he would get her a new one, but she didn't want a new ring. She wanted that old one.

Sighing, Amaria stopped in front of the nursery, stepping inside. Immediately, nannies and servants curtsied.

"Leave," Amaria barked, watching Lysander play with horses in the corner. She loved him so much. He would be one year old soon. He was so big. Where had the time gone? She wanted to be alone with him, without a simpering nanny to irritate Amaria with her mere existence.

The nannies and maids curtsied, complying with the command. Amaria lowered herself to the ground near Lysander. He was stacking the blocks on top of each other. She noted that this stack was almost as tall as Lysander was. It was impressive he did that at his age. Perhaps he would be a good military builder and engineering strategist.

It would be lovely if Lysander did not have to worry about war. Amaria knew that was stupid. They were nobles. Sons went to war and daughters made new sons to be cannon fodder. It was pointless to challenge it, as it was reality.

Reality was stifling. It was catastrophic to challenge and even more dangerous to ignore.

"Let's go for a walk," Amaria told Lysander, picking him up. Immediately, the toddler began to squirm, and Amaria's grip loosened slightly. She set him down, not wanting to drop him.

"We're going to walk," she told Lysander, crouching to his level. "Would you like that?"

Lysander giggled. Amaria smiled back at him, standing up and holding out her hand. Her son took it, and slowly they walked out of the nursery and down the corridor.

He was slow, taking uneven steps. But he was walking. Lysander wasn't even one yet. He would turn one in two weeks. Amaria's chest hurt as she looked at him. Lysander was smart, strong, and a wonderful boy.

She loved her son.

Amaria and Lysander passed the gem hall. Through the bolted doors she felt the rhythmic humming of the gems. Amaria reached out towards the door handle. She could go inside, after all, she had already absorbed some of the Raulet Ruby power, surely it couldn't hurt to have more.

Her brain felt focused for the first time in a while, and she was seeing clearly. Before she had been in a haze.

She needed more power.

Amaria needed to use the gem. She didn't know how to use it, but she felt it calling to her. It was as irresistible as a siren's song. Except the Raulet Ruby wouldn't hurt her as sirens harmed sailors. Amaria and the Raulet Ruby were the same. It was as if like was calling to like.

Amaria and the Ruby needed each other. Amaria needed more power. She needed more dark magic. She let go of Lysander's hand, him still standing close by her. She breathed in slowly as her hand rested on the polished brass handle.

She felt her magic rushing forward. She would embrace the rest of the Ruby. She had been told by the priestess of Dandar that she would be a queen among mortals. This was how that would happen—she would fully embrace her power and the power of the Raulet Ruby. She could rid herself of all of her enemies with ease if she had this power.

Amaria opened the door.

A burst of red and black energy exploded towards them. Instinctively, Amaria held Lysander, turning him away from the blast. Amaria felt as if she was being tortured again as the energy hit her. It felt as if every bone in her body was breaking. She cursed, her bones having just healed.

Lysander screamed a high pitched wail of terror as he and she were thrown onto the ground.

Amaria felt dizzy, her limbs were weak. She wanted to scream, but she couldn't scream. Instead, she was gulping down large breaths to stay quiet. Her son was screaming. What had she done?

Amaria rolled over, seeing Lysander's head bleeding on the ground.

Why didn't the magic embrace her? Why didn't she have power? Why did the gem attack her?

Her body quivering, Amaria's breath shook as it turned shallow, then deep. "Help!" she screamed through her erratic breathing. "I need a healer!"

Her hands held her child's bleeding head. She wanted dark magic. What if her desire called the gem's energy to her? She had possibly killed her son. He was bleeding because of her.

That gem had to go. She had to get rid of this dark magic. What had she been thinking?

She was sobbing, begging the gods to save her son until a healer arrived and Amaria was pulled away from Lysander.

Vividly, Amaria was reminded of a similar scene that had happened nearly two years prior. She had blamed herself for Delphina's death because the knife had been meant for her. But it wasn't Amaria's fault—she hadn't thrown the knife.

But now, she had caused this tragedy. If she hadn't reached out wanting more dark magic, Lysander wouldn't be bleeding on the ground.

Chapter Forty-Seven

Amaria sipped her tea as she watched the healers bustle around Lysander. Next to her, Theodmon cracked his knuckles. She closed her eyes, forcing herself to breathe. She counted to ten. Exhale. She counted to ten. Inhale.

The tea was a distraction. She needed a distraction. Lysander was dead. They should have never walked near the gemstone hall.

She had killed her son.

Theodmon's hand clutched her thigh. Amaria squeezed her eyes shut tight, her face turning to a grimace. Her stomach cramped, and her hands were clammy and trembling.

Lysander had to live. He had to be alright. Her mind whirled like a hurricane, and yet, she was immobilized. She could not move; her limbs would not obey her.

She had killed her son.

And so she sat with her mind racing and panicked. Yet, a small sliver of determination wove its way through the storm of emotions. Amaria knew that there must be an answer to this situation; there had to be a clever scheme or plan to halt the conflict and to tilt it in favor of herself. She wasn't a healer. She was a mage. She had the magic the Ruby had thrown at Lysander. Perhaps he lived like she had.

She barely lived. She was being stupid. Lysander was an infant—toddler really, yet what was the difference in this circumstance? But she had blocked the blow with her body.

"Marquis Chauvignon, Marchioness Chauvignon," Katerina approached, deep circles under her eyes. "Lord Lysander is alright. He's sleeping, but his vitals are fine. Something seemed to block most of the Ruby's energy."

Amaria wrung her hands. "Me," her voice was hoarse. "I think my similar magic stopped most of it."

"That's good," Katerina said. "Lysander is alright. May I look you over?"

"No," Amaria held up a hand, warning her to not come closer. "May we see Lysander?"

"My Lady, you should be checked over. You-"

"I don't want to," Amaria interrupted her coldly. "Let me see my son. Now."

Katerina bowed her head, stepping back with a disgruntled look. Amaria knew that Katerina had a point; Amaria should be evaluated after being hit with the Ruby *again*. She didn't care. She needed to see her son. She needed to make sure he was alright. That she didn't...Amaria couldn't even finish the thought, as if merely thinking it would bring the horrible possibility into a reality.

Amaria and Theodmon stepped around Katerina, seeing their toddler laid out on the infirmary bed. His chest slowly rose, and his head was bandaged.

Amaria sat next to him, her fingers gently brushing over a curl. Her heart threatened to burst from her chest as she looked at his fragile body. She had wanted to protect her child, and she had, instead, shattered him. Her hand hovered over the bloody bandage near his head.

"There'll be no permanent damage," Katerina said softly. "Lord Lysander is fine. It looks worse than what it is. I'm changing the bandage once you leave."

"Are you sure?" Amaria croaked. Salty droplets rolled down her face.

"Yes," Katerina said gently, but firmly. "You blocked the blow. Children will get hurt. He has stitches. He'll survive with no damages other than maybe a slight scar."

"A scar?" Amaria gasped, feeling her lungs tighten. She had permanently deformed her child.

"A man should have scars," Theodmon said, firmly grasping her shoulders. "He'll have several more over the years." He lowered his voice so low she could only hear. "It's fine. Chauvignons have a sort of rugged charm, I've been told."

He was joking to help her feel relaxed. Amaria knew this. But she didn't feel relaxed. She wanted to scream at herself for hurting Lysander. But she had to maintain the limited decorum she had left.

Curtly, Amaria nodded, before leaning over to kiss Lysander's head gently, avoiding the bandages. She met Theodmon's eyes knowing that she had to leave now, or else she would be inconsolable. Amaria didn't know if she would scream or cry, but she knew the actions she would take would be completely embarrassing.

She didn't want to leave.

Theodmon understood, gently guiding her away from Lysander. When they were out of the infirmary, she started to sob. He squeezed her shoulder. "We're near our chambers. Can you make it there?"

Amaria hugged herself, forcing back tears. She would have to.

"Yes," she said.

After Amaria had sobbed for a solid hour, she was sipping a cup of tea in her chambers as Theodmon paced around her. She was glad they dropped the pretense of him being angry with her and her being a submissive wife trying to appease her abusive husband after Lynette breached the alliance.

Amaria could not find it in her to pretend anymore. Especially not now. She needed Theodmon. The real Theodmon.

"The Ruby has to be destroyed," Theodmon said, cracking his knuckles.

Amaria nodded her assent. "How? Blasting it isn't an option; there's still a ton of energy left." Amaria didn't want to imagine the remaining dark energy escaping. It had to be infinitely more than what infected her.

"And we can't throw it in the Badlands," Theodmon said. Amaria shuddered, imagining giving the Badlands and Lynette that much power. It would be as if they received a Solstice gift from the gods.

"We could drown it in the ocean," Amaria suggested half-heartedly. She knew that was an impossibility. The Ruby had to be destroyed, and dropping it in the ocean merely diverted the issue of destruction by changing its location.

And what was to stop Lynette from retrieving it?

Theodmon groaned. "What can we do? Can the Extractors destroy it?"

Amaria shook her head. "Too risky. If it corrupted me...imagine eight more with my power level. Excuse the crudeness, but we'd be fucked. Lynette would win."

Theodmon clutched his head. "You're the mage. Could it be destroyed with powerful magic?"

"Hypothetically, I guess," Amaria said slowly. Hypotheticals were useless here. She knew that. She knew that her husband knew that. "What are you planning?"

"We could ask the faeries," Theodmon said. "I'm the current liaison between humans and them."

Amaria remembered him meeting them, well, a faerie named Oberon specifically, before the chaos of war and dark magic erupted. And faeries were infinitely more magically powerful than any human. Oberon irritated her, yes, however, the beautiful faerie with hair like starlight terrified her as well.

"Alright," Amaria agreed. "Will they help us?"

Theodmon shrugged. "I've no idea. But it's the best chance we have."

Amaria hated to admit it, but he was right. She sighed. "I'll write to my father. He'll be unhappy that we're essentially going behind his back and keeping him out loop on these major international decisions but there's no time."

She wasn't looking forward to the inevitable lecture. Perhaps dying with the dark magic would be preferable. Because Amaria would die. She realized that with a jolt, as if struck with electricity.

The dark magic overwhelmed her. It couldn't be separated from her. She had almost killed her son. She wanted to use this magic, at first, to protect her son. Amaria saw now how idiotic that notion was. Dark magic took until there was nothing more to take. She couldn't protect Lysander with dark magic; she would only cause him pain.

Amaria needed her dark magic to die. And the only way to get rid of magic this dark—this powerful—was to kill the vessel.

And Aion would definitely kill her to get rid of the dark magic. Amaria hugged herself, shaking. Could her father protect her from Aion? Maybe not. Aaron couldn't even protect her from Aion's bad marriage decisions for her—even though marriage was supposed to be her father's area to determine for her.

Amaria's eyes welled with tears. She wasn't going to die. She couldn't die. She would be alive after this war against Lynette Edrion and the Badlands. Amaria couldn't leave Lysander alone. Motherless.

Like she had been since she was seven.

And Amaria pretended that there wouldn't be demands for her head. How could there not be after her actions in Rindria. Probable deniability or not, people would be intelligent enough to piece together enough to suspect her. Theodmon and Aaron would resist Aion, but how long could they realistically stop the inevitable?

She tried to pretend she wasn't idealistic. She tried to pretend she wasn't hopeful for a beautiful world. She tried to pretend she wasn't a hindrance to that beauty.

It was easier to pretend to be completely cold and cunning than to actually kill all of her humanity. Amaria pulled her magic upwards, trying to find the fading silver strands in the black shroud.

"Amaria," Theodmon said beside her, "prepare yourself. We have to leave for the faerie lands."

Idealism would get her killed. But was she human without having a shred of it? Idealism wasn't just a childish fancy.

It was hope.

Chapter Forty-Eight

Theodmon rode hard for days, Amaria in front of him curled up on their horse, her hands clinging tightly to the saddle horn. Theodmon was leaning forward, shielding her with his body. Around them, the rolling hills, cliffs, and forests of the Westerlands flew by as if a blur of paint.

Amaria felt Theodmon's sweat soaking through his clothes. "I can summon air," she said.

"Save your energy," Theodmon told her. His skin glistened with sweat as the sun beat overhead.

Amaria looked up at him, her eyes dropping. She hated seeing him uncomfortable. She was heat resistant, a built-in benefit of fire magic, so she, despite her heavy clothes and jewels, had not broken a sweat.

That, and the Westerlands summer was mild compared to the tropics in Perivina Fluere.

It was funny to Amaria how she and Theodmon both were Thestitiunian, both of the same rank as well, and their experiences were entirely different because of how vast the empire was. She tilted her head upwards, surveying what she could of her husband from this angle.

Theodmon eyes were unbreaking from the tree line of the forest. The forest was colossal, impenetrable, and lush. From the outer borders of the forest, Amaria could feel it was a wild place.

She wasn't entirely sure she liked it.

"We need to go into the outskirts," Theodmon said. "The entrance to the faerie lands is in the forest."

Amaria nodded, her neck stiff.

The Chauvignons and the Faeries had a professional relationship, a liaisonship between humans and the more powerful, sentient magical species for over two thousand years. A Chauvignon had stepped down from being emperor after the Great Dragon and Hydra War of 917—or was it 915? Amaria had never been a great student of history. She had gained what was necessary for the present and future.

Chauvignons were the original emperors. They gave it to the Marions so as to maintain peace. The faeries and Chauvignons already had a relationship with each other.

That's why Theodmon knew where they were. That's why they let him approach them. Amaria hoped that would be enough to consider destroying the Raulet Ruby. Professional relationships didn't extend to personal favors.

Hopefully destroying the Ruby was professional. Amaria wasn't sure where the business and personal vendetta ended and began with that gem anymore. She blinked back tears from her eyes as she leaned against Theodmon as he guided their horse through forest.

The trees were thick now. So much so that Amaria felt as if the summer daylight sun was now dusk. She reached out to touch the swooping, climbing plants that dangled from the trees, her fingers brushing over the felt like blooming flowers.

"We should stop here," Theodmon said, his breathing labored. Amaria breathed in. The air was thick, but it was the sweetest air she had smelt. It felt untainted. Pure.

They were on the outskirts of the faerie lands.

"I, Theodmon Chauvignon, descendant of Lysander Chauvignon the first who made the peace with humans and Faeries, come as a liaison. I respectfully ask to be allowed to meet with a representative of the faeries. With me is my wife, Amaria Chauvignon, who the faeries have met before," Theodmon said as he dismounted.

He turned towards Amaria, placing his hands firmly around her waist as he lifted her off the horse, helping her steady herself on solid ground.

"Theodmon Chauvignon. Amaria Raulet," a musical voice wove through the trees.

Immediately, they both kneeled to the tall, green-skinned man entering the clearing. Amaria shut her eyes. She could feel his magic spiking off of him in waves, and he had split in two as her magic tried to compete with his.

She wondered if other mage's felt that way around her magic.

"Rise," Oberon commanded. "Why are you here, Theodmon Chauvignon?"

"I'd never risk our relationship," Theodmon told him. "I understand the precarious nature humans would be in. And so, know this is not a selfish request. We need your help with the Badlands. Dark magic will break through soon."

"You have dark magic," the faerie hissed at Amaria, gripping her wrist. Amaria could have imagined it, but she swore the faerie's eyes glazed over momentarily.

"Yes," Amaria looked at Oberon, remembering her lessons on how she should never lie to a faerie. "I have dark magic. It isn't by choice, however. I tried to contain the gemstone's power when the gem was damaged." Amaria laughed bitterly. "It didn't go well."

"But you contained the power," Oberon said, his long hair floating in the wind.

"Barely," Amaria said. "I had help; other mages—"

"You self-sacrificed," the faerie said. "I thought humans didn't do that."

"It was startlingly out-of-character for me," Amaria admitted. "Well, I suppose not, actually. I cared about some people there. I wanted Theodmon, Haerdnor, Henri, Lucas, and Aloysius safe."

"Not the others?" the faerie questioned.

Amaria pushed back a scowl. Why did he need to know? Still, remembering her manners, and prudence being advised when dealing with this species, Amaria responded. "They could have rotted for all I cared."

"This magic will fester," Oberon said. Amaria knew this. Why did this faerie care? Why did this faerie think she cared?

"Why are you here?" Oberon asked.

"To ask for help," Theodmon said. "Dark magic threatens humans and fae alike. I am a Chauvignon. We have been the family to act as a liaison between humans and fae for millenia—thousands upon thousands of years—and with that, my family has recognized that our interests are not always contrary. I believe the fae have also realized this. I only ask for you all to intervene for our mutual survival. Our interests are aligned."

Theodmon pulled out the gem. "It's leaking dark magic and has to be destroyed. Can the fae do it?"

"Yes," Oberon hissed, taking a step back from the gem. "Put that *thing* back in its bag."

"Thank you," Amaria whispered. She hated that gem. She still saw Lysander's unconscious body—she knew she had looked like that when she had taken the gems hit the second time.

"You have the gem's energy," Oberon said, still watching Amaria.

"Yes," Amaria admitted, knowing it was unwise to lie to faeries.

Oberon sighed, his skin turning from blue to silver to bronze. "Have you ever heard of ulaniza?"

Amaria and Theodmon looked at him blankly. Amaria had never heard of ulaniza before. She had no idea what it was. She had no idea why it was relevant.

Where was this conversation going?

"You might call it differently," Oberon continued. "It was when strong human female mages were given to us as brides."

"That was centuries ago. A myth," Theodmon said coldly.

"Theodmon Chauvignon," Oberon shook his head. "You're our liaison and you still believe in myths?"

"What about those brides?" Amaria interrupted. The faerie had brought this up for a reason. She needed to know why.

"Our lands are a magical place. Time moves differently. The air we breathe is different. Powerful mages can tolerate it in small bursts, which is why we meet the Chauvignons on our borders." Oberon looked at her. "These brides, as to best provide us with our needs, were transformed."

"Into fae?" Amaria gasped, moving away from him and towards Theodmon.

"No," he said sternly. "Into more powerful human mages. Though the ones who survived, they had physical manifestations of the gift."

"The ones who survived?" Theodmon repeated, his arms crossed.

"I offer you this gift," the faerie ignored Theodmon, addressing Amaria.

"No," Theodmon snapped. "Absolutely not."

Amaria took a gulp of air, forcing down her nausea. "Will I...will I be able to have human children? Will I have to be a faerie wife?"

"You can have children. And no," the faerie said. Amaria's eyebrows raised. She didn't believe him. There was a catch. There was always a catch.

"You're pregnant with a daughter now," Oberon continued. "If you survive, she'll be predisposed to have powerful magic, and even if she doesn't, she'll still have a higher chance of survival in becoming ulaniza."

Amaria couldn't help it. She laughed. She wasn't pregnant. And even if she was, how could this faerie know the gender so early?

"I touched you and saw the life you carry. I saw that life's future. It'll be a daughter. She'll have water magic. You will show pregnancy symptoms in a few weeks."

"That's..." Amaria stopped. She wanted to say that was impossible. But powerful seers could see into the future in a similar way. And faerie magic dwarfed human magic. Amaria was one of the most powerful human mages and she would easily be defeated in a mage battle by even the weakest faerie.

"So my daughter is marrying a faerie?" Amaria asked.

"She'll marry me," Oberon scoffed. "It's only fair that I reap the rewards of this gift, right?"

Amaria did have to admit it was logical. She wet her lips. She needed to know more.

"And my magic, I won't lose it?" Amaria's voice filled with panic. Her eyes widened as she looked at this beautiful, inhuman man in front of her.

She would rather die than give up her magic.

"If you survive, yes."

"No. It's dangerous," Theodmon said roughly.

Amaria turned towards him, her eyes watering "And I'll die without it. At least with this I have a chance. Please, Theodmon, please try to understand." She needed him to agree. Only he could make a binding marriage agreement. Without this, she would have dark magic forever.

She realized that she didn't want that. She wanted to be herself.

She didn't want to risk Lysander's or this daughter's lives ever again. She supposed she was risking her unborn daughter's life, but this was the same as any marriage agreement between nobles. It was just that instead of a different kingdom, their daughter would live with a different species in a different realm.

It seemed closer to home than Tressidil did at least.

"I don't want dark magic," she whispered. "Let me come home to you, Theo. I want to be myself again."

The only noise was the stream bubbling. Amaria held her breath. She realized that would go either way, however, she wished to avoid a row. And potentially breaking all social conventions by brokering a marriage alliance in violation of the father's wishes.

That would be difficult to navigate.

"We'll offer assistance to the humans against the Badlands," the faerie said to Theodmon. "But let her have this choice with your blessing."

Theodmon curtly nodded to the faerie before he ran to Amaria, picking her up in his arms. "You'll survive this. If you don't survive this, you're not the most stubborn woman

I ever met, and I'll be convinced you've hidden my real wife in some dark dungeon and I have to find her. For the other prisoner's sakes."

Amaria kissed him, crying. She wanted to say a million things. She didn't know what to say.

He touched her stomach. "I didn't mean to impregnate you after you were tortured."

Amaria laughed harshly through her tears. She tasted snot. "Occupational hazard, I guess." She hiccuped. She was scared. She didn't want to go.

Amaria couldn't wait to go and have the dark magic torn from her. She couldn't wait to meet her old magic and embrace the silver as if it were a long-lost friend.

"Amaria Chauvignon," Oberon commanded. "Come."

Chapter Forty-Nine

Oberon led her through the forest. It could have taken a minute or perhaps a year—Amaria's concept of time became fuzzy as she surveyed the lush landscape. Vibrants colors painted the world, and Amaria had never seen such bold reds, purples, and oranges.

The air was warm and humid but pleasantly so, and a sense of calm melted over her. Her muscles relaxed and she took a deep breath. Perhaps this world was what she had needed this entire time.

Amaria shook her head, trying to clear her thoughts. There was something in the air affecting her mind.

In the nearby forest she heard songs and growls of strange creatures. They were feathered creatures, scaly creatures, covered in fur; all were animalistic yet seemed human. However, they were not human; they were stronger, more beautiful, and infinitely more dangerous.

She felt their eyes on her. She stared ahead, trying to force back the realization that she was a caged animal in a menagerie.

Oberon stopped in the middle of the clearing. "Help me make a circle of stones," he directed Amaria.

Her mouth went dry. "Why?"

"To contain your magic," he dismissed.

Amaria's hands were clammy as they quivered slightly. If the faeries were going to kill her...she shook her head. No, they could make her a bride though. No human could escape them. What was she doing here?

"Why are you helping me?" she blurted out, her hand hovering over a rock.

"All magic will be needed against dark magic," Oberon said as more faeries joined him.

Amaria relaxed. His logic was cold. It was brutally practical. She understood that and found comfort in that mentality. She placed her rocks down in the circle.

"Step in," he directed her. As she stepped into the circle, he placed the final rock down, a purple haze going over them.

"This will hurt," Oberon said. "You have strong magic, for a human at least. You'll survive."

Amaria ground her teeth. "Just do it. Don't tell me when."

She couldn't afford to lose her nerve. She wouldn't live with dark magic anymore, but she wasn't planning on dying either.

A group of three faeries, each more beautiful and unnerving than the last, circled her, raising their hands.

Deep within her, the dark magic bubbled. Within seconds Amaria was screaming, clutching her head as all her worst memories flooded her mind. She was eighteen, covered in blood as she pulled a knife from her stomach. Vypren had stabbed her. Vypren laughed, telling her father she would be worthless now and he would not retake her. If he couldn't have her, nobody could. She felt rage as she lashed out at Vypren with her magic before she quickly fainted from blood loss.

She was being chastised by Aion for that act publicly. Aion was ordering nine-year old Amaria to marry forty-year old Lyseno Vypren, and then to kill him when she had ample children. Aaron protested. Aion did not care.

Why were the faeries forcing her to remember this?

Amaria remembered Delphina's death. She could almost smell her blood again. Amaria sobbed, her body shaking. She wanted this to end. She wanted to claw her brain out of her skull. Amaria would do anything to stop this mental pain.

She was in the prison beneath Bria Hall again, screaming in terror. She couldn't do this. She pressed her eyes shut as she tasted salt.

A light pressed against the inside of her eyes, forcing them open. Amaria saw Lysander. Amaria despised herself so much her anger turned to bile in her mouth.

She had almost left Lysander motherless as she dove towards the cracking Raulet Ruby in Rindria, absorbing a small part of its magic. She had almost killed him with her stupidity. With her quest for power. She wanted more dark magic, and Lysander had almost paid the price.

Smoky black tendrils came out of Amaria's mouth, eyes, and nose. The world seemed to spin around her. A sharp, throbbing pain racketed over her body, so much so that all Amaria wanted to do was vomit and hoped the pain would come out with it. Cold shivers shot through her body, and her hands and legs were trembling.

She screamed. Sharp pains pierced her chest. Her chest was being torn open. The darkness was overpowering and she couldn't see.

"Stop!" Amaria sobbed as she thrashed on the ground. She gasped for air and the world seemed to spin around her.

The faeries said something, but Amaria couldn't distinguish the words. Her head spun, nausea crept up slowly, and then suddenly it was overwhelming. For a moment, Amaria thought about giving in to the pain, letting it consume her completely. For a moment she focused on the pain, homing in on every sensation. Where it came from, how badly it hurt, and how badly she wanted it to stop.

Then there was nothing. A pause in where she was numb and nothing existed.

And as light and gentle as starlight, the small silver plant sang in relief. The plant rooted itself in her heart and Amaria sobbed. Her magic. It was beaten, suffocated, and weakened, but this plant was her magic.

She had missed it. She called it as if it were an old friend. She mourned how the dark magic had hurt it but also how she had suffocated it for years. She promised to nurture this beautiful silver flower and grow it into a tree as strong as the ancient ones in the faerie lands.

Her magic sang, answering her promises. She felt warm. They would be okay. Amaria and her magic would survive this.

And then the world exploded in silver light that centered itself from Amaria's heart.

Chapter Fifty

Faint moonlight peeked softly through the shimmering leaves and bathed Amaria in a silver cradle as she stared up at it, stars shining on her deep brown hair. Everything was peaceful, with the moon rays giving life to the night and the animals bounding away on their blissful adventures.

Amaria's eyes fluttered open. There was something heavy on her.

The lights were brighter. The air tasted sweeter. Her entire body was sore.

She rolled her neck, cracking it as she raised herself from the bed. The heavy feather blanket came with her. Amaria thought it was weird, but who knew what the faeries customs were. It wasn't going to be her who took the initiative to question them. Especially not when she was in their lands.

"You survived," a female faerie said, causing Amaria to jump. She hadn't realized she was being watched. "You're the first in three generations."

"Of humans?" Amaria rubbed her temple. That didn't seem quite right, but her head was splitting in two.

"It's disorienting," the female faerie approached, her lavender skin glistening. She handed Amaria a drink that bubbled gold. "Drink, it'll help. And, no, you're the first human to survive in three generations of faeries."

Amaria's mouth dropped as she stared at the faerie. Faerie's life spans were much longer than humans. How long had it been since they had a faerie bride? What did that mean for Amaria?

Amaria's stomach dropped. Her hands flew to her stomach. She was pregnant. She hadn't shown symptoms or missed her period, yet the faeries knew that there was something in her. Amaria twisted her memory to remember when she last had sex. It had been recently, with limited sex beforehand due to her imprisonment.

The child could only be three or four weeks. It should be impossible for the faeries to know she was pregnant. Let alone the sex of the child.

She was pregnant with a daughter and she had signed her away into marriage already. Marriage to another species.

Amaria had to compartmentalize. This was a future issue. If she didn't deal with the impending issues, this issue would become obsolete.

"How'd you know I was pregnant?" Amaria still couldn't stop herself from asking.

The female faerie laughed. "Oberon can feel all life, growing seeds or full trees."

"And he could see the baby's sex?"

The female faerie held Amaria's hands, her own firmly ensuring the drink wasn't dropped. "Drink," she commanded. "And yes, life is like a river. It doesn't stay in one place at once to those who are in touch with it. Oberon can see all stages of a living thing's being at once."

He was an intensely powerful seer. Kind of—Amaria couldn't explain the power. But she felt small. Her magic, even when most powerful, was a drop compared to a faerie's.

Amaria looked at the vial of gold liquid suspiciously in her hands. What if they wanted to kill her?

Don't be ridiculous. She told herself. *They need your daughter to breed for them in two decades. Less? More? That part wasn't specified.*

A burst of pain shot across her entire body and she felt as if her bones were being ground to dust. If they wanted to kill her, they would have already done so.

Amaria lifted the vial and drank. The liquid tasted like licorice and lavender. It was a horrifying combination.

The world stopped spinning. Amaria blinked, finally being able to take in her surroundings for the first time. She was in a room with a bed and a dresser. Gossamer sheets hung from the ceiling and lightning bugs flitted around them.

"Your magic is stabilizing," the faerie's voice sounded sweeter. "You can dress; we left you something on the dresser."

Amaria noticed that she was naked. She rubbed her hands over her stomach. Her scars were gone. She stretched out her arms and she could not see any lashes of the whip.

It made sense, she supposed. If this was a process to make her able to conceive and breed with faeries, she would have to look the part.

"Can I have human children?" Her mouth turned dry. "Or only faerie."

"Both," the faerie said. "If you want, we can let you stay here, find someone to mate with you." Amaria noticed that she was only looking at her stomach and hips. She had the sinking realization faerie brides had likely been bred into non-existence.

They probably didn't exist because of the agreement between humans and faeries. Legend said that Ghagyn bound the agreement herself. Fairies, though powerful, could not defy a goddess.

"No," Amaria said hastily as she moved over to the dresser. "I have a husband."

"Oberon said so," the female faerie said. "But each human generation of Chauvignon will give us a bride to keep our population strong. Oberon and the human liaison agreed to do so to strengthen the alliance."

Amaria's hands shook. It wasn't much different than a daughter being married off to another family in another country. Even in human lands, noble daughters' main purposes were to further the line.

"Please leave," she asked the faerie. "I'd like to change alone."

The faerie's eyes narrowed, however, she departed.

Amaria sighed in relief as she reached the dresser. It was painful to speak with the faeries. They acted so differently, so, well, *not human*. Shaking her head momentarily, Amaria's hands brushed over the silver dress laid out in front of her. The dress was sleeveless and backless from what Amaria could already tell. She sighed; it was better than being naked.

Amaria looked up into the mirror and she saw a hauntingly beautiful face that looked like her but wasn't her. She had always been beautiful. But the woman in the mirror was so beautiful she didn't look fully human. This woman's skin was as smooth as seaglass. Her silver eyes shone brighter than Amaria's ever had.

And she had silver wings, as beautiful as starlight, coming from her back.

The brides had gained physical manifestations of the gift. Amaria remembered Oberon had said that. She remembered him saying that the human brides—uzala or something similar, Amaria couldn't remember what he had exactly called them—were human but with powerful magic and a gift that physically showcased that.

She moved slowly towards the mirror, hesitantly stretching out her wings. Amaria had always been the most comfortable with air, and she had always wanted to fly. Amaria tried to flap her wings to get herself off the ground, aware that she likely looked ridiculous.

It was ridiculous—having wings made her look not human. Like a monster from a tale told to scare children. She was beautiful, angelic almost.

But Amaria was deadly, and that fact was well known. Furthermore, it was absurd to believe she could escape that reputation—not after Rindria. She was a unicorn, silver and bloody. And she was going to have to deal with more absurd, small-minded rumors.

"Get your dress on," the female faerie returned. Amaria immediately dove towards the dress, turning around with her back towards the faerie as if her wings could cover her. "We will train you before we go to war. You're as clumsy as a newborn."

Amaria backed up slightly, stumbling as she raised her hands defensively. "Let me see my husband." She would do what they wanted—she supposed she had agreed to that arrangement in this battle along with giving them her daughter.

But she needed to see Theodmon. A lot had happened, and Amaria needed him. She needed to process that they would have a daughter soon, that they had gambled their daughter's future, and that Amaria had giant silver feathers coming out of her back.

"He's still outside our lands," the faerie threw her shimmering hair over her shoulder. "I'll take you to him."

Amaria didn't lower her defensive stance, although her arms shook. Her lips pursed. Why was the female faerie agreeing to let Amaria see Theodmon? Amaria couldn't fathom why—it might be a trick—but she forced down the bile in her throat, standing straight. She'd risk it to be with Theodmon.

"Thank you," she told the faerie, gently inclining her head.

The faerie laughed, rolling her eyes. "Human politeness is so odd. Come on, let's go see the liaison. Oberon has things to discuss with him as well."

Chapter Fifty-One

Amaria felt the air shift as the leaves crunched under her feet. Previously, she could almost taste the honeysuckle in the air—it entwined with spun sugar and other sickly sweet scents that should have made Amaria gag. Instead, her body felt comfortable within it.

Now, the air was no longer sweet and the colors were less vibrant.

"We're entering the human realm," Oberon said.

Amaria blinked. Why did it seem so different? This was her home. She was human. "Will I ever be the same?" She didn't want to change this much.

However, Amaria couldn't bring herself to regret the change. She no longer felt the dark magic coursing in her veins. The Raulet Ruby was taken care of. She was alive, she was powerful, and she wouldn't hurt her loved ones further.

Arguably, engaging her unborn daughter would strengthen faerie-Chauvignon bonds. That was good for humans, well, Thestitiunians at least. Amaria pressed her eyes shut; that was an issue for the future. Not now.

She still wanted to be human and for home to feel like home.

"You're ulaniza," Oberon said. "We're exchanging your ulaniza requirement of birthing faeries to your daughter; she's ulaniza now, as she went through the ritual with you."

"So, no," Amaria scowled, her eyes watering slightly as she realized the human lands would never be the same to her.

"Not what ulaniza means," Oberon said. "You're still human. Faeries struggle with conception; humans, well, you don't have an issue there. The ulaniza process lets you keep your ability to multiply."

Amaria's skin crawled. That just sounded...crude.

"You're a human. With increased magic ability and magical tolerances, but human nonetheless. In time, your body will adjust to the human world with its blunt colors and crass sounds."

Amaria's nostrils flared. This was her home, and Oberon was insulting it.

She forced herself to breathe. She was going to see Theodmon soon. This insult wouldn't matter. They still needed the faeries' help against the Badlands. The faeries had promised that, but faeries were tricky. Amaria wasn't stupid enough to anger them.

"Your husband is ahead," Oberon said.

Amaria squinted her eyes, seeing an outline of a bulky man in the distance. He was screaming her name, sounding distant, as if a tunnel separated them. Her eyes drifted around the forest, and she saw a golden shimmer in the air. It must have been the protective barrier the faeries had to keep out those they didn't want in their lands. Amaria had never been able to see it before.

Perhaps being ulaniza changed that as well.

"Theodmon!" Amaria called out to him, not wanting to be alone in her thoughts any longer.

"Amaria!"

She was running through the trees, her lungs burned, her legs were cramping, and her wings were a heavy weight dragging behind her. She ignored this, for Amaria needed to get to Theodmon. He was all that mattered now.

She no longer saw the gold shimmer. Snow covered her feet, causing her to slow down.

Amaria paused. *Snow?* It had been summer when she left the human realms, her home, to go with the faeries.

"Gods," Theodmon collided with her, embracing her in his large arms. "You're alive. It's been months. I had to leave to make war plans—You have wings."

Amaria kissed him on the mouth, her eyes shut as she embraced everything about him: how his stubble felt against her palms, how he smelled like musty frankincense, how his breath was warm against hers. She missed everything about him.

It was easier than acknowledging how different time had moved in the faerie lands; Amaria didn't think she had been there for months. It had felt as if she was there a week, if that. She looked down at her stomach. In the human world, she now realized her stomach had grown—she had a bump. Why didn't she notice it before?

"Oberon, he's coming to discuss plans with Badlands with you," Amaria hastily breathed out. "They want me to train with them. Theo, I need to. These wings...I don't know how to do anything with them."

Theodmon hugged her. "I know," he whispered. "Do what you need to do."

"Do you hate them?" Amaria's expression became pained, her eyes clouding. "I know they're weird—"

Theodmon kissed her passionately. "No," he said as he pulled away. "I love them. They suit you."

Amaria snorted in disbelief. How could he love her wings? They were very much distinguishing her as other, a non-human. Someone who was different from Theodmon.

"I promised you I'd always love you," he said, brushing the top of her hair with his palm. "This changes nothing. Besides, we're going to fight Lynette. I think this can be a morale booster. You look righteous, like an angel from the gods."

Amaria shook her head, a shaky laugh escaping her. "Angels haven't done the things I've done."

Theodmon silently pulled her closer to him.

Exhaling softly, Amaria leaned against his shoulders, feeling her wings pull as they pressed against each other. She ignored the discomfort, instead forcing her face against his chest, listening to the rhythmic beating of his heart. It was nice being with Theodmon. They loved each other; that much hadn't changed and couldn't be changed—ulaniza or not.

She snuggled up closer to him, the cold biting at her nose and arms. He moved his cloak to cover her, protecting her exposed skin from the wind.

Amaria wasn't dressed for this weather and she would have to reenter the faeries' lands soon. She saw Oberon approaching—he must have lagged behind to give her and Theodmon a private moment.

"An angel of death then," Theodmon whispered into her ear. "I've always loved how ruthless you could be."

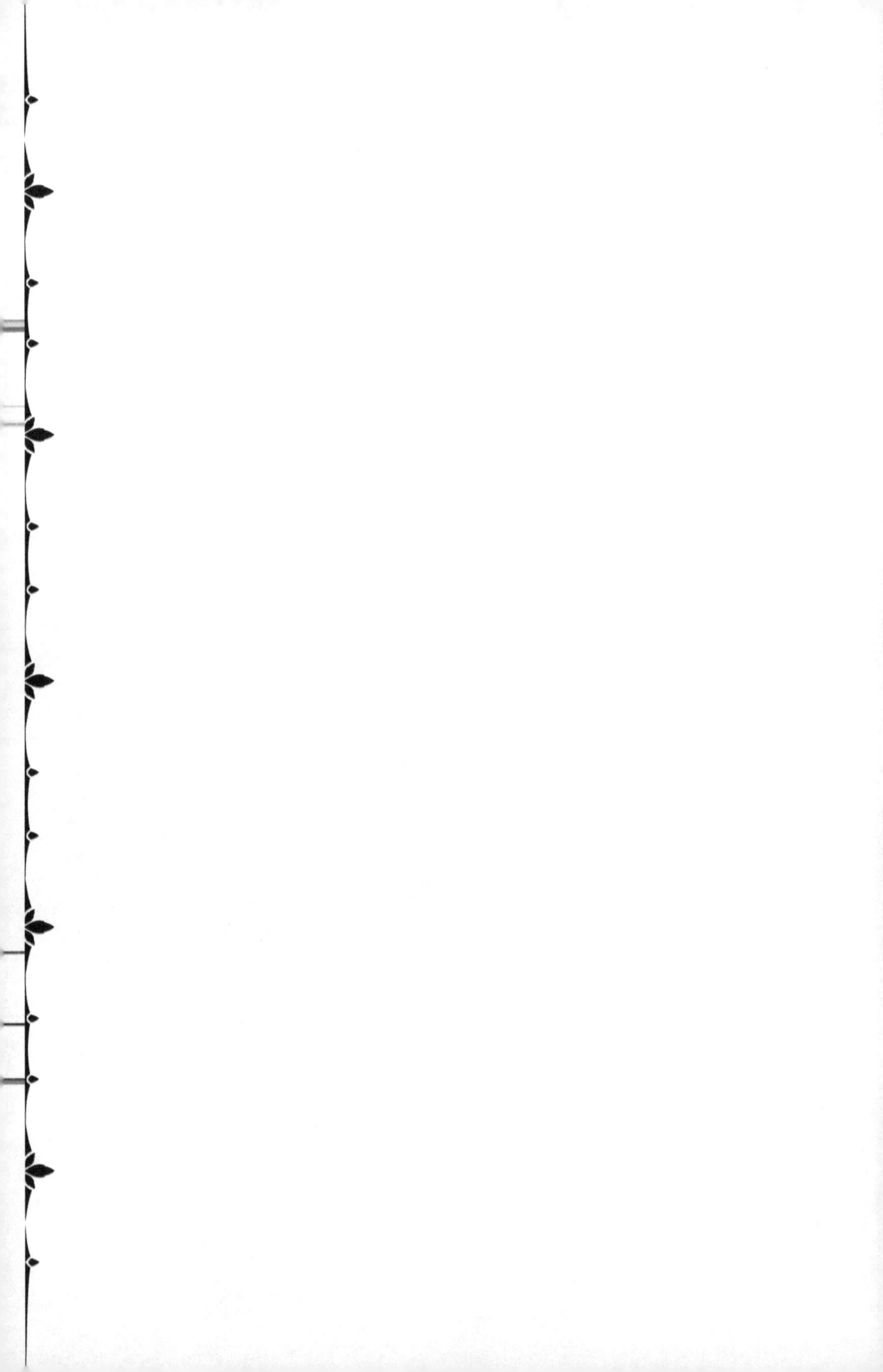

Cast of Characters

Nicoletta Astasuel (Nicoletta As-tas-u-elle): A Countess. Previously Nicoletta Lemaire. She was born in Raulle, in Perivina Fluere, Thestitiunia. She has been a lady-in-waiting and friend to Amaria Raulet since she was a child. Her husband is a Westanni Earl. They don't speak much.

Stephan Belamy (Stef-fan Bell-am-me): An Earl from the Westerlands, Thestitiunia. A war mage with the ability of precognition regarding the opponent's battle plans. He is an Extractor.

Juliette Bécharil (Juliette Beh-char-ill): She is originally from Minelle, Avondra. She married Lucas Bécharil and is lady-in-waiting and friend to Amaria Raulet. She is a water and earth mage, commonly called "Hydra Blessed."

Lucas Bécharil (Lucas Beh-char-ill): Currently an untitled Lord. Will be a Marquis once his father dies. He is one of Theodmon Chauvignon's closest friends and bannermen. He is talented with a sword, torture, and tracking.

Ophelia Belegines (Oh-feel-ee-ah Bel-lee-ginny): Previously Ophelia Chauvignon. Eldest daughter of Agatha and Raphael Chauvignon. She is married to Duke Lancelin Belegines of Skeletosa, Avondra.

Agatha Chauvignon (Agatha Chauv-ing-non): Widow of Marquis Raphael Chauvignon. Mother of Aloysius, Celestine, Ophelia, and Theodmon. She is from Morroek, and she hates magic and Thestitiunia to a degree.

Aloysius Chauvignon (A-lee-soy-us Chauv-ing-non): Youngest son of Agatha and Raphael Chauvignon. A war mage who can harden his body into a shield. He is a party boy.

Celestine Chauvignon (Sell-est-tine Chauv-ing-non): Youngest daughter and child of Agatha and Raphael Chauvignon.

Lysander Chauvignon (Lie-sand-der Chauv-ing-non): The firstborn son of Theodmon and Amaria Chauvignon.

Theodmon Chauvignon (They-od-mon Chauv-ing-non): Marquis of the Westerlands of Thestitiunia. He is the equivalent of a Duke for all intents and purposes, however, due to the faerie lands on his lands; his acreage is shy of what's needed for the legal title of 'Duke'. He is a liaison for the humans and Faeries as his father was before him, and his father was, and so forth. He is married to Amaria Raulet. A talented military strategist and swordsman.

Henri Delaluna (Henry De-la-luna): An Extractor. He can read minds, control and alter thoughts, and change memories. He is from the Westerlands, Thestitiunia, and while currently an untitled Lord, once his father passes he will be a Marquis.

Lynette Edrion (Lynn-et Ed-ree-on): The Queen of Avondra. Years ago, she killed her brother in a coup. She is a dark mage, set on bringing chaos into this world.

Delphina Ginsery (Del-fein-na Gin-ser-ray): Deceased. Thestitiunian noble-woman from the Perivina Fluere province who is murdered during the attack on Provincia Palencia in which the Raulet Ruby is stolen.

Fylla Gauthier (Fie-laa Gaa-the-eer): Midwife who works for the Chauvignons at Forteresse les Blanche.

Edward Fayley (Edward Fay-lee): Deceased. In line for the Riam throne.

Gabriel Fayley (Gabriel Fay-lee): Deceased. In line for the Riam throne.

Justin Fila (Justin Fee-laa): Deceased. A co-conspirator in stealing the Raulet Ruby. He has fire magic. He killed Delphina Ginsery.

High Priestess of Dandar: A refuge from Avondra. Can see the future. Is a powerful mage.

Andrew Hull: Deceased. In line for the Riam throne.

Annalise Hull: Deceased. In line for the Riam throne.

Brandon Hull: Deceased. In line for the Riam throne.

Josef Hull: Deceased. In line for the Riam throne.

Faelyn Laurellanza (Fae-lynn Laurel-lan-zaa): Duke of Lierre Fideles, Thestitiunia. An Extractor. A powerful healing mage.

Anthony Lyncan (Anthony Lie-can): Deceased. In line for the Riam throne.

Christopher Lyncan (Christopher Lie-can): Deceased. In line for the Riam throne.

Victoria Lyncan (Victoria Lie-can): Deceased. In line for the Riam throne.

Aion Marion (A-On Mare-ree-on): The Emperor of Thestitiunia.

Elena Marion (Elena Mare-ree-on): A Princess of Thestitiunia. She is Aion's sister. She is an Extractor. She is blind. A powerful mage who can manipulate others energies and emotions.

Katerina Montersatt (Cat-err-ein-ah Mon-teer-saat): Healing mage who works for the Chauvignons at Forteresse les Blanche.

Clarissa Nalaeny (Clare-iss-aa Nale-aah-len-knee): Deceased. The sister of the king of Rindria. She is vain, self-absorbed, and petty. Mother of Liara and Tesden Nalaeny.

Liam Nalaeny (Lee-amm Nale-aah-len-knee): Deceased. Distant Raulet cousin through his mother. Riam Duke. Married to Clarissa Nalaeny.

Liara Nalaeny (Lee-are-ah Nale-aah-len-knee): A political prisoner to Thestititiunia after she ran away from home from her mother, Clarissa Nalaeny.

Tesden Nalaeny (Tes-den Nale-aah-len-knee): Ninth in line to the Riam throne.

Oliver Neremoux (Oliver Nare-aah-Moo): A minor noble from Perivina Fluere, Thestitiunia. He is in a secret relationship with Haerdnor Raulet.

Oberon (Obb-ber-on): A male Faerie.

Aaron Raulet (Aaron Raul-lay): The Duke of the Perivina Fluere Province of Thestitiunia. Cold, ruthless, and cunning, he is efficient in getting his political goals accomplished.

Amaria Raulet (Am-mar-ree-ah Raul-lay): Also known as Marchioness Amaria Chauvignon. She is an Extractor, a powerful elemental mage, able to control the elements of water and earth ("Hydra Blessed") as well as fire and air ("Dragon Blessed"). She is the wife of Theodmon Chauvignon and mother of Lysander Chauvignon. She is Aaron and Illyana Raulet's oldest child and the twin of Haerdnor.

Catalina Raulet (Cat-ah-lein-ah Raul-lay): The youngest daughter of Aaron and Illyana Raulet. She survived a deathly childhood illness that left her with golden scars over her face and throat. She is training to enter a Temple of Ignoia (the healing goddess).

Haerdnor Raulet (Hair-den-noir Raul-lay): The oldest son of Aaron and Illyana Raulet. A hot headed fire mage, he is brave and arrogant. The younger twin of Amaria. In a secret relationship with Oliver Neremoux.

Illyana Raulet (Ill-ee-ann-aah Raul-lay): Deceased. A Duchess. Married to Aaron Raulet. Originally from Tressidil, her brother is the current Lord Prime Minister of Tressidil. Mother to Amaria, Haerdnor, and Catalina Raulet.

Edward Riarl (Edward Ree-are-el): Deceased. A formerly Sickly child. Died during the blast of the Raulet Ruby in Bria Hall. Riam Prince. Son of Tristan Riarl.

Jenna Riarl (Jenna Ree-are-el): Deceased. Riam Princess. Daughter of Tristan Riarl.

Karissa Riarl (Car-is-saa Ree-are-el): Deceased. Riam Princess. Daughter of Tristan Riarl.

Tristan Riarl (Tris-tan Ree-are-el): Deceased. The King of Rindria. His sister is Clarissa Nalaeny.

Durek Svilas (Dur-rek Civ-vil-az): A Morrian Duke. He married the eldest daughter of the Morrian King. Due to the Morrian King having no sons, he is the presumptive heir. Amaria Raulet, Aaron Raulet, and he have engaged in business relations. Talented with a bow and arrow.

Michel Valois (Mic-chel Val-roy): An Extractor. A power mage who can transform into other people, a bear, an eagle, and a dolphin. He is an untitled minor Thestitiunian Lord. He is the one who bound Giuliana Vero to await her Extraction in the Imperial Palace.

Giuliana Vero (Jul-lee-ann-naa Veyr-oo): Deceased. A co-conspirator in stealing the Raulet Ruby. She has hypnosis magic.

Pierre Vero (Peer-ree Veyr-oo): Deceased. A co-conspirator in stealing the Raulet Ruby. He dies of a broken neck during the attack.

Lyseno Vypren (Lis-sen-no Vie-pren): The Duke of Darcassa, Avondra. Amaria Raulet's ex-fiancé. He is an angry, bitter man, feeling as if he were embarrassed internationally because of it.

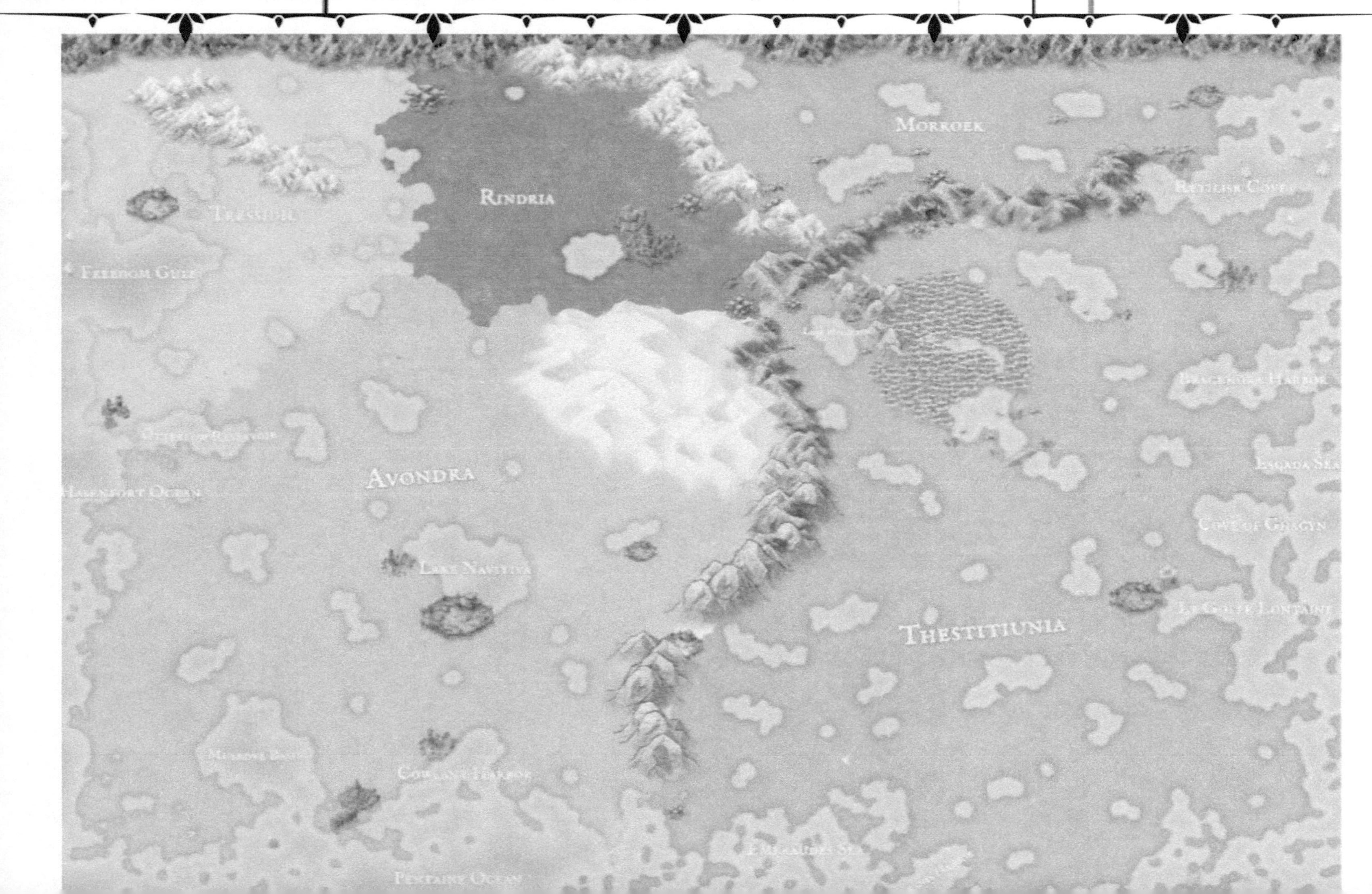
MORROEK
RINDRIA
TRENDOR
BETILISK COVE
FREEDOM GULF
AVONDRA
LAKE NAUTICA
HALENDAT OCEAN
THESTITIUNIA
ESQADA SEA
CAPE OF GRIGIN
LE GOLFE LONTAINE
COLLANT HARBOR
EMERAUDES ST
PENTAINE OCEAN

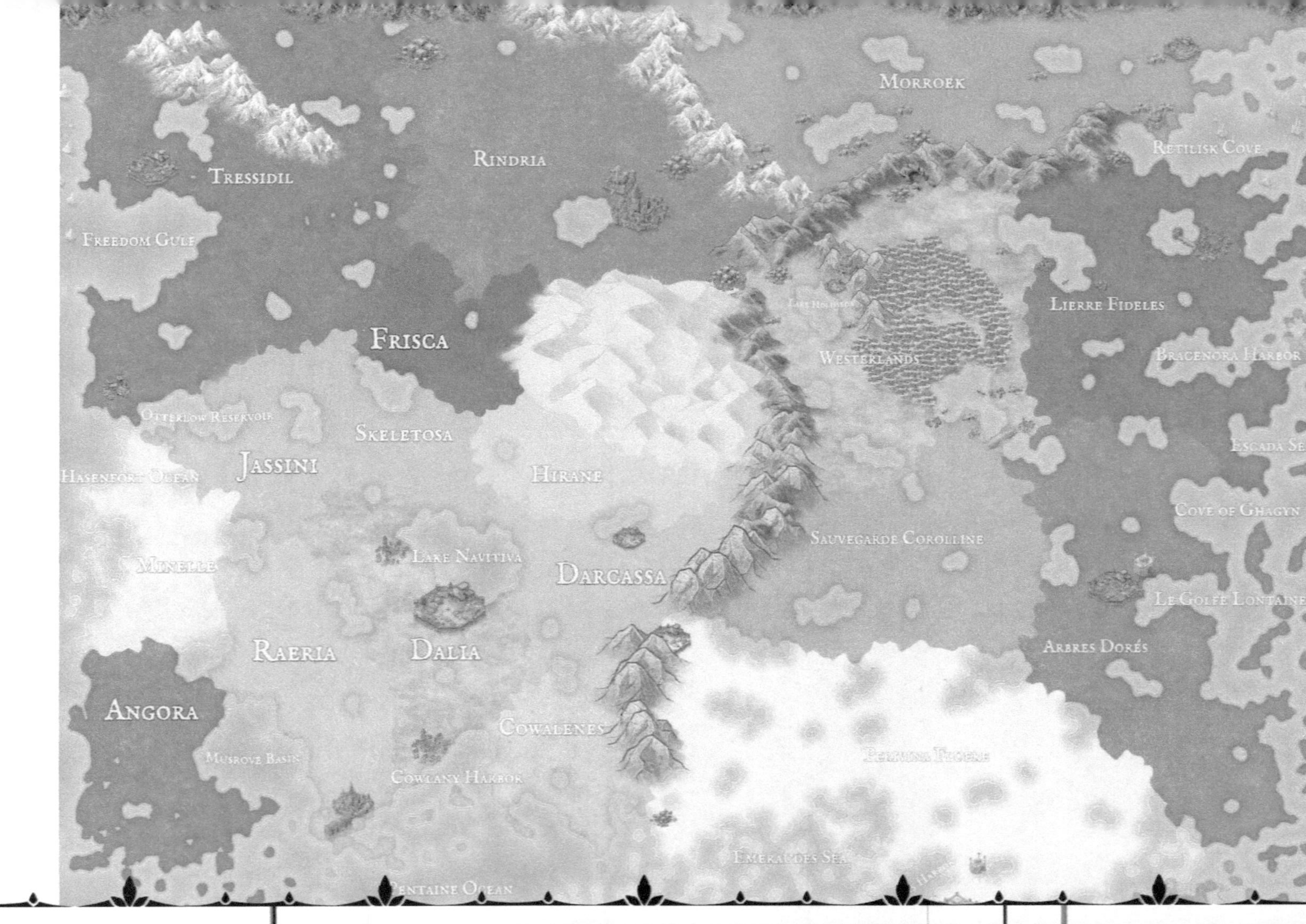

Morroek
Retilisk Cove
Rindria
Tressidil
Freedom Gule
Frisca
Lierre Fideles
Westerlands
Bracenora Harbor
Otterlow Reservoir
Skeletosa
Escada Sea
Jassini
Hirane
Hasenfort Ocean
Cove of Ghagyn
Sauvegarde Corolline
Minelle
Lake Navitiva
Darcassa
Le Golfe Lontaine
Raeria
Dalia
Arbres Dorés
Angora
Cowalenes
Musrove Basin
Petruna Tigera
Cowlany Harbor
Emeraude Sea
Pentaine Ocean

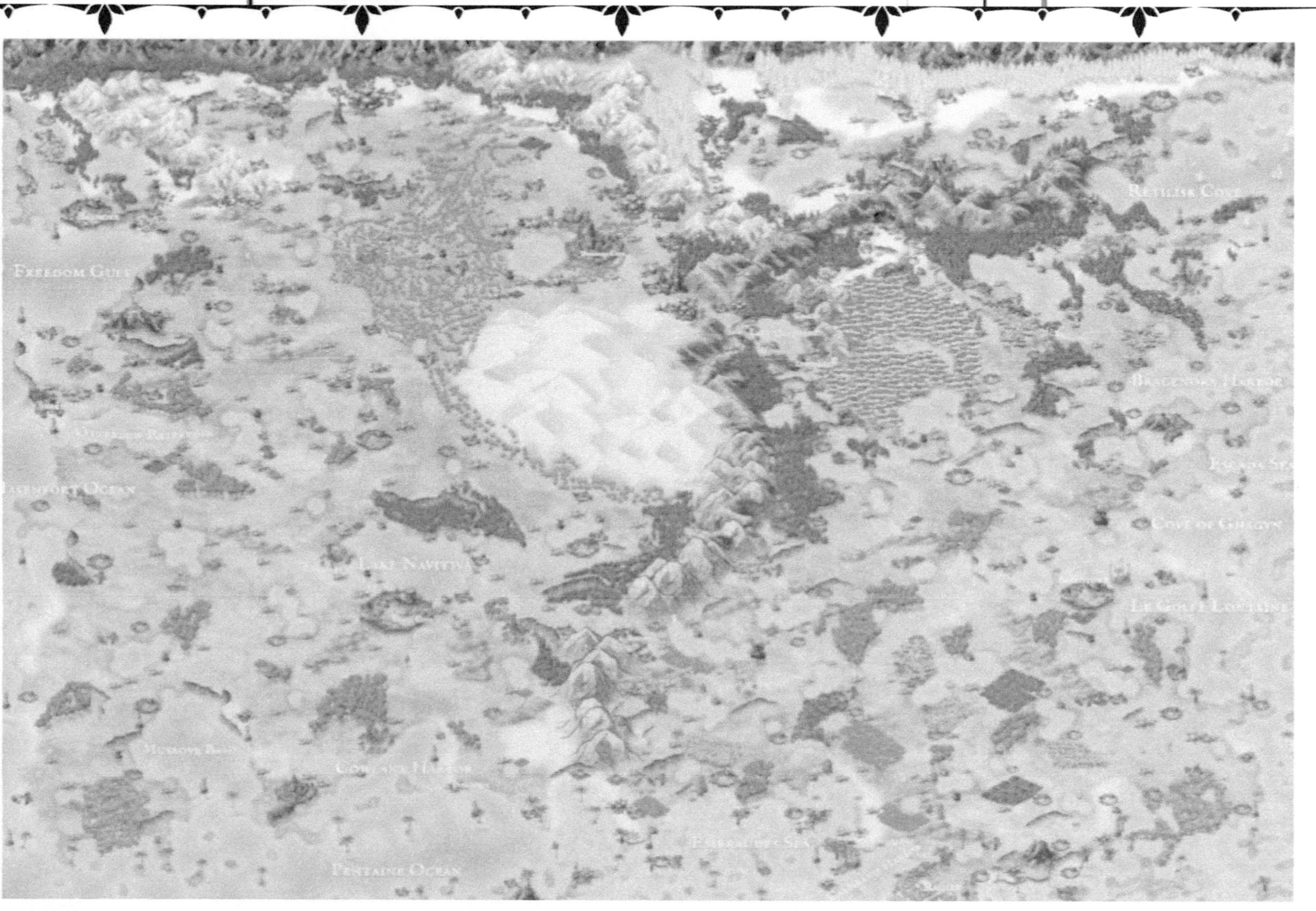

FREEDOM GULF
REVELER COVE
BRIGANTINE HARBOR
KRAKEN SEA
COVE OF GIBBONS
LAKE NAVITIVE
PENTAINE OCEAN
EMERALD SEA

Author's Note Regarding Previous Book and Thank Yous

Hello, and thank you for reading. To anyone who has read the original novel, "The Traitors Schemes," consider the events as non-canon. It is best explained as an alternative universe with the question of "What if?" regarding Liara. She is a catalyst character, not a main character, however. The true story of this series follows Amaria and Theodmon and their scheming in Thestitiunia.

I'd like to thank Scarlett D. Vine, Bell Cutler, Bobbie Hudson, Brianna Tsitsera, Emily Palmer Haddock, Chris Afanador, Lauren Maybin, Becky Puff, Hannah Ingalls, and to all my friends and family who I could write a book in gratitude for allowing me to whine to them and for all their support. Thank you to Crab, from Crab Editing, for being a wonderful editor. To my son, Augi and my husband, Alex—you guys are the true MVPS. I do it for you.

And for those who read as betas, as ARCS, or as regular readers, thank you most of all.

About the Author

Emily Almanza is a reader, tv-enthusiast, and cat lover. She lives in the mountains of North Carolina with her husband and son where she hikes, goes to wineries, and ziplines.

<u>Books by E.A. Almanza</u>
The Guileful Rose
Winterthorne's Shards
The Griffin and the Rose: A Curoria Chronicles Novella
The Topaz Crown (TBD)